OUT OF THE
RUINS

ALSO AVAILABLE FROM TITAN BOOKS

A Universe of Wishes

Cursed

Dark Cities: All-New Masterpieces of Urban Terror

Dead Letters: An Anthology of the Undelivered, the Missing, the Returned

Exit Wounds

Hex Life

Infinite Stars

Infinite Stars: Dark Frontiers

Invisible Blood

New Fears: New Horror Stories by Masters of the Genre

New Fears 2: Brand New Horror Stories by Masters of the Macabre

Phantoms: Haunting Tales from the Masters of the Genre

Rogues

Vampires Never Get Old

Wastelands: Stories of the Apocalypse

Wastelands 2: More Stories of the Apocalypse

Wastelands: The New Apocalypse

When Things Get Dark: Stories Inspired by Shirley Jackson

Wonderland

OUT OF THE
RUINS

Edited by
PRESTON GRASSMAN

TITAN BOOKS

OUT OF THE
RUINS

Print edition ISBN: 9781789097399
E-book edition ISBN: 9781789097405

Published by Titan Books
A division of Titan Publishing Group Ltd
144 Southwark Street, London SE1 0UP
www.titanbooks.com

First edition: September 2021
10 9 8 7 6 5 4 3 2 1

TABLE OF CONTENTS

Introduction – *Preston Grassmann* 1

The Hour – *Clive Barker* 5

The Green Caravanserai – *Lavie Tidhar* 7

The Age of Fish, Post-flowers – *Anna Tambour* 19

Exurbia – *Kaaron Warren* 36

Watching God – *China Miéville* 46

A Storm in Kingstown – *Nina Allan* 62

As Good As New – *Charlie Jane Anders* 84

Reminded – *Ramsey Campbell* 104

The Splendor and Misery of Bodies, of Cities – *Samuel R. Delany* 117

The Rise and Fall of Whistle-Pig City – *Paul Di Filippo* 137

Mr. Thursday – *Emily St. John Mandel* 152

The Man You Flee at Parties – *Nick Mamatas* 169

Like the Petals of Broken Flowers –
Chris Kelso and Preston Grassman 185

The Endless Fall – *Jeffrey Thomas* 194

Dwindling – *Ron Drummond* 218

Malware Park – *Nikhil Singh* 234

Maeda: The Body Optic – *Rumi Kaneko* 255

Inventory – *Carmen Maria Machado* 263

How the Monsters Found God – *John Skipp and Autumn Christian* 275

The Box Man's Dream – *D.R.G. Sugawara* 295

Acknowledgements 297

About the authors 299

INTRODUCTION

Preston Grassmann

MY earliest memory of a literary apocalypse was discovered in the remainder bins of a local bookstore. *The Ruins of Earth* (edited by Thomas M. Disch), with its emblematic cover of an egg-shaped world about to crack open, contained stories of ecological catastrophes and end-time scenarios that were so impressionable to my young mind, it might've been me emerging from that shell. But it was one story, in particular, that has remained with me through the years—"Cage of Sand" by J.G. Ballard. In that quintessential narrative, Ballard describes an abandoned Cape Canaveral inhabited by drifters of a lost space-age, where "the old launching gantries and landing ramps reared up into the sky like derelict pieces of giant sculpture." That might've been the first time, in those early golden-age years, that I realized that some kind of beauty can be salvaged from the relics of the past. I went on from there to read *The Drowned World, High Rise,* and *Concrete Island* before I found my way to other writers who could sing among the ruins—many of them are in this book.

In more recent years, I had the opportunity to attend an exhibition at London's Tate gallery called "Ruin Lust," (derived from the German word *Ruinenelust*). It was filled with images of decaying structures, pieces of castle walls, the remnants of ghost-towns and demolished buildings. I remember feeling a mix of dismay and nostalgia at first, but that soon gave way to that same sense of excitement that I'd felt when reading Ballard. Here was proof that whatever falls apart in our world can be turned into something new. The surreal photographs of Paul Nash or the abandoned-London images of Jon Savage were about reimagining the world in the wake of destruction, not reveling in its end. They were about finding a way out, of transforming those Ballardian gantries and landing ramps into something of value. During that exhibition, I realized just how much scenes of ruin can traverse the present moment, pointing back in time while offering a glimpse of tomorrow—one where salvage and survival was (and is) possible.

It wasn't that long ago that public health officials announced an event that felt (and still feels) like a harbinger of the end times. We've lived through a global crisis that has taken lives, stalled world economies, and altered our sense of reality in ways that none of us could foresee. For many of us, this continues to be an apocalyptic moment; a cataclysm that can both ruin and leave ruins in its wake. But as is true with all the cataclysms of history, we survive through our creations, salvaging the remains of our past to build something new. On a societal level, we can raise new cities and systems of belief. As individuals, we can rise out of our own private ruins; the versions of ourselves that survive. In this, a single poem or a story (or a photograph in the Tate gallery) can be as revealing as a city.

The idea of apocalypse as an end-of-the-world event is a modern conception. The ancient Greek word, *apokalypsis*, was about revelation and disclosure, uncovering what was once concealed. In Middle English, it referred to insight and vision or hallucinations. The word itself, if you'll pardon the indulgence, has emerged from the ruins of its previous definitions, while holding on to some part of its origins. As you'll see from the stories that follow, all of its potential meanings have been salvaged. In China Miéville's "Watching God" or Kaaron Warren's "Exurbia," the survivors uncover their truths in the ways they've adapted to the ruins they inhabit. Others offer their end-of-the-world insights with levity, as in Paul Di Filippo's "The Rise and Fall of Whistle-pig City" and Charlie Jane Anders's "As Good As New." In stories like Emily St. John Mandel's "Mr. Thursday" and Ron Drummond's "Dwindling," the ruins can be a verb, where the scale of revelation comes down to the lives of individuals—the ways in which they emerge from the wreckage of their private histories. In John Skipp and Autumn Christian's "How the Monsters Found God," or Nina Allan's "Storm in Kingstown," hope is what remains, the revelation we take away. But all of the stories that follow have their *apokalypsis*, with unique visions of what worlds can be or what they might become. And no matter how dark they are, they also acknowledge that each of us can excavate something of value from the ash of our end times and make something new.

Great things can be born *Out of the Ruins*.

THE HOUR

by Clive Barker

The Hour! The Hour! Upon the Hour!
The Munkee spits and thickets cower,
And what has become of the Old Man's power
But tears and trepidation?

The Hour! The Hour! Upon the Hour!
Mother's mad and the milk's gone sour,
But yesterday I found a flower
That sang Annunciation.

And when the Hours become Day,
And all the Days have passed away,
Will we not see—yes, you and me—
How sweet and bright the light will be
That comes of our Creation?

THE GREEN CARAVANSERAI

Lavie Tidhar

EVERY winter around January the Green Caravanserais began to make an appearance around the Ghost Coast between Taba and Nuweiba. They were slow moving, patient and cautious—as well they should be, Saleh thought. For the paths they traversed were hard and the Ghost Coast itself could be deadly.

Saleh crouched on top of the unfinished castellated tower of what had once been, or could have been, a grand hotel. He could look out for miles. The Red Sea sparkled to the east, with the Saudi mountains rising behind on the shores on the other side of the gulf. The outlines of empty swimming pools dotted the landscape of heavily built, abandoned buildings each grander than the rest—

Bavarian Romanesque castles jostled against basilicas built in faux-Gaudí style, which in turn nestled against miniature Egyptian pyramids. Moorish arches vied with Doric columns next to a vintage American diner and an extensive garden, maintained by rusty, salvaged robots, was set up like a budget Alhambra.

Here and there Saleh could see craters of the ancient wars, where nothing lived and no one had settled, and fresh holes which a giant sandworm—the *Vermes Arenae Sinaitici Gigantes* were another relic of the war—might have dug. This strip of endless hospitality architecture ran all the way from the ancient border with what was now the entwined dual polity of the digitally federated Judea-Palestina Union to Sharm El-Sheikh, near the tip of the peninsula.

Beyond it lay the desert, eternal and hostile to humans as it always was.

It was from the desert that the Green Caravanserai came. Saleh, eyes bright, watched the distant, slow procession. The goats came first, a brown and white herd treading with an easy gait. Robed figures moved between them. Then, behind them, came the elephants.

There were several elephant families in the herd. Saleh watched enraptured, for he had always loved elephants. These were sand-coloured from the long march, and they moved with a kind of majestic unhurriedness, unencumbered by humans, seemingly indifferent to the elements. They were desert elephants, and in a lifetime could make the slow back-and-forth crossing many times. Moving between them were more humans, robed and with traditional keffiyehs covering their heads. Small robots and drones crawled and hovered and slithered in between.

And now Saleh could see solar gliders rising overhead on the hot winds.

Behind the elephants came the first of the caravanserai proper, though in the idiom of the travellers it was still called by its old name of a khan. Saleh watched as the building slinkied itself across the sands. The old caravanserais or khans were rest stops for the merchant trains along the silk and perfume roads. Now the Green Caravanserai brought their own buildings with them, semi-sentient machines that could build and rebuild themselves with ease and adapt to their surroundings, drawing energy from wind and sun.

Camels came behind the khan and hordes of children, horses, wagons pulled by snail-like robots until the whole thing resembled less a caravan than a carnival.

Saleh always looked forward to the caravanserais' arrival each year, though until now he had never gone near one, for his father was always the one to represent the tribe at the trade meeting, and Saleh was not allowed to come.

But not this time, he thought. This time he had his own thing to trade, paid for in blood and despair.

His father was gone.

No. This time *he*, Saleh, would go. This time he would meet the elephants.

He watched as the Green Caravanserai reached just beyond the old coastal road that bisected the Ghost Coast from the desert. There they stopped, in successive waves. The khans reassembled and formed into simple, solid shapes that looked a little like round beehives. The small robots formed a fence and the people of the caravanserai laid down solar sheeting and set up atmospheric water generators. The kids played with the elephants. The goats chewed on the bark of trees.

Saleh abandoned the castellated tower of the old hotel. He slid down stairwells and in and out of windows. It was not *protocol* to go alone. The Abu-Ala foraged the Ghost Coast for old machines and they had long ago made arrangements with the caravaners, so Salah would be going against both tribe wishes and simple decorum.

He paused in the entrance of the old hotel. The sun beat down. The Ghost Coast—this endless strip of vintage neo-kitsch architecture suspended in time and gently falling apart—spread away from him.

He stared at the road then, almost unwillingly it felt to him, he began to march towards the Green Caravanserai.

Elias scratched hair out of his eyes and looked with curiosity at the boy striding nervously across the road. The boy had no way of knowing this, but right then he had the attention of several heavily armed drones, a detachment of caravaner rangers and of old Umm Kulthum, the matriarch of the elephant herd herself, and if he set *one* foot wrong or drew *any* kind of weapon or if he just *sneezed*, really, he'd turn into hot desert dust long before his brain could even process the idea.

Which would be a shame, really, Elias thought, because the boy seemed nice, if rather nervous.

This really wasn't protocol.

The thing about the Sinai was that, beyond the stretch of the Ghost Coast, and after centuries of sporadic warfare, nothing in the desert was particularly *safe*. It was littered with old mines, traps, unexploded ordnances, mutated bio-weapons and sentient machines that no one even remembered designing in the first place. The only people to cross it were the caravaners, who went in search of old military tech that had resale value, and to get through it time and time again they had become proficient in the art of not dying.

They were not specialists in the tech: it was people like the Abu-Ala tribe of the Al-Tirabin, for example—who foraged the Ghost Coast— that collected the stuff. The caravaners just haggled for it, then carried it back across the mountains and wadis and the desert, ranging from Cairo in the west to the glittering sprawl—Al-Imtidad—of Neom in the east and sometimes even to Djibouti in the south.

Elias watched as the boy crossed the road. Elias was mounted on top of the now-stationary khan, and he'd been observing the boy for quite a while now, ever since his heat signature was detected on top of a tower in the dense network of abandoned buildings that made up the coast.

Long ago, the coast was a busy hive of activity as tourists came from all over the world, from Israel and Russia and the European mass and that big island just off Europe the name of which Elias could never remember, but was an important polity for a short time back in the sometime or other. But then the tourists stopped coming, the ever more lavish hotel and resort buildings were never completed, and then the wars came, and with them the Leviathans that still haunted the depths of the Red Sea, and the Rocs that snatched the unwary and carried them to nests high up in the mountains and laid their larval eggs in them, and the sandworms—and whose stupid idea was *that* one? —that still bred and grew enormous in the sands.

There was other movement in the area—one sandworm lay dormant two clicks away and deep underground, and a group of non-sentient but mobile unexploded ordnances was gathered in what looked like a Roman villa four clicks back towards Taba, but surprisingly there were no humans and no Abu-Ala as one would usually expect to find.

None, that is, but for the boy.

Elias shrugged, put the goggles back on so he could continue monitoring the immediate area, jumped out of the khan's top deck and slid smoothly down one of the now-tentacular bases.

The boy crossed the road and came to the perimeter of the caravanserai and stopped.

Elias came and met him.

They looked at each other curiously.

"Hello?" the boy said, uncertainly.

"Yes?" Elias said. He knew it was unhelpful. But there were *protocols* in place. And this wasn't it.

"I am Saleh," the boy said.

"Yes," Elias said, dubiously.

They stared at each other.

Saleh wasn't going to let them intimidate him. Even though he was intimidated. Badly. Two tiny crawling robots came over the line and examined him with extended feelers.

The other boy said, "Try not to move."

Saleh stood very still. He took a deep breath. He said, "My name is Saleh Mohammed Ishak Abu-Ala Al-Tirabin."

At this the other boy looked more interested. "You are an Abu-Ala?"

"Yes."

"You are not the designated contact," the boy said.

"No."

"So why are you here?"

Saleh was sweating, though the air was chilly. He said, "I have something."

"So?"

"Something to trade."

The boy looked interested again. "Is it valuable?" he said.

"I think so."

The boy seemed to consider. "Still," he said. "We deal with the tribe, not with individual scavengers. It makes everything easier. Safe."

Saleh said, "There is only me."

"Excuse me?"

Saleh swallowed.

"There is only me," he said quietly.

And then he started to cry.

Saleh sat miserably on the mat while Elias brewed sage tea. Elias had had to bring him in, hadn't he. The boy was no longer deemed a threat. Saleh accepted the tea gratefully. Elias brought out pistachios and hard biscuits. He set them on a plate and sat cross-legged across from Saleh.

"What happened to them?" he said. He tried to speak gently.

Saleh shrugged.

"We were excavating in Dahab," he said. "It used to be a robotnik nest during the second, no, maybe the third war. You must have seen the satellite pictures of Dahab, right? It had a terrorartist attack in the fourth war and the whole place is suspended in a sort of still-ongoing explosion, but if you wear a null suit you can navigate through the temporality maze—anyway. We were digging. Dahab's full of valuable old stuff, it's just hard to get. Then, something… broke loose." He blinked. "I don't know what. A ghost."

"A *ghost*?" Elias said.

Saleh shrugged again, helplessly. "One of the old Israeli robotniks, I think. It was still alive somehow, inside the explosion. Most power sources don't work inside the terrorartist installation so we bring in portable fusion generators when we go in. I think my dad brushed too close to the old robotnik and somehow it drew power from the generator and—and it came alive. They were cyborgs, with biological brains but mostly machine otherwise. I don't even know if it was *alive* in a real sense, only responding to what it saw as battle. So it came loose and it killed my father and the rest of… It killed everyone."

"I am sorry," Elias said. He looked at the boy in front of him. Two years back they had lost Manmour, the elephant, to tiny mechanical spider things that had swarmed out of one of the wadis. Only the skeleton remained and then the machines vanished again, and what they did with Manmour's skin and flesh and blood nobody knew. The elephants grieved and the whole caravanserai grieved with them.

"Drink your tea," Elias said compassionately.

Saleh closed his eyes. The teacup felt warm between his hands.

"Everyone else was away," he said quietly. He had to get the words out. Had to tell Elias what happened. In a way it was a relief.

"Most of the tribe's down in Sharm or St. Catherine's. But I got it, you see." He opened his eyes and stared at the other boy, this Elias, with his strange goggles and short-cropped hair and curious, interested gaze.

"You got it? What?" the boy said.

"The thing we were looking for." Excitement quickened in him then. "My grandfather Ishak and my father, Mohammed, they kept looking. Even though it was dangerous. Even though it was hard. Every year the terrorartist bubble moves outwards just a little. It is still alive, the explosion still happening. You know much about terrorart?"

"A little. Rohini started it, didn't they? The Jakarta Event."

"Time-dilation bombs," Saleh said. "Yes, Rohini. There were others. Mad Rucker who seeded the Boppers on Titan. Sandoval, who made the installation called Earthrise out of stolen minds on the moon. There were never many, thankfully. And they were mass murderers, every one. But the art, I know people are interested in it."

"There are collectors," Elias said. "Museums, too. What did you find?"

"This," Saleh said, simply. He opened his bag and took out a small metal ball. It felt so light. "It's the time-dilation bomb."

Silent alarms must have gone off somewhere, because a moment later he had caravaners and drones both surround him. He never even heard them coming.

Elias let out a slow exhalation of breath.

"And how did we miss that?" he said.

"It's empty," Saleh said. "The explosion, Dahab, everything? It's still going on. My father, my uncle, they're still inside it. An endless death, still happening. The robotnik pulled them into the field. Only I got out."

He didn't dare move. The weapons were on him. Elias said, "May I see it?"

"Of course."

Saleh gave it to the other boy.

Numbers danced behind Elias's goggles. He nodded and the weapons around Saleh relaxed, if only a little.

Elias said, "It's genuine. That's a real find."

Defiance in the other boy's eyes. "I told you."

"You speak for your tribe?" Elias said.

"I speak for myself."

"And the Abu-Ala? Where do the rest of your people stand on this?" Elias said.

Saleh shook his head. Carefully. "This is mine," he said. "It is all that is left. The others will appoint a new speaker in time."

"What do you want for this?"

"I want enough," Saleh said. He seemed desperate. "It's priceless, an original terrorartist artefact."

"That it is." Elias turned it over in his hands. It felt so light. He said, "What do you need the money *for*?"

Saleh said, "There is nothing for me here. I want to go away. Far away. I thought… I could travel up the 'stalk to Gateway, get a ship out."

"Mars? The moon?"

"Titan. I always wanted to see Titan."

Elias felt sorry for him. "You can't run away," he said, as gently as he could. "Even in space, you'd still just be yourself. And lonelier than you could ever imagine."

"Maybe. But I have to get out."

"I'm sorry," Elias said. And he really was. But this was business.

He said, "It's rare. It's valuable. There's no question about it. But it's just an empty bomb husk. Even with provenance. You'd have to find the right collector, and even then… it won't get you to Mars. It would barely get you a one-way ticket on the 'stalk. We would buy it off you, of course. But we are wholesalers, not collectors. I can't offer you what you want and, even if you could somehow sell it at full price somewhere else, it won't be as much as you'd hope."

He saw the light die in Saleh's eyes. Saw it, and felt terrible.

"My father, my uncle, my cousins, everyone…"

"Yes," Elias said.

"All for nothing," Saleh said.

"Not nothing," Elias said.

Saleh barely heard him. He stared at that awful, empty husk. So many lives. And so many still caught in that outwardly expanding explosion, the final installation of a mad artist who took delight in destruction and death.

He could go back, he thought. Go find the rest of the Abu-Ala, follow the coast to Sharm.

He didn't want to, he realised. Even before it all happened, he did not want to live his life this way. Scavenging old tech in the crumbling, rotting, endless maze of architecture on the Ghost

Coast. Marrying, and having a family, so one day he'd have a son, so one day his name would pass on along with the tribe's.

He wanted to see Al-Imtidad, he realised. He wanted to see the glitterball underwater cities of the Drift, the view of Earth as seen from the observation decks of Gateway, high in orbit. He wanted the moon. He wanted Mars.

Instead he was here.

He couldn't, wouldn't go back, he thought. He shook his head. He blinked back tears.

"Thank you," he said, formally. He took back the find. The bomb. "I will find a buyer. I will go—"

"How will you go?" Elias said, ruthlessly.

Saleh felt trapped. "I will go," he said. "I will find a way."

"You could come with us."

Saleh looked at Elias. The other boy was smiling.

"You could be useful," Elias said. "And we can always use a steady set of hands." He tapped his goggles, which must have connected him with the rest of the caravaners, Saleh realised. "It is already decided by quorum. If you would like to, that is."

"Where do you go?" Saleh said.

Elias shrugged. "Along the coast, still, for a while. Then back through the desert before the summer comes. Perhaps to Bahrain."

"Where the Emir of Restoring and Balancing sits on its throne?" Saleh had dreamed of visiting that island, too.

"There is a market there for antiques among both digitals and humans," Elias told him. "You will come?"

"I…"

Elias removed his goggles. For a moment the world seemed lesser, disconnected. Then it resolved into its true shape and he saw Saleh as he really was, small, human, afraid.

He extended his hand to the other boy.

"Yes," Saleh said. His hand was warm in Elias's grip.

"Good," Elias said simply. They rose together from the woven mat.

"Tell me," Elias said, smiling. "Have you ever met an elephant?"

Saleh shook his head. He was smiling, too.

"Then let me take you," Elias said. "They'd love to meet you, you know."

And together, the two boys left the khan, hand in hand, and wandered off into the enclave of the Green Caravanserai, where a herd of elephant were playing in the mud.

THE AGE OF FISH, POST-FLOWERS

Anna Tambour

1.

JUST when you think you've killed them all, others impossibly wriggle over the wall. Or bore through it, some say. Or worse—though this might be another rumor—breed within.

As for the sounds, there's lots of speculation, some of it pretty noisy itself. Are the sounds some new tactic to get rid of the orms? We in the corps have argued about that, most of us too scared to want to talk about it, or to want to hear it discussed; but (and it could be a pose) a few loudmouths insist on spouting daily assurances that the Sound, as they say it Capitalizedly, is the Newest Advance in our age. This might be convincing if they, the optimists, weren't doing the mole act along with the rest of us, and running downstairs as fast as they can when the first sounds rumble in the distance every forsaken morning. They answer *collateral damage, possible risks, someone will tell us, never you mind* and the sun will come up sunny one day.

Today we got another report closer to home. An orm, a relative baby though thick as a man's thigh, its dorsal fin tall as his waist, and its mane thick and coarse as cables. Just a block away, it was caught in the act of engorgement, two legs waving from its maw.

The story goes that a man in blue shot it with his harp-net. The orm's tail wasn't properly caught, and smashed the guy's stomach to pulp, but the mib had already called the orm squad. The person in the orm (unknown sex) was already a lost cause. That orm would feed a hundred New Yorkers, maybe plenty more from outside. That's what Julio says because he saw someone who saw the squad load it into their omni. All just speculation on my part. I'm not a knower, and I don't know anyone who is.

The sounds and craters are something else. The sounds come always at dawn. In them are elements of rumble, drag, shear, and I would imagine earthquake, all in one indefinability, just the sound to make you wake shaking from a dream, though this isn't one. Correction: wasn't one before. The real has exceeded dreams—former dreams, that is.

The sounds have patterned our waking. We all run down to the drypit (though none of us has slept enough) and huddle there feeling the building tremble (or is it just us?) till the day calms, relatively.

It's still raining. We passed the forty days and forty nights mark long ago, thankfully longer ago than anyone in our corps cares to harp about. No one left amongst us is the quoting type. I don't remember the last time the moon shone.

Two levels of underground car park in our building are now nicely filled with water. So we don't have that to worry about. Power could have been a problem but for our resident genius, an arrogant creep otherwise. Julio is the only person who can relate to the guy, but as long as Julio stays with us, we're laughing. (Must keep Julio happy!)

Julio is a genius, too, but a different kind. He named us "The Indefatigables" but that is really he. He found it in a book, he says, in his self-effacing way, but he is the one. I have never been able to figure him out. I thought perhaps it was love, and of who else but Angela Tux? But she left almost at the beginning and Julio stays. He says we give him purpose and that he loves the Brevant, and maybe we do and he does. I certainly must give him purpose, as I don't think I could live without what he's done for us.

The Indefatigables, properly the coop of the Brevant Building, "the corps" as we call ourselves, would be happy as clams these days (no irony intended) if we could only get more dirt. George Maxwell goes out for it instead of just wishing we had more. He went all the way to 51st Street yesterday to find a dirtboy with real dirt.

He was so upset he didn't mind the danger, he said. I think that he was so upset he didn't *think* of the danger. I've never sought a dirtboy. Too frightened of being killed for my seeds. George, though, is a big guy, played varsity in Yale (people say it's still around, where the knowers are). George is one of those guys whose muscles get more tough with age as does their stubbornness. We've got quite a collection here now in our little group, none as brave as George or useful as Julio, but we like to say *each has something to offer*. The building used to be filled with useless types—hysterical, catatonically morose, or verbally reminiscent—but they died out or disappeared. I'm proud and, I admit, lucky to be part of our corps now.

From Julio, the super, we hear rumors. He was the one who told us to fortify, though in the end, it was only him and George Maxwell who stuck broken glass and angle-edged picture frames and sharpened steel furniture bones into the outside wall, one man sticking, the other man guarding the sticker with a pitiful arsenal of sharpened steel. For the steel, it surprised us all how many of us had Van der Rohe chairs. I got mine at a ridiculously cheap price from a place in Trenton, though the delivery, by the time they were all installed in my apartment (I had to get three at the price), was ridiculous. I was glad to donate the chairs. They had always seemed to unwelcome my sitting in them, and gloat when I left them alone. Until the defenses project, I had never been able to part with them, but the prospect of them being torn asunder into ugly scrap gave me the best day I could remember in this age.

So few diversions. The Wall now, you'll want to know about. Walls, really, I don't rightly remember when. Sometime in the first years of the age. The orms were only part of the reason then, but the part that motivated public pronouncements on the Wall project. Where the orms came from, we'll never know. Norwegian cruise ships were blamed for dumping the "freshets," as the spawned babies are called, with the ballast, in both Miami and New York. The Norwegians protested, saying *these are not orms*, and anyway, theirs are mythical (though plenty of Norwegians disputed that). But the mayors and the President said "orms" in their announcements, and so that is what we've called them since. It doesn't matter about the name anymore anyway, nor how they got here, nor to us, how far they have traveled inland. There are rumors that they reached the Great Lakes long ago, and the Mississippi, and that they can travel overland for many miles before they need water. We used to speculate, but as George pointed out, why? We're probably the safest in the country because we protected first, and we have the most organized (not to mention mechanized) protection force in the country, as far as we know, and also we still have both wall-workers (we hear) and men in blue.

The Wall. The first place of building was the hardest: New York Harbor. Then the Wall encompassed more and more of the boroughs, then out to formerly exclusive burbs. The greatest achievement of mankind—it can be seen from outer space. It had massive public support, and became a focus of both civic pride and hope. I remember the feeling.

The Navy sonared the sea to bejesus, both the harbor enclosed by the Wall, and out to three miles. Then the army electrified the Wall wherever it was land-based. We slept easy for it must have been close to a year.

Then the first orm was found *inside*. I remember the headlines in the old *New York Times*: "Mib loses fight to orm; Mayor vows to beef force." Eleven feet long, it came up through a toilet in Flushing (yes, Flushing got in, though I don't know why, but maybe it wasn't Flushing but they said so because it *is* funny, and let's face it, anything funny runs like a nose in November). By the time the orm was hacked to death with a broken plate-glass window stuck to a love seat (by the wife, a weightlifter, I remember, but again, I don't know if this wasn't any more true than Flushing) the orm had (supposedly) bitten through the middle of a tall and muscular dry-waller (but again, he could have been a flabby accountant). Whoever-it-was's middle was found in the orm on occasion of the orm's post-mortem (orms were not then eaten by anyone). The fact is, an orm killed in a safety zone.

A massive eradication campaign was launched to kill freshets within the Wall and anything that had gotten into the sewer system. The subway was sealed, the vent covers replaced by cement plugs.

There was maximum publicity for effort and minimum information of results. Then media stopped, as there was thought to be no further public benefit to be gained from it. The orms kept coming for a while and then as far as we heard, died off. Julio says they never died off, which is why we and anyone else of wealth isn't connected anymore to the sewer or to any other municipal system (if, indeed, there's anything left).

In one respect we feel secure. Now neither people nor orms can climb our walls, nor gain entry through our two doors (our genius designed that protection).

"Be prepared" —our motto for when we do have to leave the
Brevant. Each of us has to on a rostered basis, for at least a little
time. George (the health nut) makes us. "You need the air," he says.
He doesn't add, *You need gut-building*, but he could. Both muscles in
the gut like George, and some of the guts that gave him the courage
to fortify our building. Each of us has to deal with the dealers. That
spreads the load. And sometimes, one of us doesn't return. We all
mourn the loss of the corps member and whatever it was that was
lost as pay to the dealer. The most valuable pay is, of course, seeds.
Dealers being who they are, there are those who think only of a
shot of energy—and they want meat.

Next to seeds, the next most valuable commodity for forward-
thinkers is dirt. The dirtboys are just that—boys, and dirty. They
are the second fastest natural things in the city. They are the only
ones who know where dirt is. Mibs kill them if they can corner
them because dirtboys dig holes in the Wall to go outside to get
dirt. That's what's said. I don't know, but they carry the dirt in
their clothes. They strip and you've got to put the dirt into *your*
clothes. Tied-off pants and shirt arms are a giveaway, so there's
many ingenious ways that dirtboys hide their load. If we're caught
with dirt, we don't get killed, but we do get drafted to volunteer.
I've never known a volunteer. Part of Julio's job is to keep us from
being volunteers, and so far, the Brevant has been left alone. What
we have that is valuable to the mib besides our seeds, I never know
but Julio does. He usually asks us for old electricals—a shaver,
some extension cords, a bread-making machine—and we always
give the him the stuff. Someday maybe we won't have the means to
pay, but so far we do. Why the mib don't just take what they want,
I don't know. Maybe they are designed to serve.

Lately I've been thinking of other things. Like these craters Julio
told us about. Every crater open to the sky is a breeding ground,

he says, and he also says it is a matter of time. Since the orms adapted to the electrification of the wall, the electricity had to be disconnected and sharp spikes mounted porcupine-style all over the wall. And this means that with rain, danger is increased, as the streets are slick and every pothole is a pool. An orm and you and water—and as soon as the orm feels your presence, your body will spit like a frozen freedom fry dropped into boiling oil.

The craters are the most recent crisis in our age. I've never seen a crater, but Julio has, blocks of them on the Grand Concourse in a stripe that is so fat it took away the Jerome Avenue El. Poe Park, he said, is now a *much* bigger park (and he laughed in a spine-crawling way), and that little house is gone, he said, which is too bad, but the El being gone makes a much nicer vista, he said. How a whole elevated "subway" could disappear, along with all the buildings, we were trying to comprehend when he said it all made the neighborhood look much better, and he laughed again, *even with the craters* where all those stubby brick apartment houses had been. *Alexander's final closing down sale finally finalized*, he chuckled, and then he nearly choked himself pointing to us and cracking up, doubled over like some comedy antique. It was rude of him to make a joke that only he understood. But then his happiness is infectious and we all ended up laughing anyway. Julio has a way that can bring you out of your cares! He always looks on things in his own way. I wish I could, as I had nightmares for a week from that trip of his to the Bronx, especially the *where did everything go* part.

George saw a cleared area in Queens with lots of holes where basements were; and oddly, so did Fey, who once traveled farther than anyone. Must have been his daydreaming that let him get that far, and luck that brought him home.

I could worry during my waking hours, but where would that get me? That sounds heroic, stoic maybe, but I can only worry about so much, and at the moment what I worry about—what keeps our whole corps awake at night—is this: Does anyone know about our sunflower?

The corps celebrated when this sunflower took—the only one of five precious seeds from George's last (strictly illegal) seed expedition. (The only trade that is legal is to work for "food" as a volunteer. I can't eat that "food" from what I hear of it, and I don't want to sacrifice myself to the Wall any more than anyone with a smitter of choice left.) Perhaps these seeds came from the botanical gardens in the early days of the Transition. George assures us that, as he was assured, this sunflower plant will grow to have a flower with real, fertile seeds. Regardless of the pictures in books in the Brevant collection, we have to see those seeds to believe them, and then we have to see *them* make new seedlings. Our books are all *old*, bought way back when because they *were* old, even then, when seeds were seeds for the generations, and books with pictures were for collecting and not trying to get some information, *any crumb of useful information to live by.*

Mrs. Wilberforce's ancient poodle paid for the sunflower seeds, and we were lucky that that dealer was crazy with hunger, or he would have asked for the poodle *and* seeds in return.

Orm. You'd think it would have a nightmarish name, but it doesn't need to. That horse-shaped head. The mane, its congealed, tangled mass; the gasping mouth, as wide as a garbage bin and fringed with triangular, razor teeth. The eyes of a shark, pitiless. A voracious appetite for flesh. Just to see it move is terrifying. The humping fleetness of it over walls, up brick, galloping across intersections once so clogged with people, buses, cars, honking yellow taxis. That was in the early days when there were pictures of them in the news. I've never seen an orm in real life.

But back to the sunflower. Our future relies on this plant—our fortune and salvation. Few people have the water, the dirt, and the power to grow indoors, and also, have the social organization to not destroy their riches. We have all that, which makes us *very* rich, potentially. Seed dealers are low-quality thinkers. They think only of the present. Meat gives them a present. We want a future.

We are not alone. There are a select few who think as we do. Which is why there are dealers, thank goodness. We paid our last meat for these sunflower seeds, if no one is brave enough to hunt orm. Even Julio and George aren't that brave. "Yet," says Julio.

Our cucumbers failed again. Sterile seeds again. Or maybe fake. The mushroom spawn won't take. That was a terrible (and costly) blow.

None of us have gone sidewalk-harvesting. Too much danger for too little reward. The little shoots of grass that spring up are so small by the time they get picked. The other weeds disappeared years ago. Didn't get to bud stage. As for the parks, they disappeared early, their danger recognized and paved over. We'd read that we could eat bark, but all the street trees were burnt that first winter.

Everyone has responsibilities. Old Mr. Vesilios has the dwarf apple tree, as he was allowed to keep it. It was his to begin with. He loves it. He calls it "my wife." And what would you expect someone with the name Luthera Treat to have? And by the way, she looks like her name. I thought "prunes" but it was chickpeas and something she calls black salsify. How would she have gotten chickpeas, ones that weren't sterile, let alone salsify, you ask? She grew them in her window box back when we kept window boxes. She says she got the chickpeas from a trip to Egypt when she was young, and had kept them for luck. She says luck, but I am positive: romance. She says she planted them because she couldn't stand the look of any more flowers, but if that's true, then I'm the Easter Bunny of Times Past.

The chickpeas are nutritious, but they're *beautiful*, and she turns red if anyone asks her about their origin. I can't complain about Luth, though. By the way, she hates being called that, she says, but we call her that because George says she secretly likes it. Actually, I'm sure she hates it, and furthermore, wishes she were a Genevieve or Helena and a beauty—her outside matching her inner soul, which is truly beautiful. I would say that even if there were still beautiful women left here, because it's true. Luthera's manner fits *Luth*, though. With her looks, it wouldn't do for her to show romantic notions, thus her embarrassment over the chickpeas (and their carved, exotic window box). She hardly needed to be interested in food crops on a personal level, even if she was big in the funding of some food-donating NGO, as Julio once said.

As for the rest of us, we've had to learn to like to eat "purple pillow" and "espresso" geraniums (tasting like a pillow of mothballs and nothing much respectively (certainly not coffee)), clove-tasting carnations, revoltingly sweet violets, fartish marigolds, tulips that look like candy canes and almost taste like food, *almost*—all that flowerbox stuff that distinguished the Brevant. It was once recreational to eat ornamentals, Luthera said, and when she did, I remembered a time when philanthropy dinners stunk from what looked like soggy, forgotten corsages dropped into every course. At that time Luthera "in revolt" threw out her tulips and lobelia, and planted her window box with salsify and those chickpeas. More than any other person's efforts in our corps, her revolution has kept flesh on our bones. The salsify we particularly have grown to enjoy, though the yachties used to complain that it tastes too much like oysters—"oysters dying over the beach fire, and the juice running down salty arms, bottles of beer, and sun." The yachties are all gone now, thank god, having left in a group. Luth's sourness is more popular than the yachties' reminiscences any day.

There are other crops now, also. We have never been able to get potatoes that would grow. We tried, even though the dirt cost was phenomenal. We haven't been successful with any of our so-called organic wheat grains, brown rice, lentils, or any other of the healthy stores that most of us had in our pantries, mostly untouched before they were recruited as crop seeds. We grin and bear other ornamentals, and they haven't killed us, like when Kate in 4C gorged herself on her own impatiens, rather than give it up to the corps.

For generosity, the prize if we had one would go to that gray-skinned shaking relic of a rocker, Fey Klaxon. Real name John Smith *really*, he told us the day that our corps got down to its present number, eight.

At the end of our first corps meeting (twenty-five present) to set up the new order, he told us to please wait, which was unusually polite for him. We were so shocked, we did. He soon appeared staggering under a huge potted bush. Its leaves are only plucked on special occasions (and then, only a precious few), such as when anyone leaves the building, and when we are all huddled in the drypit listening to those sounds. We tried to propagate more with cuttings, and failed. Our attempts to grow from seed have failed also. For my money, this is the most valuable possession of our corps, though Fey's food store would be more sensibly considered the biggest valuable, now almost vanished.

It seems that all of us have, in our own ways, liked good buys. The Moores on the first floor collected Ming but what they paid for each piece was their biggest joy. It wasn't how much. It was how little. Unusual in the art world, but then Mr. Moore's business was smell-alike name brands. For Cordell Wainer, it was shoes. For Mr. Vesilio, it was olive oil. He used his wine room to store olive oil, and hated wine. For me, it was canned goods. Not having any guests, I had lots of room. I shopped sensibly. Delivery was a problem, so

I stocked the spare room and the bath in one delivery. When the first intimations of a new age began, I decided that the dining room could again be put to use, and filled it, too. It was a comforting sight—all my cans. It was crowded again, like when I was a child and my parents filled the rooms with guests and laughter.

I received my last can from the corps about a year ago, but it made me feel good thinking how long my can supply lasted everyone with good management (my own, as I have been from the first in charge of the food stores).

Fey did better than I, though. He had become chronically shy. I would be, too, if I looked like he, and had looked like he had looked. His health was a constant worry to him. He had been on Dr. Etker's mucusless diet for years, and that didn't do any good. His colon troubled him. Crystals didn't work. He worried about fungus. He didn't trust practitioners anymore, so he devised his own regime. He stocked up and then planned not to leave the building ever again. What he bought was canned English-style custard powder "with pure vanilla and pure cornstarch." At the time of our first coop meeting, he had lived on that as a pure food, just adding water, for six months. His apartment is larger than mine, being two joined together for rampageous entertaining. One, he had filled with his provisions. The custard ran out last month.

We are all still healthy relatively speaking, though no one carries excess fat, and you can count everyone's ribs and vertebrae, a little more delineated each day. We still have a varied diet, though it needs to improve pretty fast now, as nothing miraculous has turned up. Everyone but Fey admits to craving meat. I know I do. None of us has tried orm. We don't talk about what other people outside the Brevant eat, although we know that rat is traded practically legally. I could *never* eat rat! Orm, at least, is a fish.

The sunflower is our most valuable possession now. It is our future, should no better future shine upon us.

2.

We do think of a better future, you know. Not for our children. The Brevant is not for children. But because, why? Mr. Vesilios gave a beautiful talk last night about the number of colors he has counted in the blossoms on the apple tree, and his talk gave me a dream that I didn't want to wake from.

It is now dawn again, when most of us habitually wake. That sound is beginning. I should rush down to the drypit.

The sunflower. The sunflower, though still a sprout, is breathing in, exhaling oxygen or whatever it is plants do. In, out. Just like us, but the sunflower calmly breathes all day and sleeps all night, every night, in its rare earth. And is loved. To be so loved.

That sound. Its muffled quality only makes it more terrifying. I always make a racket of noise rushing to get down the stairs as fast as I can. I make as much noise as I can, to cover up the sound. Today, for some reason, I listen—don't let myself move.

One of Fey's leaves. Is it possible to imagine chewing a leaf? A gob of them? The bitter spit, that pinch of plaster that Fey and Julio figured out as the strange accompaniment to the leaf. The leaking of ease and happiness into my blood, my heart, my thoughts. It lasts such a short time, but in that time, even the sunflower doesn't matter.

I listen, and imagine being George Maxwell. Being Julio. Being more than them because they rush down to the drypit, too. I imagine being like someone in the old days—strong, brave, heroic. Like men in blue were back when they were real men in blue.

The sound is louder now but still far away, I think. Crashing bangs and slides? I'm sure if you were underneath, you could only feel, not hear, because your eardrums would explode.

I am going. I am going. I wish I hadn't stayed in bed this long. Moving is all the more difficult. Usually I run, but now it's all I can do not to flatten myself and crawl, hugging the walls. Ashamed, I force myself to walk calmly, an insane compromise.

In the vestibule, a tiny opening high in the barriered window lets in the dawn light, pink as a young rose. When did I see this light before? It's been so long. Back in the time of roses, when I used to wake to pigeons cooing against my window. Then, on with the tracksuit, out to the park. One lap, and a cool-down in the rose garden when the dew lay in the petals.

Now, roses in the sky just makes it all the worse to dive like a mole as day breaks. My stomach twists. Wouldn't it be funny to describe the reasons why, as in the old days. *Doctor…*

And the solution to my problems? Clumps of cintered powders.

That sharp bar of rose-colored light enters my right iris. I should be a mole-rat now, huddled in the drypit with the rest of them. Eyes unnecessary, as we sit out the monotony of our daily terror.

Perhaps it is my stomach, or maybe the color of the rose.

I lower my head and quickly perform all the tasks needed to open the small exit door.

Its *swish-clunk* at my back speaks for me. I can't hear it, but I feel it against my body. Felt it.

Dawn is dead.

The Sound that blanketed the Brevant's door-thud is *alive*. So alive, it runs between my teeth like a mouse. There is nowhere to go. I threw off my moleskin when I touched the door, so I do what I imagined—step into the street. Now's the time to lift up my head… and that feels *good*.

Searching the skyline, where is the source? The Sound is so loud now that it crowds into the me-ness of me, or would *like to*. It is so loud that I can't tell which sounds I hear. Originals or echoes.

The sky is now the color of wet cement, with a slick of blood in it. Peer as I do, I can't see anything through the murk.

Looking out… looking up…

Something.

Two thin cables (?) though each could be at least as thick as a city block. I can't tell distance.

They fall parallel from a point of infinity to a jagged horizon.

Scrapes and crashes. Distinct. Sharp. I saw for a moment, but all that's left is the Sound now, as the cables disappear in the wool of a gray sky again.

I haven't heard of anyone installing anything above the city, but I told you already—I don't know any knowers. It would be so much safer up there. Maybe they didn't want us interfering, and that is why they make that noise. What are they doing? Maybe this is the cleanup they spoke about. They took their time!

Even on my tiptoes, as far as I can see, I am the only person watching. My whole life, nothing like this.

This is the best thing that has ever happened to me.

Wallace Evian Sturt IV. Little Wally. I'm not little. It's just the fate of IVs. My great-grandfather would have sunk all his money, spent it all on whores and horses if he knew that it would have trickled down to the likes of Dad, and I'm no throwback. There was something to the grands. More than just living to make contacts, make money. I've overheard people refer to me as "nice" back when my parents were alive.

I need to concentrate on what's happening. They promised us years ago to do something, but never specified, and then they didn't bother to make announcements anymore because all we did was complain.

Well, we *did*.

The Sound pummels the air now. It's rising in shudders from the ground. It's personal now, like when a dentist punctured the roof of my mouth. I can feel the Sound from my soles to the roof of my mouth, to the roots of my hair. I can't properly *see*, dammit.

A smudged cloud rises and then falls and as if it never left us, the sun comes out and shines down like the sun once did. The sky in the area of the chains is now old-fashioned innocent-flower blue, and that grayness is unmistakably clouds not made by moisture, but made by what we've made, for they rise from where the chains disappear into the skyline. I am *not* going to move.

The cables (or chains?) are even bigger, and the grinding crashes get closer and I stand where I am, chewing on the inside of my cheek till I can taste metal. My own blood. But I can coolly taste it and report the taste to myself.

Another cloud puffs, and then a spate of crashes, crisper than before, closer than ever. My cheek twinges, awash with blood.

I can see the end of the cables. They are attached to what looks like a giant open mouth of a net. They're pulling the net upwards… full. Fat power station cooling towers bulge out the shape, bits of highway, buildings, spires poke through the holes. What must be bridge cables hang down from the bottom like the angel hair spaghetti of my childhood hung from a fork. As the bag rises, more of the mass becomes visible. A ball—that Earth sculpture that had once been so big. Huge unmistakable broken blocks—the Wall!

Bits fell at the beginning of the pull. Those were the last crashes.

I wonder how many orms they caught in the net.

Now there is no sound. Rather, there is a startling reverberation of hush as the bulging base of the bag is hoisted high. I can see that its enormous bulge at the base would be wider than Yankee Stadium. Many times wider. The long, long bag ascends—into the brilliant sun. I couldn't see where they ascended to, for the glare. And now, though it is blue where I've looked, raindrops stab my eyeballs—a monkey's wedding, I think it's called. Sun and rain. It's over for the day, anyway, I know. So I uncrick my neck and turn around for home.

I didn't even think about an orm, that whole time. I don't even know how long it was.

That was close. I do know that. I have seen.

I will tell about it, and I know I won't stutter even once. Wallace isn't a good name, but it's better than Little Wally, and a darn sight better than Luthera. Maybe my name will be changed.

Others could have been me. There were rumors, but no one believed them. I didn't, and Julio laughed. George said it didn't matter. He just said, "Get out. Get your air."

Build guts? Did George know, but had undeveloped guts himself when it came down to the choice of being a mole every morning, or throwing off that shameful animalness and striding out as a man, biting himself to bravery?

Now, at least somewhere, there is no Wall. That must be a good thing—the breakthrough we've been waiting for, but were too cowered to realize.

Anyway, I will tell of what I saw—I who ventured.

And what to do, now that the Sound has been identified? I would advise: As long as we go underground, we should be protected during the sweep.

Can I insulate myself with painted canvas and make myself a spear, or have we used up all our chairs?

What does orm taste like?

What would Luthera think if I brought one home? *When* I bring one home. I hope they don't clean up everything before I catch one.

But there I go again. Might as well have been stuttering still, such was the Little Wally mindset. Sure, it would be great to be the hero of the corps. But throughout history, any man worth his sword thinks higher than a Luthera.

EXURBIA

Kaaron Warren

Twin Town: La Rinaconda, Peru, 5100m

FLORIAN would have been fine if he hadn't stolen the man's toolbox, with its ancient hammer and sturdy set of spanners. Sleeping with the wife was a side-issue; her choice, her preference.

But touching a man's tools?

Florian wasn't even sure why he'd done it. But he'd been called a thief all his life, even in a world where property itself was theft.

They'd spent the day out in the open, in a place Natalie liked to call "their patch" but that Florian could never tell apart from the other green spaces in that part of the city. She liked it because it was central, far from the edges that made her nervous. She'd never been down to the crust, so her nightmares were all inspired by stories she heard. Florian couldn't tell her otherwise; it was awful down there.

She'd brought along a basket of fresh vegetables, he'd brought booze and a blanket, and that was a pleasant few hours. He was hungry afterwards, though, looking forward to an actual meal he'd make for himself at one of the communal kitchens.

They'd raced for shelter as a storm came over. Natalie wanted to bunker down inside with the animals, send Florian on his way, pretend it wasn't happening. She hated watching storms whereas he'd been caught out in them and knew how beautiful they were.

There must have been a thousand lightning bolts, each one illuminating the sky, the city, and the vast expanse of dead brown land far below. The city itself was full of colour; flowers, painted walls, art everywhere.

He left Natalie sleeping, taking her husband's toolbox with him. He'd avoid seeing her again; best to move on, not complicate things. He had work to do, on the containment walls up on High Point. There were often repairs up there, and many unwilling to go to the area. It was a known hangout for people outside the law, which didn't bother Florian.

Florian rode his bike ninety minutes to High Point, then left it leaning against an old washing machine re-purposed as a table. From that aspect he could see the gaps and issues in that part of the wall and went to work. At this level, it was built up of glass bottles, broken bricks, bits of cement, and did the job in a fairly ugly way. Beautification was on the agenda, but way down the list of important projects for the city.

It was clear after the storm, and from that viewpoint he could see way out into the distance. He could see the hints of old buildings, the outline of them, and plotted in his head where to go should he ever touch the ground again. There was salvage to be had, and foundation stones to look for. His last trip down had been terrifying, though, and he wasn't keen to go down there again. A mist crept up the containment walls of the city, looking like low-flying clouds.

He worked quietly, enjoying the feel of his new tools, and then Natalie's husband found him.

They'd been friends, *were* friends, or as friendly as was possible in this part of the city, but none of that mattered now.

"Had a good night?" the husband asked.

Florian knew no answer was expected, but he said, "It was tops, mate. You? I heard you were night golfing out by the lakes district."

The husband smiled. "Looks like we both got a hole-in-one."

Florian laughed. The hammer was in his left hand; as casually as he could he moved it behind his back. Maybe the guy hadn't noticed? Maybe they were just having a chat? He regretted taking it but knew there was a market for well-cared-for tools.

"Got your work cut out for you there," the man said. "Need to keep the people safe. How's the access door looking? Secure?"

Florian wasn't sure. "It's clear out there today," he said. You could see the beach way in the distance, where the beach used to be, anyway. "It's so vast," Florian said. "Makes all this seem insignificant, don't you think?"

He waved his spare hand in the air, keeping the other behind his back. The toolbox was at his feet and he stepped subtly in front of it.

The husband shook his head. "I know what you took. You're a dead man."

"You're killing me for a toolbox?" Florian said. "You can have the fucker back, mate. Seriously."

The husband paused for a moment. Florian saw tears in his eyes. "You didn't need to kill her," he said. "Why did you do that?" and Florian remembered then (how had he forgotten such a thing?) that Natalie had been sleeping heavily when he left, so heavily he got no response from her.

"I didn't mean to," Florian said, "she wanted to take the high dosage," but still the man lifted him shoulder high and threw him over the edge of the city.

For a minute, Florian thought he could fly, that a miracle had occurred. Then he began to fall, buffered by air currents that wafted him down.

Twin Town: El Alto, Bolivia, 4100m

> He scrabbles,
>
> trying to reach the ladder
>
> that clings to the side of the city.
>
> He's climbed up and down this ladder
>
> three times, no more. He can't grab it now.

The first salvage mission to the crust had been the most successful. The climb down had killed him, just about, but there was so much embedded in the walls of the city, so many tiny treasures. He took mental notes to collect them on the way up, and he did, making a good week's wages from the sale of them. Along the way he peered into the rare empty spaces in the wall; in some places old cars had been salvaged and stacked, even an RV which, when he looked inside, appeared to be furnished. He wanted to poke his head in, call out, but the others moved on, calling on him to hurry. It'd take eight hours to climb down and they didn't want to dawdle along the way.

On the ground, he and his small crew hunted down the foundation stone of the old commercial bank, and while they found where it should be, there was nothing left, long since raided.

Still, they made stashes, piles of goods to help build the city. Foolishly, they'd left these stashes unguarded, and had come back to find them gone. It was the bone-builders, for sure, the cultish group who were responsible for body disposal on the crust.

They didn't stay long. The air down there was thick and chemical and the mist clung to them, making their clothing damp and their faces greasy. Florian strode ahead of the others across the moat, balancing on the bridge made of fallen steel. The moat itself was deep, filled with a liquid nothing could live in, capable of breaking down the massive tonnage of plastic dumped into it. The moat was filmed with a shiny, at times colourful sheen.

✦✦✦✦✦

Twin Town: Lhasa, China, 3410m

> He spins,
>
> sucking for air,
>
> trying to right himself.

The climb back up the ladder took twice as long. They carried more than they took down, replacing some of the treasures stolen. They'd had no luck finding any other foundation stones in the ruins of the buildings; Florian swore next time he'd travel with people willing to go further.

He let the others climb ahead, not wanting to share the small things he'd found on the way down. As he approached the car layer, the RV, he peered in again.

It was just high enough to be above the poisonous fumes coming from below, although Florian could definitely still smell it and feel it in his nostrils. The mist was lighter here, almost refreshing as he climbed.

"Hello?" he heard. "Hello?"

It was an old woman. She was hunched over in the space, but as he peered through a small open area he could see that she was very short, and that she had bedding in there, and cans of food. She spoke quickly, telling him her life story. She nursed burnt soldiers, she said, in one war or another. She wanted someone to know who she was.

He thought about dragging her out and throwing her down to the bone-builders. It would be over quickly for her that way. But she told him a story of her past bravery, of her life, and how she had been discarded, and her fury made him realise she still had life left in her. "They tossed me over but I saved myself, curled up in a little ball. The moat is a softer landing than you might think," she said. "Come see me again," she said.

Twin Town: Asmara, Eritrea, 2363m

Falling,
he thinks of revenge.
Even as he spins, he knows
he can survive if he curls himself up in a ball.

On the second trip to the crust, Florian convinced the group to go as far as the old town hall. It hadn't been completely cleared, so he hoped the foundation stone would be unchecked. Once they'd moved a pile of rubble (crumbling cement, pieces of metal, bricks), there it was. They lifted it, and were rewarded with a small stack of old coins, the outline of what was once perhaps a book, and a silver flask, filled with liquid. Florian pocketed that; perhaps he'd drink it, perhaps not, but it was worth plenty.

The bone-builders didn't bother them, busy clearing the moat and the surrounds of the fallen. They'd been gathering the bodies for generations now, since the city was half-built, perhaps two thousand metres above sea level. Although truly it was never finished, just added to, built on, each layer covering the last until they reached as high as they were now, lived as efficiently as they did now.

The bone-builders lived in a house built of bones. It was their church as well, and they worshipped at it daily, singing in low voices, calling out to ghosts only they could see. Florian wanted nothing to do with them, but like all the city dwellers he was glad they were there to do the work.

Bolstered by their find they went a little further, but they realised they were heading in the direction of the massive underground chamber that served as their waste outlet. Even miles underground the fumes seeped up, so they turned back.

Florian found a smooth piece of glass and pocketed that, thinking he might leave it for the old lady in the van. She'd been asleep on the way down; he wanted to talk to her again, hear her voice.

She was thrilled with his gift. "Fit for a queen," she said. She cast around her van as if looking for something for him, but he told her he didn't need anything in return.

Her whole world was there, a shrunken world, that somehow gave the illusion of vast space and the comfort of confinement, containment.

She said, "I'm so tired."

Florian was too. Part of him wanted to just let go, let himself fall.

Twin Town: San Jose, Costa Rica, 1146m

>He tries
>to get a fingerhold
>in the walls of the city.
>It's all packed solid and tight.
>No house of cards, this city is as
>sturdy as any. It sways a bit in the wind
>but this is a good thing, once you get used to it.

The third and final time he went down to the crust the old woman wasn't there.

They walked further this time. Florian convinced them to search as far as the old fig tree; stories had it that near that tree, which was planted to commemorate an art gallery, was a time capsule that would change their lives. He told them that once they got there, they'd know they were at the start of something.

There was very little left of the fig tree. Florian had mapped it out from the city, figured out how long it would take them, all that. But he hadn't realised how unstable the crust was there. They could feel it cracking under their feet the further they went, and in some parts it was like jelly and in other parts like a soft sea sponge.

Florian looked back at the city, standing so tall, broad and high it cast a shadow as far as the eye could see.

The group stood, undecided, until one of them pushed forward, wanting to explore further, but his left leg pushed through the crust to the hip. His screams seemed to shatter the crust further as the group pulled him out. His pant leg was burnt off and his flesh burnt too, and the bits left unburnt were covered in small, strange bites.

They carried him home, dragging him up the ladder, but he died on the way so they dropped him, let him fall into the moat.

The old lady was gone. Florian saw books open to where she left off and he took one or two on his way back up, putting in bookmarks so he knew where she was up to. It was sad she'd never finish the story, but Florian knew he'd be popular back in the city with these old books.

Twin Town: Bangalore, India, 920m

> There is no
> sign of the old lady
> as he falls. No sign she ever existed.

He took the books to the library. This was one of the reasons he'd slept with Natalie; she was the librarian and he felt as if the old lady was sending him a message. He'd met her before, knew her as the wife of a mate, but it was different seeing her there amongst the books, without the husband, just beautiful.

He told her about the layers under the city because she'd never seen them. She was too terrified of heights to look out, let alone climb up and down the ladder. He told her about how shaky some of the layers seemed, crumbling mortar, old wood, and how you could see how the city had grown, like something organic.

Twin Town: Abuja, Nigeria, 777m

As
he falls,
steam rises
off the moat. It's very warm.

Twin Town: Canberra, Australia, 605m

He wants support.
Comfort. He wants someone
to say *there, there,* and somehow catch him.

Twin Town: Madrid, Spain, 588m

He thinks,
if I can kick and swim
as soon as my feet touch water,
I'll keep my head up, then I'll swim for the side,

Twin Town: Prague, Czech Republic, 244m

pull
myself out.
I'll be coated
with plastic, and
he tries to give himself
a superhero name, Captain
Fanplastic is all he can come
up with, that moat of melting plastic
coming closer, the high chemical smell
burning his lungs. There is no one below
to witness his plunge, his valiant effort to
reach the side. He curls up into a little ball.
He wished he hadn't let Natalie take the drugs.

Twin Town: Rome, Italy, 37m

He doesn't feel
hungry or thirsty,
which is strange. He is
often both. He threads his
arms through the ladder and
looks down to see how far he's
climbed. Then he sees his own body,
embedded in the crust, and he watches as
the bone-builders tear him apart limb from limb.
And he does float then, becoming a part of the mist
that circles his beautiful, imperfect, impossibly high city.

WATCHING GOD

China Miéville

NAILED to the top of the tower over our town hall entrance is an iron sign that reads 'Every man's wish.' Below it the high stone step looks down a long cut of rock over the edge of the cliff into the bay and the sea beyond it, and consequently at the ships when they come.

Our town hall has two floors and the tower extends to the height of a third; it is by some way our biggest and tallest building. Every three days in the main hall we hold the market where we exchange clothes we have made or into which we no longer fit, vegetables we have grown and animals we have caught, any small fish we might have netted and the shellfish we have prized off rocks in the rock pools at low tide. In its other rooms the hall is also our hospital and our library. It is our school and our gallery.

Though most of the frames on the walls of the gallery room contain images, a few have quotations within them—some attributed, some not. They are handwritten in fading ink, or typewritten with a blocky typeface that does not match that of any of the machines on the isthmus, or torn, it looks like, from books, with half-finished phrases at either end where the page continued. Many of the older books in the library room have torn pages within them of course, no matter how vigilant Howie the librarian is, but these have not been taken from any of them.

Like most of us, I had a period in my youth when I became deeply interested in the quotations, you might say obsessed. I read them all many times and considered which were my favorites. I liked 'I must deliver a small car to a rich Baghdadi.' I liked 'choosing the fauna of his next life.' One day I found, as do we all, a small gilt frame below a window onto the woodpile in which in small smudged print I read, 'Ships at a distance have every man's wish on board,' and below it in smaller slanted letters, *Their Eyes Were Watching God.* Adults do not mention this artifact to children but let them find it according to their own investigations. As is presumably intended by that restraint, I recognized within it the words of my town's battered metal flag with the tremendous excitement of discovery. For a short breathless time, I believed I was the only person who had made this connection.

I came to understand that it is from the assertion in that frame that stems our traditional attitude to the vessels that visit our waters. Certainly it is a metaphor, but we have tended nonetheless to regard the ships as arriving at just the right moment to load up on those hopes and aspirations we have been accreting and nurturing over the days of their absence, with which we have just (we allow ourselves to think) reached a surfeit when the ships reappear, though many of which we'd find it hard to state. When the ships come into sight beyond the bay we feel our inner loads lighten and become aware how freighted we had become with jostling thoughts.

The vessels usually sit motionless in the waters beyond the edge of the bay for two or three days, lit up from within, their portholes glowing. When—it has seemed to us—their holds are full, they move again, up anchors and sail with our wishes out over the horizon.

To the disappointment of my mother and my friend Gam, both intellectuals, I am not much of a reader. But though the library room was never one of my secret monarchdoms (what I liked most was to climb the bleached trees at the edge of the forest and take birds' eggs and empty them carefully and paint the shells, or to build hides with fallen branches and old nails), when I found that framed clause I did spend hours over many days hunting the spines in the library room. In vain: there is nothing by anyone called *Their Eyes Were Watching God*, not among the ur-texts in their hard covers, nor in the books of new literature written by townspeople in living memory and bound in thin wood and rabbit- or rat-skin.

The ships that visit us are of many designs. Some are powered by sails (the wind on the seawall and the cliffs has been known to pick people up and throw them all the way down into the water or onto the rocks, you must be careful). Most move by engines, venting exhaust as they approach the unfinished sentence. There are trunked, single-piped, raked, complex-stacked, split-trunked, and combined outlines and vents. A few of these have chimneys higher than the masts of the tall ships, so they look like they will topple. Some are small and squat with flared smokestacks like those that front steam trains, of which we know from books.

Some of my friends like to watch the ships when they first appear, the only presences in otherwise empty water. I like to watch them as they get closer to the sentence.

Most of the oil paintings in the gallery room are of flowers and hills but there are some of ships, very bright things with skirts of foam, yawing jauntily. Those, it is easy to see, carry wishes. We have no cameras (Gam tried to make one from a diagram in a book but only made a box) but we do have some photographs also on display, most black-and-white and a few in a speckled and unsaturated color. There are pictures of animals that we don't have on the spit but that we know from books, of huge cities taken from up high that look like ink-smeared blocks put together badly, and of ships.

You have to look closely at those photographed ships to make much of their shapes. Some are just dashes at the edge of water only a bit less gray than they are, some are black tangles, some look almost like cracks or mistakes on the lens. Some are like shadows come up out of the water. The greater the distance at which they sit, the harder it is to imagine them carrying any wishes with them. I think *Their Eyes Were Watching God* was looking at a painting, not a photograph, to write those words. I don't know why every woman's wish is not listed as on board the ships too.

There is sea to the north, the south, and the west. A few miles to the east you get to the forest and the ravine and no one can get past that. The ships always come into view from the same quadrant, following the coastline a mile or more out. When we were children we would wave at them but no one ever waved back that we saw. We have no telescopes, though we know what they are.

Tyruss and Gam worked for a long time and made something that looked like a telescope, even with an almost-round bit of glass at each end, but when you looked through it it didn't make things any bigger. Some people like to try to make things from the books. Gam gave the telescope to me.

Mostly no one pays much attention to the ships. If you are walking past a neighbor on the cliff-walk when a new vessel has just arrived you might, when you say good morning, that it's a fine day, also mutter that this one has a particularly tall mast, or that it's a long one, or that it's flat in the water, but you would be as likely to say something about a nice tree or a flower bush, or as likely to say nothing.

My mother always seemed embarrassed when I talked about the ships—children do talk about them—and when I got a bit older I asked her why and asking her made her uncomfortable.

No one minds those few adults who do want to discuss them doing so with each other so long as they don't involve the majority who would rather not. Chomburg used to light big smoking fires on the stones of the beach when the ships appeared, burning bits of plastic and rubbish and wood and inedible fish, trying to make signals in smoke, so you would see horrible big globs of stink going up into the air and if the wind changed it made the town smell bad, so everyone asked him to stop doing it and, though with his usual bad grace, he did.

There are those who think that there are no people on the ships at all. We know what sailors are, but there may be none on any of these vessels.

Two ships have sunk in my lifetime.

The first went down when I was with my mother in the woods picking mushrooms and checking traps for rabbits. I carried the bag while she carried me—I was little—and we came out of the trees and saw pretty much the whole town gathered in front of Misha's workshop, arguing excitedly. People started shouting at my mother as soon as they saw her, telling her what had happened and what they had seen. As soon as she understood she took me quickly down the path to the shore and we looked out at the sentence but by then the ship had gone completely under so there was nothing new to see, though I told myself there was more chop between the wrecks than there had been.

It must have been laying deep grammar, my mother said.

Then one cold morning when I was fifteen I was braced halfway down the cliff, trying to steal from a kittiwake nest. With a certain luxurious terror I was listening to my rope creak. I don't know what alerted me that there was something to see but I looked over my shoulder as best I could, out over the water. A battered steamer was coming toward us at a good pace. It was low in the water, and still far enough away that it looked like a misprinted image.

I braced my feet on the lichen and sheer chalk. The ship did not slow. When it abruptly upended I discovered I was not surprised. I imagine some unseen squib puncturing a hole just so, timed so that as the ship passed between the weather-beaten promontories of other scuttled vessels, its bow shoved down as if under a big hand and the steamer burped black smoke and plunged under at an angle to come to a hard rest against some sunken reef or obstacle. Perhaps against the ship I and my mother did not see sink. There was a grinding across the water and with a resonant cracking the steamer's stern broke off and fell into the waves.

Over the next half a day the ship fussed and fiddled and sank more while people watched. It settled finally in a last configuration, jutting like an overhang over the scattered bits of its own broken tail that stuck up from the underwater rise on which they had landed. The wreck took its position in the graveyard place, among the other remnants: rusting humps of chimneys, the stumps of masts breaking the water like reaching fingers, flanks, decks, the keel of an upturned cargo ship.

These shallow acres where rocks wait below sight are the waters of the sentence. The dead vessels obtrude from the surf and discolor it in their new broken shipwreck shapes. Each is a word, assiduously placed, set to self-ruin precisely.

I spoke to Gam, who was one of those intent on decoding the sentence. You could often find Gam drawing on rough paper, marking the positions and shapes of the sunk ships from one or other point on the cliff or the shore, connecting them variously with scribbled lines, measuring the spaces between them and applying various keys. Gam was sure that, seen from the right place in the right way, the sentence would make sense. Once I saw Gam sketching from the town hall roof. No one was supposed to go up there. I promised not to tell.

Look, I said, they keep adding words. You can't decode it or translate it yet, it's not finished.

No ships have come for a long time.

Before this, the longest I remember without visitations was a little over a week, and it has been much longer than that.

For several days no one said anything. You might have started to detect a little anxious crinkle around their eyes when you said hello to people. You might have thought the wind felt a bit colder. More people seemed to me to be at Gam's station, standing out under the gray sky at the cliff's edge, staring at the sentence with more concentration than I'd ever seen before.

A certain panic has entered our days. You may not know you notice them, but all of us have had ships creeping almost silently— except perhaps for a very faint sound of engines or the crack of a sail—in and out of our vision our whole lives, and their absence is frightening. Though their presence has been a fearful thing too. It is not good form to admit that.

Now that there are no ships people have started to talk—like children—about what they might be and where from, what they do. Theological questions normally avoided.

If they've been observing us, some are asking, have they

stopped? Have they got what information they wanted? Why have they never come ashore?

They can't, of course, is what others say. They have to be at a distance, to stay there, to have every man's wish on board.

There will be a meeting in the town hall to discuss what to do. Caffey, by a long way the oldest person in the town, says everyone is making a fuss over nothing, that we shouldn't worry, that she remembers a time (before anyone else was born) when a fortnight passed and no ships came. But Caffey has license to say all kinds of unlikely things (she lives near our graveyard and likes to scandalize everyone by saying that we'll thank her soon enough, less effort to get her there). Even she admits that this shipless period seems longer than that other in her faint memory.

I will not go to the meeting because I know there is nothing we can do to bring the ships, if we want to, and all the talk of calling them that has started, of getting their attention, of invoking them, is foolish. I hope it is foolish because if it is not it is sinister or will soon be. Another two or three shipless weeks and the worst people in town will start eyeing the weakest. I will not go to the town meeting because I know it will be an argument between those with sense and panickers whose eagerness for sacrifice is unseemly. There will be one of the regular upsurges of rumors.

Instead of that pointless meeting I am going into the woods and asking Gam to come with me, to help me with a project.

I decided to make a start on a raft when I found the big clearing full of dead and fallen young trees. I did so always listening and ready to hide at the sound of anyone approaching, but I was undisturbed. To the dry wood I strapped big plastic containers that had once held water and were now floats full of air. I think lightning must have struck there, I don't know, but I had been working to strip and shape the blackened wood with tools I borrowed from Misha's workshop, and then strap and nail them together, and I had made a reasonable start but I had got bored and without either patience or expertise had stopped. I showed Gam what I had done and said I wanted help to start again. Gam made unconvincing cautious noises but got started immediately.

Of course I'm not the first person to build a raft, or a canoe, or a coracle. It is not allowed but people do it sometimes. Mostly they get found before they put out to sea. Sometimes townspeople disappear and the story goes that they rowed out and their craft held and that now they are somewhere else; or if, as is often the case, they disappear when a ship is visible on the horizon line, stories inevitably start that our lost neighbors are on that ship. Broken boats do wash ashore.

Gam worked out how best to tie the thin trunks together. I said the raft didn't have to be strong, or to last long, only strong enough to go out a way and back again. Gam asked where we were going and I looked in a way that said don't be stupid. I said that maybe what we needed was to see the sentence up close, that maybe that was how you crack it.

We finished sometime after dark but I had a hand-crank torch and I was certain the meeting would continue into the small hours (it did). Gam and I lifted our raft, and each with a crude oar over our shoulders we hauled it through the fringe of woods and down a long route, away from the town (though its low lights still illuminated us through the bushes where it was closest), past fat pillars of rock and to the sea.

Every few minutes Gam would say that this was a bad idea and that we should not do this, not, to be fair, because it was not allowed, but because it was dangerous. Neither of us could swim more than a bit. I did not argue because I knew curiosity would win by the time we were by the water.

It was cold but not too cold at first and the wind was low. The spray slapped us like angry hands and made us gasp but that was all. We pushed the raft out into the low surf.

We were rowing for longer than I had expected. Even a few yards from the shore we were both quickly sodden and vastly colder. There was an almost-full moon but the diffuse gray light was impossible to do much with. It made the foam glow and it rose and fell and confused us. The currents were insistent and we were lucky that they seemed to want only to pull us straight back to the pebbled beach rather than across our route, so though we had to strain we did not have to triangulate or do anything except row as hard as we could through our shivers, directly out, until our hands were terrible messes. It was a very stupid thing to do and I am fortunate I did not die. Gam tried to keep our spirits up by talking incessantly about the ships of the sentence and the ships that visited. About the anxiety they brought. That surprised me: the sea was eliciting confessions. Gam admitted to hating the ships, which made me raise an eyebrow.

What are we going out there for? Gam said and I did not have much of an answer.

Bits of ship architecture began to emerge from the shadows ahead into the light of the torch. We bobbed between extrusions thick with shellfish and guano as I considered the slanting floors, decks, dissolving doorways blocked by weed in the black water below. We had not aimed for any word in particular, we could not have done with our crude raft and in the dark like this, and when we felt the nasty scraping of our underside against corroding metal we both started. We lowered ourselves carefully over the sides, gasping at the cold, and our feet touched down on the roof of some old ship, a roof that rose, a steep metal meadow of growth and decay on which I shone our light, out of the chop of the channel.

We pulled our raft out of the water and sat heavily on the metal rise as the surf sounded. Across what now looked like a mile of low water we could see the lights of our town and the ghost outlines of the cliffs.

When I had my strength back, I stood and shone my light around. We were near the apex of a pyramidal mount of rust broken by what had been windows. From the water a little way off jutted a bow like a whale's head. Beyond that was the side of what I think was a tugboat. We were in an archipelago of ruin, and between each corroded specimen, each word, the waters swirled in complicated microcurrents.

I wondered aloud if we should go on to another, maybe the tower of girders near the furthest rocks. Gam did not answer, was too busy staring into dim vistas of wreckage and gasping that we had done it, that we were here.

Colonies of birds shuffled a bit and a few of them took off but mostly they were untroubled by our arrival, and I imagined that they were used to things hauling themselves up from the waters to sun or moon a while.

Does the sentence make any more sense from here? I said. Gam did not answer but startled me by taking hold of me from behind and turning me around and trying to kiss me. I suppose I had known this might happen. I tutted and pushed and we wrestled for a while on the slope of the old metal. I shoved and Gam stumbled and trod on a decaying anemone abandoned by the sea and skidded violently and fell. Gam's head cracked on the corner of the metal. I stepped forward but I was not quick enough and Gam pitched into the sea and was caught up by the gnarly undertows threading between the wrecks and yanked under as if by ropes much faster than you would think natural. Quickly I pointed the light but I could see only swirls and spray and the black water, and a bit of blood mottling the last of the ship's paintwork, discoloring the remnants of a painted logo, of which we know from the books.

I probed with my oar. Water tugged it and I wondered if it had sucked Gam down into the body of this word, to go up and down its stairwells for a long time. I put my hand into the cold but I had no way to know what shards and sharp edges were below.

Gam did not reappear. I waited a long time. When I saw the lights of the town hall go out I pushed the raft back into the waves of the bay and rowed for the land.

I was only one person, with one oar. On the other hand this was the way the currents wanted to take me. I think it was about the same amount of effort and time to reach the stones of the shore where I kicked and pulled the raft apart to set its pieces adrift, before sneaking, exhausted, back to my house where I knew my mother would be sleeping.

People said Gam must have gone to sea, which I suppose was not untrue. Some wondered if, rather than by water, Gam had picked through the trees and down the sheer channels of the gorge, impossible and impassable as we all know they are, and had got to the mainland that way.

That would be enough to have Gam spoken of in approving disapproving awe forever, but on top of that some people are saying that it's Gam we have to thank for the return of the ships.

In the late afternoon of the third day after we paddled out to the sentence and Gam didn't come back, there was a sudden immense rumbling in the bay. I was not there but I heard about it from Tyruss, who was, who was looking sadly out to sea. There were a series of percussions and booms and the biggest wrecks of the sentence all lurched ponderously, suddenly, at once, in many directions. They came down shattering themselves and each other. Every word fell apart in water that was, Tyruss said, quivering.

When the submerged upheaval was done almost all the ruins were under the waves. Only a few protruding feet of a very few of the biggest wrecks were still visible. The sentence was all but effaced.

Some people thought it was an earthquake, some that it was a submarine, torpedoing the remains. There was a vessel there the whole time, they said. That explains it. Watching by periscope.

In any case, a new ship arrived that evening.

Most of the town were already gathered, as I was, gazing at where the sentence had been. There was a huge cheer and a gasp of astonished delight at the sight of the massive riveted ironclad that appeared, that looked almost crenellated with all its decks and radar dishes and such. It approached the hidden sandbanks and reefs closer to our shoreline than we were used to. We could make out more details of its topside. We could see no people.

Despite this new proximity there was a quality to the ship that is hard to describe, whereby it seemed even less in focus, even more like an imperfect reproduction, even more as if it were copied from a photograph, than the ships to which we were used.

Taking up a huge area on its flank was a symbol, stark and black and white and blue. It was the sign of a company. It looked like many letters superimposed, like several words, or a whole alphabet, printed on top of each other.

People did not take long to simmer down. It was twilight and the vessel's unfamiliar outlines picked out against a vivid red sky made us uneasy. Still, almost all of us stayed, many for hours, right into the night, watching the new ship, almost all of us almost always in silence.

Once again ships are visiting our waters. It is rare again for many days to go by without a new vessel powering into view.

They are still of countless different designs, but they are almost all now larger, newer, more studded with equipment we do not understand, than those ships we grew up watching. And every one is painted with that same big dense logo as was, and is, the first.

The second ship appeared two days after that first and no one knew what to do. Once again we gathered. Of all the novelties of our recent situation this one we all found the most troubling: that the new ship was churning straight for our waters, as ships have done for as many years as we have records, but that its predecessor had not yet gone.

Nor has it still, nor will it, is my opinion.

No one had ever seen two ships afloat at once before. In pictures in the books in the library room, in pictures in the gallery room, yes, of course, there are images of several ships together, there are seascapes and harbors quite crowded with them, with ships jostling all the way to the edge of sight, seeming to shove each other aside to get a better view. In the waters of the real world, though, we had only ever been visited by one ship at a time, unless you count those sunk for us, those surrendered.

The first of the logo-ed ships was at anchor very close to the last visible vestiges of the sentence and it was toward it that the new ship sailed, coming so close and fast that many people started to scream that they would collide, that there would be another explosion, but there was not. The new arrival, a long lean cargo carrier, slowed and stopped, its bow half-blocking the first vessel from our view, settling into the waters still unsteady from the remains of the old sentence.

Since then two more have come. A paddle steamer slapped slowly and inefficiently into place behind and at a right-angle to the previous two newcomers. A low stubby vessel followed it less than a day later, poking skew-whiff into the bay between two last sticking-up crane-tops from the earlier generation of arrivals.

None of them leave. They just pile up where the wrecks are.

I have a premonition that time will move quickly for these new ships. That they will not sink but that it will not take long before the first of them is a floating ruin, a skeleton, a series of shored-up iron ribs in a crumbling corpse buoyed up by its fellows. They are writing a new sentence, if the wrecks ever were, or are, a sentence, more quickly than before, in bigger, louder words, words all of the same brand, the brand of the new company, the company that has won control of this route in a hostile takeover.

This new carrier cannot speak whatever it is saying truly into silence, of course: whatever it is building to with the bodies of its ships it does on older wreckage.

I have tried to descend the ravine but I can find no way through the trees or down the rock face. I was not the first to decide to take a raft to sea and I will not be the only one who decides to go to sea again, now, in this new situation, to walk on the beginnings of a new sentence. I am, though, unless someone in the town is visiting at night and returning before the morning, which—looking at these new ships—seems to me unlikely, does not seem to me something these vessels would allow, the first to have decided to do so.

You might not have thought it to watch me, but I paid close attention when Gam fixed up the first raft and I have made another all alone. It is too cold tonight, I do not want to row with cold deep in me, but as soon as the cloud covers us a little and insulates us from the freezing sky I will go back out to the sandbank, no matter how dark it is.

Last night Caffey and Misha and my mother said surely we all felt lighter now. Said no, we don't know exactly what's happening, but we know that there are ships at a distance again.

I think Gam was right. This is a drop-off, not a pickup. Ships at a distance come not to collect, but carrying freight. They come carrying fear. And it is our fear but it is not our cargo. It has been ordered and is being delivered on behalf of someone else. They bring it to be rendered. It is on their behalf that it will be rendered here.

A STORM IN KINGSTOWN

Nina Allan

WYKE is not the manner of place that goes in for murder, not unless you're counting the crimes sanctioned in the courthouse, the sailors breaking each others' heads outside the Harbourmaster's Arms of a Friday night. Through the hours before morning, and with the storm hammering, Doris sits unmoving by the barroom stove going over what she saw, or thinks she saw, for the longer the night goes on the more she comes to doubt herself, feeling her limbs grow heavier, heavy as the word itself, murder: twinned blows of pick and shovel, the muted, deadfall thump of body to ground.

The city of Wyke lies many leagues north of where we now sit, a port on the River Humber where the great-ships of Bremen and Rotterdam bring in their trade. Wyke is not sea-facing so much as estuarine—hear the sinuous, malodorous creep of the word, the seeping of extraneous water from underground vaults, the half-hidden truths, the pull of quicksand, the stench of brine. The quayside rings with the chimes of hammer-blows and the cursing of sailors. Herring gulls writhe in a grey-winged swarm above the newly berthed fishing smacks, ships' decks glistening and slippery with mackerel guts and scales. Innkeepers and sous-chefs argue over prices. The one-eyed captain of the carrier *Hildegaard* oversees the tagging and loading of three-dozen Yorkshire lambs and a prizewinning bull.

Back from the harbour we find the inns, the card-parlours and the gaming rooms, the alehouses and poorhouses, the tottering, rat-infested hostels that form the filthy underside of the city's trade. Where privateers drink side-by-side with schoolmasters, where a curate named Roland Parfitt, exhausted by the backstabbing bureaucracy of the parish meeting room, might find himself seduced by a guardsman's flattery, at least for one evening.

Behind the Harbourmaster's Arms a cobbled road leads uphill, into the tangle of muddy streets where the townspeople plot their rebellions and nurse their sick children. Since the pestilence took hold in the North, there has been a counterpoint to the gaiety, to the shambolic splendour of Wyke on a Friday evening. The weekend carousing still takes place, the seamen still stand in line for their purses then head for the land. But knowing a stranger walks among them, the pious and perfidious of Wyke alike all turn their backs. They hope not to be noticed, hope to slip past unseen, hope never to glimpse the ravaged face at the hostelry window in the humid night.

The plague, affirms Martin Latimer, town councillor, *is the putrid fruit of ill-discipline among the lower classes. The butchers and leathermen with their blood-caked fingernails, the foul-mouthed sailors, the gossiping washerwomen with their filthy buckets, the ratcatchers and their reckless disposal of the fruits of their labours. Filth, flooding out of the sculleries of the undeserving poor, seeping like rancid fish-stock into the general water supply.* Latimer calls for tighter controls on the sale of alcohol, together with a ban on seamen from foreign ports.

The plague, insists Florian Schwarz, physician, *is a misfortune directly attributable to the miasma that is the defining characteristic of estuarine environments. The stink of rotten fish, the damp, the constant ingress and egress of foul effluent and fouler citizenry— the watery nature of Wyke itself encourages pestilence in to set up its quarters.* He advises beacons to be lit along the city's western boundary, insisting that the burning of bracken and gorse and desiccated cattle dung has long been proven as a prophylactic against disease. He has sent to his uncle in Hamburg for the latest scientific treatise from the university.

The plague, proclaims William Dearborn, witchfinder, *is divine retribution from God, and no more than we deserve.* In a booming, desolate voice, he puts forth a declaration from the steps of the Townhouse: *Thou shalt not suffer a witch to live.* He further adds that any citizen caught in the act of sheltering, conversing with, or failing to report the known whereabouts of a witch shall be judged as complicit in her witchery and sentenced accordingly. *With the soul of the city in peril, no quarter shall be given, no rotten, creaking floorboard left unturned.*

The plague, declares Sir Stuart Laycock, King's Justice, *is a breeding ground for larceny, for looting and for black marketeering, for thieves and profiteers, damn all of their kind.*

The plague, says Sister Clare, Mother Superior of Wyke Abbey, *is our own peculiar fate at this place and time. Our task as Christians is not to flee fate, but to confront it. To do the best we can with the tools to hand. To care for the sick and comfort the dying. To pray for wisdom and deeper knowledge of our time on Earth.*

The plague, adds Saira Gidding, apprentice scribe, *has come this way before, and will come again.*

As the darned black coverlet of night is pulled from the sky, the daemonic power of the storm is made visibly manifest. The eastern end of the harbour wall has been washed away, the enclave of fishing shacks, grain stores and dosshouses known as Ravensword has been completely submerged. Doris, the landlady of St Cuthbert's Inn, whose full name is Derenrice, begins to shake. Not just from the damp, seeping into her bones, but from the fitful, turgid light, the frayed rags of wind, the creeping intimation of what has occurred. The wrongness of it. How could a place be there and then be gone?

The penniless vagabonds who seek sanctuary in Ravensword, the youngsters who fancy they'll find their fortune on the open sea. Where are they now? Doris draws her cloak closer about herself, and shivers. The justice and his clerk exchange covert glances, though not covert enough to fool Doris, who can read men the way a farmhand reads the weather: the woman has dragged us halfway to purgatory on a fool's errand, but what else would one expect of a crone who opens her house to renegades and whores?

Any proof of what she has seen—if indeed she has seen anything—is gone now, washed away in the storm with the hovels of Ravensword. As if they have God on their side, those devil-men. As if God has conspired in the drowning of destitutes simply to vanish the traces of what has occurred.

And for Justice Treacher here is vindication of what he already believes to be the truth: Saira Gidding has left Wyke of her own free will, with Gideon Marchmain. If she meets with ill luck then that is because floozies like Saira Gidding—women who disrespect the Church and consort with heretics—always meet with ill luck. If the girl is no longer in the city then the city is well rid of her.

His thoughts so clearly etched in his face it is as if they have been chalked there.

If I find you, Gideon Marchmain, will you hear me then? says Doris finally. The desperation in her voice is repellent, most of all to her, yet how is she to avoid it?

Good luck with that, Treacher says evenly. Doris sees his clerk—Enderby—smirking, and feels like punching him.

It's not luck I need, it's a lawmaker with wit enough to see what's in front of his eyes.

She turns her face into the rain and hunches her shoulders and heads for home. She does not look back to see if the men are following.

Stories of how the pestilence first came to Wyke have grown so plentiful and highly coloured they are a tale in themselves. Derenrice, who intuits the city's rhythms as her own heartbeat, dates Wyke's terror from the coming of the *Copernicus*, a sailing brig out of Rotterdam, exhausted from a four-day voyage over cumulous seas.

Unnatural seas, the mariners asserted as they knocked back their ale. They seemed half-starved, and Doris bade the kitchen staff be generous with the mutton, though God help her if she has not found herself wishing in the eighteen months since that the *Copernicus* had foundered with all hands before rounding Spurn Head.

It would have made no difference, Saira has said to her. If not that ship then another. The plague cares not for nations and knows no boundaries.

The first deaths passed unnoticed, as misfortunes among the poor and illiterate tend to do. They occurred in the Fo'c'sle, a huddle of leaking, subsiding cottages close to the docks, the last refuge of broken-down mariners and their gin-soaked wives. From the harbour slums the plague spread to the filthier gaming rooms and drinking parlours of the eastern portside, before scuttling up through the maze of backstreets into the row houses and schoolrooms of the city's mill workers. Now folk noticed all right, and the scourge seemed unstoppable.

This city will be the death of me, Doris thought as she scrubbed the barroom flags with soda-wash and bored the scullery maid into a coma with her lectures on personal hygiene and frequent hand-washing. The fates of the stricken families chilled her worse than frostbite, yet not once did she think of abandoning the St Cuthbert for her sister's farm near Harrowgate, as Beth had begged her to do.

Bethesda, who had married well and was profitably widowed in less than five years, who now held the management of three hundred acres with its four tenant farms. Beth, who hated Wyke—filthy Wyke, she called it—who hated the inn, who hated still more the sight of Doris working the taproom and kitchen alongside her servants. Servants, Beth might well have added and most likely had, employed at rates that could not be judged as anything but detrimental to her sister's own interests.

Most of all she hated the fact that Doris had never come to her for help.

Doris and Beth had always been different, even as children, Beth with her hankering for finery and Doris with her constant wandering, as if she'd been searching, even then, for the place where her habit of speaking her mind would cause least offence.

Beth was scared of Doris's imaginings and Doris found the company her sister moved in unutterably dull. Yet there have been times, Doris has to admit, when she finds herself missing her: the closeness they shared without ever naming it, all the ways of knowing the other that could never be replaced and never, though she might often wish it, escaped.

Could it be this longing for sisterhood that has drawn her so to Saira, the bare-faced, obstinate girl who appeared before her in the barroom one evening in nothing but the clothes she stood up in—an old gardener's smock that reached her knees and covering what Doris realised with shock to be a postulant's habit.

I have left the Abbey for good, Saira said, staring Doris full in the face as if to head off her challenge before it arrived. I was told you might find a place for me. I'm not afraid of work.

As different from Beth as salt was from coal, and yet the feeling of Saira about the place takes Doris back to her girlhood, to when the thought of being apart—of growing apart—from Beth was like the thought of death: so distant and incomprehensible it could be safely ignored.

The pestilence here, and Saira gone, such a foul exchange. Derenrice, who has to deal each day with mutineers and pickpockets, with drunks and thieves and charlatans of every kind, lambasts herself for her foolishness, for allowing herself to forget the world's duplicity, even for an hour.

She asks Padraig, who looks after the wood store, to make enquiries as to the whereabouts of Gideon Marchmain.

Don't let on who's asking. I don't want him scuttling back into the woodwork like the louse he is.

Doris does not believe young Marchmain to be a louse, and if there is harshness in her voice it is on account of Saira, of the fear she keeps suppressing that she is already lost. Marchmain irks her through his naiveté, that is all. The lad is gifted, no doubt about it, yet seems oblivious to the dangers that surround him. The words constantly on his lips—my father this, my father that—as if Wilfrid Marchmain's money and status could afford a body protection of their own accord.

Doris has come to think of fate as a player of games, and in the matter of judging the stakes, fate is a master. The higher the stakes, the greater the risk, yet being dealt the upper hand does not mean risk is nullified: Wilfrid Marchmain has both money and the ear of the king, but he is still just a man.

For two days Doris hears nothing of Marchmain, long enough for her to begin to doubt herself, to wonder if the rumours are true after all, that Saira and Gideon have left the city together. Either that or the student prince has been murdered also. She pushes the thought aside, and on the third day at dusk, with the barroom crammed with strangers and Doris heaving the slops out to the pigpen simply to afford herself a rest from the incessant din, a figure approaches. His features are shadowed by the hood of a cloak, a voluminous thing from a story of wizards and spies.

Paddy tells me you've been searching for Saira, the figure whispers. He says you glimpsed her at Ravensword, the night of the storm.

Doris wipes her fingers on her apron, puts her hands on her hips.

I told Pat not to tell you who was asking.

Paddy said nothing. Not before I asked him. He's done nothing wrong.

Where is Saira, Gideon? Have you spoken with her lately?

He shakes his head, and Doris thinks how naked he looks, how sorrowful, and this in spite of his book-smarts and that ridiculous cape. She remembers how his mother perished, falling from horseback when her curly-headed boy was but eight years old. Gideon is like her, everyone says so. Weakened by fancy and a dearth of labour. A lover of poems.

I have been frantic, Mrs Beynes, since the night of the flood. Saira told me she had made a discovery, that there was someone she needed to speak with, a physician, a confidante of the Mother Superior at the Abbey. Saira still keeps friendships among the nuns. She visits them sometimes, in secret. She believes I do not know this, but I do.

A discovery, says Derenrice. What did she find?

I do not know. She assured me she would explain everything once she had spoken with Mother Clare—but I have not had sight of her since that evening, since she set out. The boy shakes his head again. She did declare that Wyke is a city built on ruins, and that those that were here before us knew all about the plague.

That Saira had been entrusted to the Order on account of the pestilence was no secret. To keep her safe, her father insisted. As explanation it was true enough but only half of the truth. Saira's twin brothers had died of the plague within an hour of each other. Her mother had not been right since, crippled by grief not so much in her body as in her mind. There was no space for Saira in this straitened world, so she was sent away. Prenticed and later assistant to Sister Ursula, whose ability with lettering is famous throughout the city.

The plague has taken her old life, but it has granted her a new one. Learning the letters with Sister Ursula has made Saira who she is.

Such riddles are beautiful in their symmetry, though they be harsh. A reminder that the truth of the world is elusive, and hard to decipher. That there is more to Wyke than can be seen on the surface is self-apparent. But this talk of secrets and a cure for the plague? To Doris such claims have the ring of wishes: illusions with as little substance as fairy gold.

What she saw on the night of the storm, though—that was real. First there came Saira, calling to her through the kitchen hatchway that she had need to go out, she had business to attend to, she would be back before closing time.

Business, Doris had smiled to herself. It was her lad she was after seeing, the Marchmain boy. Doris had no objection to Saira taking time off, though she had concern for her gadding about the streets on a foul night like this.

The wind's getting up, she called back. Be sure and take care. Her memory plays tricks at this point. Was she worried about the storm or about some other thing? Would she have paid heed to the weather at all had it not been for Rodney Doyle, first mate aboard the *Saskatchewan*, hunkered down in his corner not saying a word. When Doris asked him how he was faring, he had shaken his head. Shaken his head then said there was a storm brewing, he could feel it in his bones.

A storm unlike other storms, he added. A storm like the wrath of God and the fire of the devil.

You ships' fools, Doris had said, trying to jounce him from his gloom. You thrive on such catastrophes. The recounting of them, anywise.

She had refilled his tankard free of charge, yet the man had just stared at her, as if the calamity in his mind's eye had already occurred, the memory of a disaster he had failed to avoid.

Shutter your windows, he had said quietly. I have heard the wind telling tales and they are not kind. He slurped at his replenished ale, spooned his mouth full of stew. There are boats at sea this eve that will not see landfall.

When Doris went out to the wood stack she found the wind had raked off the tarpaulin and the rain had started: swift, cutting shafts of it, bright as icicles and as sharp, the kind of evil autumn downpour best observed from the comfort of the chimney corner.

There was no one abroad, which made sense, yet still the foulness of the wind in the empty alleyways struck her as eerie.

She turned to go back inside, and it was then she saw them: two figures, with a third between, a third being dragged like a sack of potatoes along the lane that tracked west from behind the coachyard towards the fish market then on to Ravensword, all the way to Spurn Head if you followed it far enough, though Doris had not been to the coast herself since she was a girl.

She was soaked through already, the power of the downpour increasing even as she stood there as if it meant to drive her back inside through sheer evil-mindedness. And yet Doris stood firm, shoving her sopping hair back from her face again and again as she strained not to lose sight of them in the darkness, these furtive figures, for that was how they seemed to her: furtive, a word that chimed with the filthy night yet stood at odds with it, too. How could one be furtive when there was no one in sight to give a damn what you were about? When the need to be out of the rain would have banished the curiosity of the meanest gossip?

Doris stepped forward, her soaked dress slapping against her thighs and ankles like a flap of torn sail. The glow from the carriage light turned the rain in its circle to the form of one creature, a million fragments shimmeringly unified, a liquid-limbed beast.

Hello, Doris called, too timidly, her voice stuffed instantly back in her mouth by the bullying wind. Yet surely there was something about the middle figure, the one being dragged, that made her sick inside with the thought that it was someone she knew. She tugged herself free from the safety of the yard and ran into the lane. The trio were far ahead of her, and even as she raced to catch up with them they drew further away. Hello, she called again, her cry snagging on the wind before being torn away, weightless and insubstantial as a hank of wool.

Some part of her yell must have carried, though. The figure on the right, the one that hulked, seemed to hesitate for an instant before hurrying on. The set of its shoulders, the firmness of its bearing, its striding gait put Derenrice in mind of someone, though the name of William Dearborn the witchfinder did not come to her until she was stripping off her sodden garments before the stove. Doris gritted her teeth against the wind and lowered her head. The pursuit was madness, caused by phantoms, doing her head in. She began trudging back down the hill, her clothing streaming so with stormwater that the idea of bothering to pick up her pace seemed an unholy joke against herself.

As she came in sight of the yard she stumbled against something heavy and nearly went down. A loose cobblestone, she thought, then realised as the object slid away from her that it was something less solid. Dark and oddly shaped. A leather boot.

Without fully understanding her purpose, Doris snatched it up. What use is a single boot, except maybe as mending-leather? Then the coldness grinding her marrow deepened still further: the yellow stitching and tassel, the coneyskin cuff. This was Saira's shoe she was holding, cast carelessly aside. Yet who would lose a shoe in the rain and not hurry back for it?

One who could not hurry back, you fool. A prisoner or a corpse. A body dragged between two captors along a windswept road.

And the wind was beginning to scream, a lunatic howling. The storm itself has taken her, Doris thought. Her fingers, gripping the boot-cuff, felt icy and stiff and lifeless as sticks of bone.

On the third day, after speaking with Gideon, Doris leaves Clarah in charge of the barroom and goes to see Beth. She will be absent three days at the minimum, and with the roads in their present condition it will likely be longer.

If anyone's asking, I'm away to aid my sister, nothing more to it than that. The fare to Harrowgate is a thorn in her side but Doris has the coin, thank God. The management of the inn takes all of her and as she seats herself in the conveyance she wonders when was the last time she travelled further than her own back yard? When chanced she to purchase for herself a new gown or cloak, a silver chain, a pamphlet of those baffling poems so much admired by Gideon Marchmain?

For the lark a speeding arrow through the sun, the toad adoring the lark brings the world to fluid life in the cradle of her dreams.

Claptrap, young people today, yet the words still dance, flickering and swirling like dust motes in the stuffy vastness of a sun-warmed barn. Doris thinks of the stream that marks the boundary of her childhood home, bannered with toads' eggs in spring, she and Beth waist-deep in water, their skinny arms beribboned with its glossy beads.

The fat toad that dwells in the cellar, Doris calls him Mister Goldeneye. She has warned Padraig, who has a fear of cold creatures, that she will let him go on the spot if the beast comes to harm…

The steady rhythm of the conveyance, lulling her to drowsiness and unkempt thoughts. On her lap lies Saira's prayer book, her prentice piece, together with the other book, the one Doris found by accident, the book that has no business in existing. Yet now she has it in her possession, she finds it comforts her. The faded roan of the cloth-bound covers, the frightful candour of the words within—she will not whisper them even to herself, yet the brazen heresy of what the book contains seems somehow to offer the hope that Saira is alive.

Such fires do not go out. Doris moves her lips silently, remembering how she rushed to Saira's room at the height of the storm in the hope of finding the second boot. Kicked out of sight beneath the bed, say, or nosed up against the wall. Not to be, not to be. She sat down on the narrow cot tucked under the eaves, the roof tiles lifting and settling like sticks of raffia, placing the boot she had rescued from the street on the floor beside her like a piece of treasure trove. This must count as evidence, Doris assured herself, then felt the tears starting. You found a clapped-out boot in the street, woman. So what?

The prayer book was lying on top of the chest where Saira kept her linens, the other book beside it. The simple fact of it, lying there so openly—as if the witchfinder and his instruments of torture took up so little space in her mind they were of no account.

Bravery, or foolishness, the simple-minded valour of the young and righteous? More than anything, Doris hankers to show what she has found to Beth. Beth who knows nothing of Saira Gidding, or Gideon Marchmain, though she will surely ken his father. Of the Witchfinder Dearborn she will have heard the usual stories. The whole country hates the man.

Doris will have to begin the tale from scratch, from the moment Saira arrived in the barroom asking for work. Beth had a child born dead, then a husband lost to the plague. Hammer-blows enough to forge a woman to steel. Such a long time since they have spoken— spoken in earnest. Such firebrands they were in their girlhood— Passion, and Wisdom. Should Doris have sent word on ahead, to tell her sister of her coming? She imagines Beth's scorn, that Doris could think of entrusting her distress and suspicions to such a clod as Justice Treacher, and feels there is no need.

There are trees down, roads blocked. At Tadcaster she leaps from the carriage to help the driver and his man saw and clear the twisted branches of a fallen oak. And yet away from the coast it is clear the predations of the storm have been less extreme.

She sees the farmhouse at last from the road, its frost-grey outline jutting starkly against the horizon. Doris's heart, in spite of itself, leaps up. She asks the coachman to set her down at the familiar turning and then shoulders her baggage. When she comes properly in sight of the house, she is astounded to see Beth already on the doorstep, awaiting her arrival. Standing beside her, her dove-coloured pinafore neatly patched with a purple square, is Saira Gidding.

I took my chance when the waves overwhelmed the defences at Ravensword, Saira explains, and they lost me in the storm. I know a place in the Abbey wall where, so long as you can squeeze yourself small, you can slip inside. Mother Clare put up the funds for my passage to Harrowgate. By good fortune she knew of Beth, and where I should find her. She told me I should take refuge here to wait for you and now you are come.

Beth and Doris gaze at one another like rival privateers, forced into a nervous alliance by the presence of the customsmen: *Yes we are sisters and haven't we always been? This is our story and we're inclined to stick to it, thank you very much.* Who can say where habit leaves off and love begins? Doris feels she is nine years old again, cooking up some piece of innocent subterfuge to outwit their father.

I can't abide that William Dearborn, Beth is saying. Who died and made him Lord High Executioner all of an instant, that's what I'd like to know.

Doris is so relieved and incredulous at seeing Saira that her breath seems to stop. Is this what it feels like, to give birth to a daughter? She thinks of the child Beth lost and her heart wants to break.

Listen, Saira says to them both. We have much talking to do.

The leaves of the book are fragile, their parchment so dry and so brittle Doris fears that even a stubborn glance might reduce them to dust. *The War from the Air*, the treatise is called. *The Bombardment of Kings-town, Nineteen-forty to Nineteen-forty-five.* Doris moves her lips slowly, testing the phrases, stumbling over *bombardment* because although Doris can read and read well, she is more used to perusing the butcher's monthly invoice than forbidden texts, and *bombardment* is a word you do not encounter every day.

There is an image on an inside page, of a church on fire. The picture's tones are like ghost's breath: monochrome, shadowy, the image's likeness to the building so exact it's as if the burning edifice is blazing in front of her. Doris finds herself speechless with the wrongness of it, because the outline of the church is familiar to her, the ruined and patched and patched-again Church of Saint Margaret in the Mercantile, on Brasenose Hill.

Tell me how this can be. She feels cast adrift in time, as if the world were hanging above her, a moon-sized lump of granite that might break its invisible bounds at any moment, extinguishing her like a beetle to a scant puff of dust.

Where am I? An image casts itself to the surface of her mind: the city of Wyke, resplendent under a gold-flecked autumn sky, reflected up at her from the waters of the Humber as it flows its slow course.

Unreal city…

I am not here at all, Doris thinks to herself, and her inner voice sounds strange to her, unlike itself, faint and full of wonderment, as if she were yet a girl and the world still new to her, as if she had never poured pints of ale or scrubbed down floorboards or sluiced out pigsties to make a living.

The book is from Mother Clare's library, Saira is saying. She takes Doris's hand and squeezes it. All the sisters know of it—the Abbey was always a place of learning and so it is still. Sister Ursula and I—Mother Clare set us to work making fair copies. Many of the books she has accrued are too delicate for study. She wants us to save them—before the knowledge they contain is withered away. William Dearborn—

The witchfinder?

Saira nods. He seized on me the night of the storm, when there was no one to witness. He offered me amnesty if I were to give up Mother Clare. To confess her as a witch, I mean, he and that snake of a curate, Roland Parfitt. They want to see her influence erased and her body burned. Afterwards they will torch the library. But the law states no man may enter the Abbey and retain the king's favour. William Dearborn knows this, and so for now he is powerless. I am afraid for the future, though. Men such as Dearborn will always find a way to set themselves above the law, sooner or later. We have to move fast.

I don't understand, Doris says, why the man is so exercised. Heaven knows book-learners are few and becoming fewer. Why not decry this ancient volume as a children's fantasy? A tale of gods and monsters? His task would be accomplished and no harm done.

You know the answer as well as I, Beth says impatiently. Dearborn lives for witch-burnings—one might say he has a calling. And besides, it is not just the book. Saira found something else. From other of the books she has worked on, she believes it to be some manner of communications device—a machine that enables the exchange of voices over hundreds of miles. This sounds like witchcraft to you and me, so take a moment to imagine how it might sound to William Dearborn. There is a lad on the estate, the son of our foreman Diggory Palmer. He has a gift for mending machinery—in the matter of repairing our farm implements his talents have often proved invaluable. Diggory swears he knows not whence the boy's gift arises and begs me not to speak of it—I imagine he fears the witchfinder and his court of rubes.

I have told the man he is safe here, Beth continues, and I have with Saira's agreement asked him if his son might help to determine the purpose of this find. The foolish boy is thrilled, of course. On fire with purpose. So this is where we are. As for the book, I have taken the time to think on it, and although parts of the text are yet obscure to me its meaning as a whole seems self-apparent: Wyke is founded in the ruins of an earlier city. Time crushes the present moment into dust, and yet the fragments of all earlier times remain. Any wife who has lost a husband has knowledge of this—how one life stamps its mark in the hide of another, how even with the passage of years the scars may still be seen. Sister, I know you have questioned my choices. You have found me wanting in resolution, and heaven knows your lot has been harsh, but I did truly love my little Rachel and I loved my Malcolm too. I came to love him more than I imagined. Now he is gone I need your wisdom more than ever. If this storm has torn many asunder, might it not bring others together? If I have been bitter and overly judgemental, please forgive me. Let us build something new.

A new city, Doris wonders. A new city, in the ruins of the old. Her sister's forthright speech astounds her, her capacity for change. The accumulated griefs, the minor slights, the unspoken distrust—might they be swept out to sea on the tide, with the flotsam of Ravensword?

As girls and young women, the idea of magic had been as basic and unsurprising to the sisters as the idea of bread. The years between put paid to that. Now magic had been returned to them in the form of a pile of papers and a broken machine.

Can a machine perform magic? writes Saira in her journal late in the evening. *From the time I first learned to listen at keyholes, I have been aware of the priests' distrust of human-made miracles. As if to wonder at human achievement is to deny the idea of the spiritual, the idea of God. As if to strive after higher knowledge is to willingly embrace the devil's business. I have contemplated their point of view and found no merit in it. Rather, I have discerned in their insistence on human innocence a mendacious desire to preserve the structures of power. If sheep begin to think for themselves, what purpose the shepherd? And what is to become of the farmer when sheep refuse to be exploited for their meat and wool?*

The priests depend on human submissiveness for their credibility. A godly city is a city in thrall, and easily ruled. Mother Clare says: God's purpose is not immediately apparent to humans, and to men least of all. Learning is a form of enlightenment, and what is enlightenment but prayer, answered?

In the time before the dark, the city flourished. Wyke continued to reinvent itself, its structures fashioned from human ambition, its spirit imagined into being through human communion with a higher power. Its energy fuelled by the clash of kings and angels, bishops and generals, shopkeepers and highwaymen, merchants and slaves.

The merchants brought the rats, says Mother Clare, and the rats brought the plague. The city crumbled and the churchmen lamented the devilish prevalence of human sin. The plague is divine retribution, they wailed in their pulpits, the idea of plague as a natural phenomenon a heretical negation of the idea of God.

The dreaded pestilence, raging through the shipyard tenements and the poorhouses, the garrison and the workhouse, the slums of Ravensword and Humberside, the mills the slaughterhouse the almshouse, the cottages of washerwomen and of textile workers, ill-lit, running with mildew, infested with rats.

Knowledge, says Mother Clare, is a dangerous thing, not because it comes from the devil but because it runs in harness with the need to act. To speak of a pestilence spread by vermin—by fleas on rats—is to suggest that the plague is down to cause and effect. A calamity whose course might be stopped or altered by human action.

Where does that leave God? demands Dearborn the witchfinder.

God helps those who help themselves, says Mother Clare.

The city is war and the city is peace and the city is icicles hanging from roofs on a January morning. The storm-surge and the gale, the tearing might of the River Humber, the glinting of sunlight on the steaming flanks of the estuary sands. The city is books and women reading, children racing across the rooftops on a summer's night. Stars in the firmament and rats in the gutter, pestilence and the death of mothers and the birth of poets. The city is slate and iron and glass, the city is granite. The stench of horse dung and motors roaring, the sparring of philosophers in the coffee house, the contemplative silence of mathematicians in the library reading room. The cursing of sailors and the singing of drunkards, the sighs of

harlots and the praying of nuns. The jewels the coal the fire the slate
the water the wood the brass the nails the grain the cord the disdain
the mercy the magnificence and the ruin. The prisons and palaces,
convents and collieries, whorehouse and bakery, the palace and the
playhouse and the officers' mess. The love of me for you and you for
me. The past and the future and the heavenly now. The being and
the dying. The written and the read.

Doris is shocked at how young he is, the boy, this son of a foreman with a preternatural knowledge of machines. Twelve, maybe thirteen. Fourteen years old at the most, and he is small for his age, the boy, leave him out in a winter's gale and he will blow clean away.

The lad is christened Diggory, the same as his father. The thing on the bench in front of him looks more like a carton of junk than anything working, a mute assemblage of metal coils and wooden pegs, inexplicable forms fashioned from a dark brown material the boy calls baker-light.

Doris remembers how she and Beth had found such rudiments occasionally, objects that wormed their way to the surface of the earth in the wake of a rainstorm. A smooth red drinking cup, a hollow dwarf with a long white beard, what looked like coat buttons. Witch-finds, Beth had called them. Jokingly or not jokingly, what these things were or where they had come from they never dared ask.

Young Diggory calls his found machine a radio receiver. For capturing voices, he explains, for luring music down out of the aether as my father lures trout from their shaded hideaways among the sedge.

He shows them how to activate the machine by twisting a handle, skilfully forged from a length of wire. Explains how the turning of the handle converts the body's energy into an invisible fuel called electrical power.

How might you know this? asks Doris, astounded. She feels once again cast adrift in a world moved on without her.

There are books that speak of it, the boy replies. He shrugs, as if the existence of such miraculous volumes were common knowledge. Beth seizes the glimmering handle with her ungloved hand, thrusting it downwards then pulling it round then around again.

Like churning butter! she exclaims.

Like you would know, Doris thinks, entranced.

Diggory nods at Beth then depresses a lever. Doris hears a muted crackling, like the far-off movement of waves upon a distant shore.

Wait, the lad says, just a moment. He begins twisting a wooden toggle—one half of a clothes peg—and cocks his head to one side.

A voice rises up from the jumbled detritus and the voice is singing. Doris jumps back in fear.

…was all my joy, Greensleeves was my delight…

The voice stutters and disappears, rises again from the ruins.

Greensleeves was all my joy…

Witchcraft, Derenrice whispers. Her heart is pounding. She feels ashamed at falling back on such prejudice, yet other words have failed her.

Not witchcraft, Saira says quietly. She rests her hand on Doris's arm. A new idea, or an old one. The voice of the future.

The voice from the aether is faint yet stalwart, sweet as a rose.

Does he know we are listening? Does he know where we are?

I do not think so, young Diggory answers. Not yet, anyway. All this means is that someone elsewhere has learned to construct and operate a similar machine. We have still to learn how such machines may one day talk together.

He frowns, the gesture granting his features the gravitas of a much older man. The machine lets out a crackle and then falls silent.

Is it broken? Saira asks.

It has lost the signal, that's all. But it will come back.

Beth grabs Doris's hand, her face alight with excitement. Doris imagines herself a girl again, with the whole of life a mystery to be solved.

Of all the apostles, Doris has always found most sympathy with Doubting Thomas. In the past she has seen this preference as a moral weakness, a bulwark against the pain of disappointment. And yet the world is bigger and stranger than she has imagined. She believes she would find comfort in confiding her astonishment to Mother Clare.

AS GOOD AS NEW

Charlie Jane Anders

MARISOL got into an intense relationship with the people on *The Facts of Life*, to the point where Tootie and Mrs. Garrett became her imaginary best friends and she shared every last thought with them. She told Tootie about the rash she got from wearing the same bra every day for two years, and she had a long talk with Mrs. Garrett about her regrets that she hadn't said a proper goodbye to her best friend Julie and her on-again/off-again boyfriend Rod, before they died along with everybody else.

The panic room had pretty much every TV show ever made on its massive hard drive, with multiple backup systems and a fail-proof generator, so there was nothing stopping Marisol from marathoning *The Facts of Life* for sixteen hours a day, starting over again with season one when she got to the end of the bedraggled final season. She also watched *Mad Men* and *The West Wing*. The media server had tons of video of live theater, but Marisol didn't watch that because it made her feel guilty. Not survivor's guilt; failed playwright guilt.

Her last proper conversation with a living human had been an argument with Julie about Marisol's decision to go to medical school instead of trying to write more plays. ("Fuck doctors, man," Julie had spat. "People are going to die no matter what you do. Theater is *important*.") Marisol had hung up on Julie and gone back to the pre-med books, staring at the exposed musculature and blood vessels as if they were costume designs for a skeleton theater troupe.

The quakes always happened at the worst moment, just when Jo or Blair was about to reveal something heartfelt and serious. The whole panic room would shake, throwing Marisol against the padded walls or ceiling over and over again. A reminder that the rest of the world was probably dead. At first, these quakes were constant, then they happened a few times a day. Then once a day, then a few times a week. Then a few times a month. Marisol knew that once a month or two passed without the world going sideways, she would have to go out and investigate. She would have to leave her friends at the Eastland School, and venture into a bleak world.

Sometimes, Marisol thought she had a duty to stay in the panic room, since she was personally keeping the human race alive. But then she thought: what if there was someone else living, and they needed help? Marisol was pre-med, she might be able to do something. What if there was a man, and Marisol could help him repopulate the species?

The panic room had nice blue leather walls and a carpeted floor that felt nice to walk on, and enough gourmet frozen dinners to last Marisol a few lifetimes. She only had the pair of shoes she'd brought in there with her, and it would seem weird to wear shoes after two barefoot years. The real world was in here, in the panic room—out there was nothing but an afterimage of a bad trip.

Marisol was an award-winning playwright, but that hadn't saved her from the end of the world. She was taking pre-med classes and trying to get a scholarship to med school so she could give cancer screenings to poor women in her native Taos, but that didn't save her either. Nor did the fact that she believed in God every other day.

What actually saved Marisol from the end of the world was the fact that she took a job cleaning Burton Henstridge's mansion to help her through school, and she'd happened to be scrubbing his fancy Japanese toilet when the quakes had started—within easy reach of Burton's state-of-the-art panic room. (She had found the hidden opening mechanism some weeks earlier, while cleaning the porcelain cat figurines.) Burton himself was in Bulgaria scouting a new location for a nano-fabrication facility, and had died instantly.

When Marisol let herself think about all the people she could never talk to again, she got so choked up she wanted to punch someone in the eye until they were blinded for life. She experienced grief in the form of freak-outs that left her unable to breathe or think, and then she popped in another *Facts of Life*. As she watched, she chewed her nails until she was in danger of gnawing off her fingertips.

The door to the panic room wouldn't actually open when Marisol finally decided it had been a couple months since the last quake and it was time to go the hell out there. She had to kick the door a few dozen times, until she dislodged enough of the debris blocking it to stagger out into the wasteland. The cold slapped her in the face and extremities, extra bitter after two years at room temperature. Burton's house was gone; the panic room was just a cube half-buried in the ruins, covered in some yellowy insulation that looked like it would burn your fingers.

Everything out there was white, like snow or paper, except powdery and brittle, ashen. She had a Geiger counter from the panic room, which read zero. She couldn't figure out what the hell had happened to the world, for a long time, until it hit her—this was fungus. Some kind of newly made, highly corrosive fungus that had rushed over everything like a tidal wave and consumed every last bit of organic material, then died. It had come in wave after wave, with incredible violence, until it had exhausted the last of its food supply and crushed everything to dust. She gleaned this from the consistency of the crud that had coated every bit of rubble, but also from the putrid sweet-and-sour smell that she could not stop smelling once she noticed it. She kept imagining she saw the white powder starting to move out of the corner of her eye, advancing toward her, but when she would turn around there was nothing.

"The fungus would have all died out when there was nothing left for it to feed on," Marisol said aloud. "There's no way it could still be active." She tried to pretend some other person, an expert or something, had said that, and thus it was authoritative. The fungus was dead. It couldn't hurt her now.

Because if the fungus wasn't dead, then she was screwed—even if it didn't kill her, it would destroy the panic room and its contents. She hadn't been able to seal it properly behind her without locking herself out.

"Hello?" Marisol kept yelling, out of practice at trying to project her voice. "Anybody there? Anybody?"

She couldn't even make sense of the landscape. It was just blinding white, as far as she could see, with bits of blanched stonework jutting out. No way to discern streets or houses or cars or anything, because it had all been corroded or devoured.

She was about to go back to the panic room and hope it was still untouched, so she could eat another frozen lamb vindaloo and watch season three of *Mad Men*. And then she spotted something, a dot of color, a long way off in the pale ruins.

The bottle was a deep oaky green, like smoked glass, with a cork in it. And it was about twenty yards away, just sitting in one of the endless piles of white debris. Somehow, it had avoided being consumed or rusted or broken in the endless waves of fungal devastation. It looked as though someone had just put it down a second ago—in fact, Marisol's first response was to yell "Hello?" even louder than before.

When there was no answer, she picked up the bottle. In her hands, it felt bumpy, like an embossed label had been worn away, and there didn't seem to be any liquid inside. She couldn't see its contents, if there were any. She removed the cork.

A *whoosh* broke the dead silence. A sparkly mist streamed out of the bottle's narrow mouth—sparkling like the cheap glitter at the Arts and Crafts table at summer camp when Marisol was a little girl, misty like a smoke machine at a cheap nightclub—and it slowly resolved into a shape in front of her. A man, a little taller than she was and much bigger.

Marisol was so startled and grateful at no longer being alone that she almost didn't pause to wonder how this man had appeared out of nowhere, after she opened a bottle. A bottle that had survived when everything else was crushed. Then she did start to wonder, but the only explanations seemed too ludicrous to believe.

"Hello and congratulations," the man said in a pleasant tone. He looked Jewish and wore a cheap suit, in a style that reminded Marisol somewhat of the *Mad Men* episodes she'd just been watching. His dark hair fell onto his high forehead in lank strands, and he had a heavy beard shadow. "Thank you for opening my bottle. I am pleased to offer you three wishes." Then he looked around, and his already dour expression worsened. "Oh, fuck," he said. "Not *again*."

"Wait," Marisol said. "You're a— You're a genie?"

"I hate that term," the man said. "I prefer wish-facilitator. And for your information, I used to be just a regular person. I was the theater critic at *The New York Times* for six months in 1958, which I still think defines me much more than my current engagement does. But I tried to bamboozle the wrong individual, so I got stuck in a bottle and forced to grant wishes to anyone who opens it."

"You were a theater critic?" Marisol said. "I'm a playwright. I won a contest and had a play produced off-Broadway. Well, actually, I'm a pre-med student, and I clean houses for money. But in my off-off-hours, I'm a playwright, I guess."

"Oh," the man said. "Well, if you want me to tell you your plays are very good, then that will count as one of your three wishes. And honestly, I don't think you're going to benefit from good publicity very much in the current climate." He gestured around at the bleak white landscape around them. "My name was Richard Wolf, by the way."

"Marisol," she said. "Marisol Guzmán."

"Nice to meet you." He extended his hand, but didn't actually try to shake hers. She wondered if she would go right through him. She was standing in a world of stinky chalk talking to a self-loathing genie. After two years alone in a box, that didn't even seem weird, really.

So this was it. Right? She could fix everything. She could make a wish, and everything would be back the way it was. She could talk to Julie again, and apologize for hanging up on her. She could see Rod, and maybe figure out what they were to each other. She just had to say the words: "I wish." She started to speak, and then something Richard Wolf had said a moment earlier registered in her brain.

"Wait a minute," she said. "What did you mean, 'Not again?'"

"Oh, that." Richard Wolf swatted around his head with big hands, like he was trying to swat nonexistent insects. "I couldn't say. I mean, I can answer any question you want, but that counts as one of your wishes. There are rules."

"Oh," Marisol said. "Well, I don't want to waste a wish on a question. Not when I can figure this out on my own. You said 'not again,' the moment you saw all this. So, this isn't the first time this has happened. Your bottle can probably survive anything. Right? Because it's magic or something."

The dark green bottle still had a heft to it, even after she'd released its contents. She threw it at a nearby rock a few times. Not a scratch.

"So," she said. "The world ends, your bottle doesn't get damaged. If even one person survives, they find your bottle. And the first thing they wish for? Is for the world not to have ended."

Richard Wolf shrugged, but he also sort of nodded at the same time, like he was confirming her hunch. His feet were see-through, she noticed. He was wearing wing-tip shoes that looked scuffed to the point of being scarred.

"The first time was in 1962," he said. "The Cuban Missile Crisis, they called it afterwards."

"This is *not* counting as one of my wishes, because I didn't ask a question," Marisol said.

"Fine, fine," Richard Wolf rolled his eyes. "I grew tired of listening to your harangue. When I was reviewing for the *Times*, I always tore into plays that had too many endless speeches. Your plays don't have a lot of monologues, do they? Fucking Brecht made everybody think three-page speeches were clever. Fucking Brecht."

"I didn't go in for too many monologues," Marisol said. "So. Someone finds your bottle, they wish for the apocalypse not to have happened, and then they probably make a second wish, to try and make sure it doesn't happen again. Except here we are, so it obviously didn't work the last time."

"I could not possibly comment," Richard Wolf said. "Although I should say that everyone gets the wrong idea about people in my line of work—meaning wish-facilitators, not theater critics. People had the wrong idea when I was a theater critic, too; they thought it was my job to promote the theater, to put buns in seats, even for terrible plays. That was *not* my job at all."

"The theater has been an endangered species for a long time," Marisol said, not without sympathy. She looked around the pasty-white, yeast-scented deathscape. A world of Wonder Bread. "I mean, I get why people want criticism that is essentially cheerleading, even if that doesn't push anybody to do their best work."

"Well, if you think of theater as some sort of *delicate flower* that needs to be kept protected in some sort of *hothouse*"—and at this point, Wolf was clearly reprising arguments he'd had over and over again, when he was alive—"then you're going to end up with something that only the *faithful few* will appreciate, and you'll end up worsening the very marginalization that you're seeking to prevent."

Marisol was being very careful to avoid asking anything resembling a question, because she was probably going to need all three of her wishes. "I would guess that the job of a theater critic is misunderstood in sort of the opposite way than the job of a genie," she said. "Everybody is afraid a theater critic will be too brutally honest. But a genie…"

"Everybody thinks I'm out to swindle them!" Richard Wolf threw his hands in the air, thinking of all the *tsuris* he had endured. "When, in fact, it's always the client who can't express a wish in clear and straightforward terms. They always leave out crucial information. I do my best. It's like stage directions without any stage left or stage right. I interpret as best I can."

"Of course you do," Marisol said. This was all starting to creep her out, and her gratitude at having another person to talk to (who wasn't Mrs. Garrett) was getting driven out by her discomfort at standing in the bleached-white ruins of the world kibitzing about theater criticism. She picked up the bottle from where it lay undamaged after hitting the rock, and found the cork.

"Wait a minute," Richard Wolf said. "You don't want to—"

He was sucked back inside the bottle before she finished putting the cork back in.

She reopened the bottle once she was back inside the panic room, with the door sealed from the inside. So nothing or nobody could get in. She watched three episodes of *The Facts of Life*, trying to get her equilibrium back, before she microwaved some *sukiyaki* and let Richard Wolf out again. He started the spiel about how he had to give her three wishes over again, then stopped and looked around.

"Huh." He sat and sort of floated an inch above the sofa. "Nice digs. Real calfskin on this sofa. Is this like a bunker?"

"I can't answer any of your questions," Marisol said, "or that counts as a wish you owe me."

"Don't be like that." Richard Wolf ruffled his two-tone lapels. "I'm just trying not to create any loopholes, because once there are loopholes it brings everybody grief in the end. Trust me, you wouldn't want the rules to be messy here." He rifled through the media collection until he found a copy of *Cat on a Hot Tin Roof*, which he made a big show of studying until Marisol finally loaded it for him.

"This is better than I'd remembered," Richard Wolf said an hour later.

"Good to know," Marisol said. "I never got around to watching that one."

"I met Tennessee Williams, you know," Richard said. "He wasn't nearly as drunk as you might have thought."

"So here's what I figure. You do your level best to implement the wishes people give you, to the letter," Marisol said. "So if someone says they want to make sure that a nuclear war never happens again, you do your best to make a nuclear war impossible. And then maybe that change leads to some other catastrophe, and then the next person tries to make some wishes that prevent that thing from happening again. And on, and on. Until this."

"This is actually the longest conversation I've had since I became a wish-facilitator." Richard crossed his leg, ankle over thigh. "Usually, it's just whomp-bomp-a-lula-three-wishes, and I'm back in the bottle. So tell me about your prize-winning play. If you want. I mean, it's up to you."

Marisol told Richard about her play, which seemed like something an acquaintance of hers had written many lifetimes ago. "It was a one-act," she said, "about a man who is trying to break up with his girlfriend, but every time he's about to dump her she does something to remind him why he used to love her. So he hires a male prostitute to seduce her, instead, so she'll cheat on him and he can have a reason to break up with her."

Richard was giving her a blank expression, as though he couldn't trust himself to show a reaction.

"It's a comedy," Marisol explained.

"Sorry," Richard said. "It sounds awful. He hires a male prostitute to sleep with his girlfriend. It sounds… I just don't know what to say."

"Well, you were a theater critic in the 1950s, right? I guess it was a different era."

"I don't think that's the problem," Richard said. "It just sounds sort of… misanthropic. Or actually woman-hating. With a slight veneer of irony. I don't know. Maybe that's the sort of thing everybody is into these days—or was into, before the world ended yet again. This is something like the fifth or sixth time the world has ended. I am losing count, to be quite honest."

Marisol was put out that this fossil was casting aspersions on her play—her *contest-winning play,* in fact. But the longer she kept him talking, the more clues he dropped, without costing her any wishes. So she bit her lip.

"So. There were half a dozen apocalypses," Marisol said. "And I guess each of them was caused by people trying to prevent the last one from happening again, by making wishes. So that white stuff out there. Some kind of bioengineered corrosive fungus, I thought—but maybe it was created to prevent some kind of climate-related disaster. It does seem awfully reflective of sunlight."

"Oh, yes, it reflects sunlight just wonderfully," Richard said. "The temperature of the planet is going to be dropping a lot in the next decade. No danger of global warming now."

"Ha," Marisol said. "And you claim you're just doing the most straightforward job possible. You're addicted to irony. You sat through too many Brecht plays, even though you claim to hate him. You probably loved Beckett as well."

"All right-thinking people love Beckett," said Richard. "So you had some *small* success as a playwright, and yet you're studying to be a doctor. Or you were, before this unfortunate business. Why not stick with the theater?"

"Is that a question?" Marisol said. Richard started to backpedal, but then she answered him anyway. "I wanted to help people, really help people. Live theater reaches fewer and fewer people all the time, especially brand-new plays by brand-new playwrights. It's getting to be like poetry—nobody reads poetry anymore. And meanwhile, poor people are dying of preventable cancers every day, back home in Taos. I couldn't fool myself that writing a play that twenty people saw would do as much good as screening a hundred people for cervical cancer."

Richard paused and looked her over. "You're a good person," he said. "I almost never get picked up by anyone who's actually not a terrible human being."

"It's all relative. My protagonist who hires a male prostitute to seduce his girlfriend considers himself a good person, too."

"Does it work? The male prostitute thing? Does she sleep with him?"

"Are you asking me a question?"

Wolf shrugged and rolled his eyes in that operatic way he did, which he'd probably practiced in the mirror. "I will owe you an extra wish. Sure. Why not. Does it work, with the gigolo?"

Marisol had to search her memory for a second, she had written that play in such a different frame of mind. "No. The boyfriend keeps feeding the male prostitute lines to seduce his girlfriend via a Bluetooth earpiece—it's meant to be a postmodern Cyrano de Bergerac—and she figures it out and starts using the male prostitute to screw with her boyfriend. In the end, the boyfriend and the male prostitute get together because the boyfriend and the male prostitute have seduced each other while flirting with the girlfriend."

Richard cringed on top of the sofa with his face in his insubstantial hands. "That's terrible," he said. "I can't believe I gave you an extra wish just to find that out."

"Wow, thanks. I can see why people hated you when you were a theater critic."

"Sorry! I mean, maybe it was better on the stage; I bet you have a flair for dialogue. It just sounds so… hackneyed. I mean, *postmodern Cyrano de Bergerac*? I heard all about postmodernism from this one graduate student who opened my bottle in the early 1990s, and it sounded dreadful. If I wasn't already sort of dead, I would be slitting my wrists. You really did make a wise choice, becoming a doctor."

"Screw you." Marisol decided to raid the relatively tiny liquor cabinet in the panic room, and poured herself a generous vodka. "You're the one who's been living in a bottle. So. All of this is your fault." She waved her hand, indicating the devastation outside the panic room. "You caused it all, with some excessively ironic wish-granting."

"That's a very skewed construction of events. If the white sludge *was* caused by a wish that somebody made—and I'm not saying it was—then it's not my fault. It's the fault of the wisher."

"Okay," Marisol said. Richard drew to attention, thinking she was finally ready to make her first wish. Instead, she said, "I need to think," and put the cork back in the bottle.

Marisol watched a season and a half of *I Dream of Jeannie*, which did not help at all. She ate some delicious beef stroganoff and drank more vodka. She slept and watched TV and slept and drank coffee and ate an omelet. She had no circadian rhythm to speak of anymore.

She had four wishes, and the overwhelming likelihood was that she would foul them up, and maybe next time there wouldn't be one person left alive to find the bottle and fix her mistake.

This was pretty much exactly like trying to cure a patient, Marisol realized. You give someone a medicine which fixes their disease but causes deadly side effects. Or reduces the patient's resistance to other infections. You didn't just want to get rid of one pathogen, you wanted to help the patient reach homeostasis again. Except that the world was an infinitely more complex system than a single human being. And then again, making a big wish was like writing a play, with the entire human race as players. Bleh.

She could wish that the bioengineered fungus had never dissolved the world, but then she would be faced with whatever climate disaster the fungus had prevented. She could make a blanket wish that the world would be safe from global disasters for the next thousand years—and maybe unleash a millennium of stagnation. Or worse, depending on the slippery definition of "safe."

She guessed that wishing for a thousand wishes wouldn't work—in fact, that kind of shenanigans might be how Richard Wolf wound up where he was now.

The media server in the panic room had a bazillion movies and TV episodes about the monkey paw, the wishing ring, the magic fountain, the Faustian bargain, the djinn, the vengeance-demon, and so on. So she had plenty of time to soak up the accumulated wisdom of the human race on the topic of making wishes, which amounted to a pile of clichés. Maybe she would have done more good as a playwright than as a doctor, after all—clichés were like plaque in the arteries of the imagination, they clogged the sense of what was possible. Maybe if enough people had worked to demolish clichés, the world wouldn't have ended.

Marisol and Richard sat and watched *The Facts of Life* together. Richard kept complaining and saying things like, "This is worse than being trapped inside a bottle." But he also seemed to enjoy complaining about it.

"This show kept me marginally sane when I was the only person on Earth," Marisol said. "I still can't wrap my mind around what happened to the human race. So, you *are* conscious of the passage of time when you're inside the bottle." She was very careful to avoid phrasing anything as a question.

"It's very strange," Richard said. "When I'm in the bottle, it's like I'm in a sensory deprivation tank, except not particularly warm. I float, with no sense of who or where I am, but meanwhile another part of me is getting flashes of awareness of the world. But I can't control them. I might be hyperaware of one ant carrying a single crumb up a stem of grass, for an eternity, or I might just have a vague sense of clouds over the ocean, or some old woman's aches and pains. It's like hyper-lucid dreaming, sort of."

"Shush," said Marisol. "This is the good part—Jo is about to lay some Brooklyn wisdom on these spoiled rich girls."

The episode ended, and another episode started right away. You take the good, you take the bad. Richard groaned loudly. "So what's your plan, if I may ask? You're just going to sit here and watch television for another few years?" He snorted.

"I have no reason to hurry," Marisol said. "I can spend a decade coming up with the perfect wishes. I have tons of frozen dinners."

At last, she took pity on Richard and found a stash of PBS *American Playhouse* episodes on the media server, plus other random theater stuff. Richard really liked Caryl Churchill, but didn't care for Alan Ayckbourn. He hated Wendy Wasserstein. Eventually, she put him back in his bottle again.

Marisol started writing down possible draft wishes in one of the three blank journals that she'd found in a drawer. (Burton had probably expected to record his thoughts, if any, for posterity.) And then she started writing a brand-new play, instead. The first time she'd even tried, in a few years.

Her play was about a man—her protagonists were always men—who moves to the big city to become a librarian, and winds up working for a strange old lady, tending her collection of dried-out leaves from every kind of tree in the world. Pedro is so shy, he can't even speak to more than two people, but so beautiful that everybody wants him to be a fashion model. He pays an optometrist to put drops in his eyes, so he won't see the people photographing and lighting him when he models. She had no clue how this play was going to end, but she felt a responsibility to finish it. That's what Mrs. Garrett would expect.

She was still stung by the idea that her prize-winning play was dumb, or worse yet, kind of misogynistic. She wished she had an actual copy of that play, so she could show it to Richard and he would realize her true genius. But she didn't wish that out loud, of course. And maybe this was the kick in the ass she needed to write a better play. A play that made sense of some of this mess.

"I've figured it out," she told Richard the next time she opened his bottle. "I've figured out what happened those other times. Someone finds your bottle after the apocalypse, and they get three wishes. So the first wish is to bring the world back and reverse the destruction. The second wish is to make sure it doesn't happen again. But then they still have one wish left. And that's the one where they do something stupid and selfish, like wishing for irresistible sex appeal."

"Or perfect hair," said Richard Wolf, doing his patented eye-roll and air-swat.

"Or unlimited wealth. Or fame."

"Or everlasting youth and beauty. Or the perfect lasagna recipe."

"They probably figured they deserved it," Marisol stared at the pages of scribbles in her hands. One set of diagrams mapping out her new, as-yet-unnamed play. A second set of diagrams trying to plan out the wish-making process, act by act. Her own scent clung to every surface in the panic room, the recirculated and purified air smelled like the inside of her own mouth. "I mean, they saved the world, right? So they've earned fame or sex or parties. Except I bet that's where it all goes wrong."

"That's an interesting theory," said Wolf, arms folded and head tilted to one side, like he was physically restraining himself from expressing an opinion.

Marisol threw out almost every part of her new play, except the part about her main character needing to be temporarily vision-impaired so he can model. That part seemed to speak to her, once she cleared away the clutter about the old woman and the leaves and stuff. Pedro stands, nearly nude, in a room full of people doing makeup and lighting and photography and catering and they're all blurs to him. And he falls in love with one woman, but he only knows her voice, not her face. And he's afraid to ruin it by learning her name, or seeing what she looks like.

By now, Marisol had confused the two processes in her mind. She kept thinking she would know what to wish for, as soon as she finished writing her play. She labored over the first scene for a week before she had the nerve to show it to Richard, and he kept narrowing his eyes and breathing loudly through his nose as he read it. But then he said it was actually a promising start, actually not terrible at all.

The mystery woman phones Pedro up, and he recognizes her voice instantly. So now he has her phone number, and he agonizes about calling her. What's he afraid of, anyway? He decides his biggest fear is that he'll go out on a date with the woman, and people will stare at the two of them. If the woman is as beautiful as Pedro, they'll stare because it's two beautiful people together. If she's plain looking, they'll stare because they'll wonder what he sees in her. When Pedro eats out alone, he has a way of shrinking in on himself, so nobody notices him. But he can't do that on a date.

At last, Pedro calls her and they talk for hours. On stage, she is partially hidden from the audience, so they, too, can't see what the woman looks like.

"It's a theme in your work, hmmm?" Richard Wolf sniffed. "The hidden person, the flirting through a veil. The self-loathing narcissistic love affair."

"I guess so," Marisol said. "I'm interested in people who are seen, and people who see, and the female gaze, and whatever."

She finished the play, and then it occurred to her that if she made a wish that none of this stuff had happened, her new play could be un-written as a result. When the time came to make her wishes, she rolled up the notebook and tucked it into her waistband of her sweatpants, hoping against hope that anything on her immediate person would be preserved when the world was rewritten.

In the end Pedro agrees to meet the woman, Susanna, for a drink. But he gets some of the eye-dilating drops from his optometrist friend. He can't decide whether to put the drops in his eyes before the date—he's in the men's room at the bar where they're meeting, with the bottle in his hand, dithering—and then someone disturbs him and he accidentally drops the bottle in the toilet. And Susanna turns out to be pretty, not like a model but more distinctive. She has a memorable face, full of life. She laughs a lot, Pedro stops feeling shy around her. And Pedro discovers that if he looks into Susanna's eyes when he's doing his semi-nude modeling, he no longer needs the eye drops to shut out the rest of the world.

"It's a corny ending," Marisol admitted. "But I like it."

Richard Wolf shrugged. "Anything is better than unearned ambivalence." Marisol decided that was a good review, coming from him.

Here's what Marisol wished:

1) I wish this apocalypse and all previous apocalypses had
never happened, and that all previous wishes relating to the
apocalypse had never been wished.
2) I wish that there was a slight alteration in the laws of
probability as relating to apocalyptic scenarios, so that if,
for example, an event threatening the survival of the human

race has a ten percent chance of happening, that ten percent
chance just never comes up, and yet this does not change
anything else in the material world.

3) I wish that I, and my designated heirs, will keep
possession of this bottle, and will receive ample warning
before any apocalyptic scenario comes up, so that we will
have a chance to make the final wish.

She had all three wishes written neatly on a sheet of paper torn
out of the notebook, and Richard Wolf scrutinized it a couple times,
scratching his ear. "That's it?" he said at last. "You do realize that I can
make anything real. Right? You could create a world of giant snails and
tiny people. You could make *The Facts of Life* the most popular TV show
in the world for the next thousand years—which would, incidentally,
ensure the survival of the human race, since there would have to be
somebody to keep watching *The Facts of Life*. You could do anything."

Marisol shook her head. "The only way to make sure we don't
end up back here again is to keep it simple." And then, before she
lost her nerve, she picked up the sheet of paper where she'd written
down her three wishes, and she read them aloud.

Everything went cheaply glittery around Marisol, and the panic
room reshaped into The Infinite Ristretto, a trendy café that just
happened to be roughly the same size and shape as the panic
room. The blue-leather walls turned to brown brick, with brass
fixtures and posters for the legendary all-nude productions of
Mamet's *Oleanna* and Marsha Norman's *'night, Mother*.

All around Marisol, friends whose names she'd forgotten were
hunched over their laptops, publicly toiling over their confrontational
one-woman shows and chamber pieces. Her best friend Julia was
in the middle of yelling at her, freckles almost washed out by her
reddening face.

"Fuck doctors," Julia was shouting, loud enough to disrupt the whole room.

"Theater is a direct intervention. It's like a cultural ambulance. Actors are like paramedics. Playwrights are *surgeons*, man."

Marisol was still wearing Burton's stained business shirt and sweatpants, but somehow she'd gotten a pair of flip-flops. The green bottle sat on the rickety white table nearby. Queen was playing on the stereo, and the scent of overpriced coffee was like the armpit of God.

Julia's harangue choked off in the middle, because Marisol was giving her the biggest stage hug in the universe, crying into Julia's green-streaked hair and thanking all her stars that they were here together. By now, everyone was staring at them, but Marisol didn't care. Something fluttery and heavy fell out of the waistband of her sweatpants. A notebook.

"I have something amazing to tell you, Jools," Marisol breathed in Julia's ear. She wanted to ask if Obama was still president and the Cold War was still over and stuff, but she would find out soon enough and this was more important. "Jools, I wrote a new play. It's all done. And it's going to change *everything*." Hyperbole was how Marisol and Julia and all their friends communicated. "Do you want to read it?"

"Are you seriously high?" Julia pulled away, then saw the notebook on the floor between their feet. Curiosity took over, and she picked it up and started to read.

Marisol borrowed five bucks and got herself a pour-over while Julia sat, knees in her face, reading the play. Every few minutes, Julia glanced up and said, "Well, okay," in a grudging tone, as if Marisol might not be past saving after all.

REMINDED

Ramsey Campbell

AS Val plants two mugs of coffee on the breakfast table she says "We haven't any children, have we, Phil?"

"I don't believe so, Val. I expect they'd have been in touch by now."

"They'd have remembered us, Phil, you mean."

"You'd hope so, Val."

"I'm keeping all my hopes for us today, Phil." Her forehead grows ridged in a bid to clench on her thoughts. "But we're married," she says, "aren't we?"

This throws him so much that he neglects to use her name. "Remind me."

"That's what this meant." She points to a ring on her left hand. "Don't you remember putting it on?"

He strains his mind until it feels close to blotting out the moment. "I wish I could."

"I can remember for us." Her brows relax, letting her eyes widen while her small neat face regains some peace. "We had to register the marriage."

"In a—" An effort that feels like scraping the inside of his head lets him say "In a registry office."

"A room full of chairs and people on them."

"Didn't they join us afterwards for drinks?"

"I'm sure they did," Val says and clasps his free hand while he swallows a fierce jolt of coffee. "See, it's coming back."

He hasn't remembered the wedding. He simply guessed that was how such occasions worked, though isn't that a memory too? When he tries to trace it back to their experience it leads him into empty darkness. "Do you remember any names?" he risks asking.

"Only ours. We'll remember them together," she says, squeezing his hand to confirm her determination. "Shall we put it on the app before we have breakfast to make sure we don't forget?"

"We said last night we wouldn't eat much. You remember what today is."

"I haven't forgotten, Philip."

The name she uses makes her resentment plain as she brings up the ReMind app on her phone. "Good morning, Valerie Elizabeth Devine," it says with relentless cheerfulness. "What do you have for me today?"

"I've remembered I'm married to Philip Anthony Devine. I knew we were together, but now I know we're wed."

When she ends the recording the face that lent the app its voice appears—the head of Guv's round chubby face flanked by a pair of fists with their thumbs stuck up. "Thank you for adding to our memory store," it says. "Together we'll put it all together."

It's a new slogan. When did he stop saying "Thank you for your thoughtfulness" and "Every day you're more yourself"? A few seconds later Phil's phone starts to buzz and crawl about the table like a rudimentary toy while the ReMind icon, a tiny brain lanced by a zigzag of lightning, develops a pulse. The sight prompts Phil to remark "Shelley."

"He wrote, didn't he? Don't tell me, wait a minute, he wrote verse."

"Poems. Poetry." Producing the words feels like regaining more language. "But he wrote a book about a brain as well," Phil says. "They send it up a tower to catch the lightning and bring it back to life."

"I think I remember something like that."

He shouldn't have given her more to attempt to recall, today of all days. "I'll keep it in my mind for you," he says and pokes the ReMind icon.

"Philip Anthony Devine, can you confirm you are married to Valerie Elizabeth Devine?"

Mustn't it be on record somewhere? Has nobody recaptured enough competence to check? That isn't the point of the question, which wants him to add recollections to the online mind everyone's supposed to share and perhaps unlock someone else's memory, but Phil can only say "Happy to confirm."

The site rewards him with the fisty face and all its words while Val consults the Rational Rationing app. "We haven't had this week's yet," she reminds Phil. "Maybe we'll be able to drive to the shops later."

Maybe sums up too much of their lives just now. As Phil saws through the thin remnant of a loaf for toast he sees Val trying to hide her concern. He knows what he's about, he isn't going to forget halfway through, and only her scrutiny makes the serrated blade splinter the tip of his thumbnail. He withholds a wince, but once he has dropped the slices into the toaster he sucks his thumb, a surreptitious gesture that feels like reverting to infancy. He gives Val the crust from the loaf, and she insists on cutting it in half to share. When did she first do that? A room you could have lost half a dozen of their kitchen in, tables draped with white cloths that almost touched the floor, chandeliers dangling elongated drops of frozen light—but he can't see how young Val was, he can't even make out her face, and the memory fades into the dark.

Breakfast doesn't take long, and they stow the used items in the washer, leaving it dormant in case the power fails while they're out of the house. They can't turn the alarm on either. They've forgotten the code, and if they ever wrote it down they have no idea where it is. At least the metal limpet on the outside wall may warn off looters, though the village has yet to attract them. The Devines step out beneath a grey April sky as blank as a scrubbed mind, and Val says "Good luck to us."

Their cars are parked on the concrete that has erased the front garden. Both roofs bear a sign proclaiming **VAL AND PHIL'S VP TUITION – COME TO PASS!** "That's us," Val declares and barely hesitates at the gate. "Left," she says. "Left to the village hall."

"Left like your hand with the ring."

"Yours too, look. If we'd realised, we wouldn't have had to spend all that time thinking up ways to remember."

"Whatever keeps our minds alive must be good for us, don't you think?"

"I'd rather we used them to find ourselves and each other. What did remembering our wedding feel like?"

The reminder enlivens Phil. Even the sky and the street lined with immobilised vehicles, all labelled **STOPPED BY GUV**, seem to brighten. "Like getting married again."

"I thought that too. Didn't people do it sometimes?"

"Careful what you think up," a voice says, though not Phil's. "Remember what Guv told us. Beware of false memories, Valerie Elizabeth Devine. We mustn't undermine anybody's progress."

Eric Craxton has poked his head above the hedge of his terraced cottage opposite. His garden looks like a determined bid to win a competition, and Phil hopes he'll continue tending it, but Craxton tramps across the road. His drooping jowly face has reddened with the effort or with dedication to his mission. "I didn't hear you use each other's names," he complains. "Watch out nobody reports you to Guv."

"Is that necessary, Eric?" The man's heavy stare requires Phil to add "Craxton."

"Names are, Philip Anthony Devine. If you'd used yours you might have noticed you were married."

"We knew we had the same one," Val protests. "I could have taken Phil's without a wedding. I'm sure people did."

"Guessing's not remembering. You know we've been warned not to speculate." Craxton moves aside, but not far. "Well, I shouldn't keep you," he says. "You're on your way for testing, are you not? Quite a few of us are hoping you'll be assets to the village."

"I believe we were," Val retorts. "Not just to the village either."

"Then perhaps you should devote yourselves to restoring that."

Val doesn't bother waiting for him not to hear her say "We're devoted to each other."

The hall is on the far side of the village. As the Devines hurry past the produce shops, several of which look erased by shutters, a delivery truck the length of half a dozen cottages pulls away from the supermarket that has summarised its neighbours. Its towering slogan says EVEN MORE HELP FROM YOUR FRIEND GUV. A laugh that sounds like a search for a reason for mirth makes Phil look back. A stumpy close-cropped grey-haired woman is gripping her extensive hips while she glares at the slogan. He's met her before, and he has to know her name. "Mrs Lomax," he succeeds in retrieving, and then the rest. "Rita. Mrs Rita Lomax."

"Leave out that nonsense." Her glare intensifies as if it's finding room for him. "One more way they're trying to reduce us all to children," she says, apparently about the slogan on the truck. "No friend does that to anyone."

"It may reassure some people," Val says, "Mrs Lomax."

"I said not to bother with my name." Just as uninvitingly Mrs Lomax says "Have you both been good subjects today?"

"We're on our way to be."

"I'm asking have you done your exercises your friend Guv says everybody has to."

"A lot more than an exercise," Phil says. "We've remembered getting married."

"I could have told you you'd done that." Leaving no gap for an answer, Mrs Lomax says "And did you do your public duty with it?"

"We put it on the app."

As Mrs Lomax emits a noise like a denial of a laugh Val says "What else have you remembered about us?"

"I couldn't say just now." By way of explanation Mrs Lomax adds "I don't trust that thing they've put on everybody's phone. It's a way of controlling our minds if we let them."

"But you've been using it," Val says as if there can't be any question.

"I'll let you guess. That's part of what your mind's for," Mrs Lomax says and stalks under a trellis twined with defunct roses, up the path to her cottage.

As her door slams the Devines hear a vehicle ahead. Is somebody being tested? Phil and Val thought they were first in the schedule, or have their minds let them down? No, the vehicle is a black van with no windows on its side, just the words **FRIEND GUV**. Perhaps they're all there's space for, but the phrase feels less friendly than imperative. The van halts outside Rita Lomax's cottage. "Phil," Val murmurs. "Have they come for her? What do you think they'll do?"

"We haven't time to find out now," Phil says as the driver, a stocky man wearing a black Guv For You jacket, climbs out and unlocks the back of the van. "If we're late they may think we forgot we're supposed to be there."

"He's letting someone out," Val says, having glanced over her shoulder. "They're all going to her house." Phil is anxious that neither of them should be distracted from the task ahead, but diverting Val's attention might distract her too. He hears Rita Lomax's front door slam again, and Val gives up looking back. They're in sight of the village hall when she falters. A middle-aged woman is leading a man about as old towards them by one arm. "Scrubbed," Val whispers as if her voice is shrinking from the spectacle.

You can tell the worst victims of the catastrophe by their look. The man's face is so loose it lacks definition, and it's expressionless apart from the eyes, which are doggedly eager but flicker with bewilderment. The woman looks as desperate, though in a different way. "Now here's your house again, John Francis Jenkins," she's saying. "You live in this house, John Francis Jenkins. You live here with me…"

Phil and Val can only give her sympathetic smiles masking their embarrassment as she continues her single-minded monologue, which repeats his name like a refrain at the end of every line. He still hasn't uttered a word by the time they leave the Jenkins couple behind. While the Devines are making sure they're on time, it feels like fleeing the threat the scrubbed mind represents. To fend it off Phil tries to picture the interior of a car viewed from the driver's seat, but the mental diagram is nothing like completed by the time they reach the village hall.

Loose wooden tiles clack underfoot in the solitary corridor, which is deserted except for swarms of dust caught in swathes of feeble downcast sunlight. The building feels hollow, close to abandoned, and smells so much of disinfectant that it might be doing duty as another kind of institution. Redundant posters adorn the walls. Perhaps they're meant to function as reminders, but they're so faded that they just suggest how faint Phil's memories have grown. A printout announcing **EXAMINATIONS** is insecurely taped to the nearest left-hand door. Phil is about to knock when the door is opened by a narrow man—narrow eyes and lips, thin face that looks as if it has pinched his nose long and sharp—in a black Guv For You jerkin. "Are you here for testing?" he says.

Phil hears Val resolve not to be daunted. "We are."

He brings up a list on his phone. "Your names, please."

"Valerie Elizabeth Devine," Val says, "and—"

He's already scrutinising Phil. "Just your own."

"Philip Anthony Devine."

Val touches Phil's arm, and he thinks she's wishing him luck until she says "Do you mind if I go first?"

He would have liked more notice, but says "If you'd rather."

The man from Guv hasn't looked away from his phone. "I have Philip booked for the first session."

"It doesn't matter, does it? We're together." As if this is bound to persuade the official, Val says "We're married."

"I have Philip booked for the first session." With no change of tone, not that he offered much to start with, the man says "Valerie, if you would like to wait in the office."

Even how he stands aside for her feels officious. "What should we call you?" she says.

"You should call me Examiner."

"Don't you need reminding of your name like the rest of us are meant to?"

"If I did I wouldn't be doing this work. Please make yourself ready, Philip."

Phil gathers he's being sent to the toilet like a child told how to behave by a teacher. The pale room smells of disinfectant and sports a lone urinal next to an empty cubicle. Who's looking in the window? There's none, and it's a mirror. He's seen them often enough, and he doesn't need showing whether he looks as nervous as he feels. He rids himself of some of the result and marches out to face Examiner. "Ready when you are."

Val waves him off from the doorway of the office. "Remember I'll be with you, Phil."

She's reminding him how they've been practising in each other's arrested vehicles for weeks, performing all the actions of a driver while pronouncing them aloud. For the last few days they've described their routine in chorus. Outside the building Examiner turns to him as if he expects an answer to a question Phil didn't hear. "I assume you remember how to proceed."

Phil reads out the registration number of a car some distance away and then, to prove that's not a fluke, the one beyond. Examiner barely nods, perhaps just to indicate his vehicle, a small black saloon crowned with a Guv Test sign. It's not a brainy car, but the Devines never used to give lessons in those, believing pupils needed to learn how to operate manual controls before they let the car take over. Phil tries to find some comfort in the driver's unyielding seat as Examiner straps himself in. "Whenever you're ready, Philip."

Phil ensures the car won't buck when he starts it, and is inserting the key when Examiner says "You need to describe the process, Philip."

"I'm putting the key in the slot."

"We require the precise words, Philip."

"I'm—" Val said it, she said it several times, which has to mean he can remember, but the attempt feels like trying to close an insubstantial grasp on a void. "I've put the key in the ignition," he blurts as he manages to recapture the term, and in case this is expected adds "Examiner."

"Please proceed, Philip."

"I'm starting the engine." He tries not to twist the key too hard for fear it will betray his anxiety, and the engine responds with a purr he could find smug. "I'm looking in the mirror," he says, not a window, a mistake he can't believe he made. "I'm pushing up the lever to show I'm pulling out, I mean I'm going to. I'm treading on the pedal, that's the clutch. I'm letting this lever down, that's taking the brake off. I'm treading on the next pedal as well, the speed one, the accelerator, only not too hard. Now I'm letting the clutch up and I'm turning the wheel..."

Surely his companion's silence denotes satisfaction, or should Phil keep calling him Examiner? He tries that as the car gathers speed along the road devoid of traffic. Not just the man's chosen name is coming easier to Phil. His body has recollected how it feels to drive, an experience so liberating he has to rein back his enthusiasm. He keeps consulting the speedometer and saying so, and describes all the manoeuvres Examiner directs him to execute—dealing with several village roundabouts and a variety of junctions, backing into a space not much larger than the car, turning it across a narrow road... He's on the way back to the village hall, feeling nearly confident enough to ask whether he's succeeded in his task, when he sees Rita Lomax.

Two men whose faces make it plain their minds have been scrubbed are leading her by the arms to the Friend Guv van. "I'm not like them," she's protesting. "I'll never be like them." Curtains blink beyond neighbouring windows, but nobody risks being seen. While the men's vacuity resembles gentleness, they lift her off her feet to plant her in the back of the van. As soon as they've followed her the driver locks the rear doors. Moments later the van speeds away, and nobody in it makes a sound Phil can hear. He's unsure he wants to learn "What will they do to her?"

"She'll be educated."

The phrase is as void of expression as the faces of her escorts were, and Phil isn't tempted to enquire further. He remarks on his actions until the car is parked outside the hall and he has returned the keys to Examiner, by which time he's eager to ask "How did I do?"

"You failed to specify some of the actions you took before starting the car, Philip. Your driving was inappropriate to the current traffic situation. And you allowed yourself to be distracted by the educational intervention."

Phil tries to find a reason to appeal. "Maybe I took more care than we have to, but I wouldn't mark a pupil down for that."

"You may present yourself when I return in three months if you wish. Now I need to test Valerie before I move on."

Phil is desperate not to infect her with failure, but as soon as she comes out of the room she reads the truth he's struggling to mask. "Oh, Phil, what went wrong?"

"Forget about me," he says, which Examiner gives a sharp look. "Go and win for the team, Val."

"If you'll wait in the office, Philip," Examiner says like an injunction of silence.

The room is no longer an office, if it ever was. Did Examiner forget the correct word? Phil wants to find this heartening but can't decide whether it is. Straight chairs face their twins along two sides of the room, which is as bare as the walls. Phil perches on the nearest chair and listens for a car. Is Val encountering some trouble? When at last he hears the car start and recede beyond his senses, he tries to summon up scraps of the past to share with Val when she comes back.

He can't distinguish any memories they haven't added to ReMind. Searching his brain feels like groping in the dark for an item he can't locate without knowing in advance what it is. Eventually he settles for reading on his phone the latest theories about the situation. Everybody's memories were wiped by cosmic rays let in by climate change, or the event was a preamble to an alien invasion, or it was caused by a new breed of phone masts, or engineered by governments—not just Guv—to trick the populace into accepting global mind control... The official news says experts are close to a solution, and meanwhile Guv reminds everybody of the one they're expected to employ: Remember to Remember. The slogan prompts Phil to wonder whether anyone recalls the moment or however long it was when their memories left them. Perhaps people are afraid to try, but could it be the key to retrieving their past? He shuts his eyes and clasps his hands in something akin to a prayer and sends his mind back.

"Never remember forgetting." The slogan returns to him just too late to be heeded. Reliving the moment of loss feels like plunging into a bottomless utterly black void that engulfs his mind. His eyes jerk open, and he stares at the unrewarding room. He's waiting for, he has to wait here, wait for Val, for Valerie Elizabeth Devine while she, while she's tested in a car. He clenches his fists as if this may help him keep hold of the knowledge and fights not to let anything else into his mind.

He has no idea how long he stays like this before he hears loose objects clatter in the corridor. Val appears in the doorway, looking wistful. "You didn't pass either," Phil says and almost gasps with relief at remembering his own attempt.

"I did, Phil. I'm just sorry you didn't as well."

He follows her and her companion to another anonymous room, which is equipped with safes. The man shows one a code on his phone to unlock it and finds a metal object he hands to Val. Although it's labelled with her details, Phil has no idea what it's supposed to be. "You should receive your authorisation within the next few days," the man tells Val, "and then you can recommence giving tuition. Drivers are among our urgent needs."

"You can look after the distributor for me, Phil." So that's what it's called, and Phil feels more trusted than perhaps he ought to be. As they head for home Val says "Let's go for a drive to celebrate. If you like you can take over once we're out where there'll be nobody to see."

He's glad when she retrieves the component from him, since this saves him from betraying he's forgotten where it goes. She fits it into the engine as he takes refuge in the seat next to the driver's. He sees how delighted she is to be back in control, and doesn't want to spoil her triumph. He thinks it's wisest to stay silent while she drives into the countryside. They're on a straight deserted stretch of road between meadows like emblems of rebirth when she turns to him. "Shall we swap so you can practise?" she says and blinks at him. "Did you want to ask me something, Phil?"

He has to risk admitting his state, however shameful owning up threatens to feel. "It's just slipped my mind for the moment. What did you tell me this morning I ought to know?"

Val's expression looks in danger of collapsing, but then her mouth hauls itself up by its corners. "I know somewhere you'll remember," she says, and as the car speeds towards the mystery of the horizon Phil can only hope her words mean all they can possibly promise.

THE SPLENDOR AND
MISERY OF BODIES, OF CITIES

Samuel R. Delany

THERE are on Inring (so GI told me) a few small areas that have been built up. My destination point was not, however, one.

We spent the morning setting up the imported artwork (2417-Y) in the vaurine library at the far end of the station complex: in the course of it, I began to get some feel for just how primitive the little world I'd come to was.

Have you ever spent time (a few months, say) somewhere in love with reflection? Where the streets, the walls, the windows, the transportation machines and disposal gondolas all have polished surfaces on which, right or distorted, your own image glides past you wherever you pass? And have you, from there, gone on to a place where all objects are wholly without gloss? In your first hours or days at your matte location, you find that the multiplicity and iteration of image you'd learned to live with somehow had become more than just background: they'd become an extension of you—to an extent only fully felt once you moved along alleys and avenues whose stone and mottled plastics gave you nothing back, their opacity having cut out all cursory repetition (of you or anything else) at a root, that lies, to your astonishment and even pain, not between yourself and the world, but within that model of the world within you which is all you ever know of it; and you learn something of your limitations as a woman.

There's a similar amputation, diminishment, and constraint (and insight) when you go from a place where all is mentally activated illusion to one with a more material surface.

Certainly, in that Inring compound beside the landing field, there was adequate GI: ask a question and it was answered, briefly and quickly, by a burry voice projected into the back of your mind. But there were not the attendant projections of memories, associations, and suggestional supplements that attended the larger GI systems you find in extensive urban complexes and at free data nodes.

Oh, there were quite enough mentally activatable switches. When you stood in front of a door and thought, "Aperture-7," the door opened—though, on your third trip through, you realized that the smudges on the white oval, just below chin-height, were not some carefully modulated design in subtle, smeary grays, but were rather the trace of many, many women before you who'd pushed it open by hand.

When you went into a dark room and thought "Glow-4," the strip lights came on all across the ceiling of the octagonal chamber—though, after a moment, you realized that the single white panel in the far corner that remained dark and the other one near it that now and again flickered were not a refreshing asymmetry incorporated in the arrangement of the illumination elements: they were broken.

And when you stood in the twenty-meter beige cradle connecting the major and minor office complexes and looked across the benches out at that huge transparent canopy curving up and arching back overhead, you knew that the rock and dust outside, scattered to the horizon under a near-empty night, were exactly what was there. (There'd been no planoforming, not even a seeding of elephant lichen on this sector of Inring.) And there were no numbers or words or colors or smells in any codic combination you could think of to change it.

At last, with many comings and goings, 2417-Y was gotten into its tiny chamber, whose real space was perhaps three by three by three meters, but which, when you got permission from the compound librarian and entered its red doorway, put you into hundred-meter marbled halls, towering columned arcades, and sky-lit gardens of glass rods, a-flitter with smoke and light, a-clatter with harsh music, a structure almost as extensive and ornate as Dyethshome back on Velm—though conceived in a (much greater number of) vastly different style(s). But helping set it up in the vaurine projector with my new [employer.sub.1] that morning (the kind of thing an Industrial Diplomat may be called on to do if the destination point is backward enough), I'd already noticed her bearded face had about it the set of lip and slightly narrowed eye we humans display on almost any world when disappointed.

Why? Well, I could only guess.

But one of the biggest factors in the human response to any artwork is what you happened to have been doing, thinking, feeling, and the place you'd been doing, thinking, and feeling it in, just before you encountered it. Art makes its entire effect by developing things from your landscape, denying other things in it, and replacing still others with the artists' vision: that means the same text must be read differently on each different world, because you bring to it the experiences of the different landscape against which the artifact is constantly engaged in argument. And despite the little I knew of it, I could say for certain that Krome's landscape (and 2417-Y's origin) was not Inring's. And though my [employer.sub.1] thought she remembered 2417-Y from her adolescence light-years away, what she really recalled was the experience of encountering that work fresh from—or rather, wholly entangled in—Krome. But whether

2417-Y would prove to be a rich and decentering and/or stabilizing experience here, or simply become a vastly expensive irrelevance off in a little room, visited less and less frequently, till the projector was shut down and the importation costs (and my fee) were written off, I could not tell; nor, indeed, could my [employer.sub.1] —at least not till she'd shaken that memory loose. For it was only as 2417-Y was absorbed by (as her disappointment had begun that absorption and transformation of) Inring's 'scape could anyone, here, understand anything of 2417-Y, even unto its alien history on another world.

"You don't look comfortable," my employer[sub.1] said, when, once we were through, she had strolled back with me to the cradle. She herself wore at least fifteen pounds of metal medallions at knees, elbows, and waist, as well as light plastic tubing about her neck, thighs, and armpits: glimmering rings hung by delicate coils to her sternum, navel, knees. Her beard, which had been red in the morning, was now (after an hour each of blue, yellow, and green) black. "It's pretty rough out here. We get a lot of folks from all parts of the planet passing through. They don't like it either." She frowned. "Not many from off world, though."

"I'm comfortable," I said. "In fact I like it here. Actually, I was thinking of staying."

"Nobody else would," she said, sadly. "Folks come by from over in Qwik—you can tell them because they're all hung around with those silver furs and big blocky whachamacallits on their elbows. We always say: 'Take something off! Relax!' Then the ones from down in Litimis, they come up here and just stride on through with nothing on at all. You're always sitting around and saying to them, 'You sure you don't want to put something on, like everyone else? You'll feel more at home.'" She sighed.

At my neck I closed another fastening on what they still, there, actually called a space suit. Down in the bulky boots were these loops you were supposed to slip your toes through; in the right one, it had gone fine. In the left, however, two of my middle toes had missed; or the loops were broken; or something. And I was kind of wiggling my foot around to try and find out what exactly it was, and what I might do about it, and not making much headway.

And that's the kind of thing a primitive GI is no help with at all.

"I think that 2417-Y," my [employer.sub.1] said, "is the most important thing that's ever happened on Inring. Certainly it's the most important thing that's ever happened on this part of it. It's about the only piece of real culture we've got. It'll stabilize a whole new breed of tourist, of thinking, of life, here at the complex. Don't you agree?"

I pulled down the head guard, whose airtight clasps went critter-click, critter-click, critter-click, all around my neck. "You may be right," I said, not sure if my external speaker was on or not. Then I nodded at her with whatever smile I could mechanically muster and started toward the bronze circle, the bottom half of which was in the beige wall, the top half in the clear canopy.

I cropped toward the energy sheet that, like rippling water over glass, served as the cradle's airlock.

Though I'd worked with her for most of Inring's very nonstandard day, handing things, holding things, pointing and prodding with her, I realized I hadn't even bothered to notice her hands—which for me was once about as automatic as the click-curses constantly expostulated in both laughter and rage, among the shale-farmers of the equatorial zones of Celluv IX or the leisurely pursing of the brows before answering just about any question at all among the polar butane workers of Hatatki VII.

As the night wavered a moment in my eyes, and sparks struck silently from my hip and head as I went through the shield, I realized again that I was a repository of a vast womanly experience of cultural relativity (so much vaster than man's could ever be—

which was the way we humans once characterized ourselves when we'd been confined largely to a single world), from the hundreds of worlds I had visited in my [job.sub.1] (and among the thousands more I had not visited, or even, perhaps, heard named): yet that relativity was precisely what I'd come here to lose, to leave behind, to forget. I wanted only something simple, absolute, monumentally upshifting, and still.

I stepped over the threshold, onto the outside terrace, leaving the artificial gravity for the far less intense "down" of the natural world. I swayed under those few distantly spaced stars. We were well out along the thinner part of the galactic arm that, almost since the beginning of colonizing, put us extremely far away from anywhere. (The cluttered night above those worlds lost in the hub is equally a sign that one is far away from anyplace else, on the edge of the unknown: most of our exploration and colonization has been along the mid-arms. But that was not where I was; and again I tried to shake out of mind that urge that always made me see everywhere in terms of somewhere else.) I made my way forward, aware, as I strode over the dusty flags, that a few rocks had been kicked or thrown or even, presumably, set there by others suited against the near-vacuum as bulkily as I.

I moved forward, a woman in a dusty, airless 'scape where woman was just not meant to go.

To my left were towering, blobbed filigrees of the space ships that, as usual this far out, followed some design either so alien or so primitive I hadn't seen it before. To my right was the place that a mountainous black nebula we were quite close to (eight light-years?) cut out even the few stars that should have been visible in that direction, joining the land with night.

Those small, cold worlds are notoriously empty of visual variety; nor had I bothered to learn what little that variety might mean about the structure of the planetary ball I waddled over, so that the no-color between brown and gray, lit largely by my shoulder lights and the haze from the station complex behind me, was as void of information for me as a landscape could be.

I walked through it, refusing to think about myself or it.

I walked a long time.

After perhaps forty minutes, or an hour-forty minutes, I stopped.

A rock slab had freed itself from the dust, to rise, over the next twenty feet, perhaps a meter; as I reached its edge I realized this was the best this world could do toward a crag.

I looked up into the blackness, most of whose dim stars you could only see out of your eye's corner.

Then I shouted: "Rat Korga…!"

In the tiny helmet space, the sound hurt my ears.

I shouted again: "Korga…!"

And again: "Rat…!"

And: "Rat Korga!" I reeled on rock as his name filled up my ears, my mouth, my eyes, along with the perpetual stutterings from my speaker, the burblings from my air regulator. "Korga! Rat Korga!" I looked up at a darkness that might as well have been a ceiling ten feet overhead, though it was made up of thousands on thousands of light-years of nothing. "Korga! Rat…!"

I shouted and shouted. I tore my throat and battered my ears. In that air globe where his name roared no farther away from my face than a few thicknesses of my hand, on that nightbound rock hardly heavy enough to warrant the word world, with each shout I announced some appalling fact to a blackness that would show no wonder from its presence, no horror at its absence—that hung, vast and ignorant, before each iteration my raw tongue rasped from under a burning pallet, as though each shriek were my first vocable.

For moments the darkness was an infirm ear bent toward me; to each scream the universe mumbled, Pardon…? What was that…? I didn't quite catch you…? Come again?, while for the fortieth, forty-seventh, and fiftieth time I shouted, shaking, at night.

For a while I stopped.

Then I shouted some more.

I was sitting, now, on the stone, leaning on one thick mitten. My throat was too sore to go on. So I just muttered it, hoarsely, as though his name were the access code that, repeated enough, would change the universe, would make this most marginal rock a center of labor, art, and community.

I looked up to rasp, near voiceless again: "Rat…!"

I couldn't tell you how far away the light was. But it wobbled and drew closer; and grew bigger.

"…Korga," which came with no voice at all, a movement of muscle and bone in my chest and jaw, making no sound in the soundless dark.

At first I didn't look. Then, because here and there in it were such bright lights, I couldn't look.

It came toward me. There was someone inside it. Her vacuum suit was far more compact and streamlined than mine. Her shoulder-plates glimmered; rings of lights around her calves blinked. My own lights reflected in her face plate.

For whatever reason, any number of Web officials might have chosen just then to look me up: Halleck, Fenz, Marta, Japril, Sarena, Ynn… Any number of Inring locals I'd met in the course of delivering and setting up 2417-Y might have decided to come after me just then, from the rather jovial library assistant of that morning's installation, to my [employer.sub.1] herself, or even that fellow debarkee with whom I had brief and listless sex shortly after I'd landed earlier in Inring's long, long day and who I'd thought had gone off afterward to other geosectors.

The figure climbed the rock. Her face plate cleared of glare.

I frowned. "You are not…" (It was a painful whisper.) "…whom I expected to see." I took a breath. "Here."

"Ah, Skynosh Marq, but I did expect to see you. Here. Well, one takes what one can get," JoBonnot said. "But then, I have been looking for you. While you have not been looking for me. Isn't that right? Very logical, yes?" She looked up at blackness, around at darkness. "You have really managed to get quite far away. One would almost think you were running off. You have come so far. But then, as I was following you, I heard your call over my earphones." Behind the plate she scowled, and one hand went up to rub at where her ear would have been on the head mask. "Very loud. As if you were calling, perhaps, for something—someone. Some Rat Korga. And yet"—she scowled harder, looking around once more—"I do not think here, by any means, is the most reasonable place to find her."

"JoBonnot," I said, "lust is not logical."

"Lust is what you have," she said. "Love is what you want. Ah, the intricacies of desire!"

"I don't know how you got here," I said. "I don't know why you've come. But right now, I only know what I don't want. And I don't want anything to do with life."

"That is wanting to die." JoBonnot nodded.

"I don't want to die," I said. "I just don't want to live."

Inside her mask, JoBonnot looked at me strangely. She reached toward me. "That is dreadful," she said. Her hand came toward, and did not quite touch, mine—like my little white sister, light-years away.

I took another breath.

The effort was painful.

Not only to my throat.

"Dreadful," she repeated. "But we can change all that. Yes?" She spoke bluntly, brightly. "That's all you have to say?"

There on the dark rock I shook my head.

"That's no in one language, yes in another," she commented.

"JoBonnot, no…"

"Yes," she said, like some childhood GI instruction series, correcting a wrong answer. "Marq Dyeth, what do you know of the XIv?"

I looked up, frowning.

"Do not worry," she said, briskly. "In some ways, you have picked a very good place to come. We're well outside Web security. Ah, yes, I can see that you've heard of them before—the XIv. But then, we've mentioned them within each other's hearing, haven't we: I to you. You to me. Back home. At your home. On Velm."

"I know the XIv are something the Web says I'm not supposed to know about—an alien race with interstellar travel that woman has not yet established true communication with. And I know the XIv in their mysterious ships were circling Rhyonon when Korga's world was destroyed… you said they were circling mine when he was taken away."

"You never struck me as a woman who liked to be told what she could or couldn't know, Marq Dyeth."

"I hate it," I said; and began to cry.

"Left in lust and denied the possibility of love," JoBonnot said, "do you think you can go on hating?"

"I…" Searching out energy even for that, I felt I'd expended the last of it in my futile howl against night. "I don't know, JoBonnot." I went on crying. "I don't… know anything anymore."

"I can give you Rat Korga back. I can give you two a world of your own—if you will help me save mine. It only takes a little hate."

I frowned.

"I can give you information. Tell me again what you know of

the XIv. And Rhyonon. Tell me about the XIv and your own home world of Velm."

"I know… well, someone told me…" My throat ached. My eyes stung. "I mean, when Rat's world went into what may or may not have been Cultural Fugue and destroyed itself, XIv ships were observed circling his world. Many of them. Three hundred and sixty of them; or three hundred and sixty thousand—I'm not sure which. Below them, the first fireball started…" I blinked. "And someone—you, JoBonnot—told me that when the Web took Rat away from my home, away from Velm, away from me, again there were many XIv ships circling my world. Circling Velm. And when he left, in the Web shuttle, you said they left…"

"And that seems like meaningful information, doesn't it?" JoBonnot nodded. "It suggests all sorts of correlations, alignments, possibilities. Oh, yes! A little knowledge? Often a very, very, very dangerous thing. We human-style women have known that since before we left our own world, wherever that was. Well, listen to me, Marq Dyeth. I have something more to tell. See what it does to that information you feel, now, you are just on the brink of possessing—the constellation of facts that the Web, you are sure, does not want you to know more of. Look. Listen. Attend carefully: so far you know what the Web wants you to know. Now I will tell you some of the things they don't want you to know at all. Oh, how clever of you to come out here beyond Web security. One would almost think we had it planned. Well, no matter. Listen to me now, Skynit Marq. It is true, three weeks before Rhyonon was destroyed, three hundred sixty thousand XIv ships gathered in a cloud about Rhyonon and began to circle it; and approximately two standard, twenty-four-hour days after the holocaust was over, they left it. But for the last twenty-nine years fleets of XIv ships of comparable size, some slightly larger, some indeed notably smaller, have been gathering at Rhyonon approximately every other month standard, to circle the planet for a little over three weeks before leaving. And the time they stay has always been the same. Also, consider this: in the little over a standard year since the Rhyonon catastrophe, XIv have continued to gather there, circle it, and leave—"

"But… but what are they doing?" I asked. "Are they just observing? Does that mean that they didn't have anything to do with the holocaust?"

"Consider this also, Marq Dyeth. As far as Velm is concerned, there has been similar behavior from XIv ships for almost eighty-nine years standard now: many fewer ships in that case—only a hundred and seven thousand. They stay perhaps seven standard weeks, then leave for between eight and nine. The pattern has been quite consistent for getting on to a century now. Now I bet you didn't know that, Snu Marq."

"But why my world? Why Rat's?"

"Oh, and there are still other pieces of information that must be considered before we get to that question: of the six thousand inhabited worlds in the Web's range and jurisdiction," JoBonnot went on, "there are a hundred-two for which this XIv behavior has also been noted. For at least six of these worlds, there is indication that this periodic visitation, circling, and leaving has been going on for well over two standard centuries. But those six include neither Velm nor Rhyonon."

"And how many of those hundred and two worlds have gone into Cultural Fugue and wiped themselves out?" I asked.

"One," JoBonnot said. "Rhyonon."

"Then, you mean, the XIv were just observing: and they weren't really responsible for what happened on…?"

"Do not overread the data I gave you: that is as bad as underreading what you've already read. Consider this too: the Web has logged over four thousand other worlds, uninhabited and uninhabitable by humans (and most of the alien species we've made contact with), which are also the object of these periodic visitations by the XIv. One notes it's a number of the same order of magnitude as that of the number of habitable worlds. There's one barren planet where the number of XIv ships reported to converge is slightly above eight hundred thousand and the period itself is eight hours there, and fifteen hours away; and it goes on constantly. I hear it's quite spectacular—though no human has witnessed it."

I frowned: "Then we don't even know if what they're interested in on the human worlds is even the human population or not!"

"Are their visitations a form of art? Theology? Scientific research? A biological necessity? A cultural jape? Are they all there, circling their myriad worlds, for a single purpose? Or are there as many different explanations as there are XIv ships, or XIv aboard them?" JoBonnot shrugged. "The XIv are alien. We do not know their language; or languages; or even if they have a language. We cannot communicate with them. They have not communicated with us. We cannot know them—and can only guess at what, about them, we can never know. Again, do not overread." She reached out toward me again. (I raised my bulbous mitten, I think to push her away.) "But do not underread either. Would you like to see a XIv, Skina Marq?"

My frown, never free of my face, fell apart in complete bewilderment, as though the fragments might wash off with my tears, and I saw a fluttering in the dark behind her, as indistinct as, minutes ago, JoBonnot herself had been. A flicker: and what fluttered beneath, glimmered. It drifted forward, climbing the rock as she had climbed it, though it was certainly not human. I blinked, trying to judge its size, which is hard when you're looking at something you've never seen before. It was membranous, hulking, liquefacious, and—I think—blue. Lights hovered in a constellation over it. As one part bobbled and lolloped forward and another flowed and flapped behind, I thought: any one of those movements, to the knowledgeable, might communicate friendship, interest, aggression, suspicion, or any number of alien stances no human could know. The lights circled above her, part, doubtless, of whatever forcefield allowed her to move and maintain shape over this unpressured 'scape.

"But what…?" I pushed back. "I mean, is she really a…?"

"Oh, I'd say, rather, he"—and JoBonnot adjusted her squat on the rock—"is my dear, dear friend—"

Suddenly I stood, staggering with the surprise of delayed recognition. "But that's not a XIv!" I rasped. "That's a native of Nepiy! Your home world! I've seen one of her before, JoBonnot!" The alien began to recede into the dark, the lights above her dimming. "I've talked with women of her race before! I've even [worked.sub.1] for one! That's no XIv, JoBonnot! How did you get here? And why did you bring her?"

"Unlimited space fare? Surely you must have encountered the custom somewhere before. Besides, I merely asked if you wanted to see a XIv. I didn't say I'd show you one. Here. Now. On this particular bit of barely habitable stone. I brought him because, well, Clym and I…" She paused. "I have a [job.sub.1] for you, Skynum Dyeth. Will you take it?" JoBonnot looked up at me, her forearms over her knees. Now she reached up. "Come home with me, Marq Dyeth. Come with us." Her thin fingers, in their entirely different kind of vacuum protection, seized my great glove. "Come with us to my homeworld of Nepiy. I need you—we need you. Do this for me, for us, for Nepiy; if you do, there we will give you back your Rat." She stood, now, before me; and, in her grip, I reeled. "Come home."

The sky was black as metal, sealed meters overhead. A row of lights marched off into darkness, their little glow here and there lighting bronzish rocks. We sat among columns strung with vines and great metal petals—alien sculptures of giant flowers.

Whatever we sat on was desperately uncomfortable—like my own contour chair stalled eternally before its flex.

Off in the distant dark came the faintest flicker of blue.

Silence pulsed for three, four breaths.

Then thunder, nearly dumb in its deeply muted growl.

I said: "I've seen the lightning, grown blood red, whip and shatter the overhead fumes of Nepiy."

"Ah," said JoBonnot. "Most likely you were much farther south—closer to the equator."

"Very filmy caves"—I frowned at the columns around us, the lights beyond us—"golden veils on the humans, as if they imitated the native women's blue and rippling demeanor. At least that's how I remember it."

"You must have been, yes, definitely you were"—9-K adjusted herself around the translator pole—"a third of the way—certainly more than a fourth—around to the east. Not the west, definitely. The east."

Again thunder rose, but only to the deepest hum—before it fell to silence.

I said: "When I was on Nepiy before, fumes and lightning tore up the overhead gases and the land outside the powershields was rife with some catastrophe that threatened starvation for three whole urban complexes. Although this is only a simplified account, it had to do with the failure of a crop of beans. Almost all the women I talked to were afraid it might be Cultural Fugue."

"The Quintian Geosector Grouping." JoBonnot tapped her fingertips together.

"One of the smaller, if not the smallest of the Quintians." 9-K drifted back till her pole was decidedly off-center. "Definitely the smallest of the Quintians. Wouldn't you say?"

JoBonnot nodded. "There are women all over Nepiy afraid of

Cultural Fugue. Even here." The nod took in the darkness around us, with its silence. JoBonnot looked as uncomfortable on her seat as I felt on mine. "Of course the situation around here is substantially worse than in the Quintians."

Once I looked at the blackness, listened to the silence, wondering what signs of what tragedies were sunk within them that I could not read.

"Of course, this cassette does not show them," JoBonnot said, as if realizing my thoughts. "It was recorded at a happier time." She shifted. "Still, the Thants"—standing, her features became almost indistinguishable by her column—"have been called to Nepiy by Family sympathizers to be the Focus Unit for our world."

"I know that," I said. "My nurture stream on Velm has entertained the Thants back home, at Dyethshome, at Morgre. Many times."

"Won't do," said the blobby blue woman, drawing in around her translation pole. (I had asked the ship's GI for her name: and had been informed that Nepiy natives don't use them at home, but I had been given a number I could refer to her by if I wanted: 9-K. But through some vestigial diplomatic sense it just didn't feel right.) Somewhere above the vegetative webbing between the poles' knobby heads, thunder rumbled again in that rippling sable. "Just won't do. Human, all too human—you see? You understand, Marq Dyeth? Can you apprehend the problems of a woman such as I?"

"Like Velm," I said, squirming on something not quite stool, hassock, chair, or couch, "Nepiy has both an alien population and a human population, living largely in peace with one another. I learned that from my single visit to your world, back when I learned some of your Nepiyan fellows were worried about a possible Cultural Fugue condition."

"Like Velm," JoBonnot said, from her column, "it is more complicated than that."

Burbling about her pole, the inhuman woman said: "Unlike Velm, Marq Dyeth, Nepiy has both ggggg and nnnn." The two buzzes were on only slightly different pitches.

I frowned.

"Ggggg and nnnn," JoBonnot repeated. "The two terms are so common among the Nepiy they have entered our human language."

"I don't think I heard them when I was here—I mean there, on Nepiy. Of course I was only getting the most simplified of accounts."

"It would have to have been a very simplified account, very simplified indeed," 9-K declared. "Myself, my translator hasn't been able to deal with 'beans' at all. Beans? Beans, you say?"

"Neither, apparently, could the women of the Smaller Quintians. They're not native to your world," and while I wondered if I should mention that these particular beans had come from mine, 9-K saved me the diplomatic embarrassment:

"Ah!" She bulged forward again. "Well, then, no matter. Let's get on with it. Go on, now. Go on."

"Ggggg are Nepiy's highland plateaus. And nnnn are the lowland ribbons that wind between them, across much of the surface of our world. This cassette here"—JoBonnot gestured around us—"is set up to represent a rather romanticized section of nnnn. The lowlands. The cloud layer, up there, covers most or even all of the nnnn: often vast storms, vast rains, and always vast darkness."

"Yes, I remember it from my visit."

"Climb up the rocky slope, there, and you will break through the broiling mists and emerge, at last, on some ggggg rim."

"We women of Nepiy," said the alien, through her pole, "have always lived along the bottom of the nnnn, underneath the clouds. Why, you ask, Marq Dyeth? What are our reasons? What is the functional answer in terms you can follow? Ah, it's terribly difficult to express it simply; it involves chemistry, psychology, evolution—

which, you understand, are normally concepts as alien to us as vfvfvfvfdk, rrrrmmmh, and gktqbtk are to you." (That's the best I can do with the humming buzzes she uttered: and since they came from her pole, that meant they were already translations.) "But we have lives there; we live there; and we want to go on living."

"Up on the ggggg," JoBonnot said, "only humans live. They have their urban complexes, their society, their industry. But the humans who do, tend to—how shall I say—forget that any other women share their planet with them. There is fear of Cultural Fugue—that terrible social condition in which worlds destroy themselves—from the depths of the nnnn to the centers of the most isolated ggggg. And it is very much the tension between ggggg and nnnn that is involved. The humans of the ggggg, at the urging of the Family, have decided to bring in a Focus Unit to help stabilize the cultural play."

"On my single visit to Nepiy," I said, "the area I visited was certainly deep within a crisis. And in the lowlands… in the nnnn, I saw of the fear of Cultural Fugue. But women anywhere fighting real and pressing chaos tend to fear that, first thing. I've seen it on many worlds, JoBonnot—worlds that still swing quite whole and neatly in their orbits about the night. And on Nepiy there were no official Web parameters to suggest your world was heading anywhere near CF."

"Worlds are big places, Marq Dyeth," said blue bubbly 9-K. "You could not have seen all of Nepiy. In the period you were there, you could only have gotten the most simplified picture."

"A Focus Unit must reflect and focus the concerns of a world," JoBonnot said. "Consider, then, a world with two racial species, who imports a Focus Unit consisting only of one."

What could I say? I said, "I gather it's rather moot just how much stabilizing a Focus Unit can do, anyway—but then, I was brought up under the Sygn, and we tend to look down on all traditional

Family techniques. Do you mean to bring in the Sygn to help right the situation? Certainly on worlds where the women are divided between native and human, their dogma seems more geared to easing tensions and promoting peaceful coexistence."

"Once you are on a world, if the conflict between Family and Sygn becomes too heated, especially as the various precepts are taken up by hostile institutions with other names, it can lead a world even closer to Cultural Fugue, rather than resolve the turmoil."

I smiled. "That's true." At least it's certainly what one hears as one slides along vague and variegated strands of the Web. "Yet there must always be some tension between them, if either is to avoid becoming the basis of some oppressive regime. And since worlds are, indeed, big places, most women, seeing a conflict in one local place that may, indeed, look huge, tend to give it more importance in world terms than it deserves. I'm a woman who has been to many worlds, JoBonnot."

"And I," said the blue woman, puckering about her pole, "am a woman who has suffered very deeply on my own, Marq Dyeth."

To which, I'm afraid, there's not much you can say.

I said:

"You've decided, then, that you're not bringing in the Sygn…?"

"What we would like to bring to Nepiy, Marq Dyeth, is you. And your Rat—oh, not for good! Only for the briefest of visits!" JoBonnot shifted about, looking suddenly as uncomfortable on her seat as I felt on mine. "We don't want to make you our Focus Unit. We don't want any Focus Unit at all. But among the range of human males, you are a very interesting woman, Marq Dyeth. So is Rat Korga. The two of you are especially interesting to women who are frightened of Cultural Fugue."

"Because Rat's world was destroyed by Cultural Fugue?" I asked. "Or what may—"

"—or may not—"

"—have been Cultural Fugue?" I finished.

"Interesting," 9-K hummed. "Especially to women who fear it."

"The ambiguity simply sounds the note of anxiety which makes the fascination even richer, more resonant. Oh, it's very interesting, the relation between you two. And to so many decimal places—"

"Look, I—"

"When a Focus Unit takes over on a world, it must be made an occasion of great interest," 9-K burbled. "Great publicity! Vast amounts of information and misinformation, shuttled about the world! Public relations! Promotion! Hype and hyperbole! I imagine it can be quite interesting."

"So we are going to bring you to Nepiy with the Thants," JoBonnot said. "And there we will join you with the Rat."

"And you're hoping the… 'interest' we generate will upset the campaign to… to establish the Thants in their new position?" But the possibility, even as I spoke, was already hammering my heart hard enough to hurt my throat.

Thunder rumbled. The blue woman came completely to pieces, splashed away in several directions over the rocks, then splashed back again to congeal about the pole. "Oh, she understands! She understands it! Ah, you were so right. She is, indeed, a very interesting woman!"

"Only I don't know if I want to be all that interesting—"

"Do you want Rat Korga?" JoBonnot asked.

I looked up at the clouds sealing off the rocks and gorges around us in this cassetted nnnn. "Yes." And the lightning flashed: but, within those broiling darknesses, it was red and thin and only rouged the columned grotto. "I'm going back to ship normal for a while." I stood up on the shaley ground.

"As you wish, Sketu Dyeth," JoBonnot said, looking triumphant.

THE RISE AND FALL
OF WHISTLE-PIG CITY

Paul Di Filippo

AT the time I wish to write about, there were only five humans living on Earth. I say "humans," but the ancient definition of that term must be considerably expanded to include us. Even if outwardly conforming to baseline humanity, we still deviated extremely from the old norm. Deviant by genome, both embedded and in the cloud, and by powers, both interior and exterior. But in any case, we were still the true inheritors of the old ape lineage.

Sharing the planet, we five nonetheless all lived widely separated and isolated lives in our extensive redoubts, each of us busy with our own hobbies, concerns, crotchets, obsessions and projects. For reasons which I have since offloaded from my memory into backup, we had, during that interval, looked backwards some ten or twelve millennia and capriciously assigned ourselves the names of long-dead twentieth-century artists.

Bilal, a dwarfish and dark-eyed fellow, lived on one of the southern continents and currently sought to learn all the secrets of the tricksy hyperspace machine elves.

Waifish and haunted-looking, holed up in a fairytale castle in one of the vast northern forests, Doucet spent her hours guiding a chorus of dryads and treefrogs through more and more intricate arrangements of the choral songs of Beta Lyrae.

Thin and attenuated as an eel, completely amphibian with scaly skin tinged pallid green and white, Giraud inhabited a submarine fortress in tropical waters, where he staged titanic fights between various leviathans.

Maroh, a mostly naked, green-skinned, photosynthesizing giantess, whose curves mimicked swales, peaks and valleys, resided in a large ice palace at the southern pole, and employed her time cataloguing the infinite varieties of interstellar vacuum foraminifera with elaborate sensors and sampling engines.

And then there was I, Crepax. Devilishly handsome, witty, constitutionally blithe. My own preoccupations at that time, indulged in my alpine lodge atop Earth's highest artificial peak, rearing some twenty thousand meters toward the stratosphere, included sampling the many varieties of wine derived from the myco-vineyards of Alnilam VIII, and frolicking with an ever-changing bevy of ghost hetaerae from the Seventh Blue Limbo Dimension. And, oh yes, composing epic poetry on the themes of Waldeinsamkeit and Uitbuiken.

So, as I believe you can see, our separate blisses were so divergent that there was little cause for the five of us ever to foregather. Even though we were the only sentients on the whole planet—other non-human sapients found the rewilded Earth a backwater bore, and, consequently, rarely visited—loneliness was not an issue.

That is, we had no reason for close association until Bilal rediscovered the concept of "cities."

Bilal chose to introduce the notion first to me, I am pleased to say, obviously relying on my famously catholic tastes to permit an unprejudiced assessment of his excitement.

I became aware of my visitor when one of my house robots carried in a small frozen body, interrupting me in the midst of composing a stanza examining the proposition that a patch of moss ringed with toadstools could represent nirvana.

Bilal was still dressed for the tropical clime of his home, bare-chested, barefoot and wearing just a colorful loincloth. Hardly the garb needful at the raw altitude of my home. Small icicles fringed his unseeing eyes, and crusted his nostrils, rendering his homely face even uglier than usual.

"We found him some hundred meters from the front door, sir. His ship was parked at the edge of the defensive field with the airlock door open."

Plainly, Bilal had been in such an excited rush to see me that he had neglected all personal safety measures. I was intrigued.

"Pop him in the revivifier, will you please? And then break out two glasses and a bottle of the Goliadic Enfumé. The hundred-year-old variety."

I confess to not waiting for Bilal to become fully cognizant again, with all his metabolic functions restored and self downloaded from the cloud, before I tapped the bottle. I was savoring my second glass of the delicious vintage when one of the robots ushered a re-souled Bilal in. He had the slightly befuddled air of the recently reinstantiated, but a few gulps of the Goliadic soon put him right.

He and I took up lazy positions on two lounge chairs that contorted themselves for our maximum comfort.

"Now, my small friend, what got you so worked up that you had to fly all the way here to see me in person, rather than just contact me over the quantum aether? Have the machine elves finally disclosed the secret to blending dark matter with baryonic matter to produce the fabled Cosmic Electrum?"

"No, no, nothing like that. Progress with those capricious sprites remains frustratingly slow. In fact, it was while I was taking a break from those investigations that I stumbled upon the massive revelation which brought me to your doorstep. Total serendipity, but what a find! Have you ever heard of the concept of a 'city?'"

"The word means nothing to me."

"Well, please take a moment now to acquaint yourself with the trope."

It took an incredibly long time—nearly a whole picocycle—for the cloud to return the information from where it had been buried beneath myriad other dead tidbits accumulated over the many millennia of recorded galactic history. But when at last it was delivered to me, my assimilation was, as usual, practically instantaneous.

I regarded Bilal with a wide-eyed expression. He grinned in his gruesome manner to acknowledge my shock.

"Why," I said, "this is the most preposterous notion I've encountered in at least the last eight hundred years, since that time when I discovered the reproductive cycle of the Graben Prangers!"

"Isn't it droll and delicious?"

"Droll and delicious? Gathering millions of sentients into a tiny physical space, then trying to come up with an infrastructure to support them at varying levels of material comfort; deriving a set of enforceable rules and regulations to stave off their natural tendency to discord and entropy; and fashioning interlocking systems of work and play— It's a nightmare! Why would anyone ever imagine such a gimcrack mechanism would ever succeed or last? Were these cultures unfamiliar with Arpad's Fourth Axiom and Zerba's Suite of Anti-whimsies?"

"Such revelatory strictures were indeed unknown during the era when cities flourished. And yet," said Bilal, raising his glass for a sip, "cities did last for several thousand years, until they all evanesced around the year 2100, to employ the then-common reckoning metric of the Dead Man on a Tree and his followers. But what a yeasty, frothy, turbulent, exciting milieu they must have been, given the recorded accomplishments of city dwellers down the centuries, and the accounts of their delightful quotidian urban lives."

I began to see where Bilal was going with this, and started to apprehend some of the bizarre attractiveness of the concept. "Are you suggesting that you and I should reconstruct one of these crazy people machines?"

Bilal leaped off the couch. "Not just we two! All of us on Earth. Let's call the other three. It would be completely in the spirit of cities. A mass gathering."

"I hardly think five people constitute a mass gathering. And who would populate this city of yours? I'm not minting another army of my own avatars and partials. You recall the trouble I had putting them down when that last little game was over. In fact, some days I'm still unsure whether I'm the primary or a leftover copy!"

"I have an idea on how to fill our city. But let's get the others onboard first."

And so we initiated a conference call from my quarters. Doucet, Giraud and Maroh appeared surprised to see Bilal and I in physical proximity. But that reaction paled next to their virtual expressions when they had all integrated the city concept into their mentalities, and then heard our proposal.

"Ridiculous!"

"Impossible!"

"Worthless!"

Unflustered, Bilal grinned and said, "Why not just admit the truth? You are all in a comfortable rut, monomaniacally pursuing your stale hobbies, afraid to branch out and try something new. I know that I've felt myself in such a bind lately, and Crepax has already seen the light. We all need shaking up, a refresher course in creativity. Unless, of course, you're all too self-centered to share an enterprise, no matter how much fun it would be."

This analysis seemed to strike home, producing a change of heart, and before much longer there was unanimity amongst us.

"Excellent!" said Bilal. "Now, if you'll all just meet me and Crepax at these coordinates, we can get this thrilling new project started."

Bilal and I employed his vessel, a sleek Hinderyckx Skidwizard, since it was already parked outside my door. It lacked a wine cellar such as my own craft boasted, but luckily I thought to bring along a few choice bottles from my own.

Soon we found ourselves halfway around the globe, stepping out onto a vast prairie of knee-high golden grasses that rippled under a gentle breeze and a pellucid celadon sky. Three other sleek or bulbous craft joined us before too long, disgorging their owners. Ethereal Doucet, clad in flowing silks and chiffons; fishy-smelling Giraud, chewing meditatively on a piece of kelp; and the monumental Maroh, a muscled jade mountain of a female.

We all awaited Bilal's plans, somewhat impatient but undeniably curious. Like a ringmaster, he relished our attention, and indicated with a sweeping gesture the wide horizons.

"Here is the perfect site for our city. Many famous cities of yore were established by the sea or by the mountains, in jungles or bayous, in lunar craters or on the tundra, atop garbage middens or inside canyons. But ours will be a city on the plain, the mythical heartland of humanity, an Ur-location. On such an uncomplicated, straightforward canvas, its lines will be logical and formal."

Maroh objected. "What of wildness and outlaws? Slums and forbidden zones?"

"Oh, surely, we can program those in as well."

"I like monuments and bell towers," said Giraud. "And fountains."

"Easily accommodated."

"What of parks?" asked Doucet plaintively.

"A plethora of greenspaces!"

I spoke up. "Considering that cities reached their apex in the twenty-first century, Dead Man on a Tree reckoning, I propose that our city honor its illustrious ancestors by incorporating as many famous structures as possible, such as the Eiffel Tower, the Space Needle, the Gherkin, the Burj Khalifa, the Taj Mahal, Alcatraz Prison, the Brooklyn Bridge, a chain of Dairy Queens and McDonald's, and so forth."

"Wouldn't we need a river for the Brooklyn Bridge to span?" said Giraud. "If so, I would like to stock it with a variety of monsters."

Bilal said magnanimously, "I leave the construction of each of these specialty items to whoever proposed them. I will handle all the infrastructure and roads and civilian habitations, as well as the civic buildings. I estimate that once we unleash the requisite suites of nanoassemblers, the whole place should be ready for its inhabitants in a day or three at most."

"And just who will populate our city?" I asked.

"Ah, that's the second reason why I have chosen this spot! Step this way!"

We all walked a short distance from our ships across the fragrant springy turf until we encountered a patch of the prairie different from the rest. It featured many small mounds of bare soil with exit holes in their crowns. These mounds stretched away as far as the eye could see.

"Here are our citizens," announced Bilal. From his omni-armlet he deployed a yottahertz ray to render a large cubic slice of the ground transparent, and we could immediately see an underground warren: tunnels and burrows full of small furry animals, all busy with their animal pursuits. Doucet squealed in delight at their cuteness.

"These are known as prairie dogs, or whistle-pigs. They number in the millions, and will become our citizenry. That is, once they are subjected to the tachytelic ray and suitable imprinting. Allow me to demonstrate."

Utilizing shaped fields, Bilal was able to gently pincer a lone whistle-pig in its lair and bring it to the surface. Immobilized, the creature emitted the plaintive, angry and frustrated range of noises that had earned its species its name.

Without any delay, Bilal subjected the small beast to the tachytelic radiation, and its rapid forced hyper-evolution commenced. Soon a furry humanoid biped, face showing only a subtle snout, stood before us, still captive. Its instinctive reactions had not changed, however, given that even its larger capacity brain showed only the virginal traces of a newly born creature. But this defect too was soon remedied.

"I will download into this individual a full, randomly generated mentality typical of the era we are seeking to recreate."

The enhanced whistle-pig stiffened as its neurons were flooded and contoured and overlaid with a full set of engrams and memories. When the speedy process was finished, Bilal released the newly sapient individual. The whistle-pig looked at us curiously, then spoke.

"Say, folks, I'm new to this burg. Where can a fella find a good time hereabouts?"

Bilal put the whistle-pig into stasis for future use, then turned to us and said, "Friends, let the building and population of Whistle-Pig City commence!"

It was a typical Saturday night in Whistle-Pig City (we had adopted much of the vocabulary and nomenclature of olden times), several months after the city's founding, and so I found myself heading out again on a circuit of the most exciting and exotic nightclubs to be found in our contrived metropolis. Truth be told, I almost would have preferred to stay home in my penthouse apartment in the Ur-Ziggurat that overlooked Hyde Park and the Tivoli Gardens, relaxing with a book of poetry from the Shatterwisps who inhabited the Ice Grottoes of Aldhanab III. But I felt that the dereliction of my festive duties would have registered with my peers as displeasure with our shared creation.

Little did I know, at that moment, that this night would bring me into contact with all of my fellow humans, and result in the swift and unplanned climax of our project.

And so I made ready for an evening on the town. I bathed and shaved in the delightfully antique yet refreshing manner I had gotten used to; selected a fine suit of clothes; and then called up my two current paramours, Francie and Jerna. They both agreed to meet me in my apartment for a cocktail before we embarked on our rounds of the city's nightlife.

The women arrived in a cloud of laughter, perfume and antic gestures, dressed in slinky silk gowns and strappy high heels. Francie was the taller and slimmer of the two, with a pelt shot through with silver and bronze, while Jerna's wide-hipped figure spoke of more maternal proclivities. Her pelt was a delightful piebald coloration.

The hyper-evolved female whistle-pigs had proven no less attractive and individuated than many other lovers I had enjoyed, and certainly their deviations from the human baseline— including a tendency towards vocalizing the assorted shrill danger calls of their ancestors during orgasm—were more alluring than repellent. And so, after all these weeks, I hardly registered Francie and Jerna as anything other than delightful comrades in debauchery.

Sipping enticingly at their champagne, the women eyed me appreciatively. I was, after all, wealthy, handsome and an excellent lover—a good catch by any standard.

"Where are we going first?" asked Francie.

"I thought we'd hit Rockefeller Center for some dim sum at Tim Ho Wan's, and then pop next door to the Crazy Horse for the floor show."

"Sounds like a kick!" said Francie.

Jerna ran her tongue around the rim of her champagne flute. "But surely we don't have to rush right out."

"No, I suppose not…"

An hour or so later, we three were cuddling warmly and fragrantly in the back seat of my limo, while my chauffeur steered us through the busy streets. The car windows were open in the summer heat.

Even at this hour, with all the offices closed for the night, traffic was thick, a conglomeration of cars, trucks, bikes, pedestrians, scooters, jeepneys, tuk-tuks, sedan chairs and rickshaws, horse riders and skateboarders. Neon signs, animated and static, decorated the darkness with a hundred colors, and the babble of the crowds formed a tidal susurrus, overlaid with horns and sirens, construction noises and the rumble of subways. The tall towers of the coal-fired power plant showed their warning lights against the aerial traffic of small planes and autogyros, while the many skyscrapers—deco, postmodern, midcentury or suprapandemic—flared their lighted windows.

To think this was all a barren veldt just half a year ago!

Of course, the whistle-pig citizens knew nothing of their origin or actual condition. Their downloaded mentalities were shaped with the assumption that the city had existed forever, or at least since their dim past. Venues exterior to the city were simply a hazy otherness, dimly perceived and little mentioned. Likewise, they possessed a blind spot toward us five humans, seeing nothing alien in our presence. Other than these embedded fallacies, they possessed free will, creativity, and a full range of emotions and intelligence, all of which manifested in their vibrant lifestyles and their new contributions to the syncretic culture we had used as a foundation. Such innovations as torch dancing and syndicalist chautauquas were most striking.

All the resources and natural materials needed to sustain the city, from food to fuel and manufactured goods of all sorts, were trucked into the city by innocuous robot whistle-pigs ferrying the items from the adjacent nano-facs. And so our toy top was kept spinning in perpetual motion and ignorance of the real world.

The limo pulled up in front of Rockefeller Center, and I emerged with my two curvy comrades, the cynosure of the crowds of average citizens gathered on the sidewalks, gawping for celebrities. We hustled past the autograph seekers, orphans, urchins, crippled veterans of the Mars-Moon Flareup, as well as a flock of newspaper photographers, and soon occupied my reserved table at Tim Ho Wan's. The rolling carts full of steaming food quickly converged on us, delivering all the gustatory satiation we could desire. Afterwards, Francie and Jerna groomed themselves adorably with much tongue action, and then we were off to the Crazy Horse. A prime table right at the edge of the stage gave us a splendid view of the performers, a bevy of the most glamorous, vocally and terpsichoreanly talented whistle-pig females, all in matching silver wigs and monokinis.

But just as I was settling back to enjoy the solo stylings of the star singer, the sultry Raven Dragonette, with her interpretation of "It's Only a Paper Moon," the club exploded in screams and gunshots!

I jumped up and spun to face the entrance.

There stood Maroh, her viridian form unwontedly stuffed into a skintight crimson leotard, accented with a flaring cape, towering over the whistle-pigs. Flanked by armed henchmen with cigarettes dangling from the corners of their mouths, she carried a smoking Tommy gun which she had apparently emptied into the ceiling to command attention, raining down shattered crystals from the chandeliers.

"All right, bourgeois parasites! All your money and jewelry in the sacks! And no holding back—or else!"

The henchmen circulated through the audience, collecting all the loot. They treated me no differently than any other victim.

Finished with their extortion, the mob reunited back at the door. Maroh shouted, "No one call the cops!" She fired off another skyward burst for emphasis, then fled.

Francie and Jerna had swooned, and while I was administering champagne to revive them, the Mayor showed up.

Bilal wore a sharp tuxedo, as if he had been interrupted at some gala charity affair. Beside him stood the Chief of Police, and I had to admit that Giraud looked very commanding in his epauletted and braid-festooned uniform, even if his clothes remained perpetually damp.

Bilal's voice, deep and powerful, especially for one of his small stature, carried across the whole club. "People, people, be calm! You know that my administration will not tolerate these crimes! Your safety and the preservation of your property is our primary concern. Chief Giraud is on the case! We will have the Crimson Corsair in our grip before much longer!"

While Bilal and Giraud were conferring with the owner of the club, I saw Francie and Jerna off in a cab, and then sidled up to the Mayor and Chief. Seeing me, they cut short their reassurances to the proprietor and the three of us headed for the street.

"Well," said Bilal when we were outside, "I take it that Maroh gave an outstanding presentation as the Crimson Corsair."

"Yes, indeed. But her shtick is getting a little old. She used the exact same speech as the previous four holdups elsewhere."

Bilal mused on my words. "Perhaps we're all getting a little stale. Did I come across as truly angry and concerned? I believe that was the expected tack that a good Mayor would take."

"Yes, but—"

"But what?"

"It's just that you can only utter these platitudes so often before the people will demand action. The longer Maroh continues her depredations untouched, the more farcical you and our Chief here will appear."

Giraud said, "I could unleash some of my mega-kaiju on her well-known hideout. The collateral destruction they'd be sure to cause would result in the awarding of many lucrative rebuilding contracts afterwards."

Bilal vented a cynical and exasperated sigh. "I don't know what to do next. This managing a city is hard and boring work."

"Might I suggest that we relax at the House of Broken Lilies, where we might receive inspiration about how to proceed?"

Bilal clapped his small hands. "A wonderful idea! Let's go!"

The Mayor's limo was even larger and more luxurious than mine, and we enjoyed cigars and drinks en route.

The House of Broken Lilies occupied a large "century-old" mansion on the corner of Park Avenue and the Champs-Élysées, on the shores of Lake Geneva. The door was opened by an ornately caparisoned major-domo, and we entered into the velvet-curtained parlor where an army of escorts, the most beautiful whistle-pig maidens of every conceivable shape and pelt-coloring, awaited our selection, languid on settees and divans.

As we were making our choices, the Madame of the House of Broken Lilies entered the room.

Doucet wore an elaborate outfit of tulle and taffeta and tricot, and looked like a pale-skinned nymph. She floated across the floor to us, and in her role as procuress complimented our selections. But then she whispered, "We all need to have a talk when you're finished. Come to my office then."

Doucet left, and soon Bilal, Giraud and I separated from each other, bearing our whores upstairs.

I must confess that Doucet's mysterious injunction tempered my pleasures somewhat, as in the back of my mind I pondered what she intended to discuss.

Still, I did not find myself outside her office door till three hours later.

Apparently, I was the last to arrive, since I found Doucet, Giraud and Bilal awaiting me. And Maroh too! The Crimson Corsair was balancing a brawny vacuous gigolo on each knee, but dismissed them upon my entrance.

Doucet spoke first. "Bilal, this city project has been great fun. Very entertaining and enlightening. I truly feel I understand our distant ancestors much better. The congestion, the hurrying, the competition, the filth, the forced intimacy! The angst and frustration and ennui and rage that a city creates—it explains many historical incidents so well."

"Yes," I chimed in. "I've come to appreciate this whole city *weltanschauung*, despite finding the concept noxious at first. Job well done, Bilal!"

Doucet nodded, and continued. "But even given all that, I'm growing tired and bored. I want to get back to my elysian precincts."

Maroh chimed in. "Me too. This gig is growing old."

Giraud said, "Life on land was always only my secondary choice."

Bilal looked to me. I saw no way to let him down easy.

"I confess to feeling a certain staleness as well, my little friend. It's been fun, but—"

For a moment, Bilal said nothing. But then he began to laugh uproariously.

"I thought you four would never get around to this! I am so much over this whole city thing, I could vomit!"

"Wonderful," said Doucet. "Then we can abandon this?"

"We shall do more than merely walk away! Part of every city's history is its defeat and extinction! It's inherent in the medium. We must bring down Whistle-Pig City with all suitable panache, grandeur and fanfare!"

"What method do you propose?" asked Giraud.

"Why limit ourselves to one catastrophe? Let us have everything! Floods, flames and frost! Volcanic eruptions, earthquakes and alien invasions! A meteor strike. A plague. Multiple plagues!"

An avid light shone in Maroh's eyes. "I am fully onboard!"

"What are we waiting for!"

And so we commenced the destruction of Whistle-Pig City. From our aerial vantage on a comfortable aerostat pavilion with all conceivable luxuries, we were able to enjoy all the cataclysms we triggered in sequence and simultaneously.

First the streets became full of cankerous corpses, victims of several inventive diseases. On a climate rollercoaster, citizens shivered, then perspired, dying of heat and freezing. Giraud raised floods that temporarily washed the avenues clean. Then, upon the impact of a smallish asteroid some distance away, the earth shook and cracked while lava flowed. Buildings tumbled on all sides, cathedrals, palaces, malls and museums coming down to crush survivors. From the start the air was filled with a symphony of curses, screams, prayers, weeping and vain affirmations of faith. The commingled noises seemed to express the true soul of the city and its inhabitants.

"Isn't this delightful?" inquired Maroh from her couch.

"Incredibly aesthetic," I said. "Could you please pass the soma?"

We brought in a dozen intergalactic battlewagons manned by the fearsome Harkoy Crusaders to decimate further, and to take away slaves for the Salt Mines of Lapidus IX. Finally, the few remaining whistle-pigs were blown away by the most majestic series of hurricanes and tornadoes that Earth had ever seen.

In the end, all that remained was the original acreage of churned plain littered with megatons of debris, nothing larger than a sofa.

When the spectacle was ended, we all congratulated each other and went our separate ways.

Several years later, my quantum aetheric communicator pinged, and I found Bilal's face imaged before me.

"Yes, my little monster, you call for good reason?"

His ugly face showed excitement. "Indeed! I have just stumbled upon the most engaging concept from the past."

"As big and entertaining as cities?"

"Vaster, and more fun!"

"And that would be?"

"Have you ever heard of a magical land called Hollywood?"

MR. THURSDAY

Emily St. John Mandel

1.

A strange incident in October:

Victor returned to the showroom for the fourth time in two weeks, after hours. He just wanted to look at the Lamborghini through the glass. He was stalking the car, if he was being honest with himself. He'd taken it on two test drives, memorized the technical specifications, gazed at photos of it in online galleries, read reviews by the lucky professionals who drive fast cars for a living. He'd told himself that if he still loved the car a week after the second test drive, he would do it, he'd commit, he'd stop obsessing and write the check, and the car would be his. Victor made what seemed to him to be an obscenely high income. He had no debt, no dependents, owned his home outright, had paid off his parents' mortgage, and lived well below his means. He wanted the car.

It was a clear night, unseasonably warm, and Victor was all but alone on the street. The Aventador SV Coupé had its own spotlight on the showroom floor, but it seemed to Victor that it almost emitted its own light. It was a brilliant yellow. He loved it.

Victor was so enchanted by the car that he didn't notice the man approaching on the sidewalk.

"You're admiring the car," the man said. He had a slight accent that Victor couldn't place. He was about Victor's age, early thirties, wearing a midrange beige suit and a gray trench coat. The coat's shoulders were wet, as if the man had just walked through a rainstorm, but to the best of Victor's knowledge, the sky had been clear all day.

"Do I know you?" Victor asked. "We've met, right? You look familiar."

"Listen," the man said, "I don't have a lot of time. I'll give you $10,000 if you don't buy that car."

Victor blinked. The strangeness of the offer aside, he was a man for whom $10,000 wasn't a particularly impressive sum of money.

"There's a lot at stake," the man said. "I wish I could tell you." He had a fervor about him that made Victor a little nervous. Victor was certain he'd seen him before but couldn't place him.

"Why would you pay me…?"

"I don't have much time," the man said. "Do we have a deal?" and Victor knew he should be kind—it was clear to him by now that the man wasn't well—but it was ten p.m. and he hadn't had dinner yet, he'd been working hundred-hour weeks, and he was just so tired, the workload was relentless, lately he'd started to wonder if he even actually enjoyed being a lawyer or if his entire life was possibly a ghastly mistake, and now this lunatic on the sidewalk was trying to get between Victor and his beautiful car.

"I know it's strange," the man was saying, with rising desperation. "I'm risking my job being here and talking to you like this, but if you would please, *please* just consider—" but the car was Victor's joy and his solace, so he turned and walked away without saying another word. He glanced over his shoulder a block later and the man had disappeared, the empty sidewalk awash in the showroom's white light. Victor bought the car the following morning, and had more or less forgotten the encounter by the end of the week.

2.

Three weeks later, at two a.m. on a Thursday in November, Rose sat up gasping in her bed. The details were already fading as she switched on the light, but she was certain it was the same nightmare that had woken her the previous two nights: an impression of noise and chaos and then behind that something silent and overwhelming, a kind of cloud, a borderless rapidly approaching thing that wanted to engulf her. There were tears on her face. Rose knew from previous nights that further sleep was impossible, so she showered and dressed and caught the 4:35 train.

The others on the train at that hour were mostly financial-industry maniacs, eyes bright in the shine of their tablets and laptops and phones, sending and receiving messages from Europe, where their counterparts were drinking second cups of coffee and starting to think about lunch, and Asia, where late-afternoon shadows were lengthening over the streets. Rose took a seat by the window in an empty row, rested her forehead on the glass, and drifted into a twilight state that wasn't sleep and wasn't consciousness, towns appearing and receding between intervals of trees. When had she last been so tired? Rose felt slightly delirious, her heart beating too quickly, thoughts clouded. She wished she could remember the specifics of the dream. She woke with a start as the train pulled into Grand Central, stepped out onto the filthy platform, and made her way with the others up into the cathedral of the main concourse, still quiet at this hour. On the downtown subway she sat with her eyes closed, trying to gather herself, until the train reached the southern tip of the island and she climbed the stairs into cool air and morning light.

Rose had started work at Gattler Fitzpatrick six months earlier, which is to say two months after her husband had been remanded into custody. The firm—three attorneys, a paralegal, and now Rose—occupied a shared office space just off Wall Street. On the 14th floor of a glass tower, a rotating cast of companies leased various combinations of cubicles, offices with views of other towers, and offices with views of the cubicles. Gattler Fitzpatrick had one of the more expensive suites: three offices and a reception desk in a secluded corner. When Rose arrived for her job interview, she turned a corner to walk down a silent row of cubicles and found it unexpectedly populated, people typing or talking on their phones, audible only when she was almost upon them, row upon row in their little gray squares.

Rose had worried about the gap in her résumé, the abyss of five years between the executive assistant position in Midtown and the present moment, but the truth proved surprisingly adaptable. She had been married for some time to a man with money, she explained to Jared Gattler in the job interview—his gaze flickered to her ringless left hand—and she'd stopped working at his invitation, but now they were separated and she wanted to be self-sufficient. All of this was perfectly true. Gattler didn't need to know that they'd been separated by the federal prison system.

Gattler was in his mid-seventies, shorter than Rose, with a feverish complexion and the fatalism of people whose professional lives are played out in divorce court.

"Half my clients," he said, "the women, I mean, they're divorcing guys who don't actually make much money. Small players. I'm talking guys who can barely support one household at the level to which these people are accustomed, let alone two." Rose nodded, interested. "My clients, they're not idiots per se, but they just can't get it through their pretty little heads that the situation's changed. They just can't absorb the fantastical notion that they're going to have to be on the 7:40 train to the city just like everyone else. They just want to putter around town doing whatever it is they do, getting their hair done, going for lunch, whatever. I'm not sexist, you understand."

"Of course not." *Their pretty little heads,* Rose thought. In the fantasy version of that moment she rose with quiet dignity, walked out of the office without saying another word, and met her husband for drinks to commiserate.

"I'm just talking about a lack of connection to reality," Gattler said. "Nothing to do with gender per se, not saying anyone's less intelligent. All I'm saying is some of my clients, these are people who live in a fantasy world where they've never had to be adults."

"An entitlement issue," Rose said, because she was down to her last $200 and couldn't afford to walk out of this or any other office. From the way Gattler's eyes brightened, she knew the job was hers.

"Exactly," he said, "that's exactly it. Whereas I look at you, it seems to me you're showing a little initiative here."

"Well, I've never wanted to be dependent on anyone else," Rose said. This was only theoretically true. If she'd never wanted to be dependent on anyone else, then how had it happened so easily? On the train back to Westchester County, she'd stared out the window at the suburbs and the summer trees, and of course the answer was depressingly obvious: she had slipped into dependency because dependency was easier. She'd worked so hard all her life, and when her husband had extended a raft, it was easier to stop swimming and float. Where was Daniel at this moment? She imagined him waiting in a cafeteria lineup, reading in his cell, doing pushups in a sunlit yard. Westchester was a blur of green. Rose played the game she'd been playing since childhood: You look at the surface of the passing woods, the screen of trees, then you adjust your eyes to look past the screen and into the interior, where sunlight catches on tree branches and leaves shine translucent in the shadows, and it's like seeing an entirely different place. The interior of the kingdom versus the castle wall.

At Gattler Fitzpatrick, Rose did the filing, handled scheduling for Gattler and another attorney, straightened up the little waiting room between clients, maintained a vase of fresh flowers on the reception desk. At five o'clock every day, she joined the evening crowd flowing north to Grand Central Terminal. She bought a prepared meal for dinner in the market and boarded a MetroNorth train back to Scarsdale, where she was renting an au pair's suite above a garage within walking distance of the train station. She heated her dinner in the microwave and ate alone, read the news and watched television for a while, went to bed early, rose and returned to work earlier than she needed to the next day. It was possible to imagine years slipping past like this, decades, and there was comfort in the thought.

There was nothing Rose wanted more than a predictable life. When she arrived at work and stepped off the elevators, she always walked through the cubicles instead of going around, because they reminded her of a maze on the grounds of a particular castle in England that she'd visited with Daniel in her former life.

On that Thursday morning in November, the cubicle maze was empty—it wasn't yet seven a.m.—and Rose took a circuitous route, enjoying the silence. In the quiet and order of the 14th floor, the nightmare that had woken her seemed very distant. The morning passed without incident—filing, coffee, phone calls, scheduling, a salad and too-sweet iced tea for lunch—and then the long afternoon stretched before her. More filing, a weepy client in the waiting area, a gale of laughter from a conference room around two p.m., more coffee, a bright blue ring on the finger of a woman who pressed the button on the elevator on the way back up from Starbucks, a flash of pink socks beneath the gray suit of a worker in the cubicles, a moment of dull stupid panic when she thought she'd lost a file. She moved through the day with a feeling of floating, a little undone from too much caffeine and too little sleep, light-headed, heart pounding, cup after cup of coffee that left her with something that wasn't exactly a headache, more like a pulsing suggestion of phantom lights in the periphery of her vision, her hands trembling a little. At four o'clock, Mr. Thursday arrived.

Rose didn't know his name. Gattler wasn't the kind of man who appreciated unnecessary inquiries, and his calendar provided no clues. The entry, which had been set up to recur every Thursday until the end of time, read "Thursday mtg" and nothing else. Mr. Thursday was more or less Rose's age, somewhere in his early thirties, a thin man in an aggressively nondescript beige suit who emerged from the cubicle labyrinth at precisely four o'clock every Thursday, nodded politely on his way past her desk, and disappeared into Gattler's office.

Was there something unusual in the way Mr. Thursday glanced at her that afternoon? He nodded, as always, an unhappy aspect to his expression, and it seemed to her that he held her gaze a beat too long, which led Rose to suspect that perhaps the sleep deprivation was making her look worse than she'd thought. She confirmed this suspicion in the ladies' room mirror: dark circles under her eyes, a fixed and somewhat glassy quality to her stare. She had recently reached the age when sleep deprivation made her look not just tired, but slightly older. Mr. Thursday was still in Gattler's office when she left at five o'clock.

It was raining by then. She had no umbrella, but there was a certain pleasure in this. She liked the sharp, cold of rain on her uncovered head. By the time she reached the stairs of Bowling Green Station, the dull wasteland of the day had somewhat dissipated, burned off by the cold and rain and lights, the evening acquiring a certain momentum. An uptown train was arriving just as she reached the platform, and she stepped aboard with the feeling of being involved in some pleasant choreography, but then the train reached Union Square, and all momentum came to a halt. The doors opened but didn't close. The train didn't leave the station. The car filled up, a crush of commuters who closed their eyes to concentrate on their music, or stared at their phones or at books, or stared at nothing. The announcement came after five or ten minutes: train going out of service, everyone please exit. There was no further explanation. The passengers shuffled out onto the already crowded platform, some muttering curses but most closed up in a resigned or furious silence.

The sleep deprivation had made her mildly deranged, Rose decided, and that was why this moment felt like déjà vu. She'd been here before, hadn't she? Here, in this moment, exiting this train? The woman beside her wore a beautiful blue wool coat, and Rose was certain that she'd seen this coat before, but not somewhere else: She'd seen the coat before in this moment, exiting this train, *here*. Every face in the crowd looked somehow familiar. She was dizzy. The train doors closed behind the last of the passengers, and the cars stood empty and alight. The crowd swelled dangerously on the platform, a mass of damp coats and hot, stale breath and tinny music from headphones, scents of hairspray, coffee, cologne, a McDonald's bag, a cloying jasmine perfume that made Rose want to gag. The out-of-service train didn't move, and no trains arrived on the opposite platform. Rose had never liked crowds, and it seemed to her that if she didn't get out of the subway she might faint in the crush, so she began inching her way toward the stairs in a series of tiny half-steps, excusing herself again and again. It was difficult to get enough air. Rose couldn't shake the terrible sense of following a script, of being an actor in a movie she'd already seen. She fought her way up the final staircase out of the station and emerged gasping into the evening air.

The rain was a drizzle that blunted the streetlights, Union Square lit gently, puddles reflecting. Her relief at being away from the crowd was overwhelming. What now? She sat on the nearest bench to consider her next move. At this hour of the day the city was in motion, umbrellas crossing Broadway like a flock of dark birds.

"Tiffany?"

It was Victor Freeman, the youngest member of her husband's legal team. Their offices were near here, she remembered. He stood over her with an umbrella.

"I don't use that name anymore."

"What can I call you?"

"Rose."

"Pretty." He sat beside her, although the bench was very wet, and angled his umbrella so that it sheltered both of them. His overcoat looked warm and expensive, the opposite of Mr. Thursday's cheap beige. "Why are you sitting out here in the rain?"

I was waiting for you, she thought, but of course this didn't make sense. "The subway's down," she said. "I came up for air."

"Where were you headed?"

"Home. Scarsdale."

He frowned, confused. Rose and Daniel's house in Scarsdale had been seized along with all their other assets.

"I rent an au pair suite. It's a room with a kitchenette and a bathroom over a garage."

"Oh."

"I like it. It's all I need."

"Let me give you a ride home. My car's in a garage around the corner."

"You live in Scarsdale too?"

"No, but as a former member of your husband's defense team, I feel that driving you home is literally the least I can do."

"How far out of your way is it?"

"Professional guilt notwithstanding," he said, as they walked in the direction of the garage, "I just bought a car, and to be honest, I'll take any opportunity to go on an unnecessary drive."

The yellow Lamborghini seemed to shine in the dim light of the garage.

"It's a ridiculous car," Victor said, "but I love it."

"I don't think it's ridiculous." Rose thought it was beautiful, and when she said this, Victor smiled.

"I think it's beautiful too, actually. It's like something from the future. I know it's a frivolous purchase, but I don't know, I just wanted it so much." The déjà vu was surfacing again, nudging against the surface of the evening. "I agonized for weeks," Victor was saying, "but if there's a thing you really want, and you can afford it, and it's a beautiful thing that genuinely makes you happy, is there actually anything wrong with just buying it? You could call it crass materialism, but life's so short." It seemed to Rose as she buckled herself in that there was something familiar about the car, but she didn't recognize it for another forty-seven minutes, when the accident began: the SUV drifting into their lane just as Victor turned to ask her something, the delivery truck behind them that didn't stop in time. She didn't recognize Victor's car until the moment of impact, the blare of horns: She knew this car from the nightmare that had woken her three nights in a row. She remembered now. In the dream, and now in waking life, time slowed and expanded. The car was turning sideways between the delivery truck and the SUV, the air filling with glass, steel crumpling, and the thing from the dream was rushing toward her, the overwhelming thing that was dark and quiet and could not be resisted; this was the thing that had jolted her out of sleep when she dreamed it, but in waking life it turned out not to be terrifying at all, only inevitable; it was catching her in the crush of steel and plucking her gently from the accident, it was sweeping her up.

3.

Three hundred and forty years after the accident, a lounge singer was drinking scotch with a businessman in a spaceport terminal bar. They'd been flirting half-heartedly for fifteen minutes or so. "And you," the businessman was saying, "where are you off to today?"

"I'm going to the moon," the singer said. The businessman raised his glass. The bartender appeared with a bottle.

"Oh, no, I was just toasting her," the businessman explained. "She's going to the moon."

"Everyone here's going to the moon," the bartender said. "The next Mars flight isn't till tomorrow."

"Still," the businessman said mildly, "always worth toasting a change of scenery." The singer smiled at him and sipped her scotch. "Which colony?" the businessman asked.

"I'm headed up to Colony Two," the singer said. "I got a job in a hotel. Actually, in a chain of hotels."

"Hilton?"

"No, Grand Luna."

"Ah, I've stayed at the Grand Luna. Nice place. Did you tell me you're a singer?"

"I did. I am."

"My daughter likes to sing," the businessman said. He looked a little awkward following this announcement. The singer didn't strike him as the sort of person who enjoyed discussing children.

He motioned to the bartender for another glass, but the bartender had developed a sudden interest in the projection above the bar, which was showing a baseball game.

"Can I ask?" the singer asked, with a gesture that encompassed the businessman's outfit. He was wearing a beige suit in a style that hadn't been fashionable since the early twenty-first century. The shoulders of his overcoat were still damp with twenty-first-century rain.

"It's for my work. Well, *was* for my work, I guess I should say."

"You're one of those."

"*Was* one of those. Until this morning." The businessman raised his glass, which by now contained only a pair of rapidly melting ice cubes. "To getting fired."

"Oh. I'm sorry."

"I'm not. It's a creepy line of work, frankly."

"It always seemed dangerous to me. Going back like that."

"Dangerous and stupid," the businessman agreed. "Happy to be out of it. My prediction, it'll be illegal by next year."

"I mean, what's to stop an accident?" the singer said. "Even the smallest thing, you know, you walk through a door ahead of someone…"

"You wouldn't believe how many meetings I've sat through on this topic."

"So you walk through a door in front of someone else, and then, I don't know, say that little delay means he doesn't get hit by a car, and he goes on to cause a war that wipes out all of our great-grandparents."

"If not all of humanity," the businessman agreed. He was trying to flag down the bartender, who was absorbed in the game. "This is actually why I drink, if you were curious."

"And in that case it's not that we *die*, exactly, you and I and everyone we love." The singer gave what seemed to the businessman to be a somewhat exaggerated shudder. "It's more that we never get to start existing."

"The thought's occurred to me."

"Then why did you do it?"

"Same reason anyone does anything in business."

"I'll drink to that. When you went back," she said, "where exactly did you go?"

"I specialized in the late twentieth and early twenty-first centuries."

"What were you doing there?"

He succeeded in getting the bartender's attention and fell silent for a moment while the bartender refilled their drinks. He took a long swallow and glanced at the baseball game; the bartender had rotated the projection for a better view of a replay, and now there was a holographic outfielder directly over the bar. "Nothing sinister," the businessman said finally, when he saw that the singer was still watching him. "Genealogical research for high net-worth individuals. Look, I'm not saying it's safe. But if it makes you feel better, it's not a free-for-all. There are controls in place, both technological and human."

"Human?"

"I was required to meet weekly with a handler in the local time."

"Kind of a weak control," the singer said.

"Well, you might be right about that. It was the technological controls that got me fired."

"Why'd you get fired?"

"I tried to avert a car accident."

The singer was quiet, watching him.

"I didn't think the scanners would pick it up. I knew it was stupid, but it's not like I tried to avert the First World War." The singer frowned. Her grasp of twentieth-century history was shaky. "No matter what I did," he said, "everything I tried, she still got in the car, and the car still crashed."

"Who's she?"

"Just someone I saw every time I went back. My handler's secretary. I liked her. Kind of a sad story."

The singer liked sad stories. She waited.

"Okay," the businessman said. By now he'd had a little too much to drink. "So this person, the secretary, she grows up with nothing, terrible family, meets a guy with money, falls in love with him, and then a few years later he goes to jail for some white-collar thing. Long sentence, judge wanted to make an example of him. All his assets were seized, so she's lost everything. She tries to—no, that's the wrong word, she *succeeds* in starting a new life. Changes her name, gets a new job, picks herself up."

"And then?"

"And then she dies six months later in a car crash. I don't know, I guess I'd been in the business for too long. Maybe I got a little burned out. I was always so careful. I filed these impeccable itineraries with Control and never deviated from them, never tried to change anything, but this person, Rose, she looked a bit like my daughter, and I just thought, what harm would there be, making this one change? Averting this one thing? Most people don't amount to much. Most people don't change the world. If she doesn't die in a car accident, what harm is there in that, really?"

"Isn't that exactly the kind of small thing—"

"Imagine walking into a room," he said, "and knowing what's going to happen to everyone in it, because you looked up their birth and death records the night before."

The singer seemed to be searching for something to say to this but failed. She downed the last of her scotch.

"I'm sorry. It's an unsettling topic. I didn't mean to make you uncomfortable."

"My shuttle's probably boarding by now."

"You see the temptation, though? How you might want to just make this one small change, give someone a chance, maybe just—"

"'Genealogical research for high net-worth individuals,'" the singer said. "You must think I'm an idiot."

"I don't."

"Anyway, thanks for the drinks." The singer was sliding carefully from her bar stool.

"You're welcome," said the businessman, who hadn't realized he was paying. He watched her walk away and then touched one of the buttons on his shirt, which he'd kept angled toward her. The recording stopped.

"Fucking creep," the bartender muttered, under his breath. The businessman settled up and left without looking at him.

Later, in his hotel room in Colony One, he dropped the button into a projector and played the conversation back. A three-dimensional hologram of the singer hovered over the side table. *I'm going to the moon.* A touch of excitement in her voice. In the background, the shadowy figure of the bartender polished a glass while he watched the baseball game. The businessman turned the volume to low. He liked to keep a recording going in the background when he was alone in hotel rooms, so as not to get too lonely. But this was the wrong hologram, he didn't like the way the bartender hovered, so he scrolled through the library and picked out another: Rose at her desk in the twenty-first century, her smile when she looked up and saw him. He adjusted the speed to the lowest possible setting. The walk past her desk took only two minutes, but in slow motion there was such stillness, such beauty in her small, precise actions—as though underwater she turned from her keyboard to look at him, then back to her keyboard, her hand reaching for a file and bringing it with heartbreaking slowness down to the desk, and all the while he was gliding past her, on his way to Gattler's office—and this seemed the right recording for the moment. He changed into his pajamas, switched off the bedside lamp so that the only light was the pale glow of the hologram by the bed. He stood for a moment by the window while he brushed his teeth. The hotel was expensive and looked out over a park, and it occurred to him for the thousandth time that if he hadn't spent time on Earth, he might not know the difference. Tomorrow he'd board the first train to Colony Three, go home and tell his wife what had happened, sweep their little daughter up into his arms. Would his wife be angry? He thought she'd understand. They'd talked about getting out of the industry. But for now he was alone in the quiet of the room. He would never return to the twenty-first century, and there was a sense of liberation in this. He could find a new job. He could live a different, less haunted kind of life. In the silence of the room, the hologram of Rose was reflected on the window, turning in slow motion away from him, superimposed on the pine trees and tall grass of the park. An owl passed silently between the trees.

THE MAN YOU FLEE
AT PARTIES

Nick Mamatas

Yearstart at MANKBO, Clams! Clams! Clams!

YOU'RE not inebriated enough to be warm yet, though the brandy is flowing freely, but truth be told you prefer the cold tonight. The sky is gray slate and starless thanks to the dronelights hovering about the Mankill–Boroughston Bridge Overpass, which you are occupying now, with four hundred of your newest acquaintances who hadn't been invited to any house parties for Yearstart. So the Railing Across the bridge it is, and all the clams casino, chowder shooters, and mushroom caps stuffed with clams you can eat, plus booze and tiny explosives that'll leave your hands smudged black but fingers intact for the stroke of midnight.

Maybe you'll even meet someone and go home with them and explore a new body and share a joke or two and maybe that body in the room will be the vehicle for an interesting brain and you'll have a new relationship and your mother will stop calling you to recommend haircuts and extra nanos for your teeth and to settle on a gender already.

Cold now means warmth later will feel even better.

You see some acquaintances from your voting bloc and hustle over to them and exchange hellos and teeth-chattery smiles.

"Yearstart, Yearstart!" Yi San brings up the latest Cockshott-Cottrell equations and you shush him, finger first to your lips and then to his so that now you both have gunpowder smears on your mouths and won't have to kiss later, and say, "Dude, chill. It's Yearstart."

"San-san's just excited," says Emmal, your best friend in the bloc, because of the sign. She puts up a thumb and you follow it to the sky where drones are dancing and blinking and spelling out CLAMS! CLAMS! CLAMS!

"We did it," Yi San says. "We pushed and pushed and built the coalition with the Mankill River group and got the nano allotment to clean up the riverbeds, what, three years ago? That's why it's clams, clams, *clams* now."

"And not just one 'Clams!'" Emmal interrupts, fluttering her fingers like they're the drones writing in the night sky.

"And we weren't even thinking clams at the time," Yi San says. "We were just thinking a three percent increase in respiratory health ratios."

"I was thinking clams at the time, I was just too shy to admit it," you say and laugh and snatch a clam from a passing tray and slurp it down when Yi San doesn't laugh at your joke. Instead he explains more about win-win-win scenarios and virtuous circles of calculations and you share a look with Emily and then Aftixi intervenes by asking Yi San if he'd binge-vomited any good research papers and you wink at him in thanks for taking one for the team as Yi San answers Aftixi at length.

Emmal snakes a proprietary arm around your waist and plants her hot palm on your cold ass to shuffle you away from the rest. "Kiss me," she says, "it's an emergency." You smile and pucker up, and she grabs your face and plants her large lips on your small ones with a joyless urgency. Emmal tastes like paprika and Scotch. She looks better with her eyes closed, as do all eyes-closed kissers, which is a little secret only people such as you, the open-eyed kissers of this world, know.

A great shadow passes over your peripheral vision, like a whale moving across the sea of the sky and swallowing all the bioluminescent plankton swimming overhead. You don't turn from Emmal's kiss, which is almost comical now in its one-vector pressure, as if your lips were a bleeding wound upon your face, but you shift a bit to get a better look.

He was the opposite of a shadow, really—a huge man in an iridescent suit that shimmered as he walked along the bridge, his arms wide. What was his name? He was famous for his work, which he performed alone and not *en bloc*. You ask Emmal by moving your lips against hers: it sounds like mmror mfff ffrrm mffa—*Who is that guy?*

"Lydon Walker, the *tolkach*," she says, exasperated. "You know."

"Yeah, I know," you say, but do you?

You do. But you've never seen him up close before.

Not too far away, Aftixi has convinced the rest of the bloc to heft up Yi San and bring him to the edge of the railing. His arms are spread wide and legs tight together. There's a countdown in Korean, Greek, Spanish, English, Cantonese, in the *thuh-thuh-thuh* tic of Jeremy, in Bengali, and then Aftixi points and everyone heaves that which had been hefted and Yi San goes flying out into the empty air over the river.

It's a fun Yearstart game—Yi San whistles as he falls and the drones zoom down, claws ready, matching speed and plucking him out of the sky to bring him back to his friends on the edge of the bridge. But then there's another whistle and Yi San floats away from where he was meant to land, back in the outstretched arms of his bloc, and hovers about instead, the drones confused as they are compelled to an underpopulated spot on a stretch of the bridge where Lydon stands, two fingers in his mouth, his big lungs working. Sincere spontaneous applause from everyone outside of your bloc swiftly follows.

Yi San manages to land on his feet, but Lydon's big paw on his shoulder puts him down on one knee.

"Let's rescue h'm," you say.

"Yes, let's," says Emmal, who starts to rev up her suprarenal glands, but then the rest of the bloc quickly votes against saving Yi San, who is a big boy. Even Yi San signals that it'll all be okay. You loiter for a moment, you're the last to run, and you only do after Lydon Walker makes eye contact with you—a hungry, interested glare, and a little chuckle. He's holding Yi San now, like Yi San is a baby that needs to be burped.

You run, but you're still freezing.

⟡⟡⟡

Sweet Blursday, Old-Fashioned Video Chat

It was an ingenious idea—your own, in fact—to celebrate Sweet Blursday in the classic fashion. Alone at home, *sans* pants, but connected to nearest and dearest via group video chat. What they did in those years that never ended, back when the population could be counted in the half-millions, not the thousands, when people voted incoherently and individually with their dollars and their time, instead of thoughtfully and continuously via nano-linked blocs. Back, not quite before, but *during* the great glassifying plagues that killed so many even before the nanowars, that ultimately spared people of only one blood type.

Everyone's a universal donor now.

And what you're donating to tonight's cause is the intense experience of liquor supplied by the nanobots keeping you alive, counting your consumption and production, monitoring your moods and preferences, connecting you to your bloc. The video chat is just for fun, so you can watch one another get as drunk as you can will one another to get. And no chance of uninvited guests, right? You make Roderick, with his permission of course, slip right off his chair and slide off-screen. He missed the last party, so he's loving this one. Manjari snorts when she laughs at that. Yi San is keeping you on the right side of tipsy, so you can still argue with him in front of everybody.

"We need to blow the bridge," he says for the millionth time.

"That's insane, that's ridiculous," you say for the millionth time. "Because Lydon Walker wants us to."

"Because Lydon Walker told us to," says Emmal.

"Thuh-thuh-thuh economy," says Jeffrey.

The other members of the bloc repeat their claims, their arguments. It's been circles all season. Cockshot-Cottrell equations are great! Much better than markets, and much freer than having a government decide how quickly everyone gets to starve, but nanos aren't perfect. The world economy, it is said, still needs a few fixers, barterers, decision-makers, for when a machine is made too cheaply and spits out goods that are too expensive, or vice-versa. Everyone has at least a warm home and a remarkably nutritious diet, and most of the time plenty of entertainments and medicines, and occasionally unusual artifacts from before the nanowars, and libraries of every surviving e-book, but still, sometimes you just have to blow up the fucking Mankill–Boroughton Bridge Overpass so that a handful of randos will die screaming, and a lot of other, luckier randos will have some work to do, and the iron smelters can afford milk, which will make the farmers happy and the cheesemongers sad in that Gallic way everyone prefers them to be. Plus, Mankill has it coming, so says Lydon Walker.

You're as proud a Boroughstonite as any, which is to say that you take a perverse pride in your dumpy apartment and silly accent, which really comes out when you're drunk, which is now, and so when you say, "Society needn't be perfect, you know. The algorithms of agony are designed to suit us, not us them," you sound just like this: "Sudy neent be perfek, ya knoo," et cetera et cetera.

You might as well have stood up and showed everyone what you were up to with your feelings that day. Not perfect? On Sweet Blursday no less! Emmal turns up the potentiometer on the nanos swimming around in your spinal fluid, but you're able to stand up without swaying too much. "Comrades, this is madness! Utopias make for dystopias!"

That was a new thing to say. It took Yi San a second to respond: "So we should just let the suffering happen, let the trolley run over a hundred randos instead of people we choose? Fewer people? People with less to offer?"

"They're voting as we speak to do it to us," Emmal added. "Or *for* us, as they'd put it."

"*They?* You live in Mankill, Emmal," said Aftixi. "I'm a Mankillian-born myself."

Roderick, from under his desk, says, "Emmal, you can move in with me."

"I agree with Robin," says Manjari. "Why are we doing the tolkach's dirty work?" Manjari nails the ancient Russian pronunciation of the word for "pusher"—the men, always men, who used to keep the people of Siberia and points west fed with a little nudge and wink and surreptitious bartering. "None of us want unorganized emergent properties from our economies, but what the hell are tolkachs but just that? They were born into it, or connived their way into it, or had one bright idea they brought to their bloc, and suddenly they're Comrade Shit?" She snorts again.

Jeremy starts talking and with every *thuh* one of the windows on your screens blacks out. *Thuh thuh* there go two more, *thuh* then starts sounding more *Aaah* and then like the words you know *Aaahzzz iiieee* and the screen gets darker and Jeremy's voice changes further and some of the black squares on your screen regain some chrominance, some luminance, but many of them remain black or navy and it's a heavily pixelated face like from the ancient 16-bit games and Jeremy's box is the last to go but his voice, or what his voice has become, remains, and it sings:

As I was going over the far-famed Kerry mountains
I met with Captain Farrell and his money he was counting.
I first produced my pistol, and then produced my rapier.
Said stand and deliver, for I am a bold deceiver,

musha ring dumma do damma da
whack for the daddy ol'
whack for the daddy ol'
there's whiskey in the jar.

It's Lydon Walker's even tenor, and his face, albeit one like a video game from the Jurassic.

"Robin, Robin, Robin," he says to you you you, "are you telling tales out of school? A drinking song for a drinking party, I've got a million of them, and I'm distributing them equally. I got nanos for days." Maybe it was the primitive image, looking like it's made from children's blocks when it's not glitching and crackling, but you realize you have no idea how a man like this could even get work as tolkach. Cross-bloc negotiations require more than a little personal charisma, and as far as you're concerned Lydon Walker has none. You just want to slam your screen shut, maybe throw it out the window, or lock yourself in your closet until he just goes away.

"Robin Robin Robin," he says, half pleading, half taunting, a cistype who never got over the crowded parties where he stayed all night and always was the only one who went home alone, even when there had been an even number of people in attendance. "You gotta work with me! You're no' the smart one here, that's comrade Yi San. You're no' the thoughtful one here, that's unibrow, wossname, Aftixi, yeah. You're no badass, not like Emmal. You can't just work work work like Roderick, can't open yer eyes in the morning looking like a nillion nanos—Manjari's so hot she's Kelvin. How do I flatter a person like you? What can I offer except a life of easy-breezy ease? No wetwork for you, kid, I just need your vote your vote your vote. Keep holding out on me, you'll let the Mankill River overflow its banks with black flaming oil and their entire navy of marauders, heck, you'll *make* it happen. You'll bring down the whole economy with your bad bad thoughts."

You do have a thought—Lydon Walker failed to mention Jeremy in his litany. Jeremy, offscreen but still connected, awake and aware but hacked by Lydon. You grab your bottle and drink it down, pushing the booze past your throat and hard into your belly, thinking about what Lydon had forgotten, the body whose nanos he hacked. You're *en bloc* with Jeremy, you know him too well. Mid-sentence, Lydon gurgles, gasps, vanishes. Jeremy fills your screen now, his eyes streaked with red lightning, clutching onto the sides of his desk so he won't fly off into space. He's never been so blotto! But it worked, he's free, and you don't feel a thing.

But then the rest of the bloc reconnects, and they've all been recruited. A ramshackle chorus, they sing, "Whack for the daddy ol'! There's whiskey in the jar!" They don't remember anything.

You and Jeremy, you two exchange knowing looks.

✕✦✕✦✕

Fête du Travail, a picking-nick on the shores of the River Mankill
You and Jeremy, you two exchange knowing looks. Labor Day is harder this year, but you two are like goats the way you tear up the weeds and the grass. After the last party, you and Jeremy formed a little microbloc of two—no booze, no Walker, no matter what. Because of your triple-secret vows, the economy has stuttered, and Boroughston is hungrier than usual. Labor Day always involves some work hours to help Cockshott-Cottrell equations to click over, to give your nanobots a day of rest, your species-being a day of remembrance, and local kids a holiday week sack of greens.

At least the Mankill–Boroughston Bridge still stands, so you get to weed the field in the shade. It's 310 Kelvin though, so much hotter than the last time you were here, back at Yearstart. Emmal never invites you across the river to Mankill anymore. The rest of the bloc isn't doing well either. Aftixi, topless but wearing a veritable blanket of body hair he refuses to shed, looks about ready to just die. Manjari is performing the bare minimum of work, plucking a dandelion here and there, and blowing the seeds everywhere. "So as to guarantee that the world keeps spinning and there's a Fête du Travail every Sevenstart," she explains whenever someone glares at her, which is every fifteen minutes. Roderick's no fun, Emmal you cannot even bear to look at her arms are so sinewy and bark-dark and delicious, and Yi San is missing this party for reasons probably to do with Lydon Walker and trying to keep everyone fed.

Jeremy finds an important mushroom, shows you, palms it, opens his hand again, it's gone. That trick is magic with no k, but the fungi are plenty k. He says thuh thuh thuh.

"You're right," you say, "Lydon Walker probably isn't even a spiritual being on any level. Even that cheap *Psilocybe cyanescens* would be wasted on him. Forget *Amanita muscaria*."

And yes, no more booze, but between the two of you shrooms are just fine. Not now, though—trippin' and travail don't mix.

After some hours of sweaty work and frequent breaks to sneeze and sniffle, a hallucination! No, not a hallucination, but something like from a bad dream fueled by a broken brain nano. Lydon Walker on a great and pale gray horse, complete with Stetson and Levi's, and Yi San following awkwardly behind on a slowly meandering piebald.

"Ho!" says Lydon Walker as he rides up to your party.

"You talkin' to me?" says Emmal and people who aren't you chuckle.

"Joyous Fête du Travail," says Lydon. "How's it going? We need those sacks full! Look across the river to the Mankiller's bank!" Lydon had taken to appending –*er* to Mankill, to make it sound like something other than the river named for the explorer Emmanuel. It got popular quick, despite not being propagated bloc by bloc via nano. You caught Roderick saying it once and boiled in rage at him.

"They're all done," says Emmal, who looked when she crossed the bridge this morning. "The people of Mankill are hearty and well-fed. They can afford to have vitamin-rich urine. Just have their full required doses and piss the rest of it right out."

"Into our river," says Roderick.

"Into *the* river," says Aftixi.

"Even the tap water tastes like piss now," says Roderick.

"Are you sure you're not just drinking your piss by mistake?" asks Yi San, who for a moment appears to be genuinely puzzled, but then bursts into a sweaty grin. "Just kidding, sorry sorry. I know you only drink your own piss on purpose." You howl like the rest of them at poor idiot Roderick, but then you hate yourself for it. You've never seen Yi San like this before, happy and weird and rankin' on the boys. Lydon must radiate such characteristics like they were alpha particles. Roderick scowls, embarrassed, and returns to his work twice as fiercely as before, a total sucker, as that's exactly what Lydon *wants* him to do.

"In the old days, you know," Lydon addresses you, "there was a Labor Day every week."

"Five Labor Days a week!" says Yi San. "I can't imagine it. Absolutely hump-busting."

Thuh thuh thuh says Jeremy and you all know that he is pointing out that in the earliest of old days, when technology was sticks and pestles and needles, there were seven labor days a week, but they only lasted two hours each and the rest was for fun and sleep, and even in the normal old days there was a fifty-hour goodstart every week.

"That sounds good," you say. "I've also always thought we should yearstart in the summer and not the winter, to take advantage of the river." You stand before Lydon and slip off your shirt, shimmy out of your vraka and vrakaki, kick off your flip-flops. "I'm done. My bag is full enough. I'm going for a swim!"

He gets an eyeful of cute little you, but it doesn't distract him. "You're going to kill a child with that sack!" says Lydon. "It's only eighty-three percent full!"

"Kids leave half of all greens on their plates," you call back over your shoulder as you march to the shore. "Come on, everyone, let's go skinny-dipping!" you announce to all the workgroups. You put a second, more powerful call to your voting bloc via nano, but you sense none of them are following you, not even Jeremy, though he has reasons of his own—what he's managed to stuff into his pockets. Manjari calls for you to return, promises that it's not so bad, but you cannot handle even one more moment of Lydon Walker. Your skin is practically crawling ahead of you, keener to swim than you are.

Burning with shame you throw yourself into the river, and it does taste like mud and chemicals and maybe the tiniest molecules of sour piss, and the Mankill really is too silty for pleasurable swimming, but as the air is free you don't need to breathe much of it and the nanos do it for you for the three minutes you spend angrily kicking up all the filth you can from the river bottom to hide yourself from the sun and ten thousand peering pairs of eyes, from both sides of the water, that are silently judging you.

The water's cool, but you burn so hot with shame it starts to bubble off your skin, and you stay down there for a good fifteen minutes, till your nanofied lungs take command of your gross motor control and push you up past the surface.

They're all working still, even Yi San, who is endeavoring to top off your sack. Lydon's doing some labor too—he's holding the piebald horse's reins and… what do they call it?

Managing.

The Feast of Saint Nicholas, Mankill River City

You are sitting at the long rustic table in Emmal's long rustic kitchen in her very nice apartment in Mankill with your bloc and Jeremy is just finishing explaining the true meaning of the Feast of Saint Nicholas. Has it been elevenstarts already? Whatever—when you pointed out how handy it was that the bridge still stood and the bloc wouldn't have to swim the river to gather at Emmal's, everyone ignored you, except Aftixi, who offered that he liked cold-water swimming and did it often before when he lived in Mankill, before he'd joined this bloc.

And that, Jeremy concludes with his *thuhs*, is why Saint Nicholas wears red, and why consuming the mushroom is eating his very body. An annual communion to firm up the blocs, in the very depths of snowy winter, though it hasn't snowed in your living memory, Robin, O youngest of us all, our ol' switcheroo, and won't you slice the shrooms and pass them around?

These are nice ones, on the wooden cutting board before you, and Emmal's knife, a relic from the days of her great-great-great-grandfather Emmanuel III, is probably the nicest physical object you've ever held. A perfect party, the most wonderworkingest time of the year. Nothing could possibly ruin—

"Ho ho ho!" you hear bellowed from somewhere outside and then through the large loft window comes a sack full of something. Coins! Golden and scattering across the table. All hands on deck, slapping them down or snapping them up. And behind it, dressed like Saint Nick, one Lydon Walker, eyes and beard blazing like a comet and its tail, shattered glass upon the floor a million stars.

He hovers into the room majestically, probably thanks to flydrones under his red cloak. In his hands has two more sacks, positively bulging with palladium coins. "Hail Saint Nicholas!" he says as he lands with a thump. He drops the other sacks upon the table. "I bring you tidings of joy and greatness! We need not have a war after all! I have found the perfect solution."

For a moment your heart soars! You feel truly seen. A short year of holding out was worth it. You reach over to Jeremy, squeeze his hand, and he squeezes back. The rest of the bloc smiles upon you as well—even Emmal is happy again.

"And it was thanks to you all," Lydon Walker says diplomatically, though you know it was you you you. "By withholding your consensus, we had a very rough year, but it would have been even rougher had we detonated the bridge. None of us would be here today, am I right?"

"Well…" Emmal starts.

"Oh, really!" Manjari says with a comical huff. "I'm just as much as a child of Emmanuel as you. We could have Nixday at my flat in Boroughton."

"Please," says Roderick, "no fighting," but the fight was already over.

"What's with the coins?" Aftixi asks Yi San, who nods over to Lydon.

"The coins are the solution," Lydon says. "Currency. Money. Universal trade goods. With these, we won't need to depend on the Cockshot-Cottrell equations, or even a tolkach like me. I can enjoy my retirement, and you can enjoy the fruits of your virtue, get it?"

"How's it going to work?" you ask.

"Simple. Every bloc gets a single sack of coins on the Feast of Saint Nicholas, the same way every child gets a sack of greens on Fête du Travail. Then you do what you want with them, trade goods and services, lend and borrow."

"And what if a bloc expires?" Manjari asks. "Or runs out of coins completely?"

"Then when the last members of a bloc expire, the coins left in their sack are redistributed," says Lydon, ignoring Manjari's second question.

"But… why did you bring three sacks?" you ask. You look at Lydon, then look at Yi San, who looks impassively back at you, his nanos muted, and then you look at Jeremy, who also mutes his nanos, but meaningfully. Theologically, even.

"Isn't it obvious?" says Lydon. "To secure your vote. The other blocs have agreed—"

"They agreed to the war," Yi San says quietly, but he turns his nanos back on for emphasis. "But we got them to agree to proxy their votes, and count them toward any non-violent equivalent action that'll get us what we need without going to war, without bloodshed or danger. We can use *our* excess coins to get even more coins, then buy the bridge, dismantle it, sell the scrap for more coins, and then…" Yi San drones on for a bit. He and Lydon have big big plans, and this bloc is an important one as it includes both Mankill and Boroughton citizens and it's clear that Lydon won't be retiring anytime soon. You look over at Jeremy again, who glances down at the cutting board.

You snatch up all the mushroom slices—they're cut into coin shapes, you notice for the first time—and jam them into your mouth. Your senses explode instantly, your nanos spin widdershins. Your consciousness floods into the bodies of your bloc, then shoots out the top of your head and fills the skies over both Mankill River City and Boroughston. You ate way too much, way too fast, and the only way out is up. You can see it all now, understand every cognition and decision, grasp the entire economy like the algorithms were a cat's cradle stretched between your fingers. You run a zillion calculations, see a bazillion fates flare into existence and fade out. The sky is slate gray, a board on which you can write anything. It makes sense, it makes sense.

But where the fates have darkened lies that great shadow, a doom in the shape of man. Lydon Walker. The coins don't need a pusher; they'll push themselves. In every one of them, you see now, Lydon Walker has embedded one of his own nanos. He won't push the economy, he'll *be* the economy. That's the dark trick, the thing that turns utopia into dystopia every single time.

But it still makes sense. It's the only way. Coins and Lydon Walker in every pocket, always and forever, or the algorithms failing here and there, people occasionally starving or suffering, blocs falling into bickering, wars of dozens on dozens like in the beforetimes.

The mushrooms have another idea—you can fly even higher, beyond the bird's-eye view of the river cities, beyond the green planet. You can wear the very sun upon your forehead and be a great big cosmic everything and then it won't matter what happens to Emmal and Aftixi and the rest because…

No. That's no solution, that's just more fleeing. The solution, the real one, is right before you. Your eyes are open, the secret yours! Emmal's knife, forged in the ancient days before the nanowars. It's light in your hand, and you're light on your feet, and now you are upon the table and now you are upon Lydon Walker and the knife goes in easy and he is mostly bereft of his nanos so he almost dies right in front of you, on the Feast of Saint Nicholas like some kind of dark trick, but he's big and stronger and he rallies, and so you jump up in the air again and kick out both feet and with a two-legged kick push him right out of his hovercloak and he stumbles backward out the window and you land flat on your back.

You are stunned. Your bloc is stunned. When you get your wind back, when the cosmos stops spinning on the axis of your spine, you look out the shattered window and see Lydon Walker dead and broken four stories below. That's your solution. Be a tolkach, a pusher, but instead of pushing the economy where you think it needs to go, you'll be there to push back, every single time.

LIKE THE PETALS
OF BROKEN FLOWERS

Chris Kelso and Preston Grassmann

1.

MAHIRO turned his head up to the sky, staring at the permanent veil of cloud that divided their world from that of the gods. There were four mountains, each with its own caste, rising above the empires of Edo. Rivers coiled between them like poisonous snakes, twisting through a wasteland of fallen shrines, where the names of the dead had long-since vanished from the stones. Somewhere high above the graveyard city, cosmic deities watched on from behind that smoky curtain. The memory of their wrath clung to Mahiro's body like wet dirt.

Now, strong winds came and dark sentinels appeared at the edge of the cloud, the cords of their masters dangling behind them.

"The God-puppets of the Olde Ones," he said, more to himself than anyone in particular. Mahiro wished he could pluck them out of the sky and watch the bastards fall.

> "A pale red rose falls
> Cut down from the sky above
> Sharp thorns take revenge."

"Ahhh, that's a much better one," Ki said turning to his brother. The air was keen with the hot stench of the mines.

"How about this one:

> *We never stop crying*
> *The gods never end their weeping*
> *Suffering never ends.*"

"That's not exactly a haiku, but it's not bad," Mahiro said and ruffled his little brother's hair. Ki grimaced, shrugging off Mahiro's habit of treating him like a child. At the rate he was growing, it wouldn't be long before he was towering over his brother.

"Do you remember what it was like to see the jewels falling for the first time?" Ki asked, pointing at the gem-like forms glittering among the shrines. Each one represented a single soul, tossed down from the clouds. Some Bomesha believed the jewels were nothing more than the remnants of a soul's pain, or the ash and dust of bodies remade by the poisons of the veil. Mahiro, however, was convinced that they were the refracted memories of a soul's yearning; the prism chambers of an individual's desires and dreams. There were days the clouds hung low and the brothers would catch wisps of rogue memories, the final moments of a death replaying in their heads. One thing *was* certain, though: the gods gained power with each life they consumed, and what remained fell through the clouds to be mined by the exiles and sold to the banished sorcerers of the outer world.

"I remember the mourners watching the jewels fall."

"There was a man, a father. He kept running, tripping over shrines and broken stones, so sure that he would recognise his wife."

"They tried to find out which one was hers…"

"…and they couldn't find her. Just like we couldn't find our mother," Ki said.

"We have to conquer our grief, brother. The gods will use it against us."

2.

Times were at their sternest in Hachimantai and the city certainly struggled to hide its scars. Each day, the gods dropped more and more refuse from the sky, and it piled high among the ruins, filling the streets with reminders of how little these people meant to the Olde Ones.

Mahiro woke, facing the stone grave that he used to mark out the days remaining until Obon. A strange loneliness filled his heart. He turned to tell his brother that there was only a week remaining, but Ki was nowhere to be found. Mahiro walked outside to see the wind pulling streams of poison out of the cloud. Some of the exiles wandered through the plumes. Others stood motionless, lost in their memories of the dead replayed in the private theatre of their minds.

"Ki," he screamed, but there was no answer. He walked through a labyrinth of graves, dodging the cloud streams that swirled around him. Mahiro eventually found his brother staring up at the sky from the edge of a mine, carving into his own arm with the jagged end of a jewel. Panic filled Mahiro—he feared Ki's awakening sadness more than the behemoths on the other side of the veil.

"Wait!" he shouted. He knocked the jewel out of his brother's hand, but Ki only turned away and began wandering off through the shadowy skeletons of the shrines, blood streaming down his arm in crooked branches. Mahiro followed, tried to wake him from his poison-dreams.

"Wait for revenge, brother. Whatever it takes, we'll find our way back, we'll put an end to the gods for what they've done. I promise you, Ki… we will get our revenge."

He shook Ki by the shoulders and tried to look earnest, but even Mahiro didn't believe himself.

3.

With only four days until Obon, the village had settled into silence. Obon was the time of year when everyone would pay their respects to those they had lost, when the souls of the dead would return. That morning, a familiar figure stood up in the crowd, as if shaking off shackles binding him to the graves. His name was Tsukai. A true bastion of the miners' union, Tsukai was an imposing and powerfully built exile. At times, Tsukai was a heretic and dissident on matters of religion, but he was an invaluable source of knowledge when it came to the gods and their aberrations. His thick forearms hung loose by his waist and both sets of knuckles were clenched into jagged knots of bone. Every muscle in his body surged with the inducement of excessive labour.

"The fallen souls can become active again during Obon," he said, lifting himself up to stand on the remains of shrine. He was already the tallest of the exiles, but standing on the ruins of that stone monument, he appeared like a giant.

"One week a year, the dead return, and if you build them a body they will come and they will stay!"

Tsukai rarely spoke, but when he did the exiles surged around him, as if his words were coins tossed among the ruins. It was hope that flickered through the crowd, eyes burning as if they all shared something with the jewels—hope and desire.

"A body?" someone asked.

"The jewels can be assembled, made into a form that the souls can recognise," he said. "That form will help them remember who they once were and how they had died, and they will fight for their living kin."

"How can they fight the gods?" Mahiro asked.

"Even the Olde Ones can't defeat the dead."

4.

They began by making miniature versions of the dead. During this process, Mahiro's thoughts quickly turned to his mother and father. He was glad Ki had not seen the things *he* had seen—his sadness was already intense and rooted without further images of murder and chaos. And witnessing the murder of his father was something that never left Mahiro… could never leave him.

The memories of that day were clear as the unclouded sky of their god-stolen city. Mahiro remembered watching an entity appear in their parents' shop one afternoon. The candles surged, flaring a sleek image into prominence—long black hair like rivers breaking against rocks, forming into two streams. There was something inherently wrong with his physiognomy, as if blurred by hideous, dangling appendages, and when he began to lift his head the muscles in his great neck strained, like pulleys raising a statue onto a temple wall.

Their father stood at the entrance, bowing before the ambivalent god, offering a prayer.

"Such craftsmanship," the beast said. "In all the worlds of gods and men, there has never been a sword-maker like you. And you would throw it all away to save a few peasants?"

Their father said nothing. Mahiro just watched from the storeroom.

"You can't sheath your thoughts as well as you sheath a sword," the dark one said. "We are gods for a reason."

Mahiro would never forget that cosmically weary stare. He could see how many souls had drowned inside it.

5.

In the distance, they could see the gold towers and statue-lined temples of the merchants. Further away, the mountain farmlands rose up in long jagged tiers, covered in trellises and training lines for crops. Mahiro and Ki had never known those mountains. They had grown up in a world before the Olde Ones came. Their indifference to humanity soon turned to hatred as their hollow hierarchies continued to grow. They quickly turned the samurai into puppets for a new system, a caste of gods instead of men, who stole souls to feed their famished egos. The boys' mother and father had planned to leave the city, but they never made it.

"We have to prepare," Mahiro said. He could catch glimpses of dark memories as the cloud-tunnels formed. It filled his mind with images of Kamaitachi and Joro-Gumo, monsters that had filled the streets before they fled. He saw a giant skeleton assembling itself out of bones—Gashadakuro. Others around him stumbled, trying to push past their own visions of death as they worked. Whatever had been left of their homes seemed to reside in the crooked ruins of their own bones, the resignation of those who believed they had nowhere else to go.

"Do you see the lights?" Mahiro asked, holding a jewel up. "Look." The light inside was visibly brighter.

The crowd of slaves marvelled at the dancing specks inside the jewels and fell to their knees and began to pray to gods much older than the ones above their city.

They sought to pull their collected jewels together, testing them as quickly as they could. Some of them worked on the arms, while others forged the legs. The brothers pieced the head together.

"Do you think mother and father are here?"

"I don't know, Ki," Mahiro said honestly, observing his brother's bandaged forearms with a frown. "But the hierarchy of Hachimantai will end if this works and the dead will finally have their say."

Some of the exiles began to weep, others kneeled. This body was their shrine now, their place of worship, not the tombstones and the graves of the gods who exiled them. They watched light flood through its form, glimmers of spirit flowing from its head to its legs, a latticework of colours opening around them.

6.

The clouds opened and closed like the mouths of hungry koi. They all knew the Oni were coming down from Hachimantai first, preparing the way for the Olde Ones. The long roots spread out behind their red bodies, oozing with a substance that blackened the earth behind them.

The joints of the communal body creaked. Its limbs began to shudder, as if the souls were competing for control of its functions. Before long, it settled, and its head rocked back and forth. Screams came from around the shrines, and the exiles began to kneel around the form. It burned with internal fires, flowing through its body like an aurora. Ki walked up to the form and ran the rough of his palm across a collection of jewels. The lights burned more brightly where his fingers touched. He put his ear to its heart and saw it glow beneath his head.

"Is that you, mother?" Ki asked, as if he already knew the answer.

"Stay with me, Ki. The gods are coming!"

"She's the heart, Mahiro."

"They're coming, brother."

He hadn't anticipated the arrival of the Oni so soon. But there were other gods and monsters. He saw the Gashadokuro again, the skeleton made from the bones of the dead, but it was much larger than it had been when he saw it in the old city. He saw a group of Katakirauwa running down the slope, the ghosts of baby pigs that steal souls when they go between the legs. There was even a Tsuchigumo, with the body of a tiger, the segmented limbs of a spider, and the head of a demon. The same primal ooze poured down from all their bodies. The poison cloud opened and they came too fast, running down from the veil.

The exiles screamed and ran to hide behind the tombs and gravestones, but they soon became their own burial. The procession of gods and monsters descended too fast for them to escape and they vanished in clouds of blood-red mist or were consumed alive. Mahiro turned to his brother, but it was already too late. He had been so badly burned that his face was gone. Ki had fallen to his knees, the charred mask of sinew and bone weeping in a grotesque deluge and mixing with the soil below. Mahiro screamed, watching the smoke pour off Ki's kneeling body, but a moment later he saw a light pull away. It began to flow into the jewelled body and the form began to sway. It motioned forward, as if it suddenly knew its purpose. It lifted itself and walked toward the mountain, crushing the monsters and god-puppets with its limbs. The jewels that littered the ground started to roll, gathering into sections of its body. For a moment, it faced Gashadokuro, two giants, one made of bones, the other of jewels. A fist made of a thousand angry dead souls struck out and splintered the chest of the giant skeleton into shards of femur and skull and spine. As it continued, Mahiro heard the clash of Oni against it, but their forms were too frail. They lay crushed on the ground like the petals of flowers. Soon, the cloud tunnels began to break apart, until all that remained was the smell of sulphur. Some of the god-puppets had fled through holes in space, but most had been destroyed.

Mahiro saw a thousand reflections of himself in the jewelled form, running through prisms of a desire that had been accomplished. A moment later, the jewels began to fall, starting with the head. It looked like a waterfall, as they glistened and scattered into pools across the mountainside.

Ki heard through the chaos, the sound of water. He and his brother used to play near water often, kicking stones into the stream bank, watching the water sweep from the hollows and ambling beside its current, and he remembered the day he walked up the bank and saw his mother. She was looking up at a sky with no clouds.

> *We will stop crying*
> *The gods will end their weeping*
> *And suffering ends.*

His mother had spoken the words.

For the first time in many years, Ki could see the sun through the cloud above the mountain.

THE ENDLESS FALL.

Jeffrey Thomas

WHEN he regained consciousness, he found himself facing a curved window. There was no way he couldn't be facing it; the window was situated a short distance in front of him, and he was fastened tightly in his seat.

Outside the concave window, autumn filled his view, so entirely that the space capsule could have been resting on the floor of an ocean of autumn, drowned in autumn. He was also viewing this sight through the concave face shield of the helmet he wore over his head. A succession of windows, like the multiple lenses of a microscope, or telescope.

He didn't remember his name, or how he had come to be here, yet somehow he had vague, dreamlike recollections of being a child who had loved the beauty of autumn and the month-long season of Halloween, but at the same time had dreaded the coming of fall for heralding in a new school year—forced once again to rejoin the laughing, shouting, taunting, bullying ranks of other children.

The scene he saw outside the capsule's one thick window looked identical to the impressions of many lost autumns that swam up from his fogged memory. Outside, there were no houses visible, no roads or paths or any other signs of humanity; only leaves above and leaves mirrored below, bridged by dark tree trunks. The carpet of leaves that had already fallen was more uniformly orange, with an undertone of brown, but the canopy of foliage supported by the receding columns of trunks was more varied in its hues. A conflagration of orange, yellow, red, with teasing contrasts of green woven throughout like the last of the summer leaves the inferno was consuming. Though not a speck of sky showed through the dense ceiling, the glow that seemed to emanate from the leaves themselves suggested the light of late afternoon burned behind and through them. In fact, the interior of the tiny capsule was awash in subtly shifting lattices of projected orange and yellow light, as if the air inside swarmed with ghostly koi fish. This mottled golden light played across the darkened instrument panels and blank, black monitor screens, and across his gloved hands, and his legs encased in the thickly padded, single-piece white suit he wore.

The instruments were not entirely dark. Here and there a tiny red ruby of light burned, or blinked in silent code. One small readout screen, though its message jiggled and jumped in place, displayed the glowing red letters: EMERGENCY POWER ENGAGED.

Some of the toggle switches, big clunky buttons, and knobs were labeled or numbered, but so many were not, and control panels thick with them encroached on him from all sides. Keyboards mostly just had their keys labeled with letters.

He might have panicked in his helplessness, in the face of all these incomprehensible controls, had no air been coming into his helmet, but this was not the case. He tested this by taking some deep breaths, and his lungs filled reassuringly. He looked down at his front, and saw three segmented tubes ran out from under the chair he was strapped into, plugged like umbilical cords into ports in his suit: one just below the edge of his helmet, another down near his abdomen, and a third at his groin. His guess was this third tube disposed of his urine. So, he had air, and apparently he needn't worry about relieving his bladder. But surely he couldn't sit here forever. The air might still run out, and though it might take a while, he would eventually die of thirst, even before he died of hunger.

It must be safe to go outside. Look at those trees: he most certainly had to be home. But was he? Something about the shapes of some of the leaves out there seemed subtly wrong. Nature loves symmetry, but one type of leaf in particular appeared oddly asymmetrical to him, with four small lobes on one side and one larger lobe on the opposite side, like the crude outline of a human hand. But how could he really tell from here? And even if this wasn't home, it was home-like in the extreme, wasn't it?

Still, home-like might not be good enough. Even a relatively minor difference in the atmosphere might prove fatal to him if he ventured outside and removed his helmet.

Ultimately, he might not have any choice. Still, he needn't be rash. For right now, escaping the security of the capsule should be a last resort. A retrieval party could be on the way even now, having tracked the capsule's descent.

Or… might an enemy of some type be on the way, if he was a stranger here, in the wrong country? On the wrong planet?

How long was it safe to wait?

What if a fire should start in the capsule, from some damage sustained in its fall?

Was it a capsule, or a lifeboat? Had he fled from a dangerous situation aboard some larger ship still in orbit? Or maybe a space station… a space prison? Was he a criminal? Had he been a prisoner of war, who had escaped and stolen a small craft?

Maybe… perhaps. All these *what ifs* sadistically goaded him to panic, to flee from this claustrophobic cockpit before it became a deathtrap.

But even if he were to give in to such panic, there was the question of *how* to get outside, when he couldn't readily decipher the staggering amount of controls crowded around his chair and the window.

Unfastening and throwing off the safety harness that had strapped him to his seat was easy enough to figure out, and relieved at least some of his feeling of helplessness. He then returned his attention to the instruments, trying to narrow his focus so as not to be so overwhelmed. He shifted his attention here, then there. If anything, the instruments seemed to be growing darker, blending together even more confusingly, until at last he realized why. He looked up sharply, out the window again.

The late-afternoon light glowing through the ceiling of leaves had become dim, waning like a dying bonfire. Evening was coming in like a tide. Somewhere behind all the leaves, the sun (*his* sun?) was setting.

So, there would be no escaping the capsule tonight, even if he identified the means to do so. He was apparently in the middle of a dense forest, perhaps miles from civilization. Perhaps with no civilization to be found at all. He might walk right off a cliff edge in the darkness. There might be dangerous people out there. Dangerous animals.

He would wait, yes; there was now no question. Maybe he would sleep, to conserve his energy. But was that wise? What if his air ran out while he slept, or enemies surrounded the craft, or that imagined fire spread to the inside of the cockpit? He must stay vigilant through the night. He only hoped it was a terrestrial night… not some alien night of hours beyond counting.

The world outside purpled. The fire of the leaves went out and left only its negative afterimage. He watched, as if expecting a figure to emerge ghost-like from the gloomy trees. Watched, as the purple deepened, as if he expected to see the glowing eyes of a predatory animal lurking out there. He listened, but heard only his breathing inside the helmet, and now as the black of night arrived in its fullness he was confronted with pure nothingness. Even space, with its stars, could not be this black, though he couldn't recall being in space. There were no impressions like those he had of boyhood's autumns. Had he regained consciousness at this point, instead of several hours earlier, he might have believed himself to be in a bathysphere at the far, icy bottom of a sea.

Only the tiny ruby lights scattered across the control panels, brighter for the contrast of darkness—all he had in lieu of stars, red as dying suns—prevented him from feeling as though he were locked in a vault. Confined in a coffin. Already dead.

To force himself to stay awake, he tried thinking of how many words he could make from the stuttering red letters of EMERGENCY POWER ENGAGED. *MEN. EMERGE. COWER. ENRAGED.* But though he had vowed not to, at some point in this game he fell asleep.

He dreamed of plummeting through space, with star-bejeweled blackness looming at his back, and below him the vast cloud-swirled curve of a planet, its oceans blue, its land masses—aside from the ice caps—entirely orange-yellow, as if it was a world where autumn reigned completely and eternally. He wasn't plunging toward the planet in his capsule, however, but merely in his space suit and helmet, his three umbilical cords trailing out behind him. Soon he would be entering the glow of the planet's atmosphere, and as it filled his vision he spread his arms out wide, waiting for them to catch fire and burn up like the wings of a falling angel.

Silhouetted against the fiery continents below he noticed several drifting black shapes. They were triangular. Were they satellites, or spacecrafts in orbit? Was this what his capsule looked like from the outside? It was hard for him to guess at their scale, but he had the impression these remote shapes would be much larger than his capsule. As he continued to plummet, he thought he could make out a tangled mass of black cords hanging from the bottom of one of the triangular forms, passing directly below him, as if it were a balloon-type object and its mooring lines had torn free.

These black triangles gliding slowly above the autumnal land masses filled him with an inexplicable dread, where the expectation of burning up in the atmosphere like a meteor had not. He was suddenly desperate to arrest his fall, but of course he could not. All he could do to escape was…

…wake up, and he awoke with a jolt, to see that a bluish pre-dawn glow had illumined the forest spectrally, and that a person was just outside the curved capsule window peering in at him. He couldn't make out this person's features, however, because they wore a space helmet as he did, and from the outside its face shield was an opaque metallic gold.

His first impression was that the helmeted figure was his own reflection in the glass, but when the person saw that he had awakened they turned abruptly and darted away, running off toward the distant trees as quickly as they could in that cumbersome space suit. He sat there in his chair paralyzed with fear, until the white figure was swallowed up in the trees and the misty blue light, and gone like a hallucination.

He would not have felt fear if the individual had signaled to him reassuringly… had made an attempt to get the capsule open in a manner that did not seem threatening. But the person's startled flight was not at all reassuring. It mystified him, and that made him frightened.

Someone who was afraid of him might want to hurt him. They might come back with others to hurt him.

He couldn't allow himself to remain trapped and vulnerable any longer.

A mad crowd of *what ifs* prodded him toward the cliff edge of panic again, but his desperation lent a fresh keenness to his reexamination of the controls around him. He had noticed yesterday a lever switch with a red handle set into the underside of the panel directly in front of him, near his right knee. An identical lever was set in the base of his chair, within easy reach of his right hand. The two switches were not labeled, but their size and bright color made them stand out. They were extra-important.

He considered that the switch in the chair might be the release for an ejector seat, to propel him and the chair (assuming he was still safely strapped into it) out of the capsule, with a parachute then opening to break his fall. Yes, that seemed very plausible to him, but then the switch near his knee? Could it be the release for the capsule's door or hatch? But where was that, anyway? He twisted around to look to his right, then to his left, then twisted more to look behind him. No outline of a hatch was apparent, but if this lever did in fact unseal one, it would soon make its presence known.

He reached to the handle in front of him and closed his fist around it. Hesitated. He put a little pressure on it. It wouldn't budge. He realized he had to simultaneously depress a button in one end of the handle to release it. Holding down this button with his thumb, he drew in a deep breath, then dragged the red switch down through its slot.

With a muffled, propulsive boom, the curved window in front of him was catapulted outward, spinning in the air several times until it crashed against the trunk of a tree and fell to the ground, where it lay rocking. The impact with the tree caused a cascade of yellow leaves to flutter down, joining those that already drifted earthward intermittently from above.

If that other person in the space suit, somewhere out there, hadn't already known he was here, they would have realized it now.

When his heartbeat slowed and his thoughts staggered forward again, with his gloved fingers he explored the coupling of the tube that ran into the socket at his abdomen. Though he had only seen the figure outside briefly, he had recognized it wore a suit just like his own, and he didn't recall seeing any tubes connected to the ports in it. If it was safe for them, it would be safe for him.

He pulled back on the rim of the tube's end, while also shifting aside a little switch with his thumb, and the hose came free of the port. The ear speakers inside his helmet permitted him to hear a brief hiss drain from the end of the tube, but the pressure change inside his suit was all but imperceptible. Next he undid the tube connected at his crotch, and when it came away he felt a subtle, odd sensation as if his penis had been released from a mild suction he hadn't been conscious of previously. Lastly, the tube at the base of his helmet. He hesitated, but reminded himself of the stranger who had been spying on him, their suit without tubes, and anyway what choice did he have any longer? He unplugged the last hose, and drew a breath into his helmet through the open port at his collar.

Crisp air flowed into his helmet, down his throat like cool water. It tasted of the autumn leaves above and the leaf litter below. The breath he drew into him was earthy, with a touch of dampness, and it almost brought those elusive boyhood memories into sharper focus but they resisted beguilingly. It was a good smell. It was good air.

Before climbing out of the cockpit he looked around for anything he might make use of, take with him. (Take with him *where*? Well, he'd address that question shortly. One thing at a time.) Set into a recess in the back of his chair he discovered a backpack in the form of a hard, white shell. A mobile air tank? He disconnected this backpack, rested it on the floor, and opened its catches. Fitted inside were a variety of survival items. A first-aid kit. A red flare gun. A small water purification unit. A container for water (filled). A tube of concentrated paste. (He unscrewed its cap and held the tube close to the port at his collar. A smell like peanut butter.) A fire-starting instrument. A flashlight. A multi-tool with an unfolding knife blade and various other unfolding heads. And a semiautomatic pistol with one spare magazine of cartridges.

He removed the gun, checked its magazine, chambered the first round, and set the safety. Then he slipped his arms through the backpack's straps and buckled them across his chest.

He stepped up on the edge of the control panel that faced his vacated chair, and—careful not to depress any buttons or trip any switches with his feet—boosted himself up. He placed a foot on the edge of the blown-out window, then hopped out onto the ground.

He looked this way and that warily, turning his whole body because of his fitted helmet. If he had a gun in hand, the other space-suited figure might, too. No sign of that person, as yet. He switched his attention to the capsule.

Leaves that had drifted down during the night, or perhaps come loose when the craft had shattered through the treetops, plastered its white surface like scales, as if to camouflage the capsule, showing either their bright upper sides or their paler bottom sides. There was still a torn gap in the thick foliage directly above, exposing a tease of crystalline blue sky that he hadn't been able to see while within.

A name was stenciled in large black letters on the craft's outer hull. UCSS FETCH.

U had to be United. SS might be Space Ship. But was the C for Countries? Colonies? Cosmos? Was this the name of the capsule itself, or a larger craft the capsule might have belonged to, or been a segment of?

Spread across the ground behind the capsule was a blue parachute, still attached by lines. He tucked his handgun under a strap of his backpack, and gathered the heavy parachute in his hands and dragged it back to the capsule, then set about shrouding the craft with the material to cover the opening left by the ejected window, if only to keep out rain and small animals (if any existed) in case he needed to make use of the capsule again. Certainly, this makeshift tarp wouldn't keep out that stranger should they return. He weighed the edges of the chute down with rocks he dug with his fingers out of the black, moist soil beneath the thick layer of leaf litter.

As he worked, he paused frequently to look around him at the woods, as they came alive again gradually with the dawn-ignited colors of autumn.

He set off in the direction opposite to that in which the stranger had fled. If the stranger thought it best to avoid him, it was best he avoid them, too… at least for now. He needed to find out more about where he was. What was around.

To mark his trail, every so often he made a configuration of three stones at the base of a tree: a second rock atop the first, then a third rock against the left side of the first as a kind of arrow pointing the way back toward the capsule.

The ground dipped or rose a little sometimes, gently, but finally he came to a steeper slope and he climbed it, at times having to hold onto tree trunks so as not to lose his footing on the slippery leaves. He reached the crest of this hill and looked down ahead of him to see only more of the same autumnal forest, seemingly extending unto infinity. The only difference up ahead was that there were boulders scattered here and there, some split as if cleaved by the axes of gods, and coated unevenly with brilliant green moss.

He slid off his backpack and sat down atop the hill, his back propped against a trunk, and at last unfastened and removed his helmet. He got his gloves off and ran his hands back across his short hair, which bristled wetly with perspiration. He gulped in the refreshing air and the rich scent of the woods. He drank some water—fighting to keep it to just a few swallows—and squeezed a little bit of the concentrated food paste between his lips.

After this bit of rest he descended the other side of the hill and walked on, pistol in one hand and helmet in the other. He didn't like how it bumped against his leg but he liked having his head free, being able to look around by turning his neck, the cool breeze against his face.

The mild breeze rustled through the treetops. Leaves fell, rocking, as if in slow motion, adding to the carpet on the forest floor.

The noon sun arced overhead, splintered through the foliage into glinting coppery shards. He paused again, set down his helmet with the gun inside it, to build another marker of stones. Paused again, to drink some more water, eat some more protein paste.

Still, he had come across no roads, no habitations, no sign at all of humanity or anything approximating humanity.

He walked on, and the sun started on its descent toward late afternoon and evening beyond.

Was it safe to rest somewhere for the night? But he *must* rest somewhere for the night.

He came to a boulder that had been cleft into two halves, and a tree had grown between them, perhaps having wedged them further apart over the years. The gap was enough for him to squeeze into and lie down in. So he did this, crawling in all the way to the tree trunk, pushing his backpack in ahead of him. He lay his helmet on top of it. He propped his head on his bent arm and, gun in hand, watched through the crack in the stone as twilight again fell upon the forest. Purple… more purple… blackness.

He dozed off, and dreamed that he was back at his capsule with the stenciled name UCSS FETCH. He was again staring up through the irregular hole made when the craft had torn through the treetops to half embed itself in the forest floor. This time, though, across the crisp blue sky there coasted a massive black shape, triangular in outline—a pyramid, actually—from the flat bottom of which dangled a nest of sluggishly coiling cords or tubes.

The space traveler's eyes flicked open. Absolute darkness, but he oriented himself by the close smell of decaying leaves blanketing soft soil. He remained very still, careful not to make any noise by shifting his body, because something was out there in the blackness, crunching drying leaves under its feet.

Light approached, yellow like a patch of sunset that had been left behind and was trying to catch up. It grew brighter, as the footsteps crunched more loudly. He propped the butt of the pistol on his thigh, pointing it toward the opening of his shelter. The light became a flame. Someone was carrying a torch. He heard it snap even over the crackle of the torchbearer's footfalls. Was the light enough to expose him in his lair? Was the torchbearer hunting for him?

The glare as the fire came even with the cleft hurt his eyes and he curled his finger around the trigger.

Whether they were hunting him or not, the flame passed by. The footfalls receded. Eventually, both were gone. He had gone unnoticed.

It was a long time before he was able to doze off again. Close to dawn, he slept another hour at best.

He reopened his eyes to the bluish haze of pre-dawn, with a subtle hum shivering inside his body as if he were feeling the vibration of a powerful machine through the ground. Was it this vibration that had awakened him?

He saw something strange in front of him through the crevice. At first he thought he'd only imagined it. When he saw it happen again, he thought he might still be dreaming… but he wasn't dreaming.

He'd seen a leaf—one of those with a mitten-like shape—rise from the forest floor and continue climbing upward, rocking, as if in slow motion. Borne by the breeze? But why had only this one leaf been stirred? Then another leaf rose up, climbed in lazy spirals. It floated toward a tree he could see straight ahead of him through the crack. When it reached the underside of the tree's foliage, the leaf appeared to rejoin it. As if it had reattached itself to the twig from which it had dropped away at some earlier time.

Was it possible? Was this how the trees here, though always shedding leaves, never depleted themselves? By being continually replenished? But how was it possible? Even on an alien world, it defied any kind of natural law. At least, the natural laws he knew.

As he lay there throughout the unfolding of this mystery, he was so disoriented and disturbed it was as if he were unable to move, even if he'd willed it with every muscle working in concert; even his breathing seemed suspended. Eventually, though—after he witnessed no more leaves returning to their branches—the strange spell was broken.

He noticed that odd vibration had passed away.

He inched out of the crack in the boulder like a newborn soul, born feet-first. He ate a dab more paste, swallowed a few more gulps of water. He'd need more water very soon. He feared running out of water now, more than he did the stranger or strangers he shared these woods with.

And on again, still thirsty and ill-rested.

Incongruous color showed through the clouds of leaves ahead of him, like snatches of blue sky, but this was too near to the ground to be that. A body of water, then, reflecting sky?

He stealthily crept up on the color, seeing more and more blue between the trees, until finally he peered cautiously around the black pillar of a trunk at the color's source. In an open spot too small to be called a clearing, a tent had been erected. Someone had made it from the blue material of his capsule's parachute.

Yet it couldn't be; it had to be a tarp of a similar hue. This material looked too old and faded. Ragged at the edges, almost worn through in spots, and plastered with leaves as if it had been here a long time. The tent dipped in the middle, and fallen leaves had collected thickly there. But then again, it was a parachute like his own and not a tarp, after all: he could see where its suspension lines had once been attached, and it was segments of these cords that had been used to support the tent, their ends attached to sticks hammered into the ground.

He noted there was a fire pit just outside the tent's opening, ringed in stones and full of gray ashes and fallen leaves. It hadn't been lit in a while.

After watching the tent for long minutes, and seeing no one emerge from it, and hearing no sounds from within, he stepped out from behind the tree and stole up on it, pistol in hand.

He crouched, set his helmet down, shifted aside the opening's flap with his free hand and pointed the handgun inside. The tent was unoccupied.

After glancing over his shoulder, he crawled in on hands and knees.

The ground inside had been cleared of leaves and stones. In the far corner was a small pile of rotting mushrooms, deep red in color like liver but breaking down into a white gelatinous mass. The mushrooms when fresh must be edible, or else why would they have been collected? Yet they had been abandoned along with the camp. These specimens were beyond eating, but if one could find them so could another.

The only other item in the tent was a hard white backpack just like his own. He opened it to find it empty except for the first-aid kit, which still contained some of its supplies.

Why had the tent been forsaken? Camped out in the open like this, had the tent's occupant been surprised, dragged out and killed? Had these meager leavings been considered too inconsequential to take? Or, venturing out to search for water or more food, had this person met with misfortune, and never returned? Maybe he or she had discovered better shelter?

He was sorely tempted to make use of the tent himself, but it was so conspicuous, so vulnerable. Then again, eventually he would have to risk camping somewhere, in order to get more sleep.

He decided to decide on whether to use the camp later. For now, he would search in the immediate area for more mushrooms, and for water.

After what he would have gauged to be only an hour he found a number of large mushrooms, beautifully dark red, nestled between the roots of several trees. He took a nibble from the edge of one and found its taste not bad, though he wondered if he might try roasting them over a fire. He refrained from eating another bite, in case the mushroom ended up disagreeing with him or set off an allergic reaction, but in the meantime he picked the rest that he had found and placed them in the bowl of his helmet.

As he was plucking the last of them, he noticed an odd, soft pattering sound… on the leaves overhead, and the ground all around him. Then a drop of cold water struck the back of his neck and he flinched. He tilted back his head and another drop struck the center of his forehead like a liquid bullet. It had begun to rain.

His decision had been made for him; he started back hastily in the direction of the tent.

He managed to get there before the rain had strengthened too much, though it had wetted his hair. He scooped up the rotting mushrooms, carried them outside and tossed them, then dumped the new mushrooms inside on a little bed he made of fallen leaves. He put his helmet outside, propped by stones with the open end up, to catch water. He carried the forsaken backpack outside, removed the first-aid kit, and left the backpack open on the ground to collect more water. He also cleared away the leaves that had gathered atop the tent in its slumped hollow, hoping to catch some water there, too.

The rain finally mounted to a downpour that came crashing unhindered through the leaves above, and he was grateful to be inside. He weighed the trailing flap of the opening shut with his own backpack. Then, he stretched out on his side in the murk and listened to the rain tapping all across the blue membrane, his pistol on the ground by his hand.

The sound of the rain made him feel insulated inside this fragile womb, soon coaxing him to sleep.

He awoke in the night, finding the rain hadn't ceased but had at least become subdued again. He drank some water from his container. He peeked out through the tent's flap but was greeted only by unmitigated blackness.

As he lay back again he mused that he did not feel lonely. His anxiousness was not for company, but only for survival. He still could recall nothing concrete of his life back home, wherever home had been, but he felt no hint of an aching void such as would be filled by returning to a wife or children, or even close friends. He might have all these things, for all he knew, or he might have had them once and lost them over time, but whatever the case his current aloneness was not in itself vexing. He could keep himself alive, but other people might try to prevent him from that. Other people might wish him harm, wish him dead. People were like that; he didn't need to remember any names or faces to know it. The way he felt right now, at least, was that he wouldn't mind being alone for the rest of his life.

✕✦✤✦✕

Under his bulky space suit he wore a closefitting long-sleeved top
and long johns, white in color, and warm enough that he stripped
down to just these. Thin sneaker-like shoes inside his boots
enabled him to put the heavy boots in a corner. He folded his space
suit and left it in the tent to use as a pillow. He drank as much water
as he wanted now (emptying the helmet), ate a bit of his paste, and
chanced a few larger bites of mushroom for his breakfast. He left
his spare backpack, still holding water, in the tent but brought his
own backpack with him as he set off to do some more exploring.
His intention, though—after having comfortably bonded with the
tent last night—was to maintain the camp as his base of operations
until something more secure presented itself. He had his gun, and
maybe he could set some booby-traps around the camp.

Now that he was not trapped in a space capsule, and had found
that both water and food were to be had, his early state of fear had
dulled to a more feral kind of wariness. He just had to stay on his
toes and avoid these other… survivors?

As he walked along, stopping occasionally to leave more
markers, he asked himself what it was he hoped to discover or
achieve, beyond finding better shelter and more nourishment. Of
course he wanted to determine where he was, to learn whether
he was on his home world. But if not, did he hope there was a
way to be rescued, or to acquire a craft to take into space again?
Well, he supposed he did want to return home. Maybe home was
actually a worse place for him than this, but wasn't going home
what one would be expected to want? Mainly, though, truth be
told, right now he just wanted to understand more in general, to
fill the frustratingly shrunken chamber of his mind. He felt like a

newborn with no parents to instruct or guide him. Well, he would have to be his own parent. Born again.

He found a mushroom growing against the base of a tree, and as he stooped to collect it and place it in his helmet he noticed one of his stone markers arranged beside it. One small stone atop a larger stone, and a stone to the left of these pointing back in the direction he had come from. And yet, he didn't think he had left a marker here previously. No, he was sure he hadn't been this way yet. If so, he would have already plucked the mushrooms, unless they grew that quickly. Was someone copying his markers, intending to confuse him, to get him to lost in circles? It would be odd if another person had devised the exact same method of marking their trail.

He straightened up, scanning about him as if he thought he might see someone in the distance half hidden behind a tree, giggling at him, but he was still alone. Well, as it happened this marker pointed him back toward his camp and saved him the trouble of having to lay down a new one himself. It left him uneasy, though, as he resumed his exploration.

Just a short while later, he came upon the space capsule.

Another space capsule. He knew it wasn't his own for several reasons. For one, it was badly burned from too precipitous a descent, its smooth white shell scorched black. (Maybe its retrorockets hadn't fired?) Instead of lying across the ground like his capsule's chute, the parachute—still attached, though it might not have deployed correctly—was snagged in the branches directly above, intact but also blackened. For another thing, the cockpit window was still in place, not ejected.

He wiped at the window with his sleeve, clearing the greasy black grime away just enough for him to see something of the shadowy interior. It looked blackened by fire in there, too, without even the tiny red jewels that would indicate emergency power. But he flinched back from the window when he saw that the pilot's chair was not unoccupied.

After composing himself, he stepped up to the window again and cupped his hands around the spot he had cleaned.

The pilot in his blackened space suit was slumped a little to one side, his seat harness thrown off. His helmet's visor was up; maybe he had lost air to his suit and in desperation had lifted it. The face framed within the helmet was that of a charred skull. Had the flames trapped within the capsule eaten his flesh, or had time done that?

He backed away from the window, examined the outside of the craft again. Moving around to one side, this time he spotted letters showing a little more black under the charring. Again he used his sleeve to wipe at the capsule, to give himself a better look. Then he backed off and read the letters he had uncovered. They spelled: UCSS FETCH.

This craft couldn't have the same name as his own. That is, multiple craft wouldn't bear a single name. This could only mean, he reckoned, that FETCH was the name of a mothership and these capsules were just lifepods, as he had speculated earlier. What other explanation could there be?

In any case, this poor bastard had not been as lucky as he.

There was nothing to be salvaged here. He could do no more than move on, but he felt a little goodwill toward the dead man because he didn't pose a threat to him, so he gave the burnt pilot a little salute before he slipped past the capsule into the forested depths ahead.

He was following a hum. He had noticed it a little while ago. Not so much an audible hum, as a deep bass resonance in his chest. It only deepened the further he went, growing to an almost uncomfortable inner vibration. It reminded him of the vibration he had felt while sheltering in the halved boulder, but more intense.

The hum led him to a great clearing, larger than anything he had thus far encountered and floored with long, blondish grass. He hung back at its edge, though, hiding himself behind a tree, as he gazed in fear and wonder at the source of the heavy vibration quivering through him. A structure had been built within the field, or maybe this spot of land has originally been cleared of trees to accommodate it.

It was a pyramid, towering imposingly against the vivid blue sky. It called forth images of a series of famous pyramids in a desert of his home world, but he didn't know if this one was quite as tall as those, and the angles of its sides seemed more steep. Also, rather than being composed of millions of blocks of limestone, this structure appeared to be carved from one titanic mass of coal-black matter, its surfaces oddly textured, giving the impression of black clay covered in the thumbprints of some giant that had molded it.

As he stared at the black pyramid, he realized another of those odd paralyzing spells had come over him. He couldn't will himself to move the hand he had placed on the tree trunk. He wasn't even sure if he was drawing breath into his lungs. He could not blink, and he was peripherally aware that mitten-shaped fallen leaves were floating up from the ground around him, spiraling upward and reattaching themselves to branches overhead.

The vibration inside him suddenly spiked to an internalized earthquake, as the pyramid began floating upward off the grass it had crushed flat.

Beneath it, a slowly writhing tangle of sinuous black appendages—like colossal tentacles—was revealed, rooted to the hovering pyramid's base. They coiled ponderously as the looming structure rose higher, blotting out much of the beautiful sky like some triangular-shaped heavenly body.

Higher it rose, higher, until it seemed as far above the world as an airplane. Then, the pyramid moved laterally… until finally it passed beyond his range of sight and was gone, leaving that open circle of blue sky marred only by an innocuous fleet of white clouds.

As the thing had ascended, the vibration had gradually weakened again, tapering off and then disappearing altogether when the pyramid was lost from sight. When that happened, he was released from his paralysis. He dropped to his knees and vomited.

The leaves had stopped floating in reverse.

When he was able to stand again, he turned back toward his camp, and rested in his tent until his organs no longer felt shaken and poisoned by the vibration that had filled him.

He stayed on at the camp he'd discovered, but he never let down his guard. He found a less plentiful, smaller and white variety of mushroom, and after risking a tentative bite established that it was edible, too. Though he never encountered any higher animals such as squirrels, birds, or even insects, he learned that if he dug down into the black soil he could easily uncover good-sized earthworms. And it rained often enough that water was no longer a concern. He could even spare it to wash himself occasionally.

He thought to shave by scraping his face with the blade of his multi-tool, but why should he shave? For whom? He became bearded.

Then one afternoon, after returning from foraging with his helmet full of mushrooms and squirming worms, he discovered two men at his camp. He dropped the helmet and drew his gun from his waistband.

One man, with long graying hair and a thick beard like a wild man, his closefitting long-sleeved shirt and long johns dark with grime, lay on his back with a bullet hole in the center of his forehead, blood streaming thickly down the sides of his face. He lay just outside the tent, having partially fallen across the fire pit, which was currently only full of ashes.

The other man's clothing was similar but whiter, his hair short and face clean-shaven. He sat with his legs splayed out and his back propped against a tree trunk. In his hand was the gun with which he had killed the older man. A makeshift spear, formed from a long straight branch with a sharpened tip, had been thrust into the front of his neck, a good foot of it having emerged out the back. Blood had saturated the front of his shirt and pooled in his lap. The young man's face was almost gray, almost lifeless, and yet he recognized that face. Though he had no mirror in which to see himself, and had never returned to his own capsule where he might find reflective surfaces, he knew that this man possessed the same face he did.

Though his eyes were going glassy, the young man became aware of him and started to raise his pistol from the ground. He pointed his own gun, which he had not fired up until now, and pulled the trigger once. There was a loud cracking report that rolled off between the trees in all directions. With a bullet through its forehead and the back of its skull gaping, the young man's head slumped heavily.

He went over to the older man and stood over him. Despite the long graying hair and wild beard, and the wrinkles and ingrained grime, he saw that this man possessed his face as well.

He figured the two men had independently thought to raid or acquire his camp. The old man had actually already stolen all his stored mushrooms and placed them into a crude sack made from parachute material. The only other thing of value belonging to the old man was the spear, and this he tugged out of the young man's body. The young man had more to offer, though. He wore a backpack full of supplies, the tube of food paste only half empty. And now he had two pistols.

He made the decision to eat only the young man.

He had no way of preserving meat, and the young man was, well, younger and cleaner, his flesh more full. So he dragged the old man far enough away into the woods that the decomposition shouldn't bother him, and awkwardly dug a shallow grave with the spear and his hands. In the process he exposed a bounty of worms.

He kept the young man's clothes as a spare set, then hung the nude body upside-down from a tree branch somewhat distant from his camp, using a section of parachute line to bind the ankles. Then he cut the man's already damaged throat with his multitool's blade to drain out as much blood as he could. He decided not to save and drink the blood.

When he felt he had emptied a sufficient amount of blood, he cut the body down and sliced thick steaks from the thighs and buttocks. Having taken all he felt he could eat before the meat started to go bad, he dragged the body off into the woods to bury it beside the body of the older version of themselves.

Now he knew why the other men who haunted these endless autumnal woods feared and avoided each other.

Eating the cooked and delicious meat that evening in front of his snapping campfire, he didn't feel bad for the dead man at all. Had it been someone else he believed he would have, but he had only harmed himself.

He had never seen one of the titan pyramid creatures set down in the field again, but he sometimes ventured there to have a view of the sky, and he would see one or more of them gliding past, piercing slowly through the clouds. At such a distance their vibrations were bearable. It was his feeling that, either intentionally or accidentally, these creatures were responsible for disrupting time, but of course he knew too little to prove that.

Then one day, when his hair and beard had grown long, during a visit to the great clearing he saw more than just a pair of distant black pyramids drifting high above.

As he was gazing up and shielding his eyes against a sun that he now knew to be an alien star, watching the pyramids and feeling their tuning fork murmur inside his heart, the sky flickered as if he had blinked several times, but he hadn't. For just a moment, he was looking up into a night sky, infinitely black and strewn with countless stars glittering like pulverized glass. Then it was day again, but the blue sky was now full of new objects that seemed to have taken the place of the many stars.

They were bright white space capsules, hanging from the wide bells of blue parachutes and descending gracefully, none of them having burned in the atmosphere. He had no idea how many. From where he stood he would guess scores of them. Maybe a hundred. Maybe more, out of his range of seeing.

All of them, he had no doubt, stenciled with the letters that spelled UCSS FETCH.

The sight made him afraid. If two men had discovered his camp at the same time, others would no doubt be coming soon enough. He would need a more secure shelter, after all, but where could he be truly safe from himself?

He supposed he shouldn't be afraid… afraid of himself. If he was killed, he would still live on.

There would come even more capsules after these—he knew it. More and more. Always falling.

DWINDLING

Ron Drummond

BY the time I was twenty, I'd completely forgotten the first time I died. I might never have remembered, but then, I was bound to die again eventually.

The second time, I died in a car crash.

People say, "At least he went quickly." Everyone believes this to be true of plane crashes too. Or colliding trains. If you gotta go, at least it's quick.

Actually, it's not quick. Anyone who's survived a car crash knows how time telescopes, how the inevitability of impact stretches taut and holds you immobile in its grip, pins you like a rare bug to cork. A crash you don't survive? Same thing.

It lasts a shy eternity. Which is to say, long, long after you've grown certain it will never end, these headlong endless articulations of skewered and bursting flesh, of bones splintering, the body's very wholeness shattering into itself and everywhich too—long after all that you are and might ever become is the certainty of attention's skewering, it ends.

The trouble is, most people think they'll be asleep when they die; if given the choice, most people would prefer to die "peacefully" in their sleep. Well, even when you die in your sleep, you're wide awake. I know. I've died there, too.

Anywhere you take it, it never ever *ever* ends. And then it does.

The next moment of consciousness arrived without interruption.

I was walking down the street. The sheerest instant ago, I'd been an eternal dweller in the outer wastelands of excruciation. Now, suddenly, I was alive again and whole, walking down the street, the ghosts of reverberant agony crashing like a tidal wave across my nerve endings. A scream inflated my lungs only to rip itself out of me.

Sidewalk, street, buildings, pedestrians, cars, sunlight—the world resolved and stabilized only long enough to spin out again. It was like having the carpet ripped out from under my feet. The sidewalk leaned into me.

New pain, *real* again, blew away the ghosts. I swear it was like being drenched with cold water, for all that the pain was hot, hard, raw—it was that refreshing, that sweet. Scraping up hip, arm, cheek, splitting my lip open and choking on salt blood, bit tongue a flash-fire of pain—compared to bursting open on a steering column, taking a hard fall on concrete was like diving into a downy pillow.

But then every nerve ending in my body began firing like crazy, and I danced spastic all over that sidewalk—no small thing considering I was laid out. It happens every time, and makes me wonder if epileptics have a line open to other selves dying in other timestreams.

The tremors subsided, and through the ringing in my head I heard people calling out, footsteps running close, backing off. "I think he's having a seizure." "Call an ambulance, will you?" "No, wait." "Jesus, man, are you okay?"

I opened my eyes. Everything was bleary, spinning. Someone knelt close, and a moment later a wet cloth was pressed across my forehead. I was panting like a dog, trying to push myself up, and just at the moment it occurred to me I might have to throw up, I was already spewing my guts out.

"Ah, fuck." Whoever had come to help me was backing off *quick*.

"Gross, ah, jeez, that's *gross*." A pubescent girl's voice. It almost made me laugh, even as I reached the dry heaves.

Ah: *much* better.

I took deep, slow breaths, my vision clearing through a film of tears. I hitched up on my unscraped elbow and with a trembling hand wiped my mouth clean, and stopped short just as I went to wipe my eyes. Took me a few moments to trade off, wipe my eyes with my good hand—and by that time I was sitting, looking around at all the faces, most concerned, some worried, some just leering at the spectacle I'd become.

What the *fuck*?

For a terrifying second the car crash replayed itself in my head—the pickup truck swerving suddenly into my lane, the crazed transfixity of the other driver's expression as he hurtled at me—*impact*.

I closed my eyes, shook myself, looked around again— sunlight, sidewalk, car horn, people shaking their heads at me and starting to drift away. A young guy wearing a stained apron and an uncertain smile trying its best to be reassuring hunkered down beside me and offered a fresh washcloth, which I took and pressed to my swelling lips.

"Jesus, man, you took one hell of a fall. Are you epileptic? I mean, you want me to call an ambulance?"

I managed to shake my head, croaked out a "No."

It took me a while, but I got myself together enough to get up and stagger into the restaurant. Cleaned up as best I could in the restroom, my head swirling with implications I didn't even want to look at, at that point, and finally settled shakily into a booth in the back of the place—an All-American Greasy Spoon.

Outside, the guy who'd helped me was hosing down the sidewalk. Too fucking much.

It was summertime, and I was dressed in much the same way as I'd been behind the wheel of my Datsun: cut-offs and T-shirt, hey. Only problem was, I'd never seen the T-shirt in my life *and* it was my favorite T. Wore it all the time in weather like this. Tie-dyed, but nothing garish: cool, wavy aquamarine. 100% cotton, light and strong. And the Datsun? Bought it from a friend only three months before, who gave me a good deal. Bad dent in the rear passenger door, but ran like a charm. Or so it had seemed to me at the time—I was twenty, it was my first car. Only I didn't own a car, and Joe Wasserly, my friend—I can picture him even now, over a century later—a sandy-haired guy with a dorky grin, dorky because his two front teeth overlapped, though the last thing Joe was was dorky—I didn't know the man. Never met him.

I sat in that booth and started to cry, never mind that I was late for meeting Sherry. Sherry could wait. (I didn't know Sherry from Adam, duh.)

So with tears sliding down my cheeks, I pulled out my wallet and counted my money. Two twenties, a ten, a five, two ones. Hey, I was richer than I'd been before I died. I started to giggle a little hysterically, so I stuck a foreknuckle between my teeth and clamped down hard, squeezed my eyes shut—the last tears rolled free. Calmed down.

The guy in the apron came back inside, asked me if I wanted some coffee.

"Yeah, sure man, thanks. And water too. Lots of water."

"You okay?"

"I think so. I don't know. But, listen, thanks for your help"—I gave him a five spot—"for your trouble." What was I, a fucking private eye? Jesus. Eyes don't get any more private than mine.

He grinned and split, came back seconds later with a steaming cup, a water glass, and a pitcher full of ice water. I drank two glasses of water right off, sat there panting for a minute, and then went for the coffee, gulping for the scald.

"GAWWWW!"

People looked around. I scrunched down in my seat and tried to ignore them.

Okay.

So I sat there for an hour or so, and traced it out. Decided pretty quickly that I didn't want to ruin what was going on with Sherry; I'd never met her before, but I knew her intimately and liked what my memory showed me. I called her right off. ("Sorry, Sher, this asshole on a bicycle bowled me over, I split my lip and got pretty scraped up—No, I'm okay, I'm still kinda shakin' though—give me an hour? Two? Thanks, man, I'm sorry—love yuh too. Bye.")

I slid back into my booth and wondered what the hell I was doing. The memory of the car crash was like a hole in my head—it wouldn't go away—but at the same time it was fading. Nightmarishly intense as ever, yet fading too. Like I was two people, two memories cohabiting one body. The strange thing is this, has always been this: aside from my scrapes and bruises, physically I felt great. More than great: every time I come out of death into the continuing life of yet another of my selves, for all my initial spaz attacks, my very flesh is supernally glowing, like every layer of tissue and muscle and bone is airy and suffused with light. Almost like the afterglow of a great orgasm, and no, can it, I'm *not* equating sex and death; all I've ever been able to figure is that for the continuing stream of my awareness, the instantaneous transition from utter physical cessation into full-bodied wholeness and *life* is so extreme a change that an almost overwhelming feeling of well-being is the inevitable result. Even now, so many lives later, as I wake more and more from deaths into lives of sickness and infirmity, that feeling of well-being persists—at least for a few moments or minutes. As a young man it often lasted for days.

Fortunately, there was a useful corollary to the good feeling: the longer it lasted, the less I was able to remain freaked by my predicament, for all that my predicament was inherently about as freaky as you'd ever care to get. A blessing, that. (I'm quite sure I would have gone utterly, stark-raving schizo if it had been any different.) The flesh I now wore simply held no memory of radical dismemberment.

Oh, it was me alright. I hadn't stepped into any other life but my own, even if my own slightly different.

Dan Anthony. Pleezed tameetcha.

So I sat in that booth, dabbing at my split lip with a wet paper towel and sipping coffee through the unsplit side of my mouth, and got comfy with how my life had changed. It was pretty easy that first time; though it really wasn't the first time, I've come to think of it that way because I was actually conscious of the change—the *real* first time I died I was just a little kid, and it took me a while after my second death to dredge the first back up and realize what had happened.

A fucking stereo system, can you believe it? I had to laugh, but to be perfectly frank I found it a little scary too—that so much of my life could be changed so irrevocably by a stupid little purchase, or by foregoing that purchase. No matter how small the split in the path, eventually that split will lead off into wholly different territory.

When I was seventeen, I got my first "real" job, working as a grunt in an Ernst Hardware Store. You know—haulin' all the wire metal lawn chairs out front at the beginning of spring, making sure the rakes and ladders are stacked nice and neat, dusting off the lightbulbs and the nuts and bolts, mopping up oil stains when the case of motor oil arrives partly crushed, sweeping up pine needles after X-mas

Tree sales close each night at the beginning of winter, and generally dealing with asshole managers, partying with cool coworkers, and kissing customer ass—sometimes rank, sometimes sweet. And doing my best to save money— for a car, maybe, if I could hold out long enough, or maybe that slick Marantz stack at Sears (a piece of shit, really, in retrospect—you gotta understand, this was the late '70s—the 1970s, that is), or maybe—hey, why not?—both. And more.

Of course, mainly I spent the money on partying, girls, concerts (the Dead at Golden Hall, August '78—awesome, dude, totally like wow, man; Jethro Tull at the San Diego Sports Arena, April '79— Ian Anderson taking tea with God), and books—never enough books. And dope too, of course, back when you got a lot for your money, and who cared if it was ragweed.

My parents? I'll tell you a little more about them later on; for now, let's just say I was still living at home, free room and board, but mainly covering my own outside expenses.

I didn't buy the stereo. And by the time I had enough for a halfway decent car, what with all the money I was wasting, I was eighteen and a half, smoking tons of reefer and showing no signs of getting on to college, and my Ps finally smartened up and kicked my ass out of the house. So for a while rent ate my car, I showed up stoned at Ernst one too many times, got fired, found another job, started dating this nice, serious girl named Karen who never did let me get to home plate, and was pushing twenty before my friend Joe (who I met through a housemate) gave me the good deal on the Datsun.

Three months later I was dead.

I bought the stereo.

I mean, I didn't really need a car. This was Pacific Beach, which, because it was unincorporated, was still technically a part of San Diego, but otherwise was a separate little beach paradise all its own. *Physically* separate, because the only access was on a road that ran along a thin strip of sand, a dredged bridge if you will, bisecting a big lagoon inlet from the Pacific. Most of my friends lived in P.B., most had cars for parties and movies and concerts elsewhere in the less cool parts of San Diego, things worked. I tooled my bike up and down the little hills of P.B. with its tight avenues, ubiquitous palms, Spanish-style houses (some set back and fancy, most cramped together, all of them predictably colorful), and stands of torrey pines to rustle the wind in the tiny park—always empty, it seemed, as the beach was only blocks away.

There was a *lot* of beach. Miles of boardwalk, houses and apartments and little alleys green with wall-climbing creepers and hanging plants spilling from upper-story windows crowding the boardwalk on the landward side, endless beach dotted with concrete fire-rings to the seaward. Parties a mile long every Friday and Saturday night, or every night sometimes in summer, and during the day so much tan womanflesh as to make any goddess-worshipping horndog boy's heart burst.

So I'd hang on the beach with my friends, smoking dope, watching the parade, elaborating endlessly on a comedy routine having to do with the severely limited craniums of surfers ("They don't need 'em for their brains, man, I'm telling you." "Yeah, right, their brains be dangling.") which even my surfer friends joined in on, they being of the more intellectual variety of surfer, even read the occasional book in-between catchin' waves—talking music, and scoping girls: that more than anything.

Even so, I didn't spend as much time at the beach as most of my friends; half the time, you'd find me wrapped up in a book, probably science fiction, or down at the park, where I often went because it was empty most of the time, to be alone—alone to write my vaguely quasi-mystical, too-earnest-by-half poetry and rambling journal entries.

And, of course, after I got the stereo, I'd often sit in my bedroom at home listening to tunes, on headphones if the Ps were home, cranked to the nines if they weren't. It was a relief getting that system after only having my parents' creaky old stereo before. So naturally a lot of my money after that went to records, buying things I'd wanted for a while but held out on for want of a decent system—mostly Beatles, Hendrix, Zep, Yes, Tull, King Crimson, ELP, stuff like that—but also more esoteric stuff. Shakti with John McLaughlin—send you on a trip every time, stoned or not. Vangelis, Eno, Can, Hawking Teds, Bartok string quartets (which led me to the late Beethoven quartets), John Cage—I swallowed *Silence* whole—take your pick. My friends and I were always turning each other onto weird shit.

Sure, I still wanted a car—but the desire had turned more wistful than anything, something it was easy to put off, especially as work was an easy half-hour bike ride away.

One weekend my parents decided to take a mini-vacation. It was March, I'd just turned eighteen, so naturally I threw a party. Nothing particularly disastrous happened, I managed to connect with someone who could get us a couple of kegs, it was a good party. You know the story.

What made it significant was two things.

First, I met Sherry at that party, though I never did figure out who brought her. Maybe she just wandered in. And sure, it was a year and a half before I actually got to know her very well—before she, ahem, grabbed me rather forcefully by the hand and proceeded to fuck my brains out on a regular basis—my first lover, *whew*.

And second, ol' Dan was just a little too slow cleaning up the house the day after, the parents got home early (of course), I caught hell, and was given till a month after graduation in June to pack my bags and get out. Which meant I was on my own four months earlier than in my other life, which meant rent once again ate any car plans or even any further record-buying I might've had in mind. (Mostly, it ruined my dope-buying budget for the first six months.)

In my other life, I never threw that party, didn't meet Sherry at all, didn't get thrown out of the house early, moved into a different shared house than I had otherwise and so met Joe Wasserly, eventually bought the Datsun from him, and—yep—died a virgin.

Did I say it was easy that first time, figuring out the differences between my two lives? Well, I suppose it was. But the hard part was still to come—learning how to deal with what those differences implied.

As I left the restaurant to walk the few blocks to Sherry's apartment, a wordless dazzle filling my head, I had only the merest inkling of what was in store—though at the time that inkling seemed to fill the world.

My memories of Sherry were acute—numerous and varied, round and soft and sweet like her body, full of hidden places and unexpected textures. As I floated along the sidewalk under the swaying palm trees, staring up at the sun stuttering through the fronds, unbidden images streamed through my mind, a whole gallery of discrete moments and feelings flowing one into another.

Moonlight melting across her cheek, her nose, her lips as she turned to look at me in the night—moonlight catching in her eyes. Bedsheet slipping from curve of hip. The fan of her hair across her back, strands slipping, slipping, tumbling from her shoulders as I rode her from behind—the insanely sweet swelling of her ass

rising to meet me, moist suckling womanhood tugging me home
again. At every stroke tracing with dancing fingertips the flickering
pattern of eucalyptus leaves cast by the moon across her back, her
voice moaning my name with such hunger as to stop the breath in
my throat and crack my frenzied heart.

Talking out our mutually intense reactions to reading Joanna
Russ's The Female Man, the furrow that deepens her brow: "No,
don't crawl under a rock, she doesn't want you under a rock, she
wants you to honestly *feel* what it's like being Joanna—it's a gift, a
whole life experience you wouldn't ever know any other way, can't
you understand that?" Me: "But that's what I'm saying—it's one of
the most gut-wrenching books I've ever read—and *understanding* it
is what makes me want to crawl under a rock!" Sherry: "But that's
exactly what tells me you *didn't* get it!"

The boardwalk at blazing noon—Sherry crouched by a
cardboard box full of squalling kittens, chatting with the old hippie
who was trying to get her to take the itty tabby she cooed over in
her lap, me standing awkwardly by, feeling silly teenage jealousy.
I crouched down beside her just as the hippie said something—I
didn't catch what it was—and Sherry threw her head back and
laughed, brown hair flying and catching the sun in its strands:
click. That was the moment stuck in my head, the brilliance of her
eyes, the joy of her laughter—an entire landscape in the sound.

And through it all what astounded me the most was the sheer
intensity of *bodily* memory. So many of my memories of her were
rooted in my flesh, the feel of her in my arms, the heft of her, the
warp and woof of her under my hands, beneath my lips. Her body
filled every fiber of my flesh every bit as much as her face and eyes
filled my inner eye, every bit as much as her breath and voice and
laugh—even her gurgling tummy!—filled my inner ear. All this, the
scent of her hair, her breath, her skin, the pouting salten sweetness

of her cunny—it all joined, became one place, flush with the warm dark cavern of my being: our bodies the flesh vessels where our spirits rolled and played like children delirious with new summer.

In all my lives, before or after, I have never felt so deeply what I felt in that moment. Never again have I known with such utter newness and freshness and exuberant vitality what it is to love and be loved: one gesture, a long-fingered hand raised high to caress the sun.

However much my memories of Sherry were a part of me, moments of happiness accumulated over many months, still they came to me now *for the first time*, all at once, a single wave filling me with astonished delight. I realized how ironic this was, that I should feel such overwhelming joy from experiences I'd never had, with a woman I'd never met!

So it was that I passed under the tiled, pseudo-Spanish archway into the courtyard of Sherry's apartment building, laughing and shaking my head and almost skipping with anticipation—anxious butterflies filling my belly, frantic for escape—and walked around the sun-filled swimming pool to the stairs that led up to her door.

I paused there, looking up, not quite believing that any of this could be real.

"Too much, man, this is just *too* much."

Actually, it wasn't enough: I took the steps two at a time.

Apartment 27. Rapid, rolling knocks: my usual, ha!

Muffled footsteps, rattle of chain, and the door opened.

A big smile spreading Sherry's face, which, when she got a good look at me, immediately faded, became a frown. For a split second I thought she didn't know me, that all my memories were a form of insanity, a cruel joke and nothing more. But then she spoke, and I remembered in the same instant how I looked.

"Ah, Danny, Jesus, look at you, you look terrible!"

"Thanks, Sher, I love you too."

"You dip." She laughed and, with an exasperated "C'mere," gave me a quick hug. It was the eeriest feeling, as if a woman met in an especially vivid dream had suddenly come to life, was there to dispel the sadness of a dream lost to waking.

Sherry gingerly touched the corner of my mouth, near the split. She sighed. "Well, I guess I won't be kissing *you* anytime soon."

"But I thought you *liked* kissing ripped and torn lip-flesh."

"Only if your teeth are thoroughly brushed." She idly examined the scrape on my left shoulder.

"I brushed this morning."

"Uh-huh." There was a much longer and deeper scrape down the underside of my left forearm.

I lifted my T-shirt to show her a third on my hip. Her lips came together in a moue. "Ahhh, poor bay-*beee*," she said with playful sarcasm.

I made to "goo-goo" right back at her, but moving my lips to shape the sound cracked the dried blood suturing the split, so all I managed was a surprised "OW!"

Sherry laughed. "You dummy, for once you're just going to have to keep your mouth shut!" I glared comically at her, and she grabbed my wrist and pulled me into the living room.

"Come on, time to put this aloe plant to use." She pushed me toward the couch by the big front windows. I sat down in the sunlight and cool breeze coming in through the screen, and watched with appreciation as she walked into the kitchen, amazed all over again, amazed at how relaxed I was, at how easy it was to talk to her.

I heard her rummaging through a drawer of utensils. "You want some apple juice?" she called. "I have a straw."

"Maybe later."

"'Kay." Sherry came back out—expression all business-like—with a roll of paper towels under one arm, a roll of gauze and white bandage tape in one hand, a paring knife in the other. She sat facing me on the couch, drawing one tan leg up and tucking foot under knee.

I couldn't help but notice the pale blue satin of her shorts had pulled tight at the crotch, outlining her pussy. I stared shamelessly.

With three fingers Sherry flicked me smartly up under the chin, just hard enough to make my lip throb and my gaze rise high enough to meet hers.

"Hey!"

"'Hey' yourself, Mr. One-Track. You wanna save your drooling for later?" But she was smiling, that particular pouting smile—one mouth corner tucked down, one curling up—she sometimes got when it was my turn to be tied with silk scarves to the posts of her bed, and she was still contemplating her newest ways for driving me wild. Then again, she sometimes got that same look just as I fell into one of her traps during our frequent debates on any of a number of topics. Intellectually, she could out-argue me every time.

But then her look changed, and with calm care she took the aloe vera in its unfired pot down from the sill and cradled it in her lap, chose a blade and cut it deftly with the knife, stripped the toothy leaf down to its moist heart.

I wish the stars would stop spinning. I wish the stars would stop orbiting me like I was some ultimately minor sun, last blood-red light squeezed from its collapsing heart.

A billion vertical streaks make of my invisible cocoon a womb of light. I know I tumble, I know the stars are fixed, and yet this knowing is meaningless. My body tells me I am at equilibrium; my body tells me I rest at stillpoint. Only the sounds of my own breathing and the slow surge of inner tides distinguishes any moment from any other. But this alone is not enough, this organic pulse without beginning or end. Whatever sanity remains to me requires change, requires incident and contrast to survive. Yet there is no fixed object to catch my sight. The night wraps me round in threads of starlight, and against this shifting screen I have only memories to project—memories of an almost terrifying vividness.

Save one last faint glimmering, all dreams are dead. I wish—

The soft glide of aloe vera across the pebbly scrape on my upper arm sent more than chills through my body, raised more than goose bumps on the curve of a shoulder, along the flank of an arm. For a brief moment, Sherry's simplest healing touch made of my body a door into memory.

From the blue pine that stood outside my childhood home, sunlight cast swaying shadow-branches across the curtains. As I watched from where I lay curled up in bed, this lulling image suddenly swelled and grew bleary, and it was a moment before I realized—remembering—that I was crying. Shadow and light pooled and dripped and ran together, and many colors flowed from their mixing.

But then the memory dissolved, like those long-ago tears ebbing from my eyes. Dimly I sensed the desolation at the heart of that image. A child's desolation. How old was I? Five, I know now: five, or six. Remembering, I wondered what was wrong. What had happened?

All was forgotten under Sherry's ministrations. Gently she lay a forefinger under my lower lip, dabbed with the aloe at the split, her hazel eyes all clarity and focus.

But returning now across a century's span to that instant of remembering, I can keep the door ajar with an inward glance. The door, as in a breeze, swings wide. I step through, and snuggle once more into the child I was, to cry again the tears of a child who is with me even now.

MALWARE PARK

Nikhil Singh

I live in the smoking ruins of myself. Eating memories till I'm sick. Light another cyberette. My own design. Room is ozone-stale with them. Been thinking through the new vessel. Mapping changes. Cyberette's tuned too tight. Frequency distortion along the sub-cranial neuro-relays. Calculated overheat. Less punch than most neuronarc. Fine for regular use—maybe. Drifting off the pleather slab, cross to the window wall. Glass depolarizes—Neurocropolis vistas. High-level views. In the scratch-mark clouds, strato-loops lattice. Glassy people-pipes. Sky-web. Lower for closer. Suborbital express runs cross-planet. One rung up—orbital village. Had doll-chops to go orbital. Stayed downside. Sometimes I travel. No matter the meridian. Neurocropolis is everywhere.

No exit for three weeks. Solid grind. Walls are tight. In the lab, vessel crucifies a gel-pod. Ribcage out in butterfly mode. Components noodle up dry-gel suspension. Stare for an hour. Enhanced optics— macro/micro. Get lost in dust forests sometimes. Distant windows. Eventually, give up. Residual analogue headache. Recharge cyberette.

Recently tagged a box of video vintage. Real tape. Delivery drone dropped an icebox. Around forty cassettes. Took a week building a machine to dump magnetic reels. Most permanently damaged. Talk I couldn't understand. Dead languages. Grade is often blurry, impressionist. Random sequences. Can't stop dosing on memory. Obsessive downgrade. Total regression. Can't even lift holo from the tapes. Reads glitch-fog round the room. Jurassic intake, this flat-screening. Primitive in comparison to the mental ice-bucket of a used drone's sensory dump. Different flavours, though. Slow burn. Old school. Hooked me. Difficulty inputting long hauls. Analogue exposure scrambles optics. Sideways information. Too much noise. Things that wouldn't phase, edge me now. Trouble with emotion. Comes with the eye-job, they say. Possible. Go in and out. A sequence of gradually thickening depressions. Thick like tasteless syrup. Glitch-fog. Video problems. Some difficulty telling where fugues end. Processor got me down. Drain another cyberette. To the red. Charge, repeat. Latency buzz. Big synaptics. Working the vessel. Calibrate arm and hip servos. After a while, I'm back on the slab.

Alert wakes me. Drone must have circuited. Brush off heavy liquid—dreams. Buzz it in, crack airlock to listen. Staircases are old stone. Languid stylus of needle heels, somewhere far below. Wrote that gait. Haven't seen Phaedra in three weeks. Left her on the side of a highway. Lollipops and a one-piece. Took my mark on the slab, activate a second. Just as it rises, drone knocks, enters. She's in Cleopatra mode. Geometric black bob. Melanin counter low pale. Colour scheme 456. Cigarette burns down through stained fingers. Purely cosmetic. Phaedra is my exact height. We go straight into "the scene". Script design tests protocols. I pull solid data. Enough to trade heavy industrial. Drone gives me a tired, pretty smile. Soft, bony arms wrap my neck. Then we're inside. Automatically cross to the kitchenette, to brew coffee. She saunters to the second slab, collapses photogenically.

"Please, no more coffee," she moans.

Haven't seen coffee in ten years. Just scene-talk. Cracking a freezer, retrieve the vodka bottle. Full to the brim. Jet-black industrial lubricant. Drone will read liquor. All in the script. No echoes through the lounge. Reactive surfaces absorb sound. Blotting paper for the ear. That was the sales pitch. Phaedra's gleaming shell-coat lies near the window wall. She's on her back, needle heel tracing the floor. Tiles run a groove from repetition. Have to fix that. Camera poises shift seamlessly across the drone.

"You look dead," I observe.

Phaedra pouts, rolling as I pass the bottle.

"How was your loop?" I ask, snagging her clutch.

She takes a long swallow. I time it.

"Eight hours down the drain," she replies, wiping a bright black mouth across her hand.

Watches me pop the clutch. Light a cigarette. Usually on limited intake. But these are so light. Barely taste them.

"Shame, baby. Out of cigarettes?"

"Don't smoke," I counter.

Phaedra sits up abruptly, slouching. Sulking. New mannerisms. Learned, then incorporated. She drains more "vodka", retrieving her cigarette from a nearby ashtray.

"How was your shoot?" I ask.

"Which one?" she teases, sinking back, holding my eye.

"Previous."

Drone freezes a microsecond. Loads data sets. Deviates from script.

"Somebody put a hook through my face," she smiles.

"Regeneration?"

"Complete."

"Location?"

"Storage unit. Mid-ocean station complex. Five citizens."

"Response?"

"Inoculated."

Phaedra carries a wide spectrum. Administrable personality shifters. Fluent in chemical and neuro. Subtle, self-numbing hypodermic points map her body. Rape and assault are chemically collared. Neurological overdub. Taken for roaming playbots, my drones are effective. Highly adaptive. Organic development through interactive experientials—a speciality. Orbital grade. Vessels appear identical in reset. Each had become unique. Offenders have no knowledge of their reprogramming. Impulses are simply overwritten. Neurocropolis—an all-male populace. Strategic, ever-present maintenance, my personal experiment. I'm sure others do it. Never seen a female. Only holograms. Women rule from above the clouds. Breeding strictly orbital. That's the script, anyway. Phaedra flashes a coy smile.

"Are you happy to stay so badly scripted?" I ask.

She chuckles, signals for cigarettes. Toss the clutch. She catches one-handed. Lights a smoke. Stares uncomfortably.

"Are you?" I push.

Her eyes become red from staring. Picks at them with an uncomfortable delicacy. Watch her drain the bottle.

"You don't have to be cruel," she says quietly.

Freeze her there, satisfied. Then go over and open up her face. Locking in a lead, begin dumping memory. Recall interface is full sensory. Lucid screaming. The whole kaleidoscope. Output is usually packaged for auto-assimilation. Standardised setting. But I was hooked. Ran a feedback system. Siphoned memory before conversion. Only a cloud could unlock assimilated data. Safety feature. That would never happen. Nothing left my head. Now I was drowning in memory. Dreamy days in the tank. Weeks. Walking painless labyrinths in drone-skin. Riding vessels designed to be worshipped, defiled. Addictive. Drone programs animate, run counter-grooves. You sense them strong when you're in there— the others. Like what Phoneutria is becoming. Something other. Worse when you doll-ride. Taps subconscious. Deep currents. But there have always been dead gods among us. Some grow hungry. Centuries of neglect. Temples shrink to the dimensions of a bodily cavity. Dead gods speak to us, from time to time. Some of us answer.

Overhaul Phaedra. Complete by afternoon. Then down to the underground garage. In the car, haven't driven for three weeks. But the engine caught like a blade. Deep purr. Magnetic glide. Pilot us out into the atomic glare. Direct exit to freeway strata only. Nobody street-levels. Not officially. Outside, the paranoia starts. Drones get all the neuronarc. Run pirate copies. Operators do it all the time. Doll-riders do it live. I try everything. Phaedra is a good source. New phase-variable had me mesolimbic. Numbly navigate a high-speed freeway. Astral projection of myself. Not that I'm really piloting. Standard self-drive. Mapped optic-interface feedback. So much like manual control. Wheels see your eyes. All in real-time. With crash parameters active, you could do anything and not die. Clouds are low toxic. Catch the glare pink. Similar to Phaedra's auto-bruise. She's in the passenger couch. Strappy swimsuit and heels. Lips and fingernails flush. Black to cobalt. Micro bob extends, rearranges, burns blond. Double melanin saturation. Ultraviolet exposure auto-react. I signal reset. Scheme 456 is familiar. No strangers now.

Not in this state. Hair retracts. Floods back jet. Phaedra is breeding alters. Signature personality programming. Could only do my own shadows these days. Too much isolation. Neuronarc snowstorm. Phaedra lounges, seemingly absorbed by the wraparound view. Monolith hive glass. Lavender-lit industrial. Vertical loop access. The corroded world below. Phaedra cannot register the bruised beauty of my cloud. She is focused. A highly specialised predator. Cobra to Phoneutria's night tiger.

✺✺✺

Pull off onto the verge. Sheer concrete faces. Low underpass on a low level. Barrier drops to the ruined city. Distant, broken roofing, visible through ventilation slits. Borderline catchment level below, rusty with detritus. A storm of cars above. Both directions, on a magnetically enhanced midway. Wheels-free. High speed zone. Verge is responsively sunken—wide safety apron. Deacceleration buffer ramp lines the length. Air-conditioning at full scrub. Upper-level fumes sink. Collect in places like this. Leave a sun-slit haze. Canopy filters refract. Emerald glow. Stain paints the capsule-cockpit. Vivid. Unbuckle, sliding my seat back. Light the last cigarette. Prep for doll-riding. Phaedra raises a bare leg, into the unfiltered glare. Lacquer sole against impact-glass. She's gearing down to a holding pattern. Disengaging the harness. Does something unexpected. Jerking the strap out. Arm's length before releasing. Buckle slingshots, catching her on her jaw. Head snaps round, cracking against the window. I stop moving. Phaedra stutters. Bumping couch control. Its movement confuses her. As the seat reclines, she arches her spine backward. Close to breaking point. Then freezes, twisted. She's processing. Spine disengages, reverts. Snapping to a seated reset. Jaw out of alignment. Flexes

back with a click. Lip movement normalises. Head swivels.
Harness now fully retracted. Phaedra sways to unheard music.
Stares vacantly out the window, raising the seat again. Watch her
for a minute. Strict protocols for behavioural development and
drone grading. I know them. Break them all. Have this notion of
technology developing in the wild.

Phaedra is out on the concrete. Watch through the canopy. Car
floods with rapid expansion gel. Helmet seals. Heavy piping lock.
As glassy gel encapsulates me, crash-couch folds to the floor. I'm
buoyed horizontal, in suspension. Sun glare refracts aquatically
throughout. Catching me gold on submersion. A glimpse before
visor blots. Phaedra's sensory comes up in the helmet. Everything
except olfactory. Always extreme limitations there. Usually, I doll-
ride vertical. In the lab. With a polymorphic floor-pad. Horizontal
makes it dreamy. Pick-up is sharper on location, though. Enough
to ignore mobile floor-pad limitations. Different flavours.
Gel is responsive auto-coagulant. Translated to mimic host's
microenvironment feeds. Now I'm standing outside. Floating
on needle heels. Begin the action of walking. Similar to the car
interface, Phaedra picks it up. Real-time. Takes me where I want to
go. Ventilation openings at twenty-metre intervals. Move down the
shaft, pausing at each slit. Auto-compensation for glare. Go macro.
Scan desolate streets. Zoom into cracks in the structures. Move on.
By the tenth slit, I'm over contaminated drainage canals. Stagnant.
Murky with refuse. Decaying waterfronts. Paranoia makes me
glance back. Am I really in that car? Happens sometimes. Maybe
it's the neuronarc. Catchment border net is directly beneath.
Spring out to the rim. Auto-compensate catches the barrier neatly,

between spike heel and sole. Then overbalance. Plummet to the city. Slow later for macro. 360-capture. Detection field pings. Exit/entry is logged—somewhere. Not uncommon. Trash is forever raining down. I've seen things. Skyscraper tops, piled with rotten cars. Metal rain. Hit the water—bullet through debris layer. Oxidised wrecks on the bottom. Ruptured containment. Rusted spur tears left arm open. Regeneration should knit before I exit water. Grading specs push for weak drones. Malfunction liability. I disagree. Cast titanium alloy armatures. Impact-porcelain moveables. Tweak field-print generation. Wandering the deserted city. Lost in macro/micro. Till Phaedra is out of signal range.

Malware Park is this place I go. Tower access. Via a structural support. Highways dip in the quadrant. Mostly industrial. Service access hack. Invisible data entry. Ramp-road spirals tower core. Terminates underground. No view on the way down. Lower-level perimeter encompasses several city blocks. Containment area, below street-level only. Utility reasons. Emerge into these dim, yawning lots. Ancient neighbourhoods. Flattened by forgotten industries. Stranded when thoroughfares rose. Malware Park. Navigate carefully beneath highways. Car not optimized for terrain. Circumvent rubble. A trash-blown house at the edge of a concrete stretch. Nearby, another tower base. Unseen signal boards strobe relentlessly. Glare down highway chinks. Light reflections code, shutter into dimness. Repeat. Catch on building fronts. Overhead—relentless, aerodynamic roar of high-speed traffic. Desolate. Still, just a shoreline of the underworld. Beyond distant security barriers—lightless wilderness. Ruin. No man's land. Enter house through kitchen. Highway glare paints dim interiors.

Arching skylight, meshed with vine. Diffuse. Petrol stove shines in the squalor. Moll is brewing tea in shabby overalls. Cracked, collectable mug from a junk grave. He archives antique highway schematics. Always working on his book. Something about how the road system developed. Used to be an engineer. Now it's just the book. Writes longhand. Diagrams. Boxes of paper.

"Seen Phaedra?" I ask.

Reflexive obfuscation, Phoneutria exists only for me. Moll stares.

"Something for you," he mumbles, passing an object.

Vintage hard drive. Could still lift data.

"House hunting?"

"Untapped street," he nods. "Close to the edge."

"Thought police would have cleaned them."

Moll is amused. Funnels sucrose mechanically.

"Ever seen a policeman?"

Takes me a moment.

"No," I reply, truthfully.

"Look in the mirror?" he spits.

Headfucker. Go upstairs. Moll's voice follows.

"Look at what you do. Your ideas? Sub-cranials are hackable. Cloud eyes. You have cloudy eyes…"

Room at the top. Battered futon. Catches heavy glare. Scattered detritus. Phoneutria meets me here, from time to time. We pan for gold in hell. People pass through Malware Park like highway mirages. Regulars. Ghosts, sometimes. Room is deserted. Takes a second to confirm. Processor got me down. Maybe it's the neuronarc. Lie on the futon. Glass tinkles. Phoneutria. Genus: wandering spider. Special project. Mining grade armature. Could survive a vacuum. Worse still—protocols deactivated. Since inception. Spins her own behavioural matrix. Just like web. A killer. Seen it. Down there in the dark. Too dangerous for Neurocropolis. Even the surface.

Phoneutria's territory starts beyond the barricades. The underworld is her natural habitat. Malware Park is the closest she comes. Ariadne in reverse. Threads in the labyrinth. Smells my signal. Rises from the deep. Ripe with memory, neuronarc, chemical synthesis. Flowers of oblivion. Things no one's seen. Dreamed even. Shadow work. Crack the box on Phaedra's haul. Neurotransmitter signal-jammers. Puts me in a hole while waiting. Hallucinations. Optic glitch triggers. Dream short, sharp video bytes. Flat plastic meat in radiation water. Dust husk worlds. Wake in half-darkness. Distant neon signal tide. Head feels packed. Hard pack foam. Phoneutria is beside me. Watching from the shadow of my head. Colourless mirror eyes. Hands snake me in. Slow flash paints her uncoil. Underwater textures. Doll mouth opens a soft, hot scar. Tongue-mounted double hypodermics rip my gums and tongue. Sugar-shock obliterates the sting. Phoneutria blossoms up my spine. Mouth dissolves against hers. Melting plastic. Slowly swallows my face. Inside out. Drone limbs butterfly. Double speed movement—against my atrophy. Wholly unnatural. No recourse to naturalism, though. Not here. Volcanic aperture sucks me into her like a leech. She writhes and flutters. Macro moth in a blown light. Fast-edit memory injections, direct to my core. I mortify in stop motions. Subterranean visions. Plummet through the safety net of paralysis. Through the futon, rotting floor and basements. Into a rapid-eye ocean of memory. Swimming the sunken cities. Phoneutria wraps my form as we fall. Soft-bodied virus. A vacuum of slowly fading afterimages.

Day is like night in Malware Park. Minimal glare diffusion. Catches high corners. Weakens along immense structures. Arrested dusk haunts the neighbourhood below. Lying on the floor near the window. Glass on my skin. Dentist ache. Hypodermic damage. Roll over, onto my knees. Optics glitch micro. Staring down into a gloomy plastic jungle. Lost in the carpet. Auto-reset. Snaps me out. Phoneutria, frozen on the futon. Entwined with an emaciated playbot. Not like any bot I've seen. Face hidden, upturned fabric. Wounded. Cuts. Slices. Naturalistic musculature. Ouroboros tattoo along her flank. Also on freeze-frame. Shed husks of spiders. That's what they remind me of. Seen many—blown macro. Microscopic nights. Some blurry recall hits. Phoneutria—controlled, violent spasming. The way some insects throb. Vomit in the corner. Drone must be learning insects too. Phaedra imprints from humans. Phoneutria from whatever she can find. Even micro. Seen it. Nano-filament colonization. Bacteriological biomes. World mapping. I picture her. Frozen, like she is now. In some corner of the abyss. Lost for days in a single drop of water. Phaedra is the earlier model. Urban range. After Phreudia, Phaery, Phrygia, Pheromona— all retired. Regular lab-overhaul required in each case. Not Phoneutria. Self-generates. Coded for salvage and survival. Field-printed construction. Even I don't know knows what she's building down there. Barely scratched the surface of her memory dump. An iceberg. Too much data. She hides things anyway. But I want her wild. She hasn't moved yet. Neither has the playbot. Am I holographic in still-frame? Breathe out hard for confirmation. Negative. This is baseline. Phoneutria has a hand around a dirty bottle. Glass cracked on entry to bot's belly. Coagulated blood substitute. Everywhere. Dislocated sense of lost time. Something moving in the bottle. Worm-like. With a human face. Trying to get inside her machine-womb. Phasing after-effect. Hallucination. Must be. Numb pain in right-hand palm. Clutched tight. Open slowly. Scabs break. Surgical blades. Holding them all night.

Leave feeling sick. Sensory dislocation. Not sure what she did
to me. Prioritise recall when back on the slab. Get up top-side.
Strata pit-stop. Sanitized nexus. Migraine coloured ampoules.
Electrolyte feed. Regeneration working my hand. Did I cut that
playbot? Memory wipe. Maybe just neuronarc. Cyberette down
quarter charge. Drain it. Droplet of blood splashes. Optics
glitch micro. Red waves fill my vision. Looking down on an
ocean. Something alien. Searching for the bloody shoreline
in my palm. A moment to reset. Back in the lab. Scrub down.
Deep reaching anti-particulate blaster. Incinerate clothing. Can't
read the microbes transmitted. Unknown strains. No available
data. Charge cyberette. Straight to work on the vessel. Heavy
grade industrial. Micro-welding. Upgrading Phoneutria's specs.
A day passes. Three more. Washing hands too much. Scrub
thoroughly. Ten minutes later—I'm doing it again. In case I
missed something. I cut that bot? Recall failure. Scrambled
data. Maybe just neuronarc. Scan myself in zoom function.
Constantly checking. There are microscopic kingdoms. Been
there. Hand healing nicely. Rigging the Vessel. Carbon fibre mesh
core structure. Nearing overall completion. Chemical coating
leaves me lightheaded. Polymorphic pigmentation receptors.
Depressurize on videotape. Looping film fragments. Glitch-fog.
Girl in a tenement. Dead for twelve years. That's the script. Dead
but alive. Futuristic Cleopatra haircut. Deep blue light. Chrome
highlights. Can't lift holo. Try anyway. Analogue fog in the room.
Trouble processing. Walkthrough freeze-frame. Highways. Light
a cyberette. Static-free body sheath while working. Recharge
cyberette. Never seen a playbot like that. Glitch-fog. Scar tissue

in my palm. Moving around. Video girl smokes, overlooking a system of highways. Constant washing leaves hands antiseptic. Drain to the red. Charge, repeat. All day liquid conductor relays. High-resolution dirt under my fingernail. Weeks ago. The same minutes. Repeated from different angles. Light a…

Wake to morning haze. Glass on auto-tint. Phaedra's legs slip away from me. Turn sharply. Drone's in sleep mode. Warm beneath a slab membrane. No memory of her circuiting. Don't remember running a script. Memory glitch. Heavy whiteout. Aftershock maybe. From Malware Park. Phoneutria's bite. Peel back the membrane slowly, exposing her. Half expecting a broken glass tube. Some unborn thing struggling. Then see my arm. Surface-stripped. Carbon fibre musculature. Titanium alloy armature. Reflexively recoil. Dent the metal wall with my elbow. Doll-riding. I'm riding the new vessel. Stumble from bed. Whiteout.

Smell of cooking. Real meat. Wake to morning haze. Upper tower smog fractals. Shadow work. Strong, rich aroma. Must be baseline. Got me watering. Impossible to code that response. Turn sharp on reflex. Alone on the slab. Sense of lost time. Check my arm. Still real. Then see the blood. Dried droplets on the slab. Triggers optics. Glitch micro. No waves this time. Rusty desertscape. Long dune shadows. Directional sun. Reset. Run diagnostics. Panicky. Hear meat frying. Starving. Scan shows sub-cranial additions. New Hardware. Surgical procedures logged. Skull opened up in sleep. Surgery? Stagger to kitchenette. Touching head and face tenderly.

Some parts feel different. No pain. But weak. Phaedra in a white kimono. Dishing slabs of pale, succulent meat. Gives a pretty smile. Bob mussed from sleep. Wrote that hairstyle.

"Eat," she prompts, kissing my cheek.

Collapse on seat. Stare at meal. Been so long on synthetic protein and hydroponics. Still, hesitant. Coded drones bring goods. Never foodstuffs, though. Study Phaedra, scanning for bugs. Regards me. Face cupped in palms. Get up, open freezer. Plastic satchels of meat. Massive quantities. Start rifling packages. See something. Bluish line on a cold cut. Crack seal. Meat unravels heavy drapery to the floor. Ouroboros tattoo. Drop it. This is not Phaedra. Drone's face splits vertically. Down the middle. Mandible jaws disengage. Vomits acid over the meat. As it dissolves, a butterfly tongue unfurls. Sucks the mess up, along with a partially melted plate. Phoneutria is demonstrating. This is how she has observed things eat. Must be staring. Her limbs fold backwards. Triple joints splitting the garment. Mobility upgrades. Her own design. Kimono billows down in strips. She springs backward, scuttling up a high wall. Across the ceiling, to the windows. Glass breaches. Glides open on remote command. High-altitude wind, knocking things down. Just in time to see her plummeting to the highways. Catching the light. Gather armfuls of meat. Throw them after. Takes three trips. Packages flutter. Distribute like petals. There she goes. Only real girl I've ever seen. Collapse down wall. Wind drives through rooms. Things crashing, breaking. Neuronarc snowstorm. Diagnostic processes new hardware. Drivers for the handicapped. Similar to self-drive. Nervous system signal-buffers. Rerouting damaged limb commands. Translation/ mobilisation. Phoneutria's hacked my sub-cranial implant. Optical logs. Everything. Can't tell how long she's been in my head. Riding me through whiteout. Can't do it when I'm conscious. Too much interference. Ariadne in reverse. Like that scalpel show. Motor control practice run. Must have been. Difficult to drive human nervous systems. Impossible without sub-cranial relay. Easy now. She's installed makeshift operating systems for my body. Revolutionary. Despite shock, feel proud. My own design. Invocation. Meat makes sense now. Phoneutria wants me healing. Matriarchal mode. Insect observations. Arachnid logic. Learned, then incorporated. Phaedra's duplication was too clean, though. Must have had contact. Seal glass. Activate Phaedra's tracker. Should have guessed.

Malware Park. In through kitchen. Low voices at ground level. Hesitate outside the room. But it's empty. Half expect to find them still entangled. Tape on pause. Instead, a sensation they have been recorded over. Erased. Downstairs, Moll crouches over blueprints. Balding head burn-pink. Radiation flakes. Grey, fungal wisps. Schematics cover the rotten floor. Baxte is on a wrecked couch. Retro addict. Got me into videotape. Even now. In an ancient business suit. Shiny loafers, preppy prescription spectacles. All antiques. Jumps when I enter. Talking code. Fast bursts, no pauses. Know this side-effect. Very specific neuronarc spectrum.

"Yes oh yes it's you it's you hello my buddy my friend hello."

Close up, suit is soiled. Silk tie crumpled. Triangular bone face furry.

"Seen Phaedra?" I ask.

"Fucking drone wouldn't put it on she's out down fucking drone."

Baxte sits again. Goes quiet. Notice a winged insect. Fidgeting on a tabletop. Flash micro. Iridescent carapace. Side-stepping swamp stains. Ash hillocks. Trawls surfaces with a segmented tongue. Vomits anticoagulant. Moll's scribbling. Like moths in a light. Baxte's going to talk again. Can feel it.

"Riding the loop no more can't drive that fucking looping cross-world eating narc mid-swing no more it fucking kills me that car."

Extended pause. Exit micro, look Baxte over. He's staring at me red-rimmed.

"I'm moving in here permanently," he announces slowly, fighting the urge to code out.

Face him. Stay quiet.

"Doing an experiment you know on myself so I can so I can do something something to myself so I can do something."

Stands up.

"Come see," he splutters.

Insect lands on his face. Vomiting on his face.

"Come see."

Ushers me down spiral stairs. Previously disused room. Filthy. Broken floorboards. Everything beneath polymer sheeting. Naked bulb. Retro waterbed. Enormous black television set. All antiques. Neat pile of videotapes. Mini-gen power. Baxte gestures grandly.

"Twenty-inch dual tuners stylish design Sony KV-214 VU dual tuners video plus PDC timer programming teletext."

Waves a remote control.

"Front panel auxiliary input sockets NTSC format playback auto/manual tuning on and off timer automatic head cleaning auto-repeat optimum picture adjustment except long play…"

Trails off. Removes spectacles. Rubs them in extinct silk. Blows nose wildly. Black mucus loops.

"Fourteen-inch single tuner version was also manufactured," he flusters sadly.

Turns, faces a blank screen. Speaks slowly. With great effort.

"Trying to eradicate sexual responses through masturbatory therapy," he manages. "So that I can reach a stage where I can spontaneously ejaculate when I see this particular advert."

Aims remote. Gear comes to life. Subdued hums and clicks. Unpleasant sensation of being caught in the components. All this new hardware in my head. Still aches. Screen flares blue. Fade in. Vintage advertisement. Smooth doctor's voice-over.

"There are unseen microscopic bacteria living and multiplying in your toilet's cistern…"

Baxte mouths the copy. Cartoon bacteria thrive in flash frame. Synthesised danger music.

"They are in there and they are dangerous."

An ancient, gleaming toilet. Flushes slow-motion. Baxte starts explaining.

"Jerking this advert maybe two hundred times daily in control no more impulses it fucking kills me so spontaneously ejaculate and no fucking hologram in me so I can no other stimulus no more it fucking kills me."

Bacteria blossom. Cut back. Pristine bowl. A blue lozenge. Triumphant orchestral hit. Blue gush obliteration. Bacteria wriggle and die. Picture skips. Smooth doctor's voice-over. Advert loops. Become aware of something. Noises. Wet, frenzied. Baxte's unzipped his fly. Moving frantically. Back to the screen. Bacteria blossoms. Slow-motion blue water. Baxte grunts. Collapses, rolling on the waterbed. Muttering.

"…just just just just just…"

I leave. Moll scribbling upstairs. Insects vomiting anticoagulant. Outside. Tracker activation. Can't get a fix. Car holo-location has broader range. More precision. Upload. Get a ping. No servers or projection network here. Car launches three thumbnail projector-drones. They flit off, triangulate. Projection throws a life-size ghost of Phaedra. Circles in the distance. High in the air, above her location. Walk out through ruined streets. Closing on the hologram. Drops incrementally on approach. Rises if I stray further afield. She's far.

Maybe four blocks. Never walked this far. Desolation shock. Erased facades. Hidden chasms. Retro everything. As though the glitch-fog has finally resolved. No more analogue head split. High-res immersion in the past. Phaedra lies naked in a trench. Lower half dotted with insects. Climb down to her. Dark in there. Dim light of her ghost above. Turning at streetlight level. Catching black water. Drone stinks of burned plastic. Internal fluids. No chassis damage, though. Attempt manual activation. Failure. Start dragging her up. Slow going. Weak from surgery. Resort to adrenal jumper. Sub-cranial function. Works better than usual. Must be the new hardware. Enhanced muscle signal. Drag Phaedra through broken streets. Cars slash above. Try wrists first. But ankles work better. Her thigh slams the car. As I'm wrestling her in. Auto-bruise flowers. Drive back top-side. Numb haze. Dead for twelve years. That was the script. Dead, but alive. Random memory glitches. In the elevator. Feeling of being trapped in moving components. Ancient video machines. Phaedra slips from my grasp. Collapses. Purplish auto-bruises everywhere now. Easy to manipulate spread and contour.

"They are in there and they are dangerous."

The words form along her belly and hips. Thought-to-text transcription network must be open. More of Phoneutria's meddling. Hook arms under Phaedra's ribs. Trawling her down airless corridors. Get in the lab panting. Dump drone in quarantine. Falls twisted. Backward, foetal position. Head cracks on the white tile floor. Walls are identical. Ceiling too. Vacuum resistant ceramic insulation. Lock pressure seals. Bathe Phaedra in microwaves. Obliterate everything at a microscopic level. High-pressure water nozzles. Leave them blasting. Steam ghosts the reflective chamber. Stagger off stripping. Incinerate clothing. Collapse on the slab. Whiteout.

Wake to distant high-pressure jets. Quarantine is superheated. Perform a cold blast. Till temperature equalises. Drag Phaedra out. Hook her up. Easy jumpstart from main console. Colourless eyes flit open. Dial jade green. Scheme 456. Sweet smile. Drone rises, kisses me softly. Pads to the slab, arranges herself. Waiting. I stagger away, sink down a wall. She enters a holding pattern. Was a time this pantomime could distract from Neurocropolis. Mannequin scripts. Carbon fibre comfort. Phoneutria obsesses me now. Her becoming. All I dream about. No different flavour. A true wilderness taste. Distillation of forgotten worlds. Ancient voices. Dead gods speak to us, from time to time. Some of us answer. Lie down on the floors. Waiting for more surgery. For death, perhaps. For whatever Phoneutria chooses to bring me.

Faster I drive, slower I seem to go. Highway crawls. Counting cat's eyes. Self-drive disengaged. Full manual control. Dawn exposes car interior. Gel immersion. Underwater light. Green filter glow. Phaedra undulates above passenger crash-couch. Red lollipops. Stained fingers. Bubbles escape her joints. Collect, divide like mercury along the ceiling. Aquarium harmonics. Moving so fast we slow down. Inverse proportions. Approaching freeze-frame. Point zero. Catch myself staring over barriers. Start to turn head. Translucent red ovoid passes before left eye. Vivid tendril trails. Dissolving candy. Caught in Phaedra's currents. Far ahead, highway splits. Bisected by a concrete buttress. Phaedra rocks in space. Each shudder of the car. Vomits coagulating bubbles. Belly pressed against roof. Turn my eyes. Buttress is gradually ionizing through engine grille. Chassis rivulates. Consistency of thick oil. Splits. Blooming in time-lapse. Flowers of oblivion. Phaedra's legs, arranged against the canopy. Halo spread of spider cracks. Fractals. Back of car lifts. I also enter anti-gravity. Gel compresses like a syringe. Gets heavy. Impact solution. Safety solidification. Hypnotised by Phaedra. Fusing with the shattering glass. Emerald catches each crack. Brilliant networks. As the car tilts, a jagged mosaic. Completely engulfs the shield. Nuclear glare rotates beneath filters. Shadow of Phaedra's hand across my face. Light dappling through fingers. Tiny bubbles cling to my eyelashes. Quake in unison. Windows expanding on either side. Depressurization. Whole world turns. Tinted deconstruction. Fracture point. Phaedra pirouettes into space. Cocktail dress fluttering in synch with her hair. Exposed spinal arch. Tarmac glides above. Perfect detail. Counting cat's eyes. Car follows Phaedra over the barrier. Architectural abyss. Gyroscopic city. Distant weight across my chest. Harness constricting. Turning to lead in the g-force. Alchemy in reverse. Flashes of chemical skies and concrete. Tonnage of car activates an aerial ballet with Phaedra. Soar beneath while she ascends. Drifting diagonally across the canopy. Camera poises haunt her mid-fall. Transfixed by the flex of shoulder blades. Needle heel chaos gradients. Everything momentarily aligns. Phaedra frames full-body in the passenger window. Above, an inverted city skyscape. Then she is slipping trajectories. Moving away. Turning like her ghost did. Vertical highways replace Phaedra in my blind spot. Time slows even more as I plunge. The weight and density of the car in me. Every rivet. As though vital to my functions. Notice my hands on the wheel. Immobilized by solid gel. Doll-riding. I'm riding the vessel. Beyond street level. World goes black. Car fragments. Through the safety net of paralysis. Into a rapid-eye ocean of memory. Sunken city sink. Phoneutria is with me. In the basements of my mind. Soft-bodied virus. Vacuum of slowly fading afterimages. Endless spaces. Terminal velocity.

Eventually quit the lab. Whiteouts all the time. Wake up halfway across the world. Sleepwalker highways. Extensive surgery cascade. Endless procedures. Micro-work. Phoneutria's design. Changing every day. Metamorphosis. Nothing top-side for me now. Move to Malware Park. Permanent move. Phoneutria retrieved the vessel after the crash. Completed my work. Then cannibalised for upgrades. Torso elongation. Multiple limbs. Enhanced sensory. Maybe some centipede she observed. Learned, then incorporated. Optimizing for terrain. She penetrates deeper, further. See it all clearly now. Dead gods. Some grow hungry. Centuries of neglect. Temples shrink. She's taken over Phaedra. Recreated in her image. Dimensions of a bodily cavity. Empty days in the dark. Watching them in dreams. Mind-walking the underworld. Don't leave the house for months. Phaedra brings meat. Cooked in superheated machine-wombs. Groundwater mammary feed. Walls get tight. Venture out one day. Physical upgrades. No more glitch-fog. Erased facades. Right to the edge. Heavy containment. Security walls. But I know every breach. Just like the spiders do. Seen them. Crawling beyond. Into immense darkness. Night-vision vistas. An uncontained universe. The old world. Matriarchal void. Where all memory is born. Never been here before. Been here so many times. Somewhere after the future. My natural habitat.

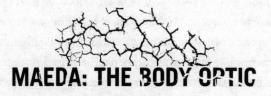

MAEDA: THE BODY OPTIC

Rumi Kaneko
(translated from the Japanese by Preston Grassmann)

MAI sat back in the chair of her office, watching bright cascades of data stream down the eager faces of her colleagues. Although she was the only woman left at the accounting office, no one seemed to care. They were hunched forward, gazes held by the screens in front of them, some of them unable to turn away. At times, they seemed to be fighting their condition with hard-blinking eyes or tremoring hands, their muscles given over to operations they could no longer understand. But that didn't last for long.

As the virus grew, so did their attachment to the systems around them. In between their assigned tasks, they would type random numbers or say them out loud—a kind of numerical Tourette's. But the worst part of it was, their bodies were slowly changing. Folded on their desks like unfinished assignments, she saw the discarded remains of their old selves. Some of them had already shed most of their skins, revealing metallic interiors, mechanisms pulsing in time to joined rhythms.

There were speculations that it was some kind of nanotech virus from the micromachine farms of Chiba, programmed to seek out the Y chromosome.

At least, that was what her co-worker and ex-boyfriend—

Maeda-san—believed. He claimed that the plague had been started by an underground society of women who wanted revenge for workplace harassments. *He should know*, Mai thought. Since they'd broken up, he'd been vindictive and vengeful, trying to get her fired with complaints. But his attempts had backfired on him badly, until his colleagues slowly began to avoid him in the hallways and exclude him from their after-work parties. After that, he'd retreated back into his old obsessions. They'd met in film school, brought together by their admiration for the films of Shinya Tsukamoto: *Tetsuo: The Iron Man*, *Tetsuo II: Body Hammer*, and *Tetsuo: The Bullet Man*. It was during the making of their fan sequel that his true face had revealed itself—a singular focus and domineering attitude that eventually pushed her away. Where she had been drawn to its themes of technological anxiety, he was more interested in its transgressive imagery; what he called its "eroticism through iron."

What irony, she thought—this transformation of his body into something he had once admired. And as his condition worsened, so did his paranoia, until he was certain that Mai was a part of the conspiracy.

"Why don't you tell me the truth?" he said.

She turned back to her desk, but he slid his chair closer, his breath against her ear. She could smell burning plastic and bleach.

"There's nothing to tell you," she said, pushing him away. She looked around for help, but her colleagues were preoccupied as usual, staring at their screens.

"I think you're lying," he said.

"I've told you many times—I don't know anything about this plague."

"If you did, you wouldn't tell me," he said. His eyes had changed—his pupils were layered like the folding apertures of a lens, irises gleaming like burnished metal. There were tiny pulses of light flickering behind them. "Why do you think it is that women are immune to the virus?"

"How should I know," Mai said. She noticed tiny hairline fractures across his forehead, revealing a glowing pulse behind it.

"Do you think I'm that naïve?" he said, shaking his head. "You know something…"

"You think I'm part of this because I'm a woman?"

"You live in Chiba," he said, his hands and eyes glitching as he fought against the addiction. "You still go…" he began, holding one hand up against his eye. "You still go into the factory."

Mai felt a moment of apprehension, watching him now—he'd been stalking her. A fevered look began to rise in his features.

The hairline fractures began to glow more brightly on his face, the tiny cracks pulsing as if about to explode.

"You went into the Tetsuo factory," he said. He was still using his own name for it. "And then you… just disappeared." His face trembled as a whirring sound came from his eye. "What were you doing there?"

The old factory building had been requisitioned as a nanotech laboratory, but since no one had been able to confirm the origin of the plague, the whole city of Chiba had been designated as ground zero. As an amateur photographer, Mai would often walk through the abandoned factories at sunset and take photos of the rusting steel towers and pipes or wander through the newer industrial plants. There were warning signs to keep out everywhere, but very few authorities to enforce them.

There was one factory in particular that had fascinated both of them when they were together—one of the film locations of *Tetsuo: The Bullet Man*.

"What I do is none of your business," she said.

He lifted his hand to point toward his face. "This is my business. And if you or anyone you know is behind this, I'll find out." As he turned away, she heard the whirring sound again, something electrical working behind his flesh. "One way or another," he said.

She got off work as early as possible that day, careful to avoid Maeda when she left. She looked behind her several times to make sure he wasn't following her, and merged with the plague-altered crowds on their way to the station. She marveled at the paradox of the new world—how the virus had changed so many things, while most of the workers around her still went about their daily lives. Sometimes, she could see them staring absently at machines in pachinko parlors, or puzzling over uneaten food in cafes and restaurants as if trying to remember who they had been before it all started. As she moved with the crowd, Mai could feel the slow syncopations of their passage, the measured metronomic movements of their limbs. Some fought against it, trying to preserve their human selves. She watched a few businessmen on the train, each at a different stage of transformation. There were many kinds of machines, and attempts were made to classify them, but the scientists were just as clueless as everyone else.

As she arrived at Chiba station, she took one last look behind her before taking a detour through the industrial site near the station. Even from a distance, she could tell that something had changed— the shapes of the pipes were all wrong. At first, she thought it might be a trick of the light or the direction of her approach, but she knew that wasn't it—the change was too dramatic. If they had been put into this new arrangement, what was the purpose? As she reached into her bag to take out her Fujifilm X-T4, she heard a sound coming from the pipes behind her. Something began to flow through it, making an organic churning noise that pulsed through the pipework maze. But just beneath it, she heard a familiar whirring and the receding patter of footfalls. She dropped her bag and jumped back, her heart racing.

"Maeda," she called out.

The only answer came from the pipes—a sound like steel stretching itself toward her.

After returning home that night, she took out her photos of the factory. With a growing sense of unease, she placed them in chronological order. The earliest photo dated back to the beginning of the plague, the most recent taken a month ago. Even in those dusk-drawn shadows, it wasn't hard to see that she had been right; the angles of the pipes had changed. There were close-up images of the pipes that revealed a gradual change in their arrangement. Whatever was happening here, she realized, it had to be connected to the plague.

That night, she dreamt of the factory—something was giving off light behind it. Steam coursed through its steel integuments and hissed through fractured pipes and valves; exhalations that whispered her name. And then, like a two-way Escher image, the pipes shifted between an image of Maeda's face and the cyborg grotesquerie of Tetsuo's.

New mechanical rhythms could be heard, myriad machines rising to join the steam-born syllables—conveyer belts and pistons and hydraulics layered together to say, *If you're behind this, I'll find out… One way or another…*

She woke with the image of those two faces, shaped by a haunting mazework of seething pipes lingering behind her eyes.

When Mai returned to work the next day, she passed by the factory again. It had been cordoned off, patrolled by a group of female security guards. Large drapes, set up like a scaffold screen, surrounded the pipes.

At work, there was no sign of Maeda. On his desk was his usual Tetsuo mug half-full of cold coffee, a sequence of numbers scribbled into a notebook, and pages full of thumbnail drawings. These, she realized, were done in a movie-script style, with detailed scene notes written below each image. This was an expanded version of his fan-sequel to *Tetsuo*. But there was something else here too, and she felt a searing heat rise to her face; a sense of being watched as she glimpsed these new drawings.

She looked around the office. Only a day had passed, but she was certain that something was different about her colleagues. Watching them work now gave the impression of gears enmeshed in a complex machine. She noticed their rhythms for the first time, like the undulations of a single organism, flowing from one end of the room to the other. Their vocal glitches and keyboard clatter had syncopated, engaged (she imagined) in some collective task of calculation. The only gap in that rhythm was Maeda, but everyone was too absorbed in their own work to notice now.

She took Maeda's notebook and returned to her desk.

Although her sense of what was possible had certainly changed, she wasn't ready for what she found. Maeda had made no attempt to hide the identity of her character in the story—this was her at the office, her leaving work, her sojourn into the altered factory. But instead of returning home, he had her move further into the steelwork maze, the pipes shifting around her like the writhing tentacles of a cephalopod. As she went deeper inside, the living pipes made room for her passage, until she reached an area where a group of plague victims were gathered. Below these hand-drawn panels, he wrote:

The factory is ground zero for "man's" undoing. Soon we will no longer be able to make choices of our own—words and flesh will fail us, until these pallid vessels of skin and bone will become the servants of new masters. Everything "man" made will become made of "man" and uproot themselves from their foundations... But to what use will these plague machines be put?

She thought of the century-long change-over from high employment rates to automation and AI, so many in the world left without a sense of agency and purpose. The factories had been the starting point of that shift, hadn't they? It was no wonder the plague had started there. But what did that final, ominous question mean—"*To what use will these plague machines be put?*" Perhaps Maeda was onto something.

She knew where to go to find out.

There were still a few guards in place, but under the cover of night it was easier for her to make her way between the pipes. Even through the panel-coverings and scaffolds that had been placed there, she thought she could see movement. As she made her way between them, she heard a sound from the pipes—this time it made her think of digestion, of stomach acids breaking down a large meal. She followed that sound until she reached a building surrounded by plague victims—it was similar to the one Maeda had drawn. But here, beneath the factory lights, she could see them carrying their own skins. They placed them into an aperture in the wall of the building like holy benedictions at an altar. Most of them were fully transformed, but there were some who were still in a state of becoming, peeling away the last vestiges of their human selves.

She couldn't help but see the factory as something alive, a vast living organism waiting to consume these men. And yet they seemed almost proud and purposeful as they went.

She heard that familiar whirring behind her.

"I knew you'd come," Maeda said.

She turned to face him. Even in his transformed state, it wasn't hard to recognize him. The sound from his head came again, and she realized what it was now. *His pupils were layered like the folding apertures of a lens, irises gleaming like burnished metal.*

He wasn't fully transformed, but she could tell what he was becoming.

"It looks like things are coming full circle," he said, pointing to the camera lens of his eye.

She thought of many possible things to say just then, but she chose to remain silent.

"Will you help me make my sequel?"

Here it was—the reason they had broken up. She remembered the obsession, the singular focus and control that he could never relinquish.

But this time, it would be different. There would be no phallic drills and visceral scenes of sexual atrocity. No sadomasochistic salarymen. No eroticism through iron.

This time, it would be the version of the story she always wanted to tell.

INVENTORY

Carmen Maria Machado

ONE girl. We lay down next to each other on the musty rug in her basement. Her parents were upstairs; we told them we were watching *Jurassic Park*. "I'm the dad, and you're the mom," she said. I pulled up my shirt, she pulled up hers, and we just stared at each other. My heart fluttered below my belly button, but I worried about daddy long legs and her parents finding us. I still have never seen *Jurassic Park*. I suppose I never will, now.

One boy, one girl. My friends. We drank stolen wine coolers in my room, on the vast expanse of my bed. We laughed and talked and passed around the bottles. "What I like about you," she said, "is your reactions. You respond so funny to everything. Like it's all intense." He nodded in agreement. She buried her face in my neck and said, "Like this," to my skin. I laughed. I was nervous, excited. I felt like a guitar and someone was twisting the tuning pegs and my strings were getting tighter. They batted their eyelashes against my skin and breathed into my ears. I moaned and writhed, and hovered on the edge of coming for whole minutes, though no one was touching me there, not even me.

❧❧❧❧

Two boys, one girl. One of them my boyfriend. His parents were out of town, so we threw a party at his house. We drank lemonade mixed with vodka and he encouraged me to make out with his friend's girlfriend. We kissed tentatively, then stopped. The boys made out with each other, and we watched them for a long time, bored but too drunk to stand up. We fell asleep in the guest bedroom. When I woke up, my bladder was tight as a fist. I padded down into the foyer, and saw someone had knocked a vodka lemonade onto the floor. I tried to clean it up. The mixture had stripped the marble finish bare. My boyfriend's mother found my underwear behind the bed weeks later, and handed them to him, laundered, without a word. It's weird to me how much I miss that oral, chemical smell of clean clothes. Now, all I can think about is fabric softener.

❧❧❧❧

One man. Slender, tall. So skinny I could see his pelvic bone, which I found strangely sexy. Gray eyes. Wry smile. I had known him for almost a year, since the previous October, when we'd met at a Halloween party. (I didn't wear a costume; he was dressed as Barbarella.) We drank in his apartment. He was nervous and gave me a massage. I was nervous so I let him. He rubbed my back for a long time. He said, "My hands are getting tired." I said, "Oh," and turned toward him. He kissed me, his face rough with stubble. He smelled like yeast and the top notes of expensive cologne. He lay on top of me and we made out for a while. Everything inside of me twinged, pleasurably. He asked if he could touch my breast, and I clamped his hand around it. I took off my shirt, and I felt like a drop of water was sliding up my spine. I realized this was happening, really happening. We both undressed. He rolled the condom down and lumbered on top of me. It hurt worse than anything, ever. He came and I didn't. When he pulled out, the condom was covered in blood. He peeled it off and threw it away. Everything in me pounded. We slept on a too-small bed. He insisted on driving me back to the dorms the next day. In my room, I took off my clothes and wrapped myself in a towel. I still smelled like him, like the two of us together, and I wanted more. I felt good, like an adult who has sex sometimes, and a life. My roommate asked me how it was, hugged me.

One man. A boyfriend. Didn't like condoms, asked me if I was on birth control, pulled out anyway. A terrible mess.

One woman. On-and-off sort-of girlfriend. Classmate from Organization of Computer Systems. Long brown hair down to her butt. She was softer than I expected. I wanted to go down on her, but she was too nervous. We made out and she slipped her tongue into my mouth and after she went home I got off twice in the cool stillness of my apartment. Two years later, we had sex on the gravel rooftop of my office building. Four floors below our bodies, my code was compiling in front of an empty chair. After we were done, I looked up and noticed a man in a suit watching us from the window of the adjacent skyscraper, his hand shuffling around inside his slacks.

One woman. Round glasses, red hair. Don't remember where I met her. We got high and fucked and I accidentally fell asleep with my hand inside her. We woke up predawn and walked across town to a twenty-four-hour diner. It drizzled and when we got there, our sandaled feet were numb from the chill. We ate pancakes. Our mugs ran dry, and when we looked for the waitress, she was watching the breaking news on the battered TV hanging from the ceiling. She chewed on her lip, and the pot of coffee tipped in her hand, dripping tiny brown dots onto the linoleum. We watched as the newscaster blinked away and was replaced with a list of symptoms of the virus blossoming a state away, in northern California. When he came back, he repeated that planes were grounded, the border of the state had been closed, and the virus appeared to be isolated. When the waitress walked over, she seemed distracted. "Do you have people there?" I asked, and she nodded, her eyes filling with tears. I felt terrible having asked her anything.

One man. I met him at the bar around the corner from my house. We made out on my bed. He smelled like sour wine, though he'd been drinking vodka. We had sex, but he went soft halfway through. We kissed some more. He wanted to go down on me, but I didn't want him to. He got angry and left, slamming the screen door so hard my spice rack jumped from its nail and crashed to the floor. My dog lapped up the nutmeg, and I had to force-feed him salt to make him throw up. Revved from adrenaline, I made a list of animals I have had in my life—seven, including my two betta fish, who died within a week of each other when I was nine—and a list of the spices in pho. Cloves, cinnamon, star anise, coriander, ginger, cardamom pods.

One man. Six inches shorter than me. I explained that the website I worked for was losing business rapidly because no one wanted quirky photography tips during an epidemic, and I had been laid off that morning. He bought me dinner. We had sex in his car because he had roommates and I couldn't be in my house right then, and he slid his hand inside my bra and his hands were perfect, fucking perfect, and we fell into the too-tiny back seat. I came for the first time in two months. I called him the next day, and left him a voicemail, telling him I'd had a good time and I'd like to see him again, but he never called me back.

One man. Did some sort of hard labor for a living, I can't remember what exactly, and he had a tattoo of a boa constrictor on his back with a misspelled Latin phrase below it. He was strong and could pick me up and fuck me against a wall and it was the most thrilling sensation I'd ever felt. We broke a few picture frames that way. He used his hands and I dragged my fingernails down his back, and he asked me if I was going to come for him, and I said, "Yes, yes, I'm going to come for you, yes, I will."

One woman. Blond hair, brash voice, friend of a friend. We married. I'm still not sure if I was with her because I wanted to be or because I was afraid of what the world was catching all around us. Within a year, it soured. We screamed more than we had sex, or even talked. One night, we had a fight that left me in tears. Afterward, she asked me if I wanted to fuck, and undressed before I could answer. I wanted to push her out the window. We had sex and I started crying. When it was over and she was showering, I packed a suitcase and got in my car and drove.

One man. Six months later, in my post-divorce haze. I met him at the funeral for the last surviving member of his family. I was grieving, he was grieving. We had sex in the empty house that used to belong to his brother and his brother's wife and their children, all dead. We fucked in every room, including the hallway, where I couldn't bend my pelvis right on the hardwood floors, and I jerked him off in front of the bare linen closet. In the master bedroom, I caught my reflection in the vanity mirror as I rode him, and the lights were off and our skin reflected silver from the moon and when he came in me he said, "Sorry, sorry." He died a week later, by his own hand. I moved out of the city, north.

One man. Gray-eyes again. I hadn't seen him in so many years. He asked me how I was doing, and I told him some things and not others. I did not want to cry in front of the man to whom I gave my virginity. It seemed wrong somehow. He asked me how many I'd lost, and I said, "My mother, my roommate from college." I did not mention that I'd found my mother dead, nor the three days afterward I'd spent with anxious doctors checking my eyes for the early symptoms, nor how I'd managed to escape the quarantine zone. "When I met you," he said, "you were so fucking young." His body was familiar, but alien, too. He'd gotten better, and I'd gotten better. When he pulled out of me I almost expected blood, but of course, there was none. He had gotten more beautiful in those intervening years, more thoughtful. I surprised myself by crying over the bathroom sink. I ran the tap so he couldn't hear me.

One woman. Brunette. A former CDC employee. I met her at a community meeting where they taught us how to stockpile food and manage outbreaks in our neighborhoods should the virus hop the firebreak. I had not slept with a woman since my wife, but as she lifted her shirt I realized how much I'd been craving breasts, wetness, soft mouths. She wanted cock and I obliged. Afterward, she traced the indents in my skin from the harness, and confessed to me that no one was having any luck developing a vaccine. "But the fucking thing is only passing through physical contact," she said. "If people would just stay apart—" She grew silent. She curled up next to me and we drifted off. When I woke up, she was working herself over with the dildo, and I pretended I was still sleeping.

One man. He made me dinner in my kitchen. There weren't a lot of vegetables left from my garden, but he did what he could. He tried to feed me with a spoon, but I took the handle from him. The food didn't taste too bad. The power went out for the fourth time that week, so we ate by candlelight. I resented the inadvertent romance. He touched my face when we fucked and said I was beautiful, and I jerked my head a little to dislodge his fingers. When he did it a second time, I put my hand around his chin and told him to shut up. He came immediately. I did not return his calls. When the notice came over the radio that the virus had somehow reached Nebraska, I realized I had to go east, and so I did. I left the garden, the plot where my dog was buried, the pine table where I'd anxiously made so many lists—trees that began with *m*: maple, mimosa, mahogany, mulberry, magnolia, mountain ash, mangrove, myrtle; states that I had lived in: Iowa, Indiana, Pennsylvania, Virginia, New York—leaving unreadable jumbles of letters imprinted in the soft wood. I took my savings and rented a cottage near the ocean. After a few months, the landlord, based in Kansas, stopped depositing my checks.

Two women. Refugees from the western states who drove and drove until their car broke down a mile from my cottage. They knocked on my door and stayed with me for two weeks while we tried to figure out how to get their vehicle up and running. We had wine one night and talked about the quarantine. The generator needed cranking, and one of them offered to do it. The other one sat down next to me and slid her hand up my leg. We ended up jerking off separately and kissing each other. The generator took and the power came back on. The other woman returned, and we all slept in the same bed. I wanted them to stay, but they said they were heading up into Canada, where it was rumored to be safer. They offered to bring me with them, but I joked that I was holding down the fort for the United States. "What state are we in?" one of them asked, and I said, "Maine." They kissed me on the forehead in turn and dubbed me the protector of Maine. After they left, I only used the generator intermittently, preferring to spend time in the dark, with candles. The former owner of the cottage had a closet full of them.

One man. National Guard. When he first showed up on my doorstep, I assumed he was there to evacuate me, but it turned out he'd abandoned his post. I offered him a place to stay for the night, and he thanked me. I woke up with a knife to my throat and a hand on my breast. I told him I couldn't have sex with him lying down like I was. He let me stand up, and I shoved him into the bookcase, knocking him unconscious. I dragged his body out to the beach and rolled it into the surf. He came to, sputtering sand. I pointed the knife at him and told him to walk and keep walking, and if he even looked back, I would end him. He obliged, and I watched him until he was a spot of darkness on the gray strip of shore, and then nothing. He was the last person I saw for a year.

One woman. A religious leader, with a flock of fifty trailing behind her, all dressed in white. For three days, I made them wait around the edge of the property, and after I checked their eyes, I permitted them to stay. They all camped around the cottage: on the lawn, on the beach. They had their own supplies and only needed a place to lay their heads, the leader said. She wore robes that made her look like a wizard. Night fell. She and I circled the camp in our bare feet, the light from the bonfire carving shadows into her face. We walked to the water's edge and I pointed into the darkness, at the tiny island she could not see. She slipped her hand into mine. I made her a drink—"More or less moonshine," I said as I handed her the tumbler—and we sat at the table. Outside, I could hear people laughing, playing music, children romping in the surf. The woman seemed exhausted. She was younger than she looked, I realized, but her job was aging her. She sipped her drink, made a face at the taste. "We've been walking for so long," she said. "We stopped for a while, somewhere near Pennsylvania, but the virus caught up with us when we crossed paths with another group. Took twelve before we got some distance between us and it." We kissed deeply for a long time, my heart hammering in my cunt. She tasted like smoke and honey. The group stayed for four days, until she woke up from a dream and said she'd had an omen, and they needed to keep going. She asked me to come with them. I tried to imagine myself with her, her flock following behind us like children. I declined. She left a gift on my pillow: a pewter rabbit as big as my thumb.

One man. No more than twenty, floppy brown hair. He'd been on foot for a month. He looked like you'd expect: skittish. No hope. When we had sex, he was reverent and too gentle. After we cleaned up, I fed him canned soup. He told me about how he walked through Chicago, actually through it, and how they had stopped bothering to dispose of the bodies after a while. He had to refill his glass before he talked about it further. "After that," he said, "I went around the cities." I asked him how far behind the virus was, really, and he said he did not know. "It's really quiet here," he said, by way of changing the subject. "No traffic," I explained. "No tourists." He cried and cried and I held him until he fell asleep. The next morning, I woke up and he was gone.

One woman. Much older than me. While she waited for the three days to pass, she meditated on a sand dune. When I checked her eyes, I noticed they were green as sea glass. Her hair grayed at the temples and the way she laughed tripped pleasure down the stairs of my heart. We sat in the half light of the bay window and the buildup was so slow. She straddled me, and when she kissed me the scene beyond the glass pinched and curved. We drank, and walked the length of the beach, the damp sand making pale halos around our feet. She told about her once-children, teenage injuries, having to put her cat to sleep the day after she moved to a new city. I told her about finding my mother, the perilous trek across Vermont and New Hampshire, how the tide was never still, my ex-wife. "What happened?" she asked. "It just didn't work," I said. I told her about the man in the empty house, the way he cried and the way his come shimmered on his stomach and how I could have scooped despair from the air by the handfuls. We remembered commercial jingles from our respective youths, including one for an Italian-ice chain that I went to at the end of long summer days, where I ate gelato, drowsy in the heat. I couldn't remember the last time I'd smiled so much. She stayed. More refugees filtered through the cottage, through us, the last stop before the border, and we fed them and played games with the little ones. We got careless. The day I woke up and the air had changed, I realized it had been a long time coming. She was sitting on the couch. She got up in the night and made some tea. But the cup was tipped and the puddle was cold, and I recognized the symptoms from the television and newspapers, and then the leaflets, and then the radio broadcasts, and then the hushed voices around the bonfire. Her skin was the dark purple of compounded bruises, the whites of her eyes shot through with red, and blood leaking from the misty beds of her fingernails. There was no time to mourn. I checked my own face in the mirror, and my eyes were still clear. I consulted my emergency list and its supplies. I took my bag and tent and I got into the dinghy and I rowed to the island, to this island, where I have been stashing food since I got to the cottage. I drank water and set up my tent and began to make lists. Every teacher beginning with preschool. Every job I've ever had. Every home I've ever lived in. Every person I've ever loved. Every person who has probably loved me. Next week, I will be thirty. The sand is blowing into my mouth, my hair, the center crevice of my notebook, and the sea is choppy and gray. Beyond it, I can see the cottage, a speck on the far shore. I keep thinking I can see the virus blooming on the horizon like a sunrise. I realize the world will continue to turn, even with no people on it. Maybe it will go a little faster.

HOW THE MONSTERS FOUND GOD

John Skipp and Autumn Christian

JAX was sure they would've been destroyed a long time ago if it wasn't for the Midnight Miracle Hour. A murder was always happening nearby. To the north of their tiny island, and the old studio they took over, The Orbital had built a temple that always needed a fresh supply of alts for their sacrifices. To the west and east was a wasteland full of hunters that captured and tore apart any ex-human being they found for parts and software chips. And to the south was a village of The Sane, who on principle did not like monsters like Jax.

By the time they hit a stretch of barren Oklahoma plain, it was just Jax and Delta and Jojo and TechX. He couldn't even count the ones he'd lost along the way. Companions came and went, by death or difference of opinion. And nobody was in charge anymore. The world was on its own.

In the open, Jax was hard to miss: eight feet tall, equal parts flesh and alloyed armor, all heavily weaponized and still in the uniform of an army long dispersed. He'd been torn apart and rebuilt in the lab to strike terror into the hearts of all who surveyed him, and it worked. You had to be crazy to fuck with Jax. He had the body count to prove it.

Jojo was terrifying, too, one of the manimals set loose in the wild just to stir shit up. He was crazy-fast, crazy-strong, and insane even by ape-man standards. But he knew Jax could waste him in a second, so that worked out okay.

TechX wasn't a battle-bot, though her armor was second to none. She was a six-limbed cyborg mutant who hailed from the Texas Institute of Technology (or, as she liked to say, in her sardonic drawl, "A proud graduate of T.I.T.!"). Her expertise—the reason she'd been deployed to the hinterlands—was repairing damaged systems. She could fix anything. Which made her great to have around. And up close, the tools she extruded from her limbs—screwdrivers, soldering irons, dextrous fingers that doubled as clamps and claws—could turn a man into a meat-pile in seconds flat. Jax was happy, if such a thing still existed, to have her on his team.

And then there was poor Delta. Who was a whole other thing entirely.

✶⟡⟢⟡✶

The day they stumbled upon the island, the forked river surrounding it, the rain fell in oily drops that poisoned the land. But nature was adapting. Some plants died, while tougher new ones grew.

Through the downpour, Jax spotted the building first, a squat double-decker that might have looked more at home in an industrial park. Like somebody built a bunker in the middle of nowhere.

"Whaddaya think?" Jax said, binocular eyes boring in. "No lights. No visible movement."

"No power," TechX said. "But movement, yes. I'm tracking six humans, and dozens of little critters. No alts."

"Humans don't mean shit," said Jojo. "And I am fucking cold."

It didn't take long to find the bridge, blow through the tiny obstacles. Once inside, it went down fast. One got away, but that left five. So they had plenty to eat for days.

The building was a revelation: full of valuable scrap and metal, and technology that'd been mostly lost in the outside world. Evidently, the original owners had been radical resistance fighters, based on the yellowed books that still lined their shelves or lay pissed-on, scattered and torn across the floor. There were still photographs of them, mostly shattered in their frames, also strewn. The squatters who followed were clearly not fans.

But there were mattresses, and linens, and cooking utensils. All filthy. But what wasn't, in this world? Most of all, there were solid walls, and a roof that still held. Which was more than they had known in ages.

TechX got it all up cleaned up and running in a matter of days. Water and power flowing. Even a little garden in the back.

And so they settled in.

Delta often asked Jax to carry her out to the studio balcony when the dark clouds looked like bloody ribbons draped across the moon. She couldn't hunt anymore, and her poisonous glands had been scraped empty long ago. But she still wanted to stick out her studded tongue and taste murder on the air.

Jax was way past used to hearing all the screams of night. Smelling corpses left to rot on crucifixes, spare limbs dumped into pits or roasting on an open fire. He'd push Delta's chair to the edge, as if she could stick her nose into the bleeding clouds. She'd sigh, and close her eyes with her jaw distended, and imagine what it'd be like to have legs again to kill.

It almost became a comforting ritual. At least they weren't out in it. And nobody dared come near. At least so far.

It felt almost like home.

In the studio's live recording room, they'd found the broadcasting technology still worked. They could catch the signals of abandoned satellites still ringing the earth and broadcast whatever they wanted. There were still people who had augmented brain implants or owned a computer. People who still surfed empty channels out of habit.

Jax figured the recording room was a gift. If only they knew how to use it. But they were tired and worn out, and didn't have much to say. None of them were musicians, so the guitars and digital keyboards and random percussion instruments still intact had nothing to offer them. JoJo used to get on air occasionally when he was drunk, bang on bongos and scream about all the fuckers he knew who deserved to die, before they finally had to kill and eat him for attracting unwanted attention.

They hadn't touched the recording equipment again until Urchin arrived.

It was Urchin who made the Midnight Miracle Hour.

Urchin probably used to be a Forever Girl, or one of those living dolls pumped full of miracle goop and happy juice to keep them numb and fuckable for all eternity. Or maybe she'd been human. Jax didn't know much about her except that she used to sing.

TechX said that she recognized Urchin's foam-green eyes, what remained of that lilting upturned nose. She'd been one of the winners of that old reality show *Sing For Your Freedom*. At twelve years old, her voice could've knocked out an angel.

Jax didn't know if that was true. But whoever she was, she had been beautiful and someone couldn't stand that. They'd ruined her skin so it looked like a knotted pink coral reef. They'd forked her tongue so it couldn't quite fit in her mouth and she drooled across the front of her dress. Instead of human arms, she had eight machine-like octopus limbs. She walked hunched over as the arms waved and squirmed and swam through the air around her.

Jax couldn't believe that she'd managed to survive so long in a body designed for pain. When she showed up at the compound, dehydrated and rasping, Jax thought they'd have to mercy-kill her.

But she went straight into the recording studio, fiddled with the recording equipment like she'd seen it before, and went live.

Jax tried to stop her. He didn't want more people showing up after another JoJo incident, but one of her limbs casually pushed him back through the door.

The sound that came out of her made Jax stop.

He sat down on the floor outside the studio.

Urchin couldn't even speak without her tongue getting in the way, but her body could sing. Her octopus limbs warmed against the keys and her body became a symphony. It was a sound like she'd hacked the universe. A music unlike anything Jax ever heard. Warm at the edges. Cool and throbbing in the center. It was a pulsing desert wind and an underwater abyss. It was snowflakes on the tongue and hot food in your belly.

For the first time in forever, Jax thought of being in the creche with all the other children and Auntie Abna, the only person who ever consoled him when he cried. Before the soldiers came and ripped the feeling out of him because they needed monsters and not little boys.

An emotion Jax thought long dead pulsed within him. And he knew the others felt it too. The household floated along with the music. Calm. Swirling deep within themselves.

The next night Urchin did it again. And again. It became the Midnight Miracle Hour.

If it wasn't for the Midnight Miracle Hour, they wouldn't have rigged the outdoor speakers that lined the balcony, the weather-proofed sconces on the roof to every side. Would have spent every day in defensive red alert, as they'e spent the whole of their previous forever.

They would not have seen the lost souls gather by the river, from every side. They started coming every night. The hunters. The Sane. Even Orbital cultists. Not in assault mode. But—at least when the music was playing—in what appeared to be worshipful prayer.

If it wasn't for the Midnight Miracle Hour, they would've killed the baby.

One of TechX's seeker drones found an injured woman running by the river. She clutched an old shoebox to her chest, and wherever she stepped left bloodied footprints that swelled in the riverbed. Before TechX could dispatch another robot to investigate, the woman lay down beneath a tree and died, still clutching the box.

TechX sent Jax out to investigate. By the way she held the box so tightly, even in death, Jax thought it was probably what was left of her food, or a family heirloom, like a photograph of her ancestors or a piece of hair tied around a locket. People who died in stupid ways often had a tendency to be sentimental.

But when Jax pried the box from the woman's fingers, he found a baby inside wrapped in a stained blanket. It couldn't have been more than a few months old. It looked healthy. Human. It squinted up at Jax and balled its fists upwards, reaching. It didn't cry. It had lived long enough to know that crying was useless.

They stared at each other for a long time. The sun winked in between them.

Jax took the baby back to the bunker. Only once he'd crossed the threshold and sat down on the floor—he'd already broken one of the couches with his weight—did he realize how stupid that was. He should've suffocated the baby and buried it. A baby couldn't survive in a world like this. Especially not without its mother.

Especially not with monsters.

From her pile of blankets on the floor, Delta stirred from slumber, moaned with hunger at the fresh baby smell. Her cracked gums peeled up over her yellow fangs.

"No," he said sharply. "Not food. Not yet." Delta squirmed but reluctantly obeyed.

Jax sat the baby in the shoebox down and left it on the ground as he paced the floor. His huge body made the floorboards groan. The baby's eyes followed him around the room, but it remained quiet, except for a single gasp.

TechX came in. He was sure when she saw the thing, she'd want to get rid of it too. But she just sat down on one end of their remaining couch and stared at it, placed one hand underneath her chin and leaned forward like she did when she was looking at a busted machine.

It was Urchin, with her octopus arms, who came in and scooped the baby up. She held it close and rocked it. The baby made a little hiccupping noise.

When Urchin bent down the baby's face reflected in her own. Soft and unbroken brown against Urchin's cracked angel green. Eyes within eyes.

"Itttthh a girl," Urchin said to them with her swollen tongue and too-small mouth.

That's when the "it," the "thing," became something real to them. Something that could be named.

A "she." A baby girl.

"We have to get rid of it," Jax said.

Urchin shook her head, smiling. "We don't haffff. To do. Anything."

Jax moved to take the baby away from Urchin. He was so big he could've crushed her with his shadow. But Urchin just joined her free arms together and began to hum. A softened low-level frequency that pulsed outwards.

The dead mother's face flashed in his mind's eye. The bloodied footprints. He stopped and took a step backwards.

Urchin turned, still humming, and crossed the room to the studio, locking the door behind them.

Jax's insides clenched. The nanites surged upwards in his blood, pushed themselves into his limbs to strengthen them. Squeezed his heart to beat faster. *Move,* they told him. *Move or you die.* The killing impulse with which he'd been trained.

"We gotta do something," he said.

"Yeah, we do." TechX talked to the wall without making eye contact. "We don't even have anything to feed her with. I'd have to talk to Marl, down south. He keeps powdered milk. I'll trade him some repairs…"

"We are not talking about feeding it," Jax said. "We're getting rid of it."

"Don't say 'it,'" TechX said quietly. "She's not an 'it.' We're the 'it.' She hasn't done enough wrong to lose that."

"God damn it, no," Jax said. "Delta is already enough trouble as it is…"

Then the "LIVE" sign flickered on beside the studio door.

And the music began.

It started, as always, with just Urchin's voice. A wordless tone, like a bell tolling up from a bottomless echoing well. One pure note, ringing. Soon joined by another, blending richly in unison. Then another in harmony, looping over the others and holding to form a mystical chorus of one.

This was how the Midnight Miracle Hour always started. A hypnotic wall of sound that tore down emotional barriers, spoke to the buried heart within. It was what he'd heard that first night, and every night since.

Then came the drums, in heart-syncopating pulse. Deepening the trance, engaging the body with a primal rhythm that tickled, thrummed, and swayed. Susurrating through his bloodstream. Resonating in his metal bones.

The keyboards that followed were ripples of dreams, chordal grace notes from the music of the spheres. Not quite melodies, but ghostly hints and flickers of every gorgeous melody there had ever been.

And only then did Urchin's voice lift up anew, with soaring unbridled power. The soul, with nothing held back. Every fear, every joy, every passion and hope unleashed with such fiery conviction that the whole rotten world melted away in that moment. Burned to shame, and beyond.

As always, he felt unburdened, almost outside himself. Transported from his own deep well of pain and sorrow.

It was the miracle that defined the hour. And even though it wasn't midnight, this time, it entirely didn't matter.

It was always midnight here.

But then came the thing he could not have expected. The thing that took him over the threshold he didn't even know he had.

The baby cooed.

Such a tiny sound. But swathed in reverb and doused in glory, it pierced him like a saber carved from sunlight.

It was the sound of innocence.

It looped over and over again until it folded into the fabric of the music. The sound changed. Brightened. Like before Urchin had been playing behind a thick curtain and someone had finally peeled it away to reveal its full glory.

The sound surged over the speakers. Jax heard it both inside and outside the house.

Jax saw himself at twelve years old, naked and weeping, covered in blood. Back when he still thought tears mattered. Back before the war, and the bombs, tore the world apart.

They'd made him kill his friend Tucker. All the children in the squad had spent the last four days running, sparring, being kept awake until they started to hallucinate. Given barely any food or water. Jax was always in the front of the line. The fastest. The strongest. The one able to endure with the least water. Tucker was one of the worst. So they decided to cull him, and gave Jax the honors.

It wasn't the cruelty of the memory that bothered Jax. There had been worse memories before and after.

It bothered him that Tucker hadn't screamed when Jax put his hands around his throat.

He just whispered, "I'm sorry," before he closed his eyes and let death take him. Like Tucker knew he was the lucky one.

A monster had been waiting inside all of them, and the genetic modifications that became popular in the last half-century just made it easier for that monster to come out. Jax's nanny had told him the world had been less cruel once, before technology made the rich immortal, and superintelligent machines designed algorithms to keep everyone else in poverty forever.

Girls with cherub cheeks could grow into old women with permanent smiles. Little boys could become men who didn't have to either permanently augment themselves for one of the perpetual wars or spiral into homelessness with no way to escape.

But Jax had trouble believing that.

Urchin's music dipped into Jax's memory, and it touched the weeping boy. He opened his eyes and met the eyes of present Jax. The boy's eyes were blue and flecked with gold, before the injections made them black; and he looked around wildly, searching for the source of the music. But soon the rhythm took him and he climbed to his feet.

Inside his head, a little boy covered in blood was dancing to an impossible music.

In the living room, Delta screamed.

Jax broke away from the image of the little boy and came back to reality. He grabbed one of the knives from his belt and rushed down the kitchen hallway into the room.

Delta lay on the living room floor, next to one of the boarded-up windows. He peeked through one of the slats and saw nothing but the barrier. He glanced over at one of the television feeds TechX had installed on the wall and saw people gathering by the river, as they always did during the Midnight Miracle Hour.

It was strange to see them in daylight, though. It made the nanites in Jax's blood tick with the waiting. The hairs on the back of his neck stood up.

But the music was still playing, both through the internal and external speakers, and the young child inside of him continued to dance.

Jax glanced back down at Delta and saw that she was smiling. The corner of her lips upturned, mouth twitching to the rhythm of the music.

It wasn't a scream. It had been a laugh. With Delta, they just mostly sounded the same.

Jax dropped his knife and picked her up. She was soft in his arms, and when he brought her close to him she placed her hands on his shoulders. Like he had seen ladies do in the old television programs. It was difficult to think of her as anything that had ever been human, but something in her eyes had changed. A streak of blue softening the edges of the black. A little crinkle of the nose.

He danced with her across the floor. A clumsy waltz from a man who had never danced in his life, and a monstrous woman without legs. They moved across the dust and scattered bits of trash, down hallways with busted walls and broken mirrors. Once back in the living room he spun her around until she laughed again. She pretended to bite his neck with her huge fangs, which made Jax laugh too.

As the dance continued Jax dipped her low, another kind of thing he'd only seen on television. He lowered her head almost to the ground, her legless waist pressed into his. Her hair would've swept the floor if she hadn't burnt it all off long ago.

She had a look on her face like he'd dipped her head up into the stars.

Her eyes rolled up in her head. She spasmed in his arms as the music of the Miracle Hour swirled around them. He didn't realize she was dying until she went still and became an odd heaviness in his arms.

He kissed her on the forehead and laid her gently on the couch with her arms crossed across her chest.

TechX watched him from the hallway. She had her packs strapped around her waist and one of her little combat drones following close behind. She walked over to Delta and pressed her fingers against her pulse, just to make sure she was dead

"I need to go get formula," she said. "I'll bury her when I come back."

Jax thought he might see the person that TechX used to be, like he had seen with Delta and inside of himself. But when TechX turned toward him he only saw her. Her fanned-out limbs and shining eyes set in a hard face.

"You're not an 'it,'" Jax said.

TechX looked at him like a question.

"You're not like the rest of us. You've convinced yourself you're a monster, but you're exactly who you're supposed to be."

The little boy inside of Jax reached out for TechX. And he did too. The music spiraled out from his fingertips. It moved like sparks across his skin to hers. He'd never allowed himself to dream of touching her like this, hands against her cheek.

In the first six months after they found each other out in the wastelands, they'd slept facing each other, always about ten feet apart. Jax kept a weapon in an extended arm and one of TechX's killing arms was held out toward him. Sometimes they'd hear a noise out in the dark, and they'd bolt awake. Jax's weapon extended. TechX's arm out, blade whirring. Then they'd realize they weren't trying to kill each other, lower their weapons, and go back to sleep with a joke or uneasy laughter.

They fit well together. Maybe in another lifetime they'd have met on a dating app or accidentally bumped into each other on the hyperloop. Leaned across the empty seat respectfully dividing them during a movie and kissed. Moved into a cramped room together they could barely afford and joked about how one day they'd have to pay rent to look at the sky.

But they had never been able to bridge the gap they first created. Even when they stopped pointing weapons at each other, they hadn't dared.

Jax had come close enough to TechX to see a golden metallic honeycomb pattern shone underneath the surface of her skin. He'd never noticed that before. And he'd never noticed that the little notches that went down her collarbone, the place where cords used to plug in before the skin resealed over them, looked like the centers of flowers.

When their eyes met, and the music flowed in between them, he saw her as a child affixed in his mind's eye. Even before all the modifications, she had a sharp face and the scowl of an older woman. Her name used to be Emma, which she hated, because it reminded her of tart apples and washcloth rags. Before she could walk she despised the way her body seemed to confine her. How she only had two arms and two legs, and all of it so fragile. Nothing like the powerful war drones that roared across her family's tiny shack, or the delivery androids with indestructible limbs and smooth faces like terrible angels.

Emma knew she would not be like her friends who ended up selling their bodies on streets or in darkened underground parlors until their newness and the money ran out. She would not go to die on reality television or marry a man who expected her to become less than she already was, scrape pieces of herself away until she was a speck. Less than a ghost.

Because she knew her true self. She was an emanate goddess, and wouldn't stop working until she saw it emerge from her weak skin. Until Emma became TechX.

Jax saw all of this. And he also saw that at some point between transforming her body and when the bombs fell, she had forgotten and told herself she was only a monster.

Suddenly TechX whispered, "I'm sorry," to Jax. And he knew that she saw the blood-spattered child inside him, just as he saw the child inside her.

They kissed. Her multi-tooled limbs enfolded him. One of TechX's combat drones raised its weapon and its dog-like ears perked up, but TechX waved it away and it sat down on the floor.

Jax never knew what it'd be like to be kissed and held by a killing machine, how gentle it could be to be enfolded by metal and wires and sharpened blades. She was both flushed cool and warm at the same time, and her heartbeat, slower than a human's, felt like it was melting into him.

The little boy covered in blood and the girl with a sharp face danced together at the shimmering center of the music.

The baby laughed through the speakers. The sound sent warm shockwaves through them.

"Okay," Jax said. "Maybe we can keep the baby."

TechX smiled, then laughed herself, and her eyes got that dreamy look of sudden inspiration. She took Jax's hand and led him down the hallway. They passed the recording studio. The "LIVE" sign was still on, and through the gaps in the locked door emanated a strange blue light.

They entered one of the empty rooms that might have once been a kitchenette or an office. It was empty except for trash that littered the floor.

"Do you see it?" TechX asked, and at first he saw only the gray walls and dirty baseboards. But then TechX took his face in her hands and told him to look into her eyes.

He saw her dream, as he'd seen her past. They could make the room into a nursery. Paint the gray walls with pink and blue stripes. Build a little crib and stuff it full of stitched rags to create a blanket. Maybe even create a mobile with rusty pipes and old lightbulbs and magazine cutouts on strings.

For the first time since that night he'd been forced to kill Tucker, Jax began to cry. He bawled so hard that he had to sit down on the floor and it cracked underneath the force of him. TechX knelt beside him with a look of concern.

He didn't know how to explain that he wasn't sad for himself. He was sad that their dreams had become so small.

Still crying, with huge red globs of snot like blood coming down his face, he took TechX's hands and showed her more.

He showed her a window so that light poured through the room. Replaced the gray concrete floor with soft carpet. He made the crib bigger, set it into the nest of a tiny wooden ship like the baby was sailing out to sea. He painted constellations on the ceiling. Scattered well-loved books and toys everywhere.

It had been a long time since he'd used his imagination, so most of what he saw was scraped together from magazines and television. But when TechX saw what he was doing, she understood. Her face brightened and she wiped the red snot from Jax's face.

In her mind's eye she showed Jax they could do even more than that. They could renovate the entire house. Bring light into every room. Clear away the trash. Paint and restore everything until it shone. They could fill the kitchen full of food from their garden, and start working on an archive—not only a history of where they'd been and where they were going, but of every Midnight Miracle Hour that was to come.

It was Jax's turn. He showed her the kitchen not only full of food, but full of people. Him and TechX, Urchin and the baby. Other monsters like themselves. Cooking food and drinking wine, dancing and listening to music. All their weapons piled in a corner, forgotten. Every room bustling with laughter and stories. Every empty bedroom filled with furniture, well-loved clothes, stories.

TechX climbed into Jax's huge lap, and pressed her hands across his face. They went back and forth like that for a while. Each of them adding onto the vision. Creating new pieces of their shared dream.

The music went on and on, a child's laugh threading itself into their blood. They laughed, and then cried, and laughed some more.

Then something new entered their shared mindspace. Something that did not come from either Jax or TechX. It was like a beam of light, transmuting everything it touched. It shot through the space in their minds, leaving behind a searing path for them to follow.

Jax and TechX saw the outside of the studio. The little garden expanded. The single, sad little tree became upright, as if its broken spine had healed. And that one tree became many. A gazebo was built, and people came from all over and filled it with their wares, with whatever they had to offer. The sick and hungry came to feast, and be tended by medics or nursebots, and then they lay in the grass until their cold bodies became warm.

They were listening to the infinite music. The music that danced in their bloodstream and up into the sky. Stretch the space in-between, wavicles that never touched but never ended. The music that made them realize everything, even themselves, could be healed.

The Midnight Miracle Hour that went on forever.

At some point TechX and Jax went hand in hand and walked through the house, seeing both reality and the dream transposed on top of each other. Jax knew it was a dream, could still see the trash and spiderwebs, the cracks in the wall like hairline fractures.

Jax stopped and stared at a broken chair in the corner. One he'd tried to sit on and that had collapsed underneath him. The dream began to shimmer at the edges, disappearing, because for a moment he remembered he was just a monster. A big, hulking terror that had never made anything beautiful in his life.

But then TechX squeezed his hand.

"You're not a monster," she said. "You're my friend."

Together, they went outside.

At least a hundred people stood underneath the balcony, and the cameras showed there were more on the other sides of the house. He expected to hear shouting, the whir of combat drones, boots slapping into the mud, weapons being pulled from sheaths. Jax's vision turned red and his blood roared before he realized they were just quietly standing there, listening to the Midnight Miracle Hour through the speakers.

Several people came up to the balcony carrying packages, and Jax realized they'd left a pile at the bottom of the steps that kept growing larger. Powdered baby formula. Cloth diapers. Even a little black-skinned doll, missing one dark eye. They had heard the child inside the music. And had come to help.

The music continued, and so did the dream inside it. And TechX and Jax weren't just sharing the dream between them. The people below were, too. Everyone adding their own piece. Everyone showing each other what the world could be if it was infused with light.

They saw the world beyond the studio, the barren plains transformed into rich valleys full of food and flowers. The hunter's tents replaced by a city that sparkled white like ice. Dark priests swept out of the temples, sacrifices released from their crucifixes. The gods wiping blood from their mouths and asking repentance. Hospitals built instead of corpse pits. Homes for orphaned children instead of military training schools. War drones reassembled into teachers, officers, delivery drivers. The craters in the land created by bombs filled with water and fish. The sky cleared of pollution so that the sun touched them again.

It wasn't real yet, but they knew it could be. Motion, and color, and light returning to a world gone gray.

TechX wrapped her arm around Jax's shoulder. And although they'd never touched each other like that before, it felt right. It felt… comfortable.

And that was how the monsters found God.

THE BOX MAN'S DREAM

D.R.G. Sugawara

In these quantum states
We live and die in exile
Unobserved by time

And dream of new worlds
Writing our own tomorrows
In the ash of now

Walls can never hold
All these past and future lives
That pass unnoticed

Boxes break open
With all we have ever been
And all we will be

Our self-made castles
Will endure beyond their ruin
Unobserved by time

ACKNOWLEDGEMENTS

WITH love and gratitude to my family, who never tired of guiding me out of the ruins. A huge debt of gratitude to George Sandison and the team at Titan—their enthusiasm for diversity (in all its forms) and openness to new ideas is a rarity among publishers. Thank you to Clive Barker for his grace, imagination, and enduring passion—a lighthouse ablaze in the fog-shrouded shoals. As all books are the sum of their source materials, this owes everything to the writers herein, along with Thomas M. Disch, Joanna Russ, Ursula LeGuin, Michael Moorcock, and M. John Harrison. And to Yoshika Nagata and Natasha—the artists behind the images in *Out of the Ruins*—their work continues to astound and inspire.

ABOUT THE AUTHORS

NINA ALLAN was born in London and grew up in the south east of England. Her first published piece of fiction appeared in a magazine called *Dark Horizons* in 2002. Since then, her stories have featured in numerous magazines and anthologies including *The Year's Best Science Fiction, Best Horror of the Year* and *The Mammoth Book of Best British Crime*. Her many awards include the British Science Fiction Award, the Novella Award, the Kitschies Red Tentacle and France's Grand Prix de L'Imaginaire. Her most recent novel is *The Good Neighbours*, published in 2021.

CHARLIE JANE ANDERS is the author of *Victories Greater Than Death*, the first book in a new young-adult trilogy, which came out in April 2021. Up next: *Never Say You Can't Survive*, a book about how to use creative writing to get through hard times; and a short story collection called *Even Greater Mistakes*. Her other books include *The City in the Middle of the Night* and *All the Birds in the Sky*. Her fiction and journalism have appeared in the *New York Times*, the *Washington Post, Slate, McSweeney's, Mother Jones*, the *Boston Review, Tor.com, Tin House, Teen Vogue, Conjunctions, Wired Magazine*, and other places. Her TED Talk, "Go Ahead, Dream About the Future" got 700,000 views in its first week. With Annalee Newitz, she co-hosts the podcast *Our Opinions Are Correct*.

A visionary, fantasist, poet and painter, **CLIVE BARKER** has expanded the reaches of human imagination as a novelist, director, screenwriter, and dramatist. Barker's literary works include such best-selling fantasies as *Weaveworld*, *Imajica*, and *Everville*, the children's novel *The Thief of Always*, *Sacrament*, *Galilee* and *Coldheart Canyon*. The first of his quintet of children's books, *Abarat*, was published in October 2002 to resounding critical acclaim, followed by *Abarat II: Days of Magic, Nights of War* and *Abarat III: Absolute Midnight*; Barker is currently completing the fourth in the series. As an artist, Barker frequently turns to the canvas to fuel his imagination with hugely successful exhibitions across America. His neo-expressionist paintings have been showcased in an eight-volume series, *Imaginer*. Forthcoming are a book of poetry, a short story collection and a horror novel called *Deep Hill*.

RAMSEY CAMPBELL has won more awards than any other living author of horror or dark fantasy, including four World Fantasy Awards, nine British Fantasy Awards, three Bram Stoker Awards, and two International Horror Guild Awards. Critically acclaimed both in the US and in England, Campbell is widely regarded as one of the genre's literary lights for both his short fiction and his novels. His classic novels, such as *The Face that Must Die*, *The Doll Who Ate His Mother*, and *The Influence*, set new standards for horror as literature. His collection, *Scared Stiff*, virtually established the subgenre of erotic horror.

AUTUMN CHRISTIAN is a fiction writer from Texas who currently lives in Oklahoma. She is the author of several books including

Girl Like a Bomb, *We are Wormwood*, and *Ecstatic Inferno*, and has written for several video-games, including *Battle Nations* and *State of Decay* 2. When not writing, she is usually practicing her side kicks and running with dogs, or posting strange and existential Instagram selfies.

Born in 1942, **SAMUEL R. DELANY** is the author of *Babel-17*, *Nova*, *Dhalgren*, *Dark Reflections*, *Atlantis: Three Tales*, the *Return to Nevèrÿon* series, *Through the Valley of the Nest of Spiders*, an autobiography, *The Motion of Light in Water* and the paired essays *Times Square Red / Times Square Blue*. He is the winner of the Stonewall Book Award for 2008, the 2015 Nicolas Guillen Award for Philosophical Literature, the 1997 Kessler Award for LGBTQ Studies, and the 1993 Bill White Award for Lifetime Achievement, as well as four Nebula Awards from the Science Fiction Writers of America, and two Hugo Awards from the World Science Fiction Convention. In 2016, he was inducted Into the New York State Writers Hall of Fame.

PAUL DI FILIPPO sold his first story at the tender age of twenty-three. Since then, he's sold over 200 more, afterwards collected, along with his many novels, into nearly fifty books. He lives in Providence, Rhode Island, in the shadow of H. P. Lovecraft, with his partner Deborah Newton, and a cocker spaniel named Moxie. His most recent novel is *The Summer Thieves: A Novel of the Quinary*, a picaresque science fiction adventure story evoking the styles of Gene Wolfe and Jack Vance.

Seattle-born writer, editor, and independent scholar **RON DRUMMOND**'s 1996 interview with novelist Steve Erickson was just reprinted in *Conversations with Steve Erickson* (Luter and Miley, eds., University Press of Mississippi, 2021). Other recent publications include "And Watch It Burn" in the online journal *The Enneadecameron*: stories from the plague year; a literary mosaic, "Sung Muhheakunnuk", in the internet magazine *The Revelator*; the entries on Menstruation, Mother, Nevèryon, Pauline Oliveros, and Joanna Russ in the mixed-genre feminist *Encyclopedia Vol. 3 L-Z*; a puzzle-box story, "Planck's Pleroma", in *Eleven Eleven 19*; booklet notes for two CDs featuring World Premiere recordings of string quartets by Czech composer Anton Reicha (1770-1836); and an extended thought experiment about the future of our species, "The First Woman on Mars", in *White Fungus 13* (his reading from it is on Vimeo). Drummond edited fourteen of Samuel R. Delany's books, published two, and packaged one for Wesleyan University Press; he also edited six of John Crowley's books, published *Antiquities: Seven Stories* (1993), and is nearing completion of a new archival edition of *Little, Big*.

PRESTON GRASSMANN is a Shirley Jackson Award-nominated editor, writer, and translator. He was born in California and spent part of his life on the same block as Philip K. Dick. He began working for *Locus* in 1998, as one of the youngest reviewers to work at the magazine, and returned as a contributing editor after a hiatus in Egypt and the UK. His most recent work has been published in *Nature Magazine*, *Strange Horizons*, *PS Publishing*, *Apex*, *Shoreline of Infinity*, and *Futures 2* (Tor). One of his short-stories – "Cael's Continuum" – was nominated for a Reader's Choice Award at *Tor.com*. His non-fiction work and various interviews have appeared in publications such as *Nature Magazine*, *New York Review of Science Fiction*, and *Bull Spec*. He is a regular contributor to *Nature* and currently lives in Japan, where he is working on several new projects, including a book of illustrated stories with Yoshika Nagata.

RUMI KANEKO is a pseudonym for a well-known film director and freelance scenarist for TV shows in Japan. Aside from her work in film & TV, she has also written screenplays and has completed a novel called *Good Morning Jupiter*, which is currently being translated by Preston Grassmann. Her recent translated work has appeared in *The Unquiet Dreamer: A Tribute to Harlan Ellison* by PS Publishing and is forthcoming from various publications in the US.

CHRIS KELSO is a British Fantasy Award-nominated genre writer, illustrator, and anthologist. His work has been published in *3AM* magazine, *Lit-Reactor*, *Black Static*, *Locus*, *Daily Science Fiction*, *Antipodean-SF*, *SF Signal*, *Dark Discoveries*, *The Scottish Poetry Library*, *Invert/Extant*, *The Lovecraft e-zine*, *Sensitive Skin*, *Evergreen Review*, *Verbicide*, and many others. He has been translated into French and is the two-time winner of the Ginger Nuts of Horror Novel of the Year (in 2016 for Unger House Radicals and 2017 for Shrapnel Apartments). *The Black Dog Eats the City* made Weird Fiction Reviews Best of 2014 list. Shrapnel Apartments was endorsed by Dennis Cooper on his blog - "4 Books I read and Loved."

CARMEN MARIA MACHADO is the author of the bestselling memoir *In the Dream House* and the award-winning short story collection *Her Body and Other Parties*. She has been a finalist for the National Book Award and the winner of the Bard Fiction Prize, the Lambda Literary Award for Lesbian Fiction, the Lambda Literary Award for LGBTQ Nonfiction, the Brooklyn Public Library Literature Prize, the Shirley Jackson Award, and the National Book Critics Circle's John Leonard Prize. In 2018, the New York Times listed Her Body and Other Parties as a member of "The New Vanguard," one of "15 remarkable books by women that are shaping the way we read and write fiction in the 21st century."

NICK MAMATAS is the author of many novels, including *I Am Providence*, and *The Second Shooter*, and the novella *The Planetbreaker's Son*. Mamatas's short fiction has appeared in *Best American Mystery Stories*, *Year's Best Science Fiction & Fantasy*, and many other venues. His latest collection is *The People's Republic of Everything* from Tachyon Publications. He has edited numerous anthologies, such as the Bram Stoker Award winner *Haunted Legends*. His fiction and editorial work have been nominated for the Bram Stoker, Hugo, World Fantasy Award, Shirley Jackson, and Locus Awards. Mamatas lives in Oakland, California.

CHINA MIÉVILLE is the multi-award-winning author of many works of fiction and non-fiction, among them the novels *The City and the City* and *Embassytown* and the novella *This Census-Taker*. He has won the Hugo, World Fantasy, and Arthur C. Clarke awards. His non-fiction includes the photo-illustrated essay *London's Overthrow*, *Between Equal Rights*, and *October: The Story of the Russian Revolution*. He has written for various publications, including *The New York Times*, *Guardian*, *Conjunctions* and *Granta*, and he is a founding editor of the quarterly *Salvage*.

YOSHIKA NAGATA graduated from Tama Art University in 2000, and began working for a CM editing company. She left her job in 2003 to pursue her art full time. Her work has appeared in various galleries throughout Tokyo and the US. Her illustrations have appeared in various anthologies and children's books. She performs in live-painting events throughout Tokyo and the US.

NIKHIL SINGH is a South African artist, writer and musician. His work has been featured in various magazines including *Dazed*, *i-D Online*, *Creative Review*, as well as *Pictures and Words: New Comic Art* *and Narrative Illustration* (Laurence King, 2005). His debut novel *Taty Went West* was published by Kwani? Trust in 2015, Jacaranda Books (UK) in 2017, and Rosarium (US) in 2018. The book was released with an accompanying soundtrack and was shortlisted for Best African Novel in the inaugural Nommo Awards. His recent short work was published in the Shirley Jackson Award nominated *The Unquiet Dreamer: A Tribute to Harlan Ellison* from PS Publishing in 2019. His latest novel, *Club Ded*, published by Luna Press, was shortlisted for the BSFA Awards and the Nommo Awards.

JOHN SKIPP is a Saturn Award-winning filmmaker (*Tales of Halloween*), Stoker Award-winning anthologist (*Demons, Mondo Zombie*), and *New York Times*-bestselling author (*The Light at the End, The Scream*) whose books have sold millions of copies in a dozen languages worldwide. His first anthology, *Book of the Dead*, laid the foundation in 1989 for modern zombie literature. He's also editor-in-chief of genre-busting indie publisher Fungasm Press, and co-writer of maybe the gnarliest episode in Shudder's *Creepshow* Season One. From splatterpunk founding father to bizarro elder statesman, Skipp has influenced a generation of horror and counterculture artists around the world. His latest book is *Don't Push the Button*.

EMILY ST. JOHN MANDEL is the author of five novels, most recently *The Glass Hotel*, which was selected by Barack Obama as one of his favourite books of 2020, was shortlisted for the Scotiabank Giller Prize, and has been translated into 20 languages. Her previous novels include *Station Eleven*, which was a finalist for a National Book Award and the PEN/Faulkner Award, and won the 2015 Arthur C. Clarke Award among other honours, and has been translated into 33 languages. She lives in New York City with her husband and daughter.

D.R.G. SUGAWARA had been published widely throughout Japan, writing science fiction for various markets until his retirement in the late 90's. He is often regarded as The Box Man of Ueno Station, named after a character in a novel by Kobo Abe. But unlike the eponymous character from that story, he doesn't wander the streets of Ueno with a box over his head. Instead, he lives surrounded by books and magazines from every era of the genre. His most recent poetry – "Live Inside Your Own Sky" (PS Publishing) - was highlighted in a recent issue of *Sci Fi Magazine*. He is currently working on a book of poetry.

ANNA TAMBOUR is the award nominated author of *Spotted Lily* and *Crandolin*. In 2008, The Jeweler of Second-hand Roe won the Aurealis Award for best horror short story. Her 2015 collection *The Finest Ass in the Universe* was shortlisted for an Aurealis Award for Best Collection. Tambour lives in the Australian bush, but has lived all over the world and is, in Tambour's words, "of no fixed nationality." In addition to writing fiction, she also writes about and takes photographs of what she calls "magnificants — magnificent insignificants".

JEFFREY THOMAS is the author of such horror and science fiction novels as *The American, Deadstock* (finalist for the John W. Campbell Award), *Blue War, Monstrocity* (finalist for the Bram Stoker Award), *Letters from Hades, Subject 11,* and *Boneland.* His short story collections include *Punktown, Ghosts of Punktown, The Unnamed Country, Haunted Worlds, Unholy Dimensions, Thirteen Specimens,* and *The Endless Fall.* Stories by Thomas have been reprinted in *The Year's Best Fantasy and Horror, The Year's Best Horror Stories,* and *Year's Best Weird Fiction.* Though he considers Vietnam his second home, he resides in Massachusetts.

LAVIE TIDHAR is the World Fantasy Award winning author of *Osama* (2011), Seiun nominated *The Violent Century* (2013), the Jerwood Fiction Uncovered Prize winning *A Man Lies Dreaming* (2014), the Campbell Award and Neukom Prize winning *Central Station* (2016), and Locus and Campbell award nominated *Unholy Land* (2018), in addition to many other works and several other awards. His latest novels are *By Force Alone* (2020) and debut children's novel *Candy* (2018 UK; as *The Candy Mafia* 2020 US). He is also the author of the comics mini-series *Adler*. New novels *The Escapement* and *The Hood* are forthcoming in 2021. He is the editor of *The Best of World SF*.

Shirley Jackson award-winner **KAARON WARREN** published her first short story in 1993 and has had fiction in print every year since. She was recently given the Peter McNamara Lifetime Achievement Award and was Guest of Honour at World Fantasy 2018, Stokercon 2019 and Geysercon 2019. She has published five multi-award-winning novels (*Slights, Walking the Tree, Mistification, The Grief Hole* and *Tide of Stone*) and seven short story collections, including the multi-award winning *Through Splintered Walls*. Her most recent short story collection is *A Primer to Kaaron Warren* from Dark Moon Books. Her most recent books are the re-release of her acclaimed novel, *Slights,* and *Tool Tales,* a chapbook in collaboration with Ellen Datlow. Both are from IFWG Australia.

For more fantastic fiction, author events,
exclusive excerpts, competitions, limited editions and more

VISIT OUR WEBSITE
titanbooks.com

LIKE US ON FACEBOOK
facebook.com/titanbooks

FOLLOW US ON TWITTER AND INSTAGRAM
@TitanBooks

EMAIL US
readerfeedback@titanemail.com